The Saddler Boys

Fiona Palmer lives in the tiny rural town of Pingaring in Western Australia, three and a half hours south-east of Perth. She discovered Danielle Steel at the age of eleven, and has now written her own brand of rural romance. She has attended romance writers' groups and received an Australian Society of Authors mentorship for her first novel, *The Family Farm*. She has extensive farming experience, does the local mail run, and was a speedway-racing driver for seven years. She spends her days writing, working as a farm hand, helping out in the community and looking after her two children.

fionapalmer.com

PRAISE FOR FIONA PALMER

'A delightful piece of rural romance.'
BALLARAT COURIER

'A rollicking romance that will have readers cheering
on the heroine . . . Evokes the light, people, atmosphere
and attitudes of a small country town.'
WEEKLY TIMES

'A moving story that reveals the beauty of the bush and
the resilience of rural communities during times of hardship.'
QUEENSLAND COUNTRY LIFE

'A good old-fashioned love story.'
SUNDAY MAIL BRISBANE

'Palmer's characterisation of the town's many colourful
identities is delightful and will bring a smile to those who
have experienced country life.'
WEST AUSTRALIAN

'A heartwarming romance about finding true love and
following your dreams.'
FEMAIL.COM.AU

'Distinctly Australian . . . heartwarming and enjoyable . . .
a well-written and engaging read.'
BOOK'D OUT

'A great addition to your shelf if you love strong
characters and beautiful Aussie landscapes.'
THE AUSTRALIAN BOOKSHELF

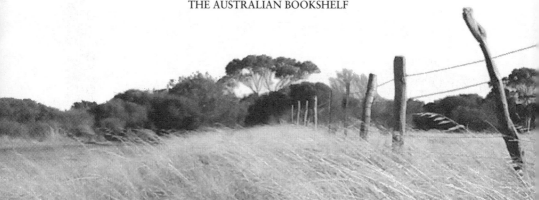

FIONA PALMER

The
Saddler Boys

MICHAEL JOSEPH
an imprint of
PENGUIN BOOKS

MICHAEL JOSEPH

UK | USA | Canada | Ireland | Australia
India | New Zealand | South Africa | China

Penguin Books is part of the Penguin Random House group of companies
whose addresses can be found at global.penguinrandomhouse.com.

Penguin
Random House
Australia

First published by Penguin Australia Pty Ltd, 2015

1 3 5 7 9 10 8 6 4 2

Cover & text design by Laura Thomas © Penguin Australia Pty Ltd
Photograph on pp i–iii © Fiona Palmer
Background credit: Peter Walton Photography/Getty Images;
Man: Sam Edwards/Getty Images; Woman: PeopleImages.com/Getty Images
Typeset in Sabon by Penguin Australia Pty Ltd
Colour separation by Splitting Image Colour Studio, Clayton, Victoria
Printed and bound in Australia by Griffin Press, an accredited ISO AS/NZS
14001 Environmental Management Systems printer.

National Library of Australia
Cataloguing-in-Publication data:

Palmer, Fiona, author.
The Saddler boys / Fiona Palmer.
9780143799795 (paperback)
Love stories.
Western Australia–Fiction.

A823.4

penguin.com.au

Dedicated to all those communities
that have lost their schools

Prologue

PEERING out her car window, she waited and watched as kids piled onto orange school buses with bundles of energy. She scanned each face for likeness, for familiarity, for features she was trying hard to remember. But she had no clue if she'd ever spot him. Would she even be able to recognise him?

The buses pulled away from the school and she followed one in the direction she knew. It was weird being back here, in Lake Biddy – a tiny outback town in the middle of nowhere. And she wasn't exaggerating; she meant tiny. A shop, a pub, a school and a few houses. It was all surrounded by empty paddocks and scrub. Being so isolated made her feel misplaced and slightly scared, like a flower petal blowing into the dry desert. Being here brought back waves of feelings she wasn't used to, memories she didn't want to remember, or deal with.

The large bus continued along the road and she kept following, knowing her boy must be on that bus. When it stopped at the familiar gate, she was overwhelmed with emotion. She reached for her cigarettes with shaky hands and quickly lit one, puffing away until the hit came.

She pulled over and waited for the bus to leave, then crept forward. A little boy with a large schoolbag walked to the bush on the left of the gate where a small tin shed was nestled. She watched him wheel out a tiny motorbike from the shed and start it. Could this really be him? He looked about the right age, but she was no expert.

He took off his school hat, and she noticed that his short clipped hair looked mousy blond. He put on his helmet. She cursed when she couldn't see his face. Did she dare drive any closer? If he turned and saw her, what would he do? Approach her? Or run? Maybe she could tell him she was lost – or would she tell him the truth?

The boy roared his motorbike up the driveway, leaving a trail of dust behind.

It was probably for the best, she thought as she sucked the last bit of life out of her cigarette and lit up another one. She wasn't quite ready yet. But soon. Soon she would be.

Chapter 1

BUGS smacked into Natalie's windscreen, hindering her view as another dual-cab four-wheel drive sporting a big roo bar whooshed past her on the endless bitumen road. That made three four-wheel drives in a row, not to mention the massive trucks that barged past, blowing her across the road like a dead leaf in the wind. Add the wayward storm of rocks flicked up off the road every time she passed a big vehicle and her sleek car was taking a serious battering. Welcome to the country.

Natalie Wright glanced out her window into the wide-open paddocks that stretched for miles in yellows and browns against a vibrant blue sky. The vista was dotted with large gangly eucalypts, their leaves shimmering in the sun as if coated in glitter. Nat's music played like a soundtrack to the scene before her. Actually, it made her want to search through her iPod for some Jimmy Barnes or Paul Kelly. The rural landscape seemed to evoke an Aussie yearning for something a little more rustic and raw. A smile grew on her face and she breathed in deeply, imagining she had her windows down and could smell the earthy, fresh countryside.

Was it the massive sky that made her feel so free? It stretched over her, uninterrupted except for one wispy, see-through cloud. Or was it the fact that she'd been driving for over three hours now, leaving the city with its bustling streets and compressed buildings so far behind? Nat tapped a manicured nail, painted in dusty rose, against the leather steering wheel.

This was her real first venture into the countryside. Sure, she'd driven down to Margaret River to taste the fabulous wines and flown up north to Broome, but never had she driven east towards the middle of Australia, where nothing seemed to live except pink-and-grey birds and bobtails that liked to sunbake on the road. The land was so hot it shimmered, and Nat wondered if she'd be able to breathe the air in. Would her skin crackle and wrinkle after her year here?

A rusty metal sculpture of wheat stood proudly on the edge of the road, followed by two more, metres apart, before a sign for the township appeared. Two years ago, if someone had told her she'd be travelling to the outback to stay in Lake Biddy, population not even three hundred, she would have laughed and called them mad. Yet, here she was. Life had a funny way of turning the tables. She grinned to herself. Out here she'd have the freedom to make her own choices, and maybe along the way she'd find out just who Natalie Wright really was.

She'd tried to research this place but couldn't find much on the internet, and what Google Maps had shown her was more paddocks than any sort of town. As she drove into Lake Biddy she noted three streets on the right before she realised she had driven right through town and was back among native bush on both sides of the road. Small was an understatement. Jogging around the block would never get her fit here. Maybe she'd have to run around the paddocks – but what if she got lost, bitten by a snake, chased by a kangaroo or eaten by some starved native animal? She should have packed her exercise DVDs. Already she missed her workouts at her local gym.

She slowed down then did a three-point turn, right next to a dead kangaroo on the side of the road. Its body was stretched tight like a balloon. She'd never seen one in the wild before but she wasn't going to stop for a closer look. Just the thought of the smell of its rotting carcass made her screw up her nose.

This time she drove even more slowly through the town, noting the large white bin structures on her right, which were situated next to a railway line. In the main street there was an old tin workshop with cars and trucks parked out the side. A Country Women's Association building with a small sign on the old bricks looked a little neglected with its flaking paint and old wire fence. Next was another shed-like structure, cream and antique red with two fuel pumps out the front, and a wide verandah. One advertisement offered a Coke and pie special while another was spinning in the gentle breeze; *Open* flashed in white then black. Three utes were parked out front, their trays loaded up with big tool boxes, wire and other things that looked farm-related. A couple had dogs waiting patiently on the back.

Nat pulled into the area and parked her Monte Carlo blue BMW next to the fuel bowser. Her fuel gauge was reading nearly empty. It was her motor, all eight cylinders, chewing up fuel. Not that she minded, especially when having to pass those long trucks. Her beautiful car had been a twenty-first birthday present from her parents last year. It was an exquisite blue with gorgeous black merino leather seats, which were so comfy. Made the long trip bearable.

Nat flipped down the mirror and reapplied her favourite lipstick, which was a similar shade of rose to her nails. Then she reached into her Gucci tote, pulled out her wallet and stepped out of the car.

Outside, the afternoon sun was blindingly bright and warm. It had been cool when she'd left the city but now it was time to discard her jersey shrug. She noticed two men standing outside the shop on the verandah, watching her. Behind her large dark glasses, she studied them back as she locked the car and walked up to the shop. They wore boots, thick socks, shorts and shirts that looked a little on the thin side. The man with the dirty hat had a big tear up the side of his shorts. She could probably tell what colour underwear he was wearing if she had a good look. Nat shot them a smile before smoothing out her printed silk wrap dress and adjusting the tie at her waist.

The heat prickled at the back of her neck underneath her long blond hair and she wished she'd taken the time to put it up. One of her high-heeled sandals slipped on the uneven dirt but she expertly gathered herself and made it to the cement verandah without a glimmer of trouble. Nat had dressed in her best for her new adventure – she hardly left the house without a good pair of heels – but only now did she wonder whether she looked too different. It seemed that old clothes and worn boots were the go.

The men nearby still watched her soundlessly, as if their tongues had frozen. She opened the glass door and walked inside the shop, pushing her sunglasses onto her head. A girl of no more than eighteen was serving a man at the counter, her face flushed as she talked to him. She wore a black singlet, torn denim jeans and had her hair up in a loose knot. An open can of Diet Coke sat nearby, along with a phone that was making tweeting sounds.

The girl was about to put a box of tissues in a plastic bag when she looked up. Her mouth dropped as she spotted Nat. The door opened and the two men from outside shuffled in. The man at the counter didn't turn; he was busy signing something. He was also in shorts and boots. At least his shorts didn't show his underwear, Nat thought.

'Excuse me, can I get some fuel?' asked Natalie.

The girl nodded. 'Um, yeah. Just turn the pump on.' She pointed to a switch on the wall behind her. Someone had written, *Turn off fuel!!!* and underlined *off* three times.

'This one?' Nat put her finger on it. When the girl nodded, she flicked it on. 'Thanks.'

'Cheers, Jess,' said the man at the counter, putting down the pen.

Jess stood up straighter and smiled. 'No worries, thanks. See you around.'

Nat checked him out when he turned around. He was tall and cute. A real-life handsome farmer. This one wasn't like the two older guys behind her with scruffy hair and worn clothes. Well, actually this one did have messy, blond-tipped hair and he wore boots, but his face was gorgeous. Something you'd normally see in a fireman calendar, with dirt smudged on his tan skin. His deep sapphire eyes found hers, he smiled, she smiled back and then he walked straight past her and out the door.

He even smelt manly and strong, salt of the earth stuff. With an appreciative sigh she went back outside to her car and opened the fuel cap. The bowser was old, the price much higher than she was used to, and the handle was covered in leaking fuel and dust. She wasn't a real princess – she pumped her own fuel. It was just a lot cleaner in the city. Nat didn't want to get it on her dress or in her car and she wouldn't be able to wash until she'd found her new house.

'Would you like me to do that?' said a warm voice behind her. Nat turned to see those blue eyes coming her way from the nearby red ute, where he'd deposited his shopping. His legs were long, lean and golden-brown, like his muscled arms. He would make a perfect Mr January. At least the blue shorts he wore weren't torn but his blue cotton shirt had a few missing buttons, revealing a golden chest with only a light scattering of hair. He stopped in front of her, waiting.

'Um, yes, please. Thank you.'

'No worries.' He grabbed the nozzle with a strong grip. 'Nice car. Are you lost?'

'No.'

He frowned as he took in her high heels. His eyes slowly made their way up along her legs to her face and Nat resisted the urge to shiver with delight. She got many appreciative looks from guys but for some reason this felt different, like he was a knight looking upon a princess.

'Are you sure you're not lost?'

Nat laughed. 'No. Lake Biddy is where I'm meant to be.' She waved to the back seat of her car, which was filled to the top with bags. 'It's my new home.' She could tell he was surprised, even though he tried to hide it. 'Actually, do you happen to know where the schoolhouse is?'

'Ah, you're the new teacher. Now it makes sense.' He smiled and it was full of sincere warmth and friendliness. He had a crooked tooth, which somehow made his grin more interesting and real. 'Sure. You go right from here then take the next right and your house is the small blue one mid-street on the left. The school is at the end of the road. You'll see it.' His brow creased slightly. 'You don't have much stuff,' he said a little sceptically.

She looked at him, amused. He didn't seem to believe she was actually here to stay. 'My brother is bringing a truck down tomorrow and helping me move in.'

He nodded as the two men from the shop came outside again. This time they talked quietly while watching her.

'Don't mind Don and Polly. They'd stare at a brand-new Holland header the same way.'

'Thanks, I think.' Nat wasn't sure what a Holland header was exactly but it sounded like these guys were harmless.

The fuel clicked full, and he put the nozzle back and screwed the cap on. 'You'll need to tell Jess how many litres so she can put it into the computer.'

'Okay, thank you.'

'No worries. I guess I might see you around then, seeing as you're here to stay.' His lips curled into a wide smile that brightened his masculine jaw. 'Welcome to Lake Biddy.' He went to extend his hand, realised how filthy it was, and tucked it into his pocket. 'I'm sure you'll love it here. You may find us all a little strange to begin with but I'm sure we'll grow on you.' With a nod he turned and walked back to his ute. 'Turbo, get up!'

A black-and-brown dog came running from a spot beside the shop and launched onto the back of the ute. Then, without a backwards glance, the stranger was gone.

Instead of making her feel like she was the odd one out or crazy for leaving the city, he'd actually made her feel welcome, like she'd made the right decision. She was determined to make this work, no matter how different or strange life out here was. Nat wasn't naive; she knew she'd be the round peg trying to fit into a square hole. But a part of her welcomed that challenge. It was time for her to experience something out of her comfort zone, something away from her family and their opinions. Something she could do alone.

She walked back inside to pay. 'Good afternoon,' she said as she passed the men.

They both smiled and tipped their hats. 'Afternoon, love,' one said. 'G'day,' said the other.

After paying for the fuel and a bottle of water, Nat followed Mr January's directions to her new schoolhouse but kept driving to the end of the street to see the school. He was right: it was easy to find. She stopped by the small fence that edged the road. There was just one wooden building, painted white, with a quadrangle on one side and an undercover area with an ablution block on the other. Was this it? It was so small and quaint. The gardens looked tended to, the lawn lush and green. There was brightly painted play equipment out the back and a flagpole near the school sign: *Lake Biddy Primary School. Est. 1923.*

Excitement, nerves and anticipation churned through her. This was her life, her year, and she couldn't wait to meet all of her kids on the first day of school. This was what she'd always dreamt about. It was finally happening.

Chapter 2

NATALIE spent her first weekend in Lake Biddy moving into her little house. And it really was little: it took four strides to get from the bedroom to the kitchen. Her brother, Jason, had taken the short journey three times, shaking his head in shock.

'The whole house is smaller than Mum's kitchen, sis,' he'd said, hands on his hips as if addressing a boardroom meeting.

'At least I won't have much to clean,' she'd replied in defence of her new home. 'Anyway, I like it. It feels snug and personal, like my own bedroom.'

'That's because it's the size of your bedroom,' her brother had teased. But he'd stayed true to his word and helped her move in. Together they had carted in the bed, couch, tables and chairs that he'd brought down in the hired truck.

'Actually, this has been fun,' Jason had said at the end of the day. 'It's not often I get to do manly jobs like this. Makes a nice change from the office.'

'Well, I appreciate you coming to help me, Jase. I know you

guys don't agree with me coming out here —'

'You mean to Woop Woop. Outback past the black stump.'

'Yeah, but it's not that bad. You'll see. I'm happy with my decision and it means a lot that you came to help me settle in. Just saying.'

Jason had pulled her into his arms. 'Anything for you, sis.'

Her first night in Lake Biddy had been spent with her brother and a meal of pasta and wine in her new home. The next day he returned to Perth, leaving her to empty her boxes: clothes, plates, photos, cleaning products, plus her laminator and coloured paper. By the end of Sunday it was feeling like her place. She'd arranged her things in each room just how she liked them, and no one else had put their two bob in. She skipped through the narrow passageway, all three metres of it, and swung from the doorways, singing as though she were in a Julie Andrews–inspired musical.

And now in the Monday morning sunshine, as Nat shut the door to her little blue house, she felt like singing again. It was her first day of school and she felt like a lamb, bouncing with each step. Nat loved getting to school early. Even as a child she had been fascinated by the long empty corridors and still rooms. Maybe it was the anticipation of what was about to begin, being able to watch everyone arrive, chatting and running around. It was no different being a teacher. Each step towards the tiny school filled her veins with adrenaline and excitement. Birds chirped in the nearby trees as a gentle breeze rattled the leaves. It was warm in the sunshine but not enough to bring a sweat – that would come later on, with a forecast top of thirty-eight degrees.

'Hello, you must be Natalie. Welcome.' A medium-height lady in a perfectly ironed pencil skirt and blue blouse walked to the school gate and pulled Natalie into a hug. 'Hi, I'm Kath, the registrar.' Kath's grey hair was short and neat, her nails filed. There was no missing the cigarette stains on her fingers and the lingering scent of smoke. 'So great to have you here. Gosh, I love your dress,' she said, eventually letting Nat go.

'Hi, Kath. Lovely to meet you finally.' Nat had been emailing Kath and felt fully prepared for her first day. She knew her kids' names, their ages, and who the rest of the staff were. Kath had said there was no need to get to the school any earlier than the kids' first day, that she'd cope just fine and would settle in within the week, guaranteed. Pulling out two sets of keys from her bag, Kath gave one to Nat and opened the school building with the other. The door caught on the jarrah floorboards and Kath used her shoulder to push it open like she'd done it a million times. Inside, the boards ran the length of the school. Long benches sat outside each classroom, where the kids would put their schoolbags, with rows of hooks above for their hats and jackets. Windows ran along the length of the outside wall, and Nat knew they would soon be filled up with the children's work.

Their heels clicked against the hard floor as Kath led Nat down the corridor. 'That's the library room, then the senior room, which is Grace's. This is the principal's office, where I sit too. And this one is yours, with the staffroom at the end.' A flutter of excitement rippled through her as they paused by the door to her classroom. Inside it was rather bleak and lifeless: white walls, blue-grey carpet and a big blackboard. It had a plain, nunnery-like feel, but the sight of the small desks and little blue chairs made her smile. Tiny bottoms belonging to bright-eyed children would soon be sitting there. There were twelve children in Nat's class and she had taken much delight in making all the nametags for their desks the previous night, along with a small sheet of the cursive alphabet for the younger ones. Her laminator had run hot, covering phonics charts, a day chart and a poster with their classroom rules. The school probably had its own large laminator but Nat hadn't been able to resist buying her own, along with an array of bright stickers and fancy paper, not to mention her own stationery. To Nat, the smell of hot melted plastic was almost as alluring as fresh flowers and she couldn't wait to get the nametags out of her large tote and start sticking them to the desks.

Kath must have sensed her eagerness. 'I'll let you get sorted. If you need anything I'll be just next door.'

'Thank you, Kath,' Nat said, getting to work. She rearranged the desks, settling on a U-shape, then stuck on the nametags and hung up her posters. She looked around – it was definitely feeling a little brighter already. Soon, with the kids' work to exhibit, it would be a room full of colour and excitement, just like her Year 1 class with Mrs Smithe had been.

Truth be told, it was Mrs Smithe who had made being a teacher seem like the grandest and most alluring job. Nat had idolised her. She'd had more attention, comfort and understanding from Mrs Smithe than from her own parents. Then, in Year 3, she'd had another wonderful teacher in Miss Parish. Nat could remember wanting to impress her so much and, right from those early years, being a primary school teacher had been her only dream. Other kids had changed their minds, but not Nat. She was finally living her dream and it was everything she'd hoped for and more.

She actually felt tingles watching kids arrive by bus, flooding into the school in a flurry of chatter and schoolbags. Her bright-faced kids came inside and crowded around her, as if she was a shiny new toy. Everyone wanted to touch her and feel her clothes, especially the girls. She took in their faces; at the moment they were all unfamiliar but soon she'd know them all so well. Then they'd really be her kids. Just thinking the words made her squeeze her hands together with joy. Sure, she'd worked in a school before, but this was her first posting, her first real class.

By Friday morning, Nat couldn't believe it had only been a week. It felt like a month had passed with all the things they'd done. Already the walls were covered in artwork and maths sheets. Just about anything she could put up she did, just to make the classroom feel more inviting. Now she was stapling the laminated titles of the books they would be reading this term to the pin-up board before the bus arrived.

'Gosh, you don't waste any time.'

Nat turned to see Kath, who smiled as she pushed back her short, grey hair. Nat admired the way Kath always came to work in a pencil skirt and blouse, stockings and nice shoes, showing that the job still demanded respect even in such a small school. The previous day Kath had mentioned she was in her sixties, and had seen all her kids through this school, as well as some of her grandkids. Nat also learnt that Jess from the shop was Kath's granddaughter. She thought of what Grace, the senior teacher, had told her: 'Kath has been here nearly longer than the school.'

'It's the best part of the day.'

'Yet another gorgeous dress. Don't you worry the kids will paint it or accidentally glue glitter to it?' Kath's face crinkled with lines.

Nat laughed, flattening the material of her designer V-neck dress. It was black down the sides, with a white centre and a beautiful rose pattern overlay. 'I have others.'

With a smile, Kath left her to her morning routine. Nat quickly finished getting her desk organised, along with her sheets for that morning's lessons.

'Good morning, Miss Wright,' said a tiny voice from the doorway.

'Good morning, Lucy.' Lucy still had her bag on her back – it was half her size and Nat was amazed that the child could carry it. She was one of the town kids who walked to school. Her green school shirt looked two sizes too big and nearly hid her black shorts. She had one pink sock and one yellow sock, and her shoelace was undone. 'Don't forget to do up your shoe-lace, Lucy,' she prompted while the child tugged on one pigtail. Lucy shrugged and Nat went over and tied it up for her. All her kids were special. Ruby had the reddest lips and a dad who sat at the table in jocks – as she'd reported for show-and-tell on her first day. Liam had all the freckles and a pet bobtail, and

Ava always had a runny nose and sniffed a lot. Jack had solid little legs like tree trunks and told her repeatedly that his dad took him shooting cans. Zara seemed to have her head in the clouds, and her uniform had been inside-out on her second day. Mallory and Seth were siblings. So were Mia and Noah. Isaac thought he was a cowboy and was constantly shooting things, and Billy was shy and wore long-sleeved shirts and pants every day despite the heat.

Natalie stepped outside as the two buses pulled up, and watched the children big and small descend on the school. Mia tripped over and a senior boy helped her up and checked she was okay.

'How have you liked your first week?' The principal, Ross, had appeared beside her, white shirt straining around his belly, the buttons threatening to pop.

'It's been wonderful. I can't get over how different it is from a city school. The size, the mixed classrooms and the way the kids all get on.'

'I know. I was a big city schoolteacher for a few years.' His thick hair hardly moved as he shook his head. The sides were greying considerably. 'The country kids seem more tolerant and helpful. Perhaps when you know everyone it's harder to get away with being a troublemaker.'

'I keep waiting for the novelty of having a new teacher to wear off but they are all just so eager to please me. I'm loving it,' she admitted.

'Good, I'm glad,' he said, before twenty kids' voices over-powered his.

With their bright morning faces, they all greeted her and the principal before going back to their lively discussions.

Natalie studied one of her eight-year-olds as he took off his schoolbag and hung up his hat with meticulous care. He was again wearing long pants and a full-length shirt. 'Morning, Billy. Don't you get hot in pants?'

The boy cocked his head to the side. 'Sometimes.' His voice was soft, unlike most of the other boys, who practically yelled.

After she gathered her class together, they began their morning by going through the day chart and then sharing their news. The children's 'news' was sometimes the highlight of her day, and also a good way to get to know them better.

It was Noah's turn. 'Last night my dad kicked our dog, Brute, because he was fighting with our other dog, Tonka, near my little sister. He yelled at them both and said swear words.'

The class giggled and Nat realised she'd been holding her breath, hoping Noah wouldn't say the swear words. 'Well, that's no good, Noah. It can be a bit dangerous around dogs when they're angry.' She nodded for him to sit back down and then clapped her hands together to get their attention. 'Now, this morning you're going to do an activity that will help me learn a little bit more about you all. So, when I'm finished, I want you to take a large sheet of paper from my desk and draw me a picture of your favourite place.' As she'd expected, kids started yelling out.

'My cubby house.'

'The tractor.'

'The water slide.'

Nat waved her hands to shush them. 'Listen. Year 1s, 2s and 3s, you will also have to write about it: where it is, why it's your favourite place and so on. I'll be around to help you. Okay, off you go.'

While paper shuffled and pencils rattled, Nat glanced at her phone. It was angled on her desk towards the window, the only spot it got good signal, and she thought of her friend Alisha, who had posted another photo on Facebook last night of herself at their favourite nightclub. It said, 'Missing my BFF.'

She gazed back over her class, their heads bent over their work. She got up and moved around the room, helping the younger ones write, asking them about their pictures. When she got to Billy she stopped and stared at the headstone and cross on his page. Surely it couldn't be a cemetery? Holding the desk, she knelt down beside him.

'Hey, Billy.' She spoke softly so as not to draw the attention of the other kids. She didn't want him teased. 'What's your favourite place?'

'It's where my nana is,' he said as he coloured with a black pencil.

'Oh, I see. Do you go there often?' Nat glanced at the nearby kids; some had turned to look but none of them laughed or teased. If anything, this seemed normal.

'Sometimes, with Dad. We sit and talk to her. Dad said that she can hear us and that she's watching over us.'

Nat swallowed hard. Billy's gentle words had moved her. She placed a hand on his shoulder. 'You must miss her.'

He turned his bright blue eyes towards her. 'I miss her butterfly cakes and poems. And her hugs.' The power of his gaze went right through her, as if he was secretly telling her all about his pain and loss. As her eyes started to gloss, he put his hand on her arm and smiled. 'It's okay.'

Nat felt strange, as if this dear little boy had tried to comfort her. Could he tell just how heartbroken she felt for him? Billy seemed wise beyond his years. His little angelic face tilted slightly. Then he frowned and looked back at his work. 'How do you spell "favourite"?'

In a flash the moment was gone, the pause button lifted, and life continued. 'I think that's a good word for the blackboard, Billy.' As Nat walked to the front, her heart ached for him. He was different from the other kids – timid, sometimes a loner, softly spoken and reserved. After just a week, she felt as if Billy was a kid with an old soul, who flitted through life like a butterfly.

She picked up some chalk to spell out the word for them all. So many schools had whiteboards or fancy projector screens these days, but having a blackboard made her feel just like Mrs Smithe. Even the smell of the chalk dust felt right. And the kids fought over who got to clean the dusters.

At lunchtime, Nat was sticking the kids' work up on the wall when Grace popped her head in.

'Would you like a cuppa? Ross has gone out on yard duty.' Grace saw the picture Nat had just put up and smiled sadly. 'Oh, is that Billy's?'

'Yes. How did you know? Did his nana pass away recently?'

Grace nodded and her shoulder-length bob swayed. Her

fringe was long but didn't quite cover the scar along her fore-head. 'About three months ago. Alice Saddler was a wonderful lady and a good friend. She was well known and loved in this community.' Grace took a moment, her eyes glistening, before she continued. 'She died from a metastatic melanoma.'

Nat's mouth dropped open. 'Is that why Billy dresses in full-length clothes?'

'Yeah. He's been a stickler for it ever since. I hear he gives his Dad curry every time he wears shorts. It's a hard lesson for a lit-tle boy.'

'He was very close to her?'

'Oh, yeah. I mean most kids are close to their grandparents around here because they all live on the farms together, but Alice was the one who helped bring Billy up.'

Nat frowned as they walked to the staffroom. Outside, kids were trying to eat their lunch quickly so they could go play. 'No mother?'

'No. She died not long after he was born.' Grace turned on the kettle and got out two cups from the cupboard.

Kath was at the table stirring a mug of soup. 'Kettle should still be hot. You talking about Billy?'

'Yeah. He seems like a gorgeous kid. Out of all of them he seems the sweetest, but . . .' Nat wasn't sure how to explain it – and what if she was wrong?

'He's a bit different?' added Grace.

'Yes. Has he been . . . tested?' Nat asked carefully as she took her lunchbox from the fridge with her homemade salad.

'They took him to doctors but they said he wasn't "bad"

enough to put under any label. Alice did a lot of after-school work with him to help keep him up with his year but now she's gone, you might find him slipping backwards.'

Nat walked across the black-and-white checked lino and sat at the table. Grace brought over their cups before fetching her lunch from the fridge.

'All right. Is there anything I should keep an eye out for?' Nat asked.

'He withdraws into himself and can sometimes have anxiety attacks but I've seen the way you are with the kids – you'll be fine,' said Grace with a smile. 'He just needs patience and under-standing. You seem to have that in spades. So are you excited about this afternoon?'

Nat groaned as she chewed a mouthful of salad. 'Not sure,' she mumbled.

Kath laughed, and it sounded like one of the birds Nat had heard that morning on her walk to school. 'You'll be fine. It's just a meet and greet and, believe me, you'd rather get it all over and done with in one go. It will save all the gawking every time you go to the shop.'

'I guess. I'm heading to Perth afterwards, though, so I can't stick around for too long.'

'Really? Are you going to do that every weekend?' asked Grace.

'God, I hope not.' Nat stabbed her fork at a cherry tomato. 'I still need a few things I forgot and everyone will want to see I'm still alive. They think I've gone to the end of the earth.' Gary, for one. 'God forbid they might actually come and visit me.' She was actually looking forward to getting back to Perth, as the annual Wright–Hutchinson get-together was on. For years they had celebrated the friendship of these two families, as far back as Nat could remember, but this year would be different: this year, Nat Wright was dating Gary Hutchinson. He was eight years older than her, and she'd had a crush on him her whole childhood. Six months ago he'd finally asked her out, and they'd been together ever since. And the families couldn't be happier.

'Ha, good luck with that,' said Grace. 'I've got friends and family in Perth who have never come out here, yet they expect me to drop in and see them all the time. I was staying in Midland once and even that was too far away for them.' She shook her head in dismay.

Nat actually hoped there was some truth to Grace's words. She liked having Lake Biddy to herself. She was worried that if her parents and friends saw how remote it was they'd try to talk her into coming home. Nat just wanted one year to herself. A year doing a job that she'd wanted to do her whole life. Was that too much to ask?

Chapter 3

'DAD, can I ride on the back with Turbo?'

'Sure, mate. Just be careful,' said Drew as he watched his son clamber up the side of the ute.

'Turbo, stop it! Don't lick. Let me get up.'

Drew tried not to laugh as Turbo showed his delight, licking madly and knocking off his son's hat.

'*Turrrboooo*.' Billy thrust his wide-brim hat back on his little head and sighed like an old man. It was still hot at four in the afternoon, the sun bearing down.

Drew lifted his own head so he could glimpse the harsh rays from under his hat. Sweat coated his neck but the gentle breeze brought some relief. He glanced at his son, sitting down on the tray beside the dog with the heat shimmering in the background. It was moments like these on their farm, Dragon Rock, that really made him feel thankful.

'Come on, Dad, the sheep are starving.' Billy's heart-shaped face looked up at him with a fierce intensity, as if to say, 'How dare we make them wait.'

Drew was continually struck by his son's beautiful innocence and energy. As if he knew Drew was having a moment, Billy tilted his head and gave him an inquisitive smile. Some days he could come across as quite simple; other days he seemed wiser than most.

'All right, Billy, let's go.' Drew jumped in his white LandCruiser and headed away from the sheds and towards the gully paddock, which had the so-called starving sheep. He glanced in the rear-vision mirror, first spotting the sheep feeder he was towing and then checking that Billy was doing as he had been told. The kid's lips were moving in an animated conversation with Turbo. Drew chuckled before stopping to open the paddock gate.

'I've got it, Dad,' yelled Billy as he jumped down, his tiny Blundy boots kicking up dirt. It was a hard gate to open, but Billy persisted until it fell to the ground and he dragged it away so the ute could drive past.

When Billy was safely back on the tray, Drew drove into the paddock towards the mob and slowed down. 'Give the rope a tug now, Billy!' he yelled.

Having done it a million times before, Billy pulled on the rope that opened the bottom of the sheep feeder. He gripped the edge of the tray and watched the wheat pour out, the sheep running towards them like kids running to Santa with his sackful of presents.

They did the same in the other paddock with the last mob. When the grain was all spent Drew got out to shut the feeder door.

'They look hot,' said Billy, nodding to the sheep in their heavy wool coats. They panted as they moved back and forth.

'It actually keeps them cool, you know. Don't worry, I'll start shearing them soon.' He gestured to Billy. 'Come here.'

Billy walked over and threw his arms around his dad's neck. Drew lifted him off the tray and hugged him tight, renewing the vow he made to himself every day: it was just the two of them now, and Drew would do his best to have Billy by his side always, no matter how hard it was to run a farm and keep a household at the same time. He let Billy slide to the ground. 'You wanna steer the ute back to the shed?'

'Oh, yes, please.'

Drew got in and Billy climbed onto his lap. He would drive the ute all by himself, if only his feet could reach the pedals.

'Dad, Miss Wright asked about Nana today,' Billy said matter-of-factly.

'Did she now? So you like this new teacher?'

'Oh, yeah.' For a moment Billy took his eyes off the dirt track to meet his dad's gaze. 'She's like one of Mallory's Barbie dolls.'

'Eyes on the road, kid,' said Drew with a chuckle.

Billy concentrated on his task but continued talking. 'She's so nice but she knows nothing about the country, Dad. She's never seen an echidna or a yabby!'

'I bet she hasn't.' Drew thought back to the woman he'd met at the shop before school started, immaculately groomed from her glossy spun-gold hair to her fancy painted toes. She was a Barbie, all right, and he'd bet his ute that this was her first real country experience. He smiled as he wondered what she thought so far. Would she last the year? Her vibrant teal-green eyes flashed in his mind and he remembered the flare of determination he thought he'd seen in them.

'Can we invite her out to the farm, Dad?'

Drew realised they were back at the sheds and brought the ute to a stop before processing Billy's question. 'Um, maybe.' Another ute was parked by the large water tank at the edge of the shed. 'Look – Uncle Matty's here. Maybe he has Seth and Mallory with him,' said Drew. It was best to distract Billy quickly before he worked up a head of steam, because when he wanted something there was usually no way to change his mind.

'Uncle Matt!' yelled Billy before Drew had even opened the door. He jumped out and ran towards the white dual-cab ute.

'Hey, kiddo, I'm here.' Matt stepped out from the shed where he'd been looking at the header. He was shorter than Drew and had a well-fed middle but could still kick a mean football and tackle with the best. He wore faded blue work shorts and a dirty brown T-shirt with holes down the front. No doubt from grinding that trailer he was making.

'Did you bring the kids?' asked Billy with his hands on his hips.

Drew had to smile at his little farmer, in work jeans, boots and long-sleeved checked shirt. He even had a little swagger.

'Aren't I good enough?' said Matt, lifting his red Elders hat and scratching his head. That worn, faded red hat was almost a part of him, like his work boots. He was hardly ever seen without either.

Billy threw his arms around Matt's waist. 'Of course you are, Uncle Matt.'

Matt patted his back affectionately. 'I know, buddy. I was just teasing. The kids are playing in the shearing shed.'

With a quick glance at Drew, who gave him a quick nod, Billy took off, running towards the shearing shed.

Drew stood by his friend in the shade as they watched Billy leave, his legs pumping in a clunky run.

'How's he been first week back at school?' asked Matt.

Drew and Matt had forged a tight friendship when Drew first came back to the farm after his father died, but it was cemented when they'd both had sons. Matt had been an honorary uncle to Billy all the boy's life. So Matt knew that school was hard for Billy and always asked how he was going – which Drew appreciated more than ever now that he was raising his son on his own.

'Surprisingly good. I was expecting a repeat of last year and was waiting for the phone calls, but he's doing okay.'

Drew didn't have to worry about getting Billy on the school bus each weekday – he happily followed his two best friends, Mallory and Seth, and had become used to the routine. But having a new teacher had upset the balance in the past. Billy didn't take to change very well, and sometimes it took him a while to build up trust. Last year he'd had a meltdown at school, as he wasn't coping with the teacher or the work. It had taken weeks of school visits and talks to help Billy settle in. Then the teacher had left at the end of the year and Drew had to worry about starting the whole process again. Only this time Billy had been great.

'He withdraws a bit here,' he told Matt. 'He feels his nana's absence the most at home. But school's been fine.'

'I'm not surprised; Mallory and Seth can't stop talking about the teacher. Miss Wright this and Miss Wright that. It's only been a week and I'm sick of hearing her name already.' Matt's smile totally contradicted his words. 'Loz has gone into the meet-and-greet thing for the parents at the school – that's why I've got the kids. I've heard around town she's a stunner. Maybe you should have gone in this arvo?' Matt wiggled his thick black eyebrows.

Drew was used to his mates' ribbing, but he didn't need or want a woman; life was busy and complicated enough. 'I've already met her,' he said simply.

Matt's mouth dropped. 'No way. When? Why didn't you tell me? Is she as hot as the gossips say?'

Drew took a moment. 'She was like something from a magazine. Well dressed, dripping of money, and she smelt . . .' Drew couldn't even describe the sweet scent that had stayed with him long after he'd left. Matt was hanging on his every word, waiting for him to continue. 'She smelt amazing. Not what you'd usually find in our little town. I thought she was lost,' said Drew with a laugh. Sure, the young lady was beautiful, but it was her eyes that had remained in his memory, and the way she held herself. It didn't mean he hadn't noticed her long slender legs or her perfectly fit form – on the contrary, he'd noticed it all. She was like something you only saw in the movies. Yet here she was in Lake Biddy. That was what intrigued him the most.

'Really? Did you speak to her?'

'Yeah, not much. Who knows if she can make it work out here, but quite frankly I hope she does last. Billy seems so taken with her. It's certainly made my life easier, not having to deal with any issues. I'd like to be a fly on the wall, though,' Drew said truthfully. He wanted to see how she engaged with Billy. Had she worked with similar children before? Was she like Drew's mum, Alice? Is that why Billy seemed so comfortable with her?

'I'd like to meet her. Damn, I should have gone in with Loz.' Matt winked. 'With a bit of luck Loz will invite her out for a meal. Maybe we'll invite you over too.'

Drew laughed. 'Don't even think about including me in your schemes.'

A motorbike whizzed past the shed at breakneck speed before doubling back to stop in front of them with a big slide, covering them in dust and sand. They both coughed and brushed themselves off.

'Thought I'd find you here,' said a voice from the cloud of rusty powder.

'Bloody hell, Kim,' Matt choked out. 'You juvenile.'

The dust cleared and Matt's sister shook out her straight brown hair. She wore a blue-and-green checked shirt with the sleeves rolled up and a big R.M. Williams belt on her jeans. 'G'day, boys,' she said with a smile.

'Hey, Kim, you mad bugger. I'm glad Billy wasn't here to see that. I saw him yesterday doing a circle on his little fifty.'

Kim's perfect teeth were bright white. 'Who do ya think showed him that, Sadds?' she said with a wink.

Drew laughed but he wasn't worried. Kim was always around and helping out, taking Billy for outings. She was a good sort, only a year older than Drew, and Billy loved her to bits. She would have made sure he had all his safety gear on and would have shown him the right way to do it. Billy had been riding his motorbike for a few years now so he'd probably already tried it.

'To what do we owe this pleasure?' said Drew. 'You didn't go in to the school thing with Loz?'

Kim flicked down the bike stand and sat propped up on the bike. 'Nah, I had a few sheep to sort out. Besides, why would I need to meet the new sheila in town? It's hard enough finding myself a bloke, let alone sharing what's left with her.'

Matt chuckled. 'Jealous much? Besides, from what I hear she'd have more chance. No guy wants a girl who can weld better than them.'

'Better than you, you mean. I can't help it if you have no skill,' Kim teased.

Drew watched their banter with joy. He missed his own sister, Amy. She was in Perth with her family and hadn't lived on the farm since she went away to boarding school. She didn't come back much – she had two young kids and a busy job.

'Matt's heard she's a stunner,' said Kim, rolling her eyes. 'Sounds too citified to me. No bloke would want a girl who's afraid to get her hands dirty. It's a prerequisite for living in the country.'

'Drew's met her. Do you think you could teach her how to get her hands dirty?' Matt said cheekily.

'I'm not even going to answer that.' Drew glanced at Kim, who was staring at her hands, picking at her dirty nails. Something was on her mind. A little crease always appeared between her eyebrows when her brain was churning. 'Kim, you still right to go fox shooting next Saturday?' he asked. As he'd hoped, she looked up, a bright smile on her face.

'Of course. Just cleaned my gun too. What's the bet this time? Loser buys a carton?'

'Sis, why do you even try? You know Drew's a crack shot.'

Kim put her hands on her hips and gave her brother a look to be reckoned with. 'Because one day I will beat him.'

And Drew knew that she bloody well would. Kim was one of the most determined, gutsy girls he knew. There wasn't a damn thing she didn't know about farming, nothing she couldn't do or learn and, to tell the truth, at times she could be a little intimidating. Drew wondered if this was why none of the single lads had claimed her. More than likely it was because she hardly ever left the farm – too busy with farm work and the sculptures she made.

One thing was for sure: he couldn't have got through the last ten years without Kim and Matt.

'You betcha. A carton for the winner. Coronas, please, and I'll meet you at the shed next Sat at seven.' Drew shot her a grin that warned her to bring her A-game.

Three kids came racing around the corner of the shed, Mallory and Seth dressed the same as Billy except for the pink tutu Mallory wore over her jeans and the sparkly headband in her hair.

'Kimmy!' yelled Billy as he ran right into her side.

Kim scooped him up and hugged him tight. 'Hey, little dude. How are ya?' She sat him in front of her, where he pretended to ride her big bike. Seth climbed on the back and Mallory pouted, left out. Kim reached out and touched her headband. 'Looking fabulous as always, Mal, my little princess.'

Drew watched the kids clamour for Kim's attention. She'd make an awesome mum one day. It's a shame he couldn't say the same for Billy's mother. He clenched his jaw but his muscles relaxed as he gazed upon his son. His beautiful, perfect boy, full of life and love. Having him was the one thing his birth mother had got right and for that, he'd always be thankful.

Chapter 4

'PLEASE have another slice, make me feel better,' said the auburn-haired woman who had a face full of gorgeous freckles that moved with every smile. This lady with the crystal-blue eyes was fast becoming Nat's favourite person at the meet and greet.

Natalie laughed and took the caramel slice offered. 'If you insist, Lauren.'

'I do. I can't afford to have any, so I'm going to live vicariously through you. I'm going to pretend I have your figure.'

Lauren giggled and Nat found her laugh infectious. Her daughter, Mallory, had the exact same laugh; she, too, had a larger-than-life personality. Even though Nat had just met Lauren, she found her to be so down to earth and real. There was nothing fake about her.

'And please, call me Loz. Everyone does – so much so that I sometimes don't answer to Lauren.' She smiled again and eyed off the last of the slice, her hand automatically going to the roll at her midriff. 'So what do you think of our little town? Have you had a chance to see the sights?'

Lauren had been one of the first to turn up, carrying in trays of yummy food, and was the first to introduce herself. She shook Nat's hand with the death grip of a seasoned fighter. She probably lifted cows or sheep for a living, thought Nat. Really, she was clueless about what farming people did.

'I'm actually loving it so far,' Nat replied – and it wasn't a lie. She was loving the space, the quiet, the freedom to do what she wanted. Just yesterday after school she'd taken a walk and stopped in the middle of the bush track around town. All she could hear were the birds. No traffic, no parents, no pressure. It was just her, the birds, the trees and the massive sky above. It was purifying. Mind you, the first few days had been a little unnerving and it had taken a bit to get used to the quiet and the fact that she had no one to answer to.

'I'm still settling in and getting to know the kids,' Nat went on, 'but that's why I'm here. I haven't had a chance to look around – hopefully I will in a few weeks when I'm caught up. I still have to head back to Perth because my boyfriend, Gary, is there, but I'll try to stay here as much as I can.' It would be a juggling act to settle into country life but also to see Gary and her family as much as she could.

'Have you been in the country before?' Lauren asked, and to her credit she didn't look Nat up and down like most of the others did, as if she was stating the obvious.

'Not this type of country. All I know about farming is what I've seen on *McLeod's Daughters*,' Nat admitted.

Lauren laughed again. 'And sometimes that was stretching the

truth a fair bit. Don't worry, when you've settled in we'll show
you around. If you ever need anything, like you find a snake in
your house or have car problems or whatever, here's my mobile
and house number,' she said, writing on a napkin. 'You call us if
you need any help, okay?'

'Snakes in my house?'

'Yep, long and slithery. The ones with legs are bobtails but
they won't harm you unless you put your finger near their
mouth.' Lauren chuckled at her own little joke.

Nat didn't find it at all funny. 'I've never seen a snake before.
Do you get many around here?' Quickly she entered Lauren's
numbers into her phone. She was tempted to put them under
'ICE': In Case of Emergency.

'Yeah, a few dugites, which are highly venomous. I'm sure I
saw a crowned snake the other day – they're poisonous too.'

Nat felt the blood drain from her head and she shivered. She
thought she could handle spiders, like redbacks, even though she
was yet to see one, or even a white-tail or a massive huntsman.
But snakes? Snakes lived in her nightmares. She made a mental
note to buy the biggest pair of gumboots she could find.

'But the good old carpet snake, he's one you don't chop up
with a shovel. You have one that lives in your car shed. Locals
have called him Rodger for years. Keeps the mice down, just like
having a cat.'

'*I beg your pardon?*'

'Rodger, a carpet python. He'll be greenish with light-coloured
diamond shapes outlined in black. Don't be afraid of him; just
let him go about his business.'

'Right,' said Nat with more conviction than she felt. From now on, she would be parking her car outside, under the big gum tree. Rodger could have the whole car shed to himself.

'It's just the black ones and the dark-spotted dugite you have to watch.'

Nat was going to google pictures of them as soon as she could – maybe even print out pictures to put by the back door just so she knew which ones could kill her. She shivered again.

'Hey, Lauren,' said a man as he approached them. He was mid-twenties and wore boots, dirty jeans and a blue shirt with a bright yellow strip across the chest. Nat was getting used to this look. The majority of the men at the meet and greet were dressed the same way, as if they'd just come straight from the farm mid-work. For once in her life she felt overdressed.

'Dicko, fancy seeing you here,' said Lauren.

His face tinged pink but his big smile didn't fade. He brushed back his unruly blond locks and gazed at Nat. 'Just come to meet the new local lady,' he said, dripping charm. 'And to eat the free spread.'

'You and all the others,' Lauren murmured, loud enough for Nat to hear.

It had felt like a bit of a meat market. Nat had met many mums and dads but also some of the single lads in town, with names like Wazza, Donk and Pansy. And there was this tall lanky bloke who had just about hoovered all the food on the table. Nat had seen him go back six times now, filling his paper plate each time.

'I think you're out of your league here, Dicko. Why don't

you go do something useful and stop your brother eating all the food?' Lauren rolled her eyes and shook her head. 'The Dixon boys: lean and lanky but they put food away like a herd of starved elephants.'

Instead of being embarrassed by this, Dicko grinned proudly, showing crooked teeth but cute dimples. 'I haven't introduced myself yet.' He held out his callused hand. 'Sean Dickson, twenty-five, single, farmer and all-round good guy,' he said, giving her a wink.

'And biggest flirt,' added Lauren, which prompted Dicko to wrap her up in a hug and kiss her cheek. 'Get out of it, you big lump.' She pushed him off but her eyes sparkled with affection. 'They're harmless lads, Nat. Plenty of teachers come to the country and never leave. They end up married to farmers. We have three in our town, and I'm one of them.'

'Really?'

'Yep, they get me in for relief sometimes but I'm needed more on the farm and at home with the kids. Now you see why there was such a great turnout. It's not often we get new ladies in the area.'

It was a big turnout – more people than Nat had thought lived in this area. And there were many who probably weren't here. She didn't see the two men from her first day at the shop, or that man with the memorable blue eyes. He could have just been passing through.

'Nor ladies as gorgeous as you,' stuttered Dicko.

'Well, I'm sorry to disappoint you all but I have a boyfriend,' said Nat softly.

'You do realise you've just broken heaps of hearts.' Loz held her hand over her mouth to hide her chuckles.

'Too bloody right,' said Dicko, looking forlorn. Then he showed his teeth, and a glint in his dark hazel eyes made her a little nervous. 'Having a boyfriend is not the same thing as being married. We might be able to win your heart yet,' he said optimistically. 'A full-blooded man of the earth, a good country bloke, could be just what you need.' Then he bowed, turned and scooped up a large handful of food before joining his brother.

Grace and Kath came over to see how Nat was doing. 'Are you heading off soon?' Kath asked. 'It's wrapping up now so it'd be okay if you wanted to leave.'

Nat checked her watch. 'I'd really like to get to Perth sooner rather than later.'

'Go on,' said Kath as she fiddled with her packet of cigarettes. 'You've met most people here and there will be plenty of time to catch up with the others later. Go on, pet. Drive safe.'

'Thanks, Kath. Bye, Grace, see you Monday. Thanks for everything, Lauren – Loz,' she quickly corrected.

'Bye,' they said as she left.

Natalie sneaked back into her classroom and grabbed her bag, then moved her way down the corridor, saying goodbyes and making her apologies. She took a deep breath when she made it outside. The day was not over.

Chapter 5

AS Nat drove through Perth it felt as if she was seeing the city with new eyes. It had only been a week, but the tall skyscrapers, the beautiful parks and the Swan River, which snaked through the centre, all seemed so much brighter and more impressive. People were everywhere, in their cars, in the trains, cruising the river in boats, jogging, cycling and fishing under the bridge. It had such a different smell from the country; in fact there were millions of different scents. The car fumes, the river, the res-taurants and fast-food chains, the hot concrete and crisp green parks. It was a mecca for the senses. The thing Nat loved the most, especially at this time of night, nearing eight o'clock, was the lights. So many twinkling colours. Her favourite place was down by the river, watching the lights reflecting on its surface and listening to the gentle lapping of water.

But she saved her biggest smile for the moment she drove into the driveway of Gary's apartment. She couldn't wait to see her boyfriend. The apartment was nestled near Kings Park and his balcony overlooked the Perth CBD and the Swan River. You could soak in the spa or sit in the pool and look across the city. Gary had good taste and he'd taken this apartment for the view alone: the designer kitchen and elegant bathroom were just bonuses.

Nat parked in the reserved parking spot and no sooner had she stopped the car than he appeared.

'Hey, baby.' Gary opened her door and she climbed out. He was Natalie's height, but he loved wrapping her up and lifting her off the ground. A few grey strands were streaked through his brown hair, which gave him a sexy George Clooney look, and if he ever let his beard grow he had some in that too, but Gary was a man who shaved religiously. He took pride in his position at work, and presentation was paramount.

Gary pulled her against his body. 'God, I've missed you,' he said into her hair as he squeezed her tight.

'I missed you too,' she said.

'Felt like you were gone for ages.'

Nat relaxed in his arms, pressed against his starched white work shirt. His spicy cologne lingered on his skin. He'd probably only just got home from the office, where he worked in the family resort and casino business.

'I know.' Nat sighed. 'But I'm here now. Let's make the most of it.'

'Hmm,' he groaned into her hair. 'Good idea. What needs taking inside?'

'I'll get it later. Right now I'm starving.'

'Me too,' he said, cupping her face and kissing her deeply.

At thirty, eight years her senior, Gary came with a lot of experience – in everything. He took her hand and whisked her inside where she found six fresh bouquets of flowers around the dining room and dinner ready and waiting on the marble table.

'Oh, Gary.'

'Welcome home, princess.'

Nat rolled over, her silk nightie riding up her legs as she snuggled closer to Gary. 'Morning.'

He was sitting up in bed with his phone but put it on the jarrah bedside table and turned to her. 'Good sleep?' he asked as he put his arm around her.

'Hmm, yep. Have you been awake for long?'

'Not long. Would you like your favourite for breakfast?' he asked.

Eggs Benedict. Just thinking about it made her mouth water. 'Sounds divine, thanks, babe.' She looked at the clock on her phone. 'Better make it quick, I'll need to start getting ready soon.' She needed a good few hours to prepare for the Wright–Hutchinson luncheon. It wasn't going to be like the casual meet and greet in Lake Biddy – there were high standards to maintain. Several years ago the *Sunday Times* newspaper had turned up and their photos had appeared in the social pages the following day.

After breakfast Nat had her nails redone and her hair blow-dried. She bought a new outfit from her favourite boutique in South Perth: a Lisa Barron cap-sleeved, form-fitting dress in a soft mint with a herringbone pattern. She did her make-up with extra care and stepped into her favourite black peep-toe heels.

'Smashing,' said Gary when she came out of the bedroom. He was wearing his favourite dark grey suit and the matching mint tie she'd got for him. 'You look incredible. Come on, darling, we'd better leave. Your mum hates tardiness.'

Nat smiled. Gary knew her parents just about as well as she did, and Nat was the same with Gary's parents, Tony and Cynthia.

Gary drove them to his parents' home on Saunders Street in Mosman Park. From the road it didn't look like much: there was a gated entry point and another for the exit, and in between was a high wall covered with crawling creepers and a lawn to the kerb. Inside the gate were six car spaces and Gary parked in his usual spot.

They walked through the house, over the familiar plush cream carpets, past matching cream-and-gold detailed furniture and through the kitchen, which was buzzing with waiters and cooks. The wall-to-wall glass doors at the back of the house opened out onto a spacious patio with an outside kitchen and seating area that overlooked the river. They were just a stone's throw away from the ocean as well. Nat spotted their parents, and further down, on the generous patch of lawn by the pool, were her brother and Uncle Kent with Gary's aunty Janice and his uncle Chris, who was holding the hand of a woman in red Nat hadn't seen before.

'Shall we?' said Gary, reaching for her hand.

'Certainly. Parents first?'

He nodded and together they stepped out into the warm mid-day sun.

'Here come the lovebirds,' said Gary's father. Tony was an older version of Gary through and through – more grey hair but the same expensive taste in beautiful suits. Gary greeted her parents, and Tony held out his arms for Nat.

'Hi, Tony.'

'You look ravishing, my dear. It's so good to see you.'

It looked as though they'd interrupted a hushed conversation between Cynthia and Nat's mum, Jennifer. Both ladies were dressed to kill, Cynthia in a soft silk dress in this season's colour of azure and Nat's mum in a similar-coloured skirt and blouse set. They'd both been to the salon that morning; their matching blonde bobs were immaculate. Cynthia gave Nat a hug with an air kiss, followed by Jennifer. Then at last Nat got to hug her father, Vincent. Nat got up on her toes to reach around his neck. He smelt like ink, his leather chair and his favourite peppery aftershave. It was easy to picture him sitting at his large oak desk, phone to his ear while he rubbed his receding hairline.

'Hey, Daddy.'

'Natalie, darling, how is it in the country?'

Tony and Cynthia added their own questions about the town and teaching, and Nat kept to the basics.

'My class is great, the kids are so adorable and so eager to please. I'm loving it. I have a quaint little house and the town is like nothing you've ever seen,' she said, trying to answer all their questions at once.

'I can't understand how you could handle the flies and country, Natalie. Are the children all unruly?' asked her mum.

Nat's eye twitched. She could have bet that within the first five minutes her mum would have something negative to say. She opened her mouth to retort but her dad picked up on her telltale sign of irritation and jumped in.

'Tell us more over lunch, darling. Tony and I are working on a special joint project and I must tell you both about it. This may be a new direction for us, something the Wright and Hutchinson families can build on together.' The conversation returned to work, as it always did, leaving Nat to calm down. Now wasn't the time to stir up her mum, not with Cynthia around. Mum would never forgive her for any embarrassing moments.

Cynthia and Jennifer got on okay, but Nat had a feeling they clashed at times. They were similar and a little competitive but made the effort for their husbands. Tony and Vincent had been through uni together and had been close friends ever since.

'We'd better go and say hello to the others,' said Gary, and he took Nat's hand as they walked over to the lawn.

'Lunch will be soon,' Cynthia called after them.

Nat practically ran to her Uncle Kent. He always made her smile. His hugs were so tight and he always took forever to let her go.

'Hello there, my sweetheart.' Kent was in a dark blue suit, even though Nat knew he'd probably prefer to be in his favourite seventies T-shirt and jeans. He was a big kid at heart and loved all the good things in life. He ate his favourite foods, he went skydiving, he spent time helping out at food shelters and loved surfing – or trying to surf, at least. He'd always been someone who saw the world through wide-open eyes. Hence he was the one who supported her the most in her decision to get her teaching degree.

Nat didn't say anything, just enjoyed the hug. Then she was introduced to Georgie, Gary's uncle Chris's new girlfriend. Chris was ten years younger than Tony, the baby of the family, and he'd spent a lot of time with Gary over the years, being the older brother he never had.

'Hi, Gary, I've heard so much about you,' said Georgie. Her little red dress had probably been the topic of Jennifer and Cynthia's hushed conversation – that and her cleavage. Georgie reached over to give him a hug and kissed his cheek, leaving a smear of red lipstick.

Chris grabbed her arm and tugged her back. 'That's enough,' he said jokingly. 'This is Natalie, Gary's girlfriend.'

They made idle chitchat until Cynthia announced lunch was ready.

Inside they all took their places around the large glass table set with fine china and glassware. Nat sat in between Uncle Kent and Gary. Georgie went to sit next to Gary but Chris directed her to a chair on the other side of the table. Chris was always rather possessive of his dates but at his age he did tend to lose a few ladies to younger men. Nat thought that he'd stand a better chance if he found someone closer to his age, not that she ever said this to Gary, as Chris could do no wrong in his eyes. He idolised Chris in the same way Nat idolised Uncle Kent.

Tony and Vincent stood up at the head of the table, both reciting stories of their uni days and how they met, being there for each other through weddings and births. And trauma, thought Natalie. Cynthia had suffered really bad postnatal depression after Gary and didn't have any more children. Jennifer had just started dating Vincent at that stage and helped her through it.

'Vincent was trying to pick up this gorgeous girl and I came in and helped seal the deal,' said Tony, giving Jennifer a wink. 'I was the older, wiser one. I told you then that she was a keeper, like my Cynthia,' he added with a grin. They never got tired of telling their stories, no matter how many times everyone had heard them. Maybe this time it was for Georgie's benefit.

Gary stood and tapped his glass with his knife. 'I hate to rain on your parade but we've all heard these stories and I'd like to start up a new one.'

Everyone turned to face Gary. Even Nat was curious to know what he was on about. Then she saw him reach into his coat pocket. A little red box appeared in his hand and a few people gasped. Or was it just her?

'Natalie, darling, I think it was meant to be – you and me. Our families are already so entwined so it seems so natural to ask you to be my wife.' He opened the box to reveal a white-gold band that held a massive white diamond, surrounded by Argyle pink diamonds.

'Oh my god, we've dreamt of this moment,' said Nat's mum. 'Haven't we, Cynthia? We just knew.' Jennifer stood up, clapping her hands together and trying to get a look at the ring.

'Bloody marvellous, son,' said Tony, turning to shake Vincent's hand. 'Our kids.' They pulled each other into a hug, patting each other's backs loudly.

'A spring wedding at the yacht club would be perfect,' Nat heard Cynthia say to Jennifer.

Nat hadn't even given Gary her reply yet. She glanced up at

him, a man she'd admired her whole life but had only just started dating. He was smiling and talking to Chris as if it was a done deal. Didn't anyone want to hear what she had to say?

She glanced around the table, at the smiles, laughter and utter joy on their faces. They were all so happy. Only Uncle Kent was looking at her. 'Sweetheart?' he said in a voice that confused her even more.

Nat clutched the table. What *did* she want to say? That this was all too sudden? That she really hadn't been with Gary long enough to get married? That she was only twenty-two and had just started her dream job? Did she really want to get married now? *Hell!*

Gary turned back to her, pulling the massive ring from the box and reaching for her hand. 'What do you say, princess?' He slipped it onto her finger before reaching for her face. 'Will you be my wife?'

Nat gave him a smile and hope it didn't wobble. She held up her hand and watched the light sparkle off the ring. It was huge, and absolutely stunning. Nat felt the pressure of the decision creating tension in her neck. She did care for Gary – loved him, in fact. He was everything she wanted: handsome, charming, romantic and generous, and it would make their families so happy. So why did this decision seem so hard? Maybe it was just nerves and excitement. Gary smiled as he caressed her cheek.

Nat gazed into his dark eyes, took a deep breath and smiled back. 'Yes. Yes, I will.'

Chapter 6

'BLOODY hell, a girl could die waiting for you, Sadds.' Kim pushed off the front of her white LandCruiser, where she'd been leaning, and walked towards Drew and Billy, who had arrived by quad bike. Her hair was tied back in a low ponytail, her jeans were clean and her blue shirtsleeves unrolled even though it was still warm.

'Sorry. I told Billy we couldn't go shooting until he finished his homework.' Drew shrugged. 'I didn't realise how tricky it would all be,' he said, ruffling Billy's hair as he climbed off the bike.

'Your dad never was very good at homework, little Sadds. If you need some real help, you can always ask me,' said Kim, bending down to Billy's level.

Billy cocked a shoulder, his focus on the dog pacing beside him. 'I'll go put Turbo in his kennel,' he said, and ran off around the side of the shed, Turbo racing beside him.

'Something I said?'

'Nah, it was a rough couple of hours. Trying to get him to stay focused without losing my cool.' Drew ran his hand through his hair. 'I had to threaten to cancel shooting before I finally got through to him. It was like pulling bloody teeth. He fought me the whole way, sobbing meltdowns and everything. I don't know how Mum managed it.'

Kim stood before him, her coffee-coloured eyes offering compassion and understanding. 'Yeah, Alice had the patience of a palace guard. I bet it's tough. You know I'm just a phone call away if you ever need help.'

'Thanks, Kimmy, I appreciate it.' He saw Kim flinch. She hated it when he called her Kimmy. It reminded her too much of the TV show *Kath and Kim*. 'Sorry, KC.' He was the only one who called her that. Not many knew her middle name, Cindy, which had been her grandmother's name, and that was how she preferred it.

She smiled. 'Well, let's get the crate on, slacker.'

'Slave driver.'

'Dumb arse.

Together they lifted the metal crate from the shed, carried it to the tray of Kim's ute and bolted it on. It was a special shooting crate with an old car bench seat that she'd made for him years ago, to stop them falling off the tray. Kim or Drew would drive, the other had the gun, and Billy aimed the spotlight. Billy took his job seriously, banging the top of the ute roof and shouting out directions when he caught sight of a fox or a wild cat.

Drew strode off to unlock his gun cabinet hidden in the shed, retrieved some ammo and carried it back to the ute along with his .243 Winchester gun and scope. Kim would have her .223 Remington in the ute on the holder behind the seat.

'Can I sit on the back now, Dad?' asked Billy as he appeared by his side.

Drew put the ammo in the special box to stop it rolling around the tray and sat his gun down. 'Righto.' As Billy climbed up, Drew poked his head into the ute, where Kim was now sitting. 'Gonna do your place first?' he asked.

'Yeah, I've seen a few around the top block.'

'Sounds like a plan.' Drew went to climb on the tray but swung back to the open window. 'Hey, can we swing past and see how your new creation is going?'

She frowned. 'No! It won't be a birthday surprise then, will it?'

'Matty told me it's huge. Said it's looking like your best yet.'

She rolled her eyes but her face flushed pink from the praise. 'I'll bust his balls if he ruins the surprise. My shed is off limits to both of you now.'

'Will it be ready in time? My birthday is only —'

'I know when your bloody birthday is, Sadds. Don't worry, I've got it covered. Now get on the back and let's go. I've got a bet to win.' She started the ute and put it into gear before shooting him a 'hurry up' glare.

'I'm going,' he mouthed before hauling himself onto the back, where Billy sat patiently. He knew he was never allowed to touch the guns, ever. Drew had strict rules around the farm, which had been in place from day one. Originally because Alice had been a stickler for safety, but it had become even more important now that it was just Drew and Billy.

'How many will we get, Dad?' Billy yelled into the wind as the ute drove off towards Lake View Farm. Kim drove on her land and Drew would drive on his – that way no one would accidentally drive over a culvert or hit holes they didn't know about.

'How many do you think?'

'Eleven.' Billy's voice was sure and his denim-coloured eyes twinkled like a pair of Mallory's glittery jeans. His hair was cut short: Alice used to trim it nicely but now it was left up to Drew and they didn't have time for hair salons and such. So it was the clippers for both of them. Drew felt his own locks blow up in the rushing wind and knew it was probably time to get Billy to wield the clippers.

When they reached the top paddock, Kim stopped as the sun was disappearing into the earth. 'God, we live in an awesome place,' she said as she got out to join them on the tray. She burst into chuckles when she saw Drew.

'What?'

Billy laughed too.

'What?' Drew asked again. 'Do I have bugs stuck to my teeth? I did feel a few hit my face.' He raked his tongue over his teeth, which only made them laugh harder.

'Cool hairstyle, Dad,' Billy managed to get out. He reached up to touch it.

'The spiked look is in,' said Kim. 'You look like one of those fancy guys advertising men's hair product.'

Drew frowned and felt the top of his head. It was standing up after having the wind blow it around like a hairdryer. 'Hey, people pay big bucks to look like this.' He waved them off and turned to watch the sunset, something they always tried to make time for.

They were all quiet as they sat on the old car bench seat on the back of the tray.

Kim broke the silence when the bright yellow circle of sun disappeared. 'I was talking to Lozzy yesterday. She was telling me most of the single blokes turned up to that meet and greet last week.'

'Oh, no,' Drew groaned. 'Who turned up? No, let me guess. Wazza, Pansy, Dicko, Trotta and Donkey?'

'Haha, yep. Lucky you have more sense than that.'

'Luck's got nothing to do with it. I'm just not interested. I don't have the time. I start shearing in a few days. Already put it off longer than I wanted.' Drew leant back on the seat and Billy snuggled into his side. 'She wouldn't be interested in any of them anyway. She's too citified.' Drew wasn't sure why he felt compelled to state this. But he felt it was true. No one seemed good enough for the new city teacher.

'They didn't even stand a chance. Lozzy said she told Dicko she had a boyfriend but you know Dicko. He doesn't give up that easy. Anyway, Loz said she came back from the city engaged now.'

'Oh, right.' Drew crossed his arms. Well, it was bound to happen, someone as gorgeous as Natalie wouldn't be single for long.

'Loz said she has a big fancy knuckleduster. Sounds like she comes from money.'

'Yep. I got that impression.'

'Can we go shooting now?' said Billy. 'This is boring.'

Kim stood up and saluted. 'Yes, sir, captain sir.' She jumped down and got in the ute.

Billy grinned and reached for the spotty. He placed a red cover over it and then wrapped his free arm around the metal bar, hanging on tight.

Drew collected some bullets for his pocket and loaded the gun, making sure the safety was on. It took half an hour before they saw their first fox.

The night air came in cool, heightening the smells of the bush and paddock stubble. Even the dirt they kicked up lingered in the still night and each shot fired cracked out like lightening.

Drew had shot three foxes before it was time to swap drivers and do his farm.

'You can do it, Kim,' Billy cheered.

An hour later Billy signalled by banging on the roof. 'Stop, Dad. There's a fox on the right,' he said.

'You got him?' yelled Drew.

'Yep,' said Kim. 'He's stopped. Got him in my sights.'

Nobody moved a muscle and Drew wondered if Kim was feeling the pressure. This would be fox number three for her if she got it.

The shot rang out. Billy whooped. 'I think you got him, Kimmy. Dad, quick, let's check.'

They found the fox where Kim had shot him cleanly.

'You got the same as Dad,' said Billy in awe. He began to dig a hole with his little shovel. He believed it was only fair that they gave them a proper burial, vermin or not.

'Do you want help with this one?' asked Drew.

'Yeah, thanks, Dad. My arms hurt.' He passed over the shovel and bent down to the fox. His little hand reached out and brushed its tail. 'He was a well-fed fox. Look at how shiny his fur is.' Billy squatted, sitting on his heels, his face a mixture of sadness and wonder as he patted the departed animal.

Drew finished digging the hole while Billy slid his hands under the fox and popped him in.

'Bye, Mr Fox.' They covered it over and Billy patted the dirt down then brushed his hands on his jeans.

'All done?' Drew asked.

'Yep.' Billy ran back to the ute, they watched him go.

'He's got such a huge heart. A real gentle soul,' Kim whispered.

'Yeah. He makes me a better person for it too.' After a moment Drew glanced at his watch. 'Well, would you look at that. It's ten, so that's it – time's up. It was a draw,' said Drew. He held out his hand and she shook it. 'Guess we get to share that carton of beer.'

Kim laughed. 'I'm going to have more than half. I'm calling this a win. I'm getting closer to you, Sadds. Better watch your back.'

'Ah, Kimberly. Just this time, I'll let that slide.'

Chapter 7

PUTTING down her marking pen, Nat gazed over the room, watching the children with their heads down as they concentrated on the maths sheets she'd given them. It was the last week in February and Nat was starting to feel settled. The kids were used to her little routine and the classroom looked amazing decorated with this term's theme of 'under the sea'. There were underwater paintings on the walls, and fish of all shapes and colours hanging from a fishing line strung across the room, with green crepe paper for seaweed. Work was pinned to each wall, and the chalkboard at the front had a big sea mural that Natalie had stayed behind to draw a few weeks earlier. With only a quiet house to go home to most afternoons, she enjoyed staying at the school and catching up on marking or organising the next lesson. And doing things like the mural was a lot of fun. She loved seeing the expressions on the kids' faces when they came to school and saw what she'd created. Their smiles and excitement were like caffeine to her bloodstream.

Noah was chewing on the end of his pencil again. 'Noah,' she called out softly. He glanced up and she shook her head. Noah would have nothing left to write with if he kept chewing his pencils as if they were strips of liquorice.

All the kids were concentrating so hard. She got up to see if anyone was struggling. The Year 1s were using coloured counters. Lucy had to separate her counters into colour groups before she would use them.

'You've all been working so wonderfully,' she said, drawing their attention. 'It's time to finish up now. Put your name on your sheets, and Isaac, would you please collect them and leave them on my desk? I think we have enough time before the bell for something fun.' And she literally meant the bell: one of the senior room kids had the job of ringing the handheld bell kept in the office. It was much better than the siren one she was used to as a kid. 'Shall we read some more of *Harry Potter*?'

The kids whooped in excitement and there was a flurry of papers and pencils being put away. Quickly, as if worried they would miss out, the kids gathered on the mat by her reading chair.

Nat picked up the soft skirt of her mushroom-pink dress and sat with the book in her lap. She wore a fine black belt around her waist, simple black heels and matching black jewellery to set off her dress. The material was so soft it fell from her shoulders and swished like butterfly wings as she walked. More than once she'd caught Mallory playing with the hem as it draped down from the chair. Mallory was a princess in the making.

'So, where did we get up to? Can anyone remember?'

Liam shot his hand up, wiggling on the spot as if busting for the toilet. 'Hagrid gave Dudley a pig's tail.' A few laughed as they remembered this.

'Harry got his letter,' said Zara.

Natalie let them all have a go at remembering what they'd read last time. They didn't know it yet but next term they would be turning their classroom into Hogwarts. Nat had just started drawing a picture of the Hogwarts castle for the classroom door. She was planning on making a sorting hat and putting the kids into houses, which they could earn points for. She had Gryffindor, Hufflepuff, Ravenclaw and Slytherin colours to hang in the room and a black cloak that the best worker of the week would get to wear on Fridays.

To say Nat was more excited about this than the kids would be was probably true. Wanting to be a teacher her whole life had meant she'd dreamt up many special activities.

Nat opened the marked book. 'Chapter five, Diagon Alley,' she said softly, which caused the kids to hush, their little ears straining to hear what came next.

A few days a week Natalie had a teacher's aide, Emily, who also worked in the senior room. She was a local, not much older than Natalie, married to the town mechanic and four months pregnant. If Nat was behind with her work then she'd ask Emily to read, but today she was glad the class was all hers. She loved having their attention: twelve bright little faces, so full of inno-cence, all so happy to please her. In the month she'd been with them she'd forged a bond with each of them, learning about every little individual and the unique ways they saw the world. Their characters were blossoming before her eyes.

Being a kid was a joyous time. Friends, fun, laughter and no huge responsibilities. Just how it should be. And then you grow up. Natalie was only twenty-two, yet she felt as if her life was all planned out for her. After she got married she would probably need to quit teaching and get fully involved in the joint family business, especially the social functions. Maybe she could teach part time – that would be okay, wouldn't it?

Looking up from the page she glanced at these darling children and vowed to make this one year with them as memorable as she could. And she wasn't going to miss a moment.

'Let's begin.'

The bell rang ten minutes later and Nat had to rush to finish the last page. The kids were fidgety, wanting to run to the buses but also wanting to hear the last bit of the chapter.

She shut the book. 'Good afternoon, class.'

'Good afternoon, Miss Wright,' the kids chorused as they ran from the room, rushing for their bags and hurrying to the bus lines outside.

Nat tidied up before collecting her things. She wasn't going to stay behind to work this Friday night. Instead she was going to the shop to buy some groceries and a nice wine and then she was going to enjoy her first weekend in Lake Biddy. Gary was away, taking board members around a new resort he was interested in, so she had no need to drive back to the city for the weekend. She was surprised at how excited she felt to be having this weekend on her own.

Nat walked out to find Billy by the bag rack in tears. 'Billy, what's wrong?'

'I can't find my hat,' he said through sobs.

'Don't worry, sweetie, it can't be far away.'

Billy's blue eyes flashed towards the window. 'I need it for the weekend.'

Kath came out from the office, wondering what the sobs were about.

'Where did you last see it?' Nat asked him calmly. 'Don't worry about the bus. I'll make sure it won't leave without you.'

The poor kid seemed to settle a little after that. 'I left it near my bag.'

'It's his red one with the neck cover for the sun. Alice got it for him,' said Kath, filling in the blanks.

'Oh.' Nat had a quick look around and couldn't see it. She bent down to Billy's level. 'Let's go and find out if anyone may have seen it.' She put her arm around him and hugged his little frame. He needed some reassurance and understanding, and whether it was allowed through a hug or not, Nat didn't care. 'Come on.' She held out her hand and Billy slid his into it. Together they walked out to the south bus, which was waiting for him.

Nat poked her head in and got everyone's attention. 'Has anyone seen Billy's red hat?'

Seth jumped up. 'I know.' He pushed his way down the aisle and out of the bus, and ran towards the school. Near the steps he bent down, then waved the hat like a flag as he ran back. 'Here, Billy. It might have got caught on someone's bag.' Seth wedged it on Billy's head.

'Gosh, we must have walked right past it,' Nat said as Billy's face lit up. 'All better?'

He nodded and wiped his face. 'Thank you, Seth. Thank you, Miss Wright,' he said politely before following Seth onto the bus.

Nat waved the bus off and then headed back inside. The school had an eerie quiet like an empty stadium hours after a noisy music show.

Kath came out of the office with a forlorn look and a letter in her hand.

'Found it, thankfully.' Nat grimaced. 'I'd hate to know what he'd be like if we couldn't find it.'

'Hmm,' said Kath. She was looking down the corridor sadly, her hand on her lips. It looked as if she was about to cry.

'Everything all right, Kath?'

'No. No, it's not.' She blinked rapidly. 'I just opened this.' Kath held out the letter, the paper rattling as her hand shook. 'They want to close down our school.'

'What? When?' Nat skimmed the letter from the Department of Education.

Grace came out from the senior room and overheard Nat's outburst. 'What's wrong?'

'They can't do that, can they?' Nat asked. She felt instant panic at the thought of heading back to her old life in the city. It was too soon; she wanted a whole year of teaching. They couldn't close it now.

'We've been on their watch list for a few years now,' said Kath, 'but when they changed the high school process it killed our numbers. Our kids didn't go away to high school until Year 8, now they have to go in Year 7. We lose nine kids in one go at the end of this year. All just to bring it in line with the eastern states.'

'What shall we do about it?' asked Grace. 'My grandson is only three years off starting here. I'll do everything I can to keep this place open.'

'Don't worry, the town will fight this. We'll fight this. Nothing is set in stone,' said Kath with determination.

'They haven't met Lauren and her team of school mums. We'll fight it all the way,' added Grace, nodding in agreement, and Nat felt a surge of relief and hope.

'It won't happen now anyway. If it does go ahead, it will be closed at the end of the school year,' Kath explained. 'Still, we don't want to lose our school. The next schools are over 60 kilometres away and it will kill our town. The shop would suffer, everything would suffer. I'm going to call Lauren and organise a meeting. Get the progress association involved too. We'll need the whole town's support to change their minds. We have to try. Our town depends on it.' Kath took the letter back and looked at it with disgust.

'Well, if there is anything I can do, I'm here to help,' said Nat.

Grace and Kath seemed surprised at her offer. 'That's kind of you, Natalie,' said Grace. 'Not many city folk would understand what it is we are trying to save out here. No offence.'

'None taken. If I wasn't working here, I doubt I would have understood either. But truly, for my kids' sake, I'd really like to help out.'

It wasn't like Nat had anything else to do while she was here. She may as well get involved. The thankful smiles she received from Kath and Grace were worth it. Natalie felt that her input was valued, which was one of the things she craved: to be needed, appreciated. To make a difference.

The small shop seemed quite busy for a Friday afternoon, with two ladies she didn't know buying groceries. Nat carried a red basket as she checked out every shelf. It didn't take long; there were only three small rows and a five-door fridge on one wall containing milk, cream and a selection of cool drinks, including beer and wine. She didn't recognise any of the labels, and there was nothing over fifteen dollars. Oh well, when in Rome, she thought, and reached for a 2014 Chardonnay by Walkers Hill Vineyard. Next she found some cheese and crackers to finish off her perfect afternoon.

'Hi, Jess,' Nat said, putting her purchases on the counter. Nat had been a little shocked her first time shopping here. She couldn't find any familiar brands and discovered that the fruit and vegetable selection was pretty basic. Apparently you had to drive to a bigger town or do big shops in the city when other items were required. Some days Nat felt as if she was on another planet. The shop could order in specific products, if you were willing to buy a whole carton. They'd soon go out of date other-wise. One thing she'd learnt about quickly was the passion and dedication these people had for their little town. They were very proud. Nat was smart enough not to put anyone offside.

'Hi, Nat,' said Jess, putting her phone away and entering Nat's items.

Everyone called her Nat in Lake Biddy – nicknames were obviously the normal way to address people.

'This is a nice wine,' she added while scanning the barcode. 'Have you been to the vineyard yet? It's on your way to Lake Grace.'

'So this is a local wine?'

'Yep, not bad either. Think this one won an award. If you're looking for a nice place to go, they do coffee there too.'

'Thanks, Jess.' Nat was getting used to having conversations while shopping. Actually, she couldn't go anywhere without having a conversation with the locals. On her morning jogs she'd met Beth, the school gardener. Beth lived in the only house on South Street and was a divorced grandmother. Then there was Scott, who owned the pub. He was often chucking boxes in the industrial waste bins out the back and had stopped her one day for a ten-minute chat. She was actually starting to think he left that job for the time she went running. To get any running done she'd had to change her route.

Nat headed home to her little blue house. She liked the fact that she only had to move a small step to reach the dining table, the fridge and the sink in her minimal, plain kitchen. It made making her meals easy, with everything so close. Her fridge had three large drawings stuck on with butterfly magnets – artwork the kids had given her to take home. On her windowsill above the sink sat glued-together gumnuts and leaves finished off with glitter sprinkles, creations from Mallory and Mia. The tea towel hanging off the old oven's handle was last year's Lake Biddy Primary School project, with all the kids' handprints. It had been part of her welcome gift pack from the Parent & Community Association, or the P & C as they called it. Nat loved each and every item, as they made her house a home. And, not to leave out the boys, she had a collection of sheep knucklebones, which Seth had shown her how to use to play a game. He'd painted them so they didn't look like bones but Nat knew what they were, which was why they were still sitting outside.

Filling up her wine glass and pulling out her cheese and crackers, she put together a feast fit for a queen. Then she took it outside and made herself at home on the back patio while she waited for the small, rattly air-conditioner to cool the house down. The back fence was waist-high, and behind it was bush and large gum trees, which swayed in a gentle breeze that carried the scent of eucalyptus and dust. Nat had no neighbours, not on this side of the street, and the only sounds were the magpies and galahs, which chattered from the nearby trees.

Everything was dry and crisp, even the air, but the bush was still a sight to behold. The changing shades of the bark, from the pale creams and pinks of the salmon gums to the reds and browns of the gimlets, bordered the scene before her like a natural photo frame. The birds in the trees were talking to each other; it was noisy yet it felt so silent. As if there was no one else for miles. Natalie had never been so remote before, and as strikingly beautiful and different as it was, she worried about what wildlife might visit her small backyard during the night. As long as it wasn't Rodger out for a slither, she should be okay.

She couldn't remember the last time she'd had a moment to herself to appreciate her surroundings. Maybe not since the picnic at Kings Park with Uncle Kent, when he'd surprised her for her nineteenth birthday. He'd spent most of the time telling her about the breeds of birds and the species of trees that surrounded them. Nat could have listened to him all day. She smiled as she raised the wine to her lips. The moment was perfect and she had the whole weekend to herself.

Bliss.

Chapter 8

THE weekend was lovely and refreshing with no one to answer to. She'd found herself sitting and contemplating her situation. Thinking about Gary and their engagement, her parents and her job. She also worked on her school plan for the kids, made up some colourful new charts and classroom decorations and finished off with some romantic comedy movies. Natalie got ready for school feeling fabulous. She dressed for the occasion with a pencil skirt, thick black belt and a matching soft grey silk top with a black collar and cuffs. Her hair was back in a sleek ponytail and she wore her favourite black red-bottom heels, and a matching red lipstick for an extra flash of colour. She was about to head off to work when her phone rang. It was Gary. She was dying to tell him how well Billy was progressing and that Seth had just aced his maths test and was entering a competition.

'Hey, how's my princess?' he said. 'Are you missing me?'

'I'm fine, and of course I miss you.'

'Enough to quit and come home to me yet?'

'Honey, you know I have to do this. No matter how much I'm missing you.'

'I know, baby. I just miss you so much,' he replied. 'And you're going to be my wife now. I want you here so I can take care of you.'

'We have the rest of our lives together. We haven't even set a date yet.'

'Next time you're home we will. Look, babe, I have to go. Jimmy is waving at me like he's dying from food poisoning. My dad must be here for the meeting. Talk soon. Love you.'

'Love you too,' she whispered, but he'd already hung up.

Nat tucked her phone away, locked up her house and walked to school, thinking things over. She had a niggling feeling that Gary's proposal had come early due to her stay in the country. Had it made him realise how much he loved her? Or was it just a way to get her to come home? Maybe it was a bit of both. Surely if he loved her he'd know she had to see the year out. She took a deep breath. The walk was just what she needed to be able to face her kids with a bright smile.

After lunch, the kids were having a great time. Sure, Isaac was play-shooting everyone more than ever because his dad had just got a new shotgun, and Ava had picked her nose for the tenth time – but it was Billy who had her worried. He wasn't his usual bright self. He hadn't spoken much that morning, not even a polite question, and now he had his head resting on the desk.

Normally she'd have a few issues trying to get him to focus on the task at hand, and it had started off like that this morning, but now it was definitely something more.

'Billy, do you need help?' Nat knelt down beside him and noticed the sweat along his hairline. 'Are you feeling okay?'

Without lifting his head from the desk he rocked it slightly while blinking slowly. His lips were dry.

Nat touched his forehead. He was hot and clammy. 'Oh, you poor boy. Why didn't you tell me you weren't feeling well? Do you want to go and lie down in the beanbag and I'll see if I can call your father?' Billy arched an eyebrow but didn't make a move. 'Come on, sweetie.' Nat took his hand and led him to the beanbag in the reading corner. 'Now, lie here and rest. I'll just go get your water bottle.'

Outside the classroom she found his bag and retrieved his water bottle, then popped her head into the office. 'Kath, Billy looks quite sick. Can you see if someone can come get him? He has a temp.' Ross was in the back corner at his desk, talking to someone on his mobile.

Kath pulled a face. 'Logan had the flu last week, it knocked him for six.' Logan was in the senior room, one of her grandkids. 'Bugger, I guess it's going to do the rounds. I'll call Billy's dad.'

Kath reached for the phone, and Nat got back to her class. 'Drink lots of water,' she told Billy. 'It will make you feel better.' She wasn't allowed to give him any Panadol to ease his fever without his dad's consent.

'Thank you,' he said softly as he tried to smile.

How could such a little man be so strong, suffer in silence

and still remember his manners? Nat felt his forehead again and didn't like how hot he was.

Keeping Billy in her peripheral vision, she went back to teaching the class. He was soon asleep.

Kath came into the classroom and told Nat quietly, 'Sorry, Nat, Drew isn't answering. He had Lauren down as an emergency and I know she's in Perth at the moment. But I'll keep trying.' She went over to check on Billy but didn't disturb him.

He woke as the bell rang for hometime. Nat went to him. 'Hey, Billy, how do you feel?'

Silent tears fell from the corner of his eyes, rolling into his damp hair. 'Head hurts.' He clenched his lids shut.

Grace came in. 'Kath still can't reach Drew,' she said.

'He can't go home on the bus like this,' said Nat.

'No, especially as he probably rides his motorbike from the front gate to the house,' said Grace. 'Do you want me to run him home?'

Nat was reeling – as a parent, wouldn't you make sure you were always available for emergencies? 'It's okay, I'll take him. I want to make sure he's okay. Can you give me directions to his place?' He was her student, her responsibility. And she was worried.

Grace drew out a map, but it didn't look too hard – a few turns and about a ten-minute drive.

Nat told Billy she was going to take him home. He seemed a little disorientated but it could have been because the school was empty; the place always felt different without kids. She put his schoolbag in her car before helping him into the front seat.

He struggled to walk and Nat just wanted to scoop him up in her arms and carry him. He didn't complain but his eyes were heavy with fatigue and pain. Billy had suffered because his father couldn't keep his phone nearby. In this day and age, Nat didn't know anyone who didn't have their mobile glued to them.

The directions to the Saddler farm, Dragon Rock, were spot on, and she had no trouble finding the winding driveway that came out by a house. Further up the road she could see sheds and machinery. For a moment she wondered if Billy's father had hurt himself. Farms were big – should she try to find him? She shook her head. Getting Billy in and settled was her first priority.

'Is this home?' she asked.

Billy managed half a smile and undid his seatbelt. Nat grabbed his bag and went around to help him out. They walked along an overgrown pathway made from old bricks through a beautiful, established garden with massive trees and roses. It was looking a bit neglected, though – Nat would have bet Billy's nana had been the gardener. Agapanthus edged the path and little metal creations in the shape of animals were scattered about under trees. A long lizard gave her a fright before she realised it wasn't real. At the end of the path they stepped up to a verandah, where they were greeted by an old black dog. Billy didn't even have the energy to greet the excited animal, who looked quite blind but recognised Billy with one sniff.

Nat opened the glass sliding door. 'Anyone home?'

Billy gave her a funny look before walking inside, his little hand pulling her after him. The house smelt quite musty, and the floor looked as if it hadn't been swept in a while. They passed the dining table, piled up with papers and unfolded washing, walked through the kitchen, where breakfast dishes still sat on the island bench, and down a passage to the first room on the right. Lightning McQueen and Minecraft posters hung on a light blue wall and the bedspread, covered in motorbikes, was unmade. Toy farm machinery lay all over the carpet. Billy crawled onto his bed.

'Here, let me take your boots off.' Nat pulled off the little farm boots, which most of the boys wore to school.

Billy reached for the doona. 'I'm cold,' he whispered.

Nat felt his forehead again: still hot. She brushed back his hair, wanting to soothe away his pain. His body began to relax.

'How about I go find you some Panadol and some water? I'll be back in a minute.'

When Nat reached the kitchen she wondered if she'd need longer than a minute. How was she going to find Panadol in this mess? She checked the top of the fridge first. No luck, but she did notice a photo of Billy with an older lady – probably Alice – stuck on with magnets. There was another one of Billy on his bike, and one of him standing with a pretty woman, both with their thumbs up, beside a metal kangaroo.

Nat went through the cupboards and found a small walk-in pantry. Up on a high shelf were the Panadol and other medication. Grabbing the one for kids, she measured out the right amount and took it back to Billy's room. She was off-duty and, quite frankly, she didn't care what was protocol any more: this child needed some help.

'Here, darling, take this. It will help.' She placed his water bottle on the bedside table after shifting paper Minecraft boxes, and held out the measuring cup of Panadol.

'Will you stay with me?' he asked as he handed the cup back and lay back down.

'Of course.' She didn't want to mention his father in case Billy got upset. Instead she knelt by his bed and stroked his hair until he was asleep.

She sneaked out of his room and went to the kitchen. Everything was in complete disarray. The sink was full and the milk was still out. The floor looked as if someone had walked around with muddy boots on and if she didn't watch where she put her feet she might end up skating across the room on Billy's toy cars and tractors. The least she could do was tidy up the dishes.

She was just about finished when she heard the sliding door open.

'Billy!' yelled a voice.

'Shhhh,' said Nat as she pulled the plug on the sink water before turning to see the man who had stormed into the house. It was Mr January. Seriously? The man from the shop on her first day was Billy's father?

'What the hell are you doing in my house?' he said, stomping towards her.

Nat's senses were assaulted. He stank of sweat and something yucky like animal poo; he was covered in grime from head to toe and had white fluff stuck to his blue singlet. There was even some blood on his forehead.

'Excuse me?' she demanded back. 'Where the hell have you been? Don't you know how to answer a phone?'

'I beg your pardon?' said Drew as he stopped a foot away from her. Dirty hands went to his hips and his arms flexed like a bull ready to charge. He glanced around the house before his eyes zeroed in on her again. 'Where's my son?' he said accusingly.

For a moment Nat was afraid, but she resisted the urge to step away. 'Your son,' she shot back, 'is sick, and if you'd answered your phone you'd know that and you could have saved him a lot of pain.'

Drew stepped towards the island bench and picked up the bottle of Panadol.

'I've just given him some,' she said defiantly. 'He needed it.'

Drew's face darkened and he strode off towards Billy's bedroom. Nat sighed in frustration. She wanted to yell at him not to wake Billy but the shouting had probably already woken the poor boy.

'A simple "thank you" would have been nice,' she muttered as she made her way to the door. The sweet guy who had helped her at the shop turned out to be a grumpy bastard. Who would have thought? She was about to slide the door closed when she saw a photo on the hall table. It was of Drew, who looked right out of high school, holding a baby with Billy's eyes. Drew's gaze was that of a devoted father, protector and carer. No matter how bad a person he was, it looked like he truly loved his son. Something in her heart told her that now Drew was home, young Billy would be okay.

Chapter 9

DREW stood by his son's bed. The sight of his boy tucked up, sleeping, with sweat beading along his hairline, turned him to mush. He knelt down, fighting back anguish at not being there for Billy when he'd needed him.

Drew had been shearing but he'd glanced at his watch around the time Billy was due home. Sometimes Billy would make himself a Nutella sandwich before coming up to the shed, so Drew hadn't thought much of it at first. When he'd checked his watch again and realised it was much later, he'd grown worried and jumped straight on the quad bike to the house.

Seeing that fancy blue car had filled him with dread, but as he'd got closer he'd remembered it from the shop. It belonged to the new teacher. Who had told him to be quiet in his own house! To see her in all her finery in his messy house, doing his dishes, of all things, had spun his head. He was ashamed, embarrassed, angry, worried and confused all at once. He brushed the damp hair from his son's brow and Billy groaned.

'Hey, little buddy, how're you feeling?'

Billy's eyes fluttered open. 'Dad.'

The smile he gave Drew melted his heart. Where had he left his mobile? Was it still by his bed, or in the ute? Damn, he should be more organised. 'I'm sorry, mate. I was shearing but I'm here now. Can I get you anything?' God, he missed his mum at times like this. He was so used to having her as backup. She'd looked after them both but now it was all down to him. Should he take Billy to the doctor? What would his mum have done?

Billy wiggled his nose. 'Dad, you smell.' He pushed his head into his pillow.

'Okay, I get it. I'll have a quick shower.'

'Is Miss Wright still here?'

Drew blinked as he studied the hopeful face of his son. 'Oh, I don't know, mate.' He went back out to the kitchen but there was no sign of her – only the clean stack of dishes she'd washed, the dishcloth neatly folded over the tap just the way his mum used to leave it. 'Huh.'

With a shake of his head he searched for the thermometer and went to check Billy's temperature. Thankfully it wasn't extreme so he decided to have a quick shower. There would be no more work today. Everything could wait. At least he'd have time to get some housework done.

Drew caught sight of himself in the mirror and grimaced. No wonder the teacher had looked aghast. He was in a right mess, with blood on his face where he must have wiped his brow after sewing up that cut sheep. The blasted ewe had kicked out, making the handpiece slip. He hated cutting them; it was the main reason he shore his own sheep instead of getting in a shearing team. That, and it also saved him a heap of money. While he was scrubbing the soap over his skin he thought back to the look on the teacher's face. She was pretty even when her face was red with anger. He had to give her points, bucketloads, for watching out for Billy. It wasn't in her job description to care for him after hours. Drew chuckled to himself. She may be a city girl but she'd done a very country thing, settling Billy in at home and tidying up. She'd got involved, sticking her nose in where it probably didn't belong. And for that, he'd always be grateful. Maybe they'd make a country girl out of her yet.

Billy wasn't at school the next day or the one after, which Nat had expected. But by Thursday she was getting worried.

'Kath, have you heard how Billy's going?' she asked at recess.

'Oh, he's fine. Should be back at school tomorrow.'

'Did you call them?'

'Oh, no, I heard it through the grapevine.' Kath raised her eyebrows. 'But that's not all I heard. Your name was getting mentioned.'

Nat was about to take a sip but put her cup down. 'Me?' Had she upset the town by going to Billy's place? Was Drew saying bad things about her? Had she overstepped the mark?

'Yes, you. Young Drew was overheard spruiking how you went above and beyond to look after Billy. He said Billy thought the world of you and I know that's true. Drew's been singing your praises.'

Nat frowned. 'That's weird, considering he was pretty angry when he found me in his house.'

'Yes, dear, but he probably didn't have time to think things through. Billy always comes first. That's why the town catch is still single.'

Nat almost laughed. How could Drew be single? Even with a kid he'd still be highly sought after. Those eyes, that face . . . that body. Nat could feel a slow burn of appreciation just from picturing him.

'I know what you're thinking,' said Kath. 'But it's true. The women around here aren't blind. It's more that he's blind. Maybe it has something to do with Billy's mother. I'm just guessing, but Drew's been through a lot and Billy's all he's got. I doubt Drew's done much for himself since that boy was born.'

Nat nodded and sipped her tea. Gary wanted children soon. He'd once told her he wanted four, and she'd agreed wholeheartedly. They would often lie together in bed thinking up names and deciding if they would have boys or girls. They were on the same page when it came to how they wanted to raise children, and Nat knew that they would make a wonderful family together, that Gary would be a great father. She just wasn't quite ready for that yet.

'Well, anyway,' she said to Kath, 'I'm glad Billy's okay. I was getting more and more worried.'

'Get used to it. These are mostly farm kids. They stay home from school if shearing is on or if they're needed in the yards. Between you and me, I think a little bit of it is good for them. They learn life skills.'

Kath got up to rinse her cup out and headed back to the office. The jury was still out for Nat, who'd been taught that school was the most important thing. Her parents had spent thousands on top schools. But, really, was she any better off than teachers who'd gone through government schools? It all depended on the child.

Nat wondered what hopes and dreams Drew had for Billy. Or was he destined to be a farmer?

When Friday morning came, she was relieved to see Billy walk into the classroom with a smile on his perky face.

'Good morning, Miss Wright,' he said clearly. 'Thank you for taking care of me when I was sick.'

He had such lovely manners. 'Thank you, Billy, you're welcome. Are you feeling better?'

He nodded, still smiling and fidgeting on the spot. His eyes danced as if filled with fireflies. He held out a small envelope.

'Dad said to give you this. It's an invitation to lunch.'

Nat took the envelope, unsure of whether she wanted to open it.

'Please, you have to come so I can show you my pet yabbies, Frank and Ben.' Billy tilted his head and pulled a face. 'But Ben is having babies.'

'So Ben could be a Benita?'

Billy giggled and nodded.

Nat opened the envelope. Was this normal out in the country? Did people invite teachers for lunch?

To Natalie,

At least he knew her name. His handwriting was a sloped print.

*I owe you an apology and a thank you. Please let me make
it up to you with lunch on Saturday. If you're free. Regards,
Drew and Billy.*

A smile tugged on her lips at the way he'd signed the note. He'd
left his home and mobile numbers at the bottom.

'Please come?' asked Billy. He stood expectantly, with his
hands clasped behind his back.

'I'll think about it. I might be going back to Perth this weekend,' she improvised. She needed time to think this through.

At recess, she waited until Ross left before asking Grace, Kath
and the aide, Emily, for their opinions.

'Do you think I should mention I'm engaged?'

Grace shook her head. 'He already knows. Everyone knows,'
she said with a laugh. 'That went through town the moment you
returned from Perth with that sparkly rock. It's actually quite
common for new teachers to be invited out to lunch or dinner.
It's just what we do.'

'Really?'

'Yes, I'm actually surprised Lauren hasn't had you over yet. I'm
sure she's working up to it. Being on the P & C board, she makes
it her business to look after the new teachers. And you don't have
to worry about Drew overstepping the boundaries. You couldn't
find a more perfect gentleman. Alice raised him well.'

Nat remembered their second meeting and was going to debate this, but then recalled how kind he was at their first encounter. 'So you think it would be okay to accept?'

'It's totally up to you,' said Emily. 'But engaged, married or not – I'd be there like a shot. Not many get to see Drew in his home environment, except for Lauren and Kim.'

Kath reached over and patted her hand. 'Go and enjoy yourself. Billy would love it. It's been pretty hard on them both with Alice gone. I bet they're both craving some female company.'

Nat sighed. 'I wouldn't mind seeing a yabby. Then the kids might not look at me as if I have two heads.' That caused the ladies to laugh. Nat smiled at her new friends as she thought of lunch with Drew. 'You know, I miss male company myself. Not having Gary here, or my brother around. And I did idolise Jason, growing up. Guys have a different take on things.'

Kath chuckled. 'Well, be prepared to hear all about farming,' she teased. 'Actually, with Drew you won't get the normal farmer routine. Being so devoted to his son makes him a little bit different. In a good way.'

'I think I could handle that.'

Nat excused herself from the staffroom and went back to class to get her mobile. She keyed in Drew's number.

'Hello, Drew speaking.' There were sheep *baa*ing in the background and Drew sounded slightly out of breath.

'Hi, Drew, it's Natalie. The teacher,' she said awkwardly.

'Hey, hi, how are you?' The background noise grew quiet, as if he'd found another spot to talk. 'I guess Billy gave you the invite.'

'Yes, he did.'

'Great. Please say you'll come out tomorrow. Let me show you that I'm not a barbaric farmer, 'cos we are actually quite normal.' He laughed. 'And I really do want to thank you.'

'Sure, why not? Billy wants to show me his yabbies and I really would like to see what all the fuss is about,' she said. 'What time?'

'How's eleven sound?'

'That will be fine. Thanks, Drew.' They said goodbye and ended the call. Her hands were shaking.

She wondered what Gary would think. His last girlfriend had left him for a friend of his, and it had really torn him up. She got the feeling that he didn't like her spending time with other guys. Perhaps she needn't tell him. It was harmless, after all.

Chapter 10

DREW shoved the vacuum cleaner back in the cupboard and turned to survey his work. The washing had been put away, the kitchen was tidy and the floors were clean. It was the best the house had looked in a while. Sure, it could still use his mother's touch with stuff like the dusting and washing the windows, but he'd done the best he could in the time he had. Billy had helped too, in his excitement. He'd made his bed and cleaned his room. After school on Friday they'd put the yabby nets in, ready for today's lunch.

'I hear a car,' yelled Billy as he ran through the house and out the sliding door.

'Shut the . . . door,' he said, but it was too late. Billy was long gone.

Drew went outside and closed the door, slipped on his boots and followed the sound of his son's voice.

'Do you wanna see my yabbies first?'

Drew came to the end of the path, the trees clearing, to find

Natalie standing by her fancy car. He stopped and smiled. 'Just settle down, kiddo, she's not rushing off straight away.' At least he hoped not. She'd run away pretty quickly last time. He held out his hand. 'Let me start this off properly. Hi, I'm Andrew, but everyone calls me Drew.'

The woman smiled. She was a breath of sweet air, literally, with an exotic splash that delighted his nose. Like a frangipani flower floating through the smelly shearing shed. She was dressed in fitted jeans, high black wedges and a pure white top, soft and light as spun sugar. Her hair fell down her shoulders in a shiny cascade as if she'd just stepped out of the hairdresser's. Suddenly Drew wondered if he should have worn something other than his blue shorts and matching King Gee shirt. At least they were clean, and he'd used plenty of deodorant.

Her hand slipped into his, cool and supple, but she shook firmly.

'Natalie, nice to meet you. Most people call me Nat.'

There was tranquillity in her eyes, which were a darker shade of teal today. Maybe they were reflecting the overcast day. It was nearly autumn; you could feel the change in the air, and the sky was filled with dark, plump clouds.

'They forecast a chance of rain for today,' he said, pointing skywards.

Natalie tilted her head up, her neck sleek, her chin shaped beautifully. He studied her as if she were a prized ram, unobtainable yet clearly worthy of praise and admiration.

She glanced back at him, catching his gaze. 'Am I dressed okay?'

Drew scratched at his stubble. 'Um . . . sort of.'

'This is Jo. She's old,' said Billy as he pushed the dog's nose away from Natalie. 'She won't bite, but if she does it won't hurt 'cos she doesn't have any teeth left.' Billy knelt down in the dirt and pulled Jo's lips back to show her small white nubs. 'See? She liked chasing golf balls and rocks.'

'Oh, I see,' said Nat as she waved away a fly.

'Come inside and we'll sort out your shoes,' said Drew. He saw the funny expression on her face but ignored it. She'd soon realise that heels didn't work on sloped dam banks – not that he'd actually tried, but he was quite certain she'd do an ankle.

'What's wrong with my shoes?' Drew heard her whisper to Billy as they got to the back door.

'Well, they are a bit impractical,' he whispered back.

'Really?' she said with a laugh.

Inside, Drew yanked out a chair on his way to the kitchen. 'Grab a seat. Would you like a drink? Cool drink, beer or water? I don't have any wine, sorry.' She looked like someone who'd probably prefer a bright-coloured cocktail with an olive or one of those umbrella things in it.

'A beer would be lovely, thanks.'

Drew stood hanging on to the fridge handle for a moment, processing her words. A beer? Right. Did he put hers in a glass? He took out two beers, slid them into stubby holders and cracked them open. 'Here, hope you like Carlton Dry.'

'We do get beer in the city, you know,' she said teasingly.

Drew felt his cheeks burn and hoped his stubble would cover it.

'But I must admit to preferring Coronas and the Crown Ambassador.'

She was letting him off the hook and he'd never even heard of that last beer. It sounded fancy.

'Place looks nice,' she added as she glanced around.

'We've been cleaning *all* morning,' said Billy, who sat right next to Natalie at the table. 'Do you want to see my yabbies now?' He put his head close to her face as he asked.

Drew noticed Natalie didn't move away from his invasion of her space. 'Sure, lead the way.'

While Billy dragged Nat into the lounge, Drew headed off to his mum's room to find some socks for Natalie. Alice's clothes were still in there. 'Just chuck everything out, give them to Good Sammy's or use them for shed rags, I don't care,' she'd said. She'd sorted through her valuables, giving jewellery away to her friends, so all that was left now were her bed and clothes. Her memory lived in everything around the house: the photos, the knick-knacks she'd bought, her collection of teaspoons.

It was still hard to wake up expecting to see her in the kitchen, making them eggs for breakfast. It still gutted him when he realised she'd never be there again, waving her spatula and telling them to hurry up before it gets cold. Or seeing her curled up on the couch with Billy in her lap as she read him poems from Banjo Paterson or his favourite Paul Jennings stories, the ones that had belonged to Drew. It was like living his childhood again, through Billy. Correction: it *had* been.

With a deep breath, Drew walked into the plain yellow room and opened a drawer, relieved to find it full of socks. He pulled out a thick black pair. His sister had told him to leave it all, that she would clear out their mum's clothes. 'No son should have to go through his mum's undies,' were her exact words. So here he was, still waiting for the day Amy would come back to the farm for a visit and clear out this room. Maybe she'd come back for the anniversary of Alice's death.

When Drew went back to the lounge, Nat had her face pressed up to the glass tank, clearly fascinated.

'Oh, they're so green. I thought they'd be a different colour.'

'They go red when ya cook'em,' said Billy. 'But we don't cook my Ben and Frank. We never eat our pets,' he said matter-of-factly. 'Nan said. Not even our chooks or pet sheep.'

'I should hope not.'

'Heads up.' Nat looked up and Drew threw her the socks. She caught them with ease. 'Nice catch.'

She smiled. 'Basketball. Leading goal scorer for three years straight.'

Drew raised his eyebrows. He hadn't seen that one coming either. 'Really? Wow. Don't let the locals know or you might just find yourself recruited for one of the teams at the end of the year.'

'That wouldn't be so bad. So . . . um . . . what's with the socks?'

Drew beckoned her to follow as he headed to the laundry room that was just off from the sliding door. He picked up his mum's Redback boots and held them out to her. 'These should fit,' he said. He'd already sized up her feet. It would be a shame to cover those cute toes painted a pretty pink, but safety first.

'You'll need them for the dam.'

He could tell she wanted to ask more questions but instead she sat down and changed her shoes. 'I feel like a clown.'

'You look great,' said Drew. 'I'll have you in farm clothes pushing up sheep before you know it.'

She shot him a dirty look and he laughed.

'Right, Billy, ready to go?'

'Yep, Dad. Come on, Miss Wright.'

'Where are we going now?' asked Natalie, taking her beer.

Drew walked to his LandCruiser ute, an old yellow one that still had more life in it than a bucking bronco. Billy had run off in front but kept stopping to check that Natalie was following.

Drew smiled. He couldn't help it; Nat was walking strangely, as if she had cement blocks on her feet. Surely they couldn't be worse than those massive wedges she'd worn here?

'Jump in.' Drew started the ute while Nat opened the door and eyed off the inside. He leant over and banged on the seat before brushing off some grain and stray dog hair. 'Sorry, it's the work ute.' He wasn't sure why he'd said that – it wasn't like he had a new ute for special occasions. This was as good as it got. She climbed in anyway and reached for her seatbelt. 'Nah, I wouldn't, unless you want a dirty mark across your top. We're not going off the farm,' he said as he drove towards the paddock after checking Billy was hanging on. Maybe inviting her back had been a bad idea. She'd go home covered in dirt and probably cursing him even more. At least she hadn't complained yet. His citified brother-in-law complained all the time. About the flies, the dust, the heat, the internet, the mobile reception, the distance, the lack of water . . . on and on he went. Drew was glad Amy preferred to travel back alone.

'Is Billy all right?'

'What? Oh, yeah, he's fine. He loves it on the back. You should try it some time. Lots of fun having the wind in your hair. Best thing about being a kid was riding on the back of the ute.' Drew checked on his son again and grinned. 'So how is Lake Biddy treating you? How are you finding it so far from the city?'

'Oh, it's lovely.' She must have seen his amused expression. 'No, actually, I'm serious. I'm enjoying that aspect of it. No freeways, no lights —'

'No restaurants, no shops, no choice of groceries,' added Drew.

Nat smiled. 'Yeah, but you guys survive. It won't kill me.'

Strands of her hair floated around her face like fine threads of silk. He should have wound up his window but he liked seeing this natural, unkempt look. 'Love your attitude. You'll be winning over the locals soon enough, just like you have with Billy. He thinks you hung the moon.'

'He's a sweet kid.'

'I, um, hope you can understand how I reacted when he was sick.' Drew knew he had to get this off his chest before he could relax. 'He's my world and I tend to forget what goes on outside of that. Plus, having a stranger in my house freaked me out a bit. So, I'm really sorry for my behaviour.' Drew glanced across, catching her eyes and holding them for a moment. 'You didn't deserve to be treated that way when you were taking such good care of Billy. I really am sorry and totally grateful.'

'Thanks, Drew.'

Her voice was light and sweet, just like her scent. Everything about her was so feminine.

They reached the dam and Drew began to drive up the side of the white bank. From the corner of his eye, he saw Nat reach for something to hold. Billy whooped with joy as if he were on a rollercoaster.

Drew stopped not far from the water's edge, where the dam levelled out at the run-off entry point. 'Let's go catch our lunch.' Jumping out, he reached for the big bucket while Billy carried the sorting tray.

Nat followed them to the water. 'I see why my shoes would be a problem.'

Billy laughed, dropped the trays and reached for her hand. 'I'll help you. We can do the first one together.'

Drew was half expecting Nat to decline but, like a child who was curious about how everything worked, she went along. Billy showed her how to pull on the rope, which was lying in the mud, and bring forth the net from the dam in a rush of water, covering their boots. Nat's were encased in mud as she struggled with the heavy net.

'Oh, there's lots. What do we do with them?'

She held the net away from herself awkwardly, but, to her credit, she didn't drop it.

'Here, I'll show you,' said Billy, taking it from her. He dumped the yabbies into the white sorting tray that Drew held over the large bucket. 'See, now Dad will shake them through so we don't eat any that are too small. We put them back in the dam along with any with eggs.' Billy emptied out the tube with the dog kibbles in it and rolled up the rope while Drew threw the small ones back in.

'Oh, no,' said Nat. She was shaking her foot, trying to dislodge the big pile of mud on the end of the boot.

Drew glanced at Billy and they began to smile.

'It's all dirty,' she added.

Drew and Billy broke into laughter. She shot them a concerned look and they laughed even harder.

Nat threw her hands on her hips. 'What's so funny?' she demanded, while fighting to keep a smile from her face.

'Miss Wright,' said Billy. 'They're boots. They're meant to get dirty. That's why we wear them.' He giggled again.

'You think that's bad – wait till I show you the photos of Billy playing in the mud, or the time he helped me in the shed and covered himself in grease,' said Drew.

Nat raised a perfectly sculpted eyebrow. 'I don't think I ever got dirty as a kid. Maybe in the sandpit or from eating, but I never did get to play in mud.'

'It's a shame you're wearing that top,' said Drew just as he felt the first few drops of rain. He looked up. It was going to bucket down soon.

'Why?'

''Cos I'd have grabbed a handful of mud and covered you in it,' he said with a mischievous glint in his eye. 'Every kid should get dirty at some point. Quick, Billy, grab the other net, I think it's about to pour.'

Billy did as he was told while Nat held out her hands as the drops fell faster. 'Should we run to the ute?' she asked.

'You can,' said Drew. 'But it's only water and I want my lunch,' he added teasingly.

For a second she watched him sort yabbies while the rain got heavier. Then she tilted her head back and held her hands out again. 'Yes, you're right. It's only water.' Then she laughed and laughed.

'Dad, is Miss Wright okay?' whispered Billy. He stood by Drew with the next full yabby net, his face screwed up in concern.

'Yeah, son. She's fine.'

Drew wondered what was going on inside her head. Something was making her feel happy and he didn't think it was wearing his mum's boots, or the rain . . . But it didn't matter because the smile on his son's face was worth it. It was nice to have something different to think about. Except he couldn't help thinking just how much his mum would have loved meeting Natalie. She would have been someone to get to know and figure out. Alice always had to put her nose in other people's business but she did it with love and she wanted to help. Drew realised it was the first time he'd thought of his mum without wanting to fall on the ground and cry. But the emptiness was still there, the ache. He was parentless and it hurt like hell.

Chapter 11

LARGE drops, cold and wet, fell with a splat on her face. One hit the corner of her lips and the sweet taste of rain ran into her mouth. It was a sublime feeling, standing in the open, new smells and sights bringing a sense of being alive and free. Had Nat ever really stopped to smell the roses, as the saying went, before she moved out to Lake Biddy? It sure felt like she'd done a lot of it since then. Maybe because she knew her time here was limited, so she was making the most of it.

The rain was coming harder now. She felt the water run down her neck, and her top felt plastered to her shoulders. She glanced back at Drew, who was staring at her but not really seeing her. He wore a sad expression that instantly tugged at her heart. It was raw, open and honest. As if sensing her gaze, Drew blinked and went back to helping Billy sort out the yabbies.

They were getting drenched. 'Can I help?' Squatting down, she watched them pick up yabbies. Big claws arched out, trying to find something to pinch. 'On second thoughts, those claws look nasty.'

'They do hurt,' said Billy as he picked one up and checked for eggs. 'But if you pick them up like this then they can't get ya.' He held up another one in his other hand and put them together so they could touch claws. 'They like to fight.'

'Once you get nipped you're pretty good at not letting it happen again,' said Drew with a smirk.

'Yeah, I bet.'

'We're nearly done. Head back to the ute and we'll be right behind you,' he said with rain dripping from his hair and chin. His long, dark eyelashes held the drops momentarily before they slid off.

Nat felt bad but did as she was told. By the time she got in and shook out her hair, Drew was climbing in beside her, Billy on his lap. Together they drove back to the farmhouse.

'I'm sorry,' said Drew when they finally stood under the protection of the verandah. 'I hadn't planned on a drenching to go with your meal.'

Nat pulled her top away from her, where it had been suctioning onto her skin. The poor bloke was probably getting more than he bargained for. 'It's fine. Like you said, it's just water.'

'Billy, can you get the yabbies ready while I just duck inside?'

Drew went inside without waiting for an answer from Billy, who carried on putting the yabbies into a wire basket.

'Copper is ready, Dad. Can I put them in?' he said as Drew came back out.

He was wearing a dry white T-shirt that was a little snug – not that it was a bad thing on Drew; it just made Nat more aware of his muscled physique. He was also carrying some clothes.

'Let me do that, buddy, it's really hot.' He turned to Nat. 'Here, in case you want to change into something dry. They were my mum's. You can keep them.'

Billy's head tilted towards them with the mention of Alice. Nat reached for the clothes and held out a pair of black track-pants and a blue fleecy checked shirt.

'Those are called trackpants. Really comfortable. And if you come back out here again this is what you can wear for farm work,' said Drew with a half smile. 'I could use a helper while I'm shearing.'

Nat scoffed at his cheek but, biting her tongue, she went inside to change.

In the laundry she tugged off her wet jeans and top. Her white silk and lace underwear weren't too damp, luckily. With nothing else under the flannel shirt, she made sure to do up every button and then pulled on the pants. She had to admit they felt soft and comfortable, but she did feel very unglamorous.

Outside, Drew was putting the basket of yabbies into an old-looking tub. Billy was watching more intently then he ever did at school. 'What is that thing?' she asked.

'It's an old copper boiler,' Drew replied. 'They used them back in the day for laundry. But they're perfect for cooking big catches of yabbies. I sure don't use it for washing. This girl can boil up in around twenty minutes. It's an electric one, so you don't have to light a fire underneath.'

Drew finally ran his eyes over her outfit. He smiled and for the first time she noticed small dimples. Would they stand out more if he was clean-shaven?

'Well?'

'You look great. Now I don't have to feel bad when you get the yabby guts and juices splashed all over you.'

Natalie frowned. She didn't like the sound of that at all.

Drew set up three chairs, handed her another beer, and brought out some bowls and newspaper, plus an old bucket. 'Sorry you have to work for your lunch, but it's all a part of the experience. It makes it taste even better, I promise.'

Nat had always liked the idea of being self-sufficient. Her nan had a small vegie garden and pots full of herbs. She also had two chooks in a little pen in the back corner of her yard, and as a little girl Nat had loved collecting the eggs.

Soon Drew was pulling out the wire basket and dumping the yabbies on the newspaper in the middle of their chairs. Then he showed her how to pull the tails away from the body and peel them. 'Keep the big claws too, as the meat's nice and sweet.'

Nat reached for the red- and orange-tinged yabby. It was still hot from the water, but as Billy had already pulled apart about six, she thought she'd better get cracking. Digging her nails into the middle, she began to pull. She couldn't help squinting and gritting her teeth.

'You got it,' said Drew. He reached over and showed her how to remove the shell.

She got the hang of it and before long the pile of yabby meat was growing. Her fingers were sore from little cuts from the shell and the yabby juices were probably splattered all over her, but she was having fun. Billy was keeping them entertained with stories from the farm and some really bad jokes. At one point Drew

97

asked him to recite his favourite poem and he did, not missing a beat.

> *In an old rocking chair on verandah boards,*
> *He sits and reminisces,*
> *Of days gone by and the work he's done,*
> *Of the wife he so dearly misses.*
> *His weather-beaten face proof of years in the sun,*
> *Eyesight that's failing him fast,*
> *His tired old body can no longer work,*
> *As it did in the years gone past.*
> *Slippers replace the work boots he wore,*
> *His big hands are now pale and tender,*
> *Arms that once rippled with muscle,*
> *Are now pale, fragile and slender.*
> *Things were so different from when he'd first come,*
> *To the land as a strapping young lad,*
> *The clearing he'd done, the homestead he'd built,*
> *'Twas a good life, the life that he'd had.*
> *Eighty years' worth of memories to share,*
> *But nobody wanted to listen,*
> *As he thought of his wife and the children they'd raised,*
> *The tears on his cheek softly glistened.*
> *And now it was done, his dreams were all dreamt,*
> *The hardship and toil all past,*
> *As he closed his eyes for the very last time,*
> *The first shadows of evening were cast.*

Natalie clapped and shook her head in awe. 'Billy, that was amazing.'

His grin was wide. 'Thanks. Nan said it's about my pop.'

'Billy, can you go inside and set up the table, please, buddy?' asked Drew. 'We'll finish up and bring these in.'

'Okay, Dad.' Billy went and washed his hands in the water coming from the gutter. It was still raining but just lightly.

'Mum taught him that,' said Drew once Billy was inside. 'She thought that giving him something to focus on, to remember and to recite, would help his learning, and that was their favourite poem. Mum liked to think that's how my dad would have turned out if he was still alive.'

'You don't have either of your parents?' Nat was shocked. Drew couldn't be that old.

'No. My father died when I was eighteen. I was away at Muresk, studying Ag Science when he crashed his car after footy one night. So I came home to run the farm with mum. That was eight years ago now.'

Nat sat there, watching him and trying to imagine what that must have been like. She had both her parents, even though some days they drove her nuts. Maybe she should go home next weekend and see them. 'So, Billy . . .?' Nat wasn't sure how to ask all the burning questions she had about his son. What happened to his mother? How old was Drew when he was born?

'My dad's name was Bill, and yeah, Billy was born the same year Dad passed away. It was a tough time but I had Mum. Now it's just us.' Drew picked up the bowl of yabby meat before continuing. 'That's what worries me about Billy. I'm not my mum and I'm not sure if I can help him as much as she did. I'm really hoping that he doesn't fall too far behind at school.'

'I'm keeping an eye on him,' said Nat.

'Thank you. You've already earnt his trust so that will go a long way in helping him get through this year. I'm not the best when it comes to homework.' Drew stood up and Nat followed. 'We can wash up in the laundry.'

'I don't want you to worry. We'll work together to help him. And you can always call me if you need. I'm not going back to Perth as much, which is giving me lots of time with nothing to do.'

'If you ever get bored there is always something to do here on the farm.' Drew said. 'Maybe I could employ you to tutor Billy?' he added suddenly.

'Yeah, if it comes to that.' Nat didn't really need the money; she'd help Billy for free.

'Dad, table's ready,' yelled Billy even though they'd just walked inside.

After washing up Nat sat at the table, which was set with a bowl of sauce and bread.

Billy sat beside her again. 'Now we have yabby sandwiches. Like this.' He grabbed some bread, filled it with the yabbie tails and covered it with the sauce before putting a top slice on. 'Would you like to try it?' mumbled Billy, shoving his bitten sandwich in her direction.

'I might make my own.' Nat usually tried to avoid eating white bread but this time she'd make an exception. 'Oh, this is yummy. The sauce really works.'

'Dad makes the best yabby sauce,' said Billy, with a blob of it on his chin. 'It's got mayo in it, and other stuff.'

'Just about the only thing I can do, hey, buddy? Mum tried hard to teach me how to cook before she . . .' Drew stared at his sandwich. 'She needed to know that we'd survive without her and wouldn't live off pies and chips.'

'Maybe one day I can repay the favour and make you guys dinner,' she said.

'Really? Can you make sushi? I love sushi,' said Billy.

Drew laughed. 'Don't be so eager to replace me, buddy.'

'Oh, no, Dad,' said Billy quickly. His face dropped.

'I was just kidding, mate. It's all good.' Drew winked at his son and Billy's face lit up again.

Billy was one of those kids who felt every emotion keenly, and Nat saw how it affected him in the playground. The other kids were obviously used to him, but she'd hate to see how he'd fare in a bigger city school. He'd be ostracised for his lack of social skills.

After lunch, Nat helped clear the plates away but Drew wouldn't let her do any dishes. The rain had stopped so they put on their boots and Billy took her to the chook pens, where they threw the yabby scraps. Nat couldn't get over how many chooks there were, or their beautiful feathers.

'These were Mum's girls. She loved her chooks. Ducks are in the last pen,' said Drew, pointing.

There were four pens in a row, with different breeds in each, plus the ducks.

'Oh my god. Chicks!' she said, squatting down to get a better look.

Billy went inside the pen and picked one up for her to cuddle.

'It's so cute. My nana used to have some in her backyard in a little chicken coop. I'd love to do the same.' Nat rubbed the baby chick against her cheek, the soft yellow feathers like nothing she'd ever felt.

'We can build you one, hey, Dad? Then you can get your own eggs.'

It was almost gut-wrenching to have to put the chick back. Maybe that's what she needed to keep her company in her little blue house.

Eventually they sloshed back through the wet dirt to the house and Nat said it was time to head home. She didn't want to outstay her welcome, even though she'd had so much fun.

The boys walked her to her car after she'd collected her shoes and wet clothes. The sky was almost clear and the sun was shining, making it hard to believe it had ever rained.

'Did you make these, Drew?' asked Nat, pointing to the metal creations along the path.

'No, Kimmy did,' said Billy as he skipped along beside her. 'She's awesome.'

'Who's Kimmy?'

'Kim Richards,' said Drew.

'As in Lauren Richards?' Nat asked.

'Yep. Loz is Kim's sister-in-law. Kim and Matty run the farm next door. They're my best mates and Kim is amazing with a welder. She also helps me out on the farm and watches Billy sometimes. I don't think I could have made it without those guys. Friends are worth their weight in gold.'

Nat had to agree. She missed her friends back in Perth, especially Alisha. Texts and phone calls weren't the same as a night out together. 'Well, thanks for a fantastic afternoon,' said Nat as they reached her car. 'I had so much fun.'

'I hope it wasn't too . . . rustic,' said Drew cautiously.

Nat chuckled. 'It does me good.' She looked down at her clothes. 'Are you sure you don't want these back?' They had been his mother's after all.

'I'm sure. And keep the boots too. I'll give you more if you want them. If you're keen to come out again I'm shearing at the moment.'

All Nat knew about shearing was that it was how you got the wool for making clothes. She hadn't the foggiest how it actually happened.

'Yeah, I can show you how to ride a sheep,' said Billy.

'Hmm, I think I'm a bit big for that,' she replied. 'But I would love to see some shearing, if that's okay with you?'

Drew nodded. 'Just understand that I may put you to work,' he said with a twinkle in his sapphire eyes. 'I'll be shearing all next weekend, so if you're bored just drive up past those sheds to the big one out the back. It has the sheep yards beside it.' Drew pointed up the road.

'Thanks, I just might. See you later. See you at school, Billy.'

Nat got in her car and drove away, glancing at them in her rear-vision mirror. Yeah, she'd come back.

Chapter 12

To my darling princess,

I miss you already. Thank you for the most amazing weekend. I hope you loved eating at your favourite restaurants – yes, I was trying to cram them all into two short days but it was worth it to see your face, especially when you ate that first mouthful of Giovani's pasta. I may have to find out Giovani's secret to his creamy sauce to win your heart forever. And I'd gladly sit through another chick movie if dessert is spent naked with you.

It's always hard to leave you to head to the office but I'm glad you had your parents to visit. I'm sorry that your mum made you feel that way. I, too, will stop trying to convince you to come home. It's just hard when I miss you so much. But your mum really does love you, Natalie. As do I. I am already planning your next visit home. I'm thinking of a picnic by the river, champagne and strawberries. Maybe we can see a play,

or I've heard Ed is coming to Perth. I'd love to get you tickets
to see him. I just want to see you happy, my love. Write to me
often, babe.

I love you, Gary xx

Nat reread the email Gary had sent after their weekend together.
He could be so romantic and thoughtful. In truth, she was feeling a little bored and she'd tried to read a book but nothing
was holding her interest. She couldn't keep reading Gary's email;
she already knew it word for word. She got up and walked to
the back door. Nat leant against the doorframe and stared into
the bush at the back of the house. It had been a quiet Saturday
morning and her mind kept wandering to Billy, who'd reminded
her about coming to see the shearing over the weekend. He'd
been like a broken record, but on the upside he'd been trying
hard to concentrate in class and Nat realised that being his new
shiny coin was a good thing. It probably took his mind off his
nan, and pleasing Nat gave him something to strive for.

Should she go out to the farm?

Did she want to? Yes, she realised she did. Being with the
Saddler boys had been a highlight of her stay and she had completely enjoyed their easygoing company. They were refreshing
and fun.

She ran to her room and changed into her oldest pair of jeans,
which she kept for around the house, a white singlet so she had
something to go under the blue-checked shirt Drew had given
her, plus the thick socks and boots. Glancing in the mirror, she
put her hair up in a high ponytail. Her new outfit felt weird but

she looked like one of the locals now. And it worked.

She stopped at the shop, which luckily was still open, and picked up some drinks, chips and dip. She wasn't sure what food you ate while shearing. Jess and the shop owner did a double take.

'Oh, Natalie. It's you,' said Frank as he flattened his hand over his comb-over hairdo. 'You look like you fit right in here. You going somewhere special?' he asked.

Nat was getting used to everyone one asking a million questions, wanting to know what she was up to or mentioning that they'd seen her car parked at the school over the weekend. 'I'm heading out to see some shearing.'

'Out at Drew's place?'

Jess's head snapped towards them, listening to their conversation.

'How did you know that, Frank?' asked Nat. The locals really did know everything, especially Frank. Running the shop seemed to give him extra intel.

'He's the only one shearing, love, and it usually takes him a while. Actually, he rang up earlier to see if I had some bale fasteners. Do you mind taking them out, love? I was going to get Jess to run them out on her way home but you'll save her the detour.'

'I don't mind,' Jess said quickly but Frank didn't even hear her. He was waiting for Nat's reply.

'Sure, Frank, not a problem.' If anything it gave her a better reason to stop in.

With her shopping and the bale fasteners – whatever they were, some sort of pointy pins – she headed out to Drew's farm.

Doing as told, she drove past their house and up to the sheds, stopping at the one at the back. It was large, made from dull grey-blue corrugated tin. On the side were old wooden rails that held some sheep, and Drew's ute was parked out the front. Nat sat in the car for a moment, trying to gather her nerves, when the old dog, Jo, appeared at the entry of the shed, barking at her. Better get out before they caught her sitting in her car like a dill.

Grabbing the shopping bag and the container from Frank, she headed up the stairs to the sliding door. The first thing that hit her was the smell. It was like nothing she'd ever experienced – unless you counted the time she'd been stuck behind a truck carrying sheep. Then there was an oil scent of some sort. Her nose twitched, and when her eyes adjusted she stepped inside. A machine that she assumed was running the shearing stuff was making a loud noise, and music was coming from an iPod dock on the opposite wall.

Drew was on the right, with a half-shorn sheep between his legs. Nat was struck by the sight and automatically moved closer to watch. Drew was wearing a blue singlet and jeans, his arms glistening with oil or sweat as he moved. She had to admit it was breathtaking to watch a man at work, especially one as attractive as Drew.

At that moment, he glanced up. His hairline was damp with sweat, his face a little grubby, but his eyes were shining.

'Hey, you made it!' he yelled over the machine. 'Just give me a tick.'

He bent his head and finished cutting all the wool off the sheep. Nat watched on in awe as he moved the cutter thing across the sheep's skin while his other hand worked in unison, guiding it along. The way the wool parted from the skin made it look like he was peeling an orange. His feet shuffled and the sheep was moved this way and that and, before she knew it, it was all shorn and Drew was pushing it down a chute behind him. A big pile of fluffy white wool sat on the floor.

Drew pulled a rope and the noise stopped. As he wiped his face on an old green towel hanging on a nail behind him, he reached out with a remote and turned down the music. 'Sorry, now we can talk. I'm glad you came. Billy will be rapt.'

'That was amazing. I didn't know what to expect. If you believed what PETA say, you'd think there'd be bloodshed and half-dead sheep.'

'Don't get me started on them or you'll never hear the end of it,' he warned with a roll of his eyes. 'It's just like getting your hair cut. I really wish these people would actually come to a farm and see shearing before shooting their mouths off. Anyway, moving on,' he finished with a smile. Then his eyes drank her in, from her ponytail to her newly acquired boots.

She flushed. 'Is this better farm attire?'

'Definitely. I don't have to feel bad when you get dirty now.' He gave her a wink and she felt like laughing.

'Here, Frank gave me these for you, and I brought some snacks.' Nat held up both and smiled.

Drew took the fasteners. 'Great, I can do up this bale now. I thought I had a spare box but I was wrong. Thanks, Nat.' He pointed to the dip in the plastic bag. 'There's a fridge in the corner to put that in if you'd like.' He walked her over to what looked like a seventies kitchen cupboard, set up with an old kettle and a microwave, next to an antique-looking fridge with drawings all over it.

A sandwich press sat open with half a loaf of bread beside it. She tried to imagine Drew working and feeding Billy at the same time. It couldn't be easy. 'Where is Billy?' she asked, putting the dip and drinks in the fridge.

'He's taken a small mob I've just shorn back out to the paddock.'

Nat raised her eyebrows in shock. 'By himself?'

'Don't worry, he's an old hand at it. He just opens a few gates and pushes them through with Turbo's help. He should be back any minute. Do you want a cuppa? Cold drink? I could use a little break,' he said, leaning back and stretching, and giving her a close-up of his six-pack through the thin material of his singlet. Farming must be pretty physical work to get a body like that. She doubted he had time to lift weights.

'Hey, Miss Wright, you're here!' yelled Billy as he came running towards them, Turbo bouncing alongside with his tongue hanging out. Billy's boots slapped against the dark floorboards of the shed. 'Have you just got here?' he panted as he stopped beside her, pulling off his cowboy hat. Turbo was panting just as much.

'I have. Are you thirsty?'

He nodded so Nat grabbed a plastic cup by the big blue water esky near the makeshift kitchen and filled it up.

He quickly drank it all. 'Thank you, Miss Wright.'

Nat bent down to his eye level. 'Hey, how about when I'm out here you call me Natty?'

'Natty?' he said, trying it out.

'Yeah. It's what my uncle calls me. But only out of school. Deal?'

'Deal. Thanks, Miss Wright . . . um, I mean Natty.' A grin spread across his face, showing off a missing tooth on the side and front ones that still seemed a little big for him. He also had dimple marks that appeared when his smile was big and genuine.

'Billy, you want to show Nat how to throw a fleece?' Drew shot her a challenging glance. 'Please say you came to help for a bit?'

Nat shrugged. 'I'm keen to give it a go.'

Drew pointed to her hands. 'You won't be going home clean if you do. I'm warning you now.'

She felt like he was testing her, seeing if she was made of tougher stuff, and he wanted her – no, he was daring her – to prove him wrong. And her whole body wanted to do it. Her fingers itched to get dirty and she felt alive. Finally someone was challenging her, making her step outside her comfort zone, and in a way, she felt as if Drew had more faith in her than anyone she knew. How could that be?

'I think it's time to go play in the mud,' she said, trying to be serious, but the corner of her lips turned up, defying her.

'I couldn't agree more. Billy, show her how it's done.'

Billy took her hand and led her to the fleece on the floor. He pointed out where the legs in the fleece were, how to grab them and fold it up, lifting it and then throwing it. 'Just like when you make your bed,' he said.

'How did he do that?' asked Nat, totally amazed at how such

a pint-sized kid could lift all that wool and throw it on a table that was almost too high for him to reach.

'My nana showed me.' He put his hands on his hips and struck a pose that would give Superman a run for his money.

'Mum was a bloody good rousie and always picked up for me while I was shearing. She taught Billy how to throw and skirt a fleece. Showed him how to grade the wool as well,' said Drew with a besotted expression. Billy ran out the back to where the sheep were, leaving them alone.

Nat loved the way his eyes shone with pride. 'What's a rousie?'

Drew almost burst into laughter but pressed his lips together and stopped it, which she was grateful for.

'Gary wouldn't believe this,' said Nat without thinking. He didn't even like it when she did the gardening at her uncle's place. 'I'll pay a man to do that,' he always said. But Nat liked pulling out weeds. It made her feel human.

'Is it okay that you're out here? Gary doesn't mind?' said Drew suddenly. 'It's just that people around here will talk and they like putting two and two together but they usually end up with five. I don't mean to scare you off or anything, because we love having you out here. We enjoy your company, Billy especially.'

Nat felt honoured and also a little taken aback by Drew's honesty. And the fact that he'd asked about Gary showed that he was aware of the situation. He was a straight-up kind of guy. 'He's an amazing kid. I mean, he struggles at school a bit but to see him here on the farm, what he's capable of, is just mind-blowing.'

'Yeah, I know.' Drew leant back on the table where Billy had just thrown the fleece and crossed his arms. 'How did you come to be a teacher, Nat?'

'I love kids,' she said simply.

'But why out here? I don't mean to be rude but most people want a city posting.'

Nat could have spun the spiel she'd told her friends and family, but for some reason, being out here, and with Drew being so honest, she felt she should be as well. 'Because I wanted time to myself, to do the job I trained for without any interference from my family. I needed somewhere far away from my mother's disapproval of my career choice. And soon I'll be married and I'll have other expectations and social commitments, so I really wanted this time out for me.' Nat chewed on the inside of her lip. Did it sound as lame as she thought?

Drew's eyes narrowed and a tingle ran up her spine, making her eager to vary the subject. 'Billy never mentions his mum. Did he not know her?'

The change in Drew was instant. He leant back and his eyes darted off to the side as he picked at the grime on the table.

'No, he didn't. I was young and stupid. But she gave me Billy so I'll always be grateful. Best get going, hey?' He walked over and picked up his shearing handpiece, ending their talk.

So he was hiding something too. But she wasn't going to pry. They were each entitled to their own secrets. 'Hey, I wanted to mention it last time I was here but I didn't want to say it in front of Billy. I guess you've heard about the school closure?'

Drew was squirting oil on the pointy end of the handpiece. 'Yeah, Loz has been chewing my ear off about it.'

'Are you going to come to the meeting next week? We need all the support we can get.'

His head tilted to the side and again he studied her as if she were a puzzle piece that didn't fit. 'You're helping?'

'Yes, Lauren and I are really going to fight this. Did you know the kids will have to be on a bus for an hour just to get to the next school? The poor little four-year-olds! How will they cope?'

Drew smiled and she wondered what she'd said to amuse him.

'So I can count on you to make it to the meeting?'

He looked uncertain but his voice was strong and sure. 'You bet.'

Chapter 13

'YOU want to have a go?' Drew asked as Nat watched him closely.

Her eyes went as big as tractor tyres and she shook her head quickly. 'It looks hard and that looks dangerous,' she said over the noise, pointing to the cutter blades before moving the fleece into position.

An hour later she was still with them. His sister, Amy, would have made up some excuse and escaped the shed by now.

'Hey, Sadds. Need a break?'

Drew glanced up to see Kim smiling down at him. She was wearing her favourite R.M. Williams jeans and belt, and a blue-checked shirt with the sleeves rolled up; her hair pulled back in a low ponytail. It was her standard work gear: she'd come to help him. He could always count on Kim to turn up when she had a free moment to see if he needed help with anything.

'Hey, KC, how are ya, mate?' Drew finished the ewe, pushed her down the chute then pulled his cord. 'Come to lend a hand, have ya?'

'Yep. Seems like you've got some help already?' Kim glanced at Nat, who was at the table with Billy, skirting a fleece.

Billy had been so busy with Nat he hadn't seen Kim yet. When he did, he ran over and Kim picked him up for a hug. She used to throw him up in the air, but now that Billy was getting older, just holding him up there was hard enough on the arms.

'Hey, kiddo.'

'Have you come to help out? Is Uncle Matt here too?' asked Billy.

'He'll be over soon with the kids.'

'Awesome.' Billy turned as Nat walked up beside him. 'Kimmy, this is my teacher. She's come out to help us.'

'Hi. Loz has told me lots about you,' said Kim, holding out her hand.

'Ah, so you're Kim. Nice to finally meet you.' Nat wiped her hand on her jeans before shaking Kim's hand.

'I'm trying to show Natty how to roustabout. Maybe you can help?' Billy turned to Nat. 'Kimmy can do everything. She's just like Dad.'

Drew chuckled. 'She can probably do more than me.'

'Except shear and shoot as good as you,' Kim said quickly.

'Now, Kimmy, you gotta leave me with something,' he teased. She already welded better than he could – she just had a bloody knack when it came to using a mig welder. She had a gift, that was for sure. Not that he could tell her that.

'Okay, short stuff. How about we throw a few fleeces before I take over from your dad?' said Kim.

Billy's toothy grin filled his face as he nodded.

Drew only shore another twenty sheep before Kim was tapping him on the shoulder. 'My turn,' she said with a smile.

Drew joined Nat by the skirting table while Kim picked a ewe from the pen.

'Oh my god, is she going to shear?' said Nat.

'Yes, our Kim is a jack of all trades.'

'She's amazing.' Nat was staring at Kim like she was some famous actress.

Drew glanced towards his best friend and tried to see what Nat saw. He probably took Kim for granted – she'd always been one of the boys, could do whatever they did and, if truth be told, her farming ideas were better than Matt's.

'Are you guys dating?'

'Huh?' Drew was confused. Was that a joke? But Nat looked serious.

'Lauren said she's single but how could you not be together? She's gorgeous, so capable and she loves Billy to bits.' Her eyebrows were raised slightly and Drew was struck by how perfect they were.

'Um, we're friends,' he said as Billy threw the next fleece on the table. Drew started skirting the fleece automatically.

'So you've never gone there?'

Nat was like a dog with a bone. Drew didn't want to have this conversation at all. He shook his head and was relieved when Seth and Mallory ran into the shed, yelling out to Billy. Before Natalie could start up again, Drew went over to Matt.

'Hey, mate. Good to see Kim is pulling her weight,' Matt laughed.

'Someone has to, 'cos you're too podgy to get down that low,' teased Drew, tapping Matt's round belly.

'You bastard,' said Matt with a smile. 'Oh, I see you already have some help.' Matt had spotted Nat, who was now encircled by the kids. 'The talk around town was right. She certainly is a looker. Man, I envy you,' said Matt quietly.

'She's engaged, Matt.' Drew was about to say, 'Besides, I'm not interested,' but he stopped. Something didn't feel right with that. Sure, he wasn't blind – she was gorgeous, funny and intriguing – but was he interested like that? Maybe if she was single he'd think about it, eventually. But life was easier with just him and Billy.

'She's good with the kids,' Matt added as he watched her listen to them intently, taking the time to hear what they had to say.

'Yeah.' Drew watched Billy put his little hand in hers as if to say he had her first. 'You hanging around for long?' he asked.

'Until the kids drive me nuts and I can take them back to Lozzy.'

'Cheers. I might get the next stand going then.'

Moments later Drew was shearing alongside Kim while the kids played in the hocks bins and chased each other around the shed, leaving Matt and Natalie to rouse. He put the music back on and the afternoon went quickly, the shed alive with action. His mum would have loved this – the shed full of people working and having fun at the same time. She would have made sure they all stayed for dinner and drinks. Drew doubted the stew he'd put on this morning would feed them all, but maybe there would be enough if just Kim and Nat stayed.

It was just after six when Matt left with Seth and Mallory, who were covered in wool and grimy dirt from the lanoline. Mallory had had a meltdown when she couldn't find her loom-band bracelet but Nat had promised to make a new one with her, which had stopped all the tears and allowed Matt to get them home. Drew sent him on his way with a few cold beers, the usual currency for his helping hands.

'Thanks, guys, I appreciate it.' Drew handed out cold beers to Kim and Nat. They sat on the bales stacked by the side wall while Billy played with Turbo in the last rays that crept along the dirty boards as the sun descended.

'It was fun,' said Nat, who looked as if it had been anything but. She had grime on her face and wool in her hair, and that perfect veneer of hers was gone, but he had to admit she was still sexy as hell. Shed work had brought real colour to her cheeks. 'Hard work, but fun,' she admitted. 'You both make it look easy.' Nat retrieved the dip and crackers she'd brought, placing them on the bale between them.

'Oh, yum, thanks. Well, we've had years of practice,' said Kim before taking a long scull from her beer. 'Ain't that right, Sadds?'

Drew smiled and raised his beer to her. 'Yep. Hey, KC, my birthday is getting closer. How's my gift going?'

'Andrew Saddler, keep that up and I'll give it to someone else. You little shit.'

Nat gestured to the food. 'Eat up.'

'Age before beauty,' said Drew to Kim.

'Shit before the shovel,' she returned before they both reached for a cracker.

'Oh, may I have some, please, Natty?' said Billy who'd spotted the food.

Nat touched his shoulder gently. 'Of course, Billy, help yourself. You worked so hard today. I was impressed.'

'And you tried really hard too,' he said, returning a compliment.

Drew couldn't hide his smile. Such well-meaning words. Luckily Nat took it all in her stride.

'Why, thank you. I know I'm not very good but I'm sure if I practise hard I'll get better.'

'Yeah.' Billy gave her a smile that was more like a grimace and they all laughed.

'Well, I'd love to stay and watch another sunset with you, Sadds, but I've got the folks over for dinner tonight,' said Kim.

'Good luck with that. Is it burnt fish or gluggy risotto?'

Kim stood up and punched his arm hard. He tried not to wince. 'Bastard. I only burnt the fish once and you kept talking so much the rice went yuck.'

'Oh, I get the blame for the rice?'

'Too damn right. And I'm taking a roady – you owe me.' Kim went to the fridge and pulled out a few more beers and left her empty one on the bench. 'It was nice to meet you, Nat. I'll see you at the P & C meeting.'

'Will do. Thanks for your guidance today. I needed it.'

'Nah, you'll be an old hand in no time. At least you gave it a go.' Kim raised her beer to Drew in a final goodbye. 'See ya, mate.'

'Later, Kim.'

Billy followed her out to her ute while Drew remained inside with Nat. They listened to Kim's vehicle driving away and then Billy calling out to Turbo as they ran around outside.

'You don't see it at all, do you?' asked Nat.

She was leaning back on one arm, her check shirt open. Drew tried to keep his eyes from wandering down to where her chest rose in soft mounds. Damn, it had been a long time between drinks. Her body was starting to mess with his head. 'See what?' he asked. He was trying not to see. How her jeans hugged her hips, or the way a loose strand of hair fell across her flawless cheek.

'Kim. She cares for you a lot.'

'Yeah. We've been mates for years.'

Nat rolled her eyes. 'God, men can be so clueless sometimes.'

Drew scratched his head. What had he done now? 'Did you want to stay for dinner?' he asked, changing the subject. 'I have a stew cooking at home. It's the least I can do to say thanks for today.'

'Ha, I thought you'd be happy to see the back of me.'

'No, really. You got the hang of it and saved me a lot of time. I really appreciate it,' he said. 'You're welcome back anytime. But I can only pay you in beer and food,' he said with a twinkle in his eye.

'Dinner sounds nice, thanks.'

Her words were music to his ears. He didn't want her to leave just yet. She brightened up the place – her smile, her gentle laugh. That killer body. It was nice to have someone new to talk to.

'Great. I'm glad.'

Nat shared a beautiful moment with the Saddler boys as the sun went down, sitting at the open door of the shed, vibrant gold and pink hues filling the sky while Billy and Turbo kicked up dust that drifted in the breeze. It was the perfect way to end the day – chatting over a beer, discussing their tastes in music. She was shocked to hear so much pop music coming from his iPod dock and he teased her for assuming he listened to country music just because he was from the country. Then, when the sun dipped below the horizon, they headed back to the house for stew and toast.

Chapter 14

WITH freshly painted nails, Nat carefully zipped up her Moss and Spy primrose dress. Her nails had taken a hammering at Drew's farm and had taken ages to get clean. But it had been worth it. She'd slept like a log that night, exhausted from the workout but exhilarated at the same time. And she'd liked being able to help Drew. He seemed like a man with a lot of pride, and asking for help was something he wasn't used to. The fact that he was trying to run a farm and raise his son all by himself seemed crazy yet amazing. To watch him interact with Billy, to see the love that radiated from him, was something special.

Nat was actually hoping he would come to the meeting tonight so she could thank him again and maybe offer to help out this weekend too. All weekend she'd wanted to head back out to the farm and practise throwing the fleece again. It was like an addiction; she wanted to perfect it. And if she was being honest, she really enjoyed the Saddler boys' company.

With a quick swipe of her lipstick she headed for the car, grabbing the blue folder from her kitchen table on her way out.

The meeting was being held in the small hall at the end of town. Weeks of advertising with fliers and notices in the local paper and school newsletter had led to this night. The kids had made up most of the posters for it too. They were hoping the whole community would turn up to support the school and to decide what action they should take. The area around the hall was filled up with cars – mostly utes, four-wheel drives and dual cabs, which were all covered in dust from gravel roads. Nat parked and walked to the hall. She could already hear the hum of voices. Men stood outside talking, some still in their work clothes while others had found time to shower and change. The hall was old, the white paint discoloured and peeling in spots. A large crack ran along the bricks, zigzagging its way from top to bottom.

A figure leant by the large double doors, in clean jeans and a white button-down shirt, his hair damp from the shower. Drew seemed too young and handsome to have a son. For a moment Nat hoped Drew had been waiting for her but then she saw Billy running around with Mallory and Seth.

'Hey, Drew.'

His eyes lifted up and he smiled. 'Natty,' he said, then apologised. 'Sorry, I've got used to Billy calling you that. It's all I ever hear around home at the moment.'

'It's okay, I don't mind.' If anything, it cemented their new friendship. 'You want a rousie for the weekend? I'm free.'

'Really? You sure?' His eyes swirled with colour, like the ocean waves around a reef.

'Only if it's okay with you. I like coming out. Better than being alone.' Not that being alone was a problem, but if it was that or the farm, then it was a simple choice.

'Yeah, sure. Just come out whenever. Cheers.'

'Oh, Nat, you're here. Great. Shall we get started?' said Lauren, who'd just poked her head outside the door. 'Drew, can you tell the kids to be quiet while we have the meeting? Thanks, darling.'

Nat waved to Drew as Lauren swept her inside to the hall, which was full of more people than she thought lived in Lake Biddy. 'Where did all these people come from?' she said, more to herself than to Lauren. So many people she was yet to meet. The older community members sat in the plastic green chairs lined up on the wooden floor while the rest stood against the walls or at the back. Lauren led Nat to the front and up some steps onto a stage with thick red curtains draped at the sides. The principal and some of the staff were already seated at a table, along with other members on the P & C committee. She didn't think she was running late, yet she felt like they'd all been waiting for her. All eyes followed her movements and she wondered what the residents were thinking. City imposter? No business being here? She wouldn't understand? Maybe all of that and more.

Nat took a seat between Ross and Kath. Lauren stood up the front and waved her hands before yelling, 'Oi! Can I have every-one's attention?'

Someone at the back whistled, loudly enough to send the

fifty-odd dogs outside nuts. But it did the trick. When the hum of voices died down Nat noticed some of the men wander in from outside. Drew was there too, standing at the back just inside the door. No doubt keeping his eye on the kids.

'Right. You've all heard about the plan to close the school,' said Lauren. The crowd voiced its displeasure.

'It's bloody stupid,' said a tall man standing up the front by the wall. He had a thick black beard and wore a blue flannel shirt. 'Our children should not be the scapegoats for the government's poor finance management. It'll kill our town,' he said in a thunderous rumble. 'And why should we be punished because they've taken away our Year 7s? They take our kids then close our schools.'

'I know, I know,' said Lauren. 'We can't let it happen. So, this is the first of what will probably be many meetings. Tonight we want to hear your thoughts, your ideas, and we'll put together a plan of attack.' Lauren gestured to Nat and the others. 'We have a dedicated team and welcome anyone else who's willing to pitch in and help. We have notified our politicians and approached the shire council. Natalie has already offered to put up a Facebook page and start a petition, as well as a census for the district to see who plans to have kids over the next five years. We'll try to get some officials out here to explain their motives. Ross is happy to take the minister around if we can get him out to our school. Kath's offered to do fliers and letters, whatever is needed. That's it from me to begin with – I'll hand it over to you.' Lauren gesture to the crowd.

'I'm happy to help out,' said a lady at the front with a baby and a two-year-old on her lap. Other hands went up and Kath recorded the helpers' names.

A man in the second row stood up, his glasses sitting in the front pocket of his flannel shirt. 'I've already written a lengthy letter to the minister regarding the Year 7s moving to high school and the effect this has on our rural schools and towns. I can give you a copy if you want to use it,' he said.

'Thanks, Mack,' said Lauren. 'That would be great. Can you get it to Kath?'

Mack nodded and sat back down.

'How about I do up a timeline of my kids getting to school and how much it will change if they have to go to Lake Grace? Point out the early starts and the extra hours on the bus?'

'Fantastic, Shirley,' Lauren replied.

There was more discussion and Nat was impressed by how easily Lauren mediated the room. She knew every local and kept the crowd under control.

'Tom, go and get a beer and take a breather,' Lauren called to the tall man with the beard who'd been getting angrier as the night went on.

'It's okay,' Tom yelled back. 'I've already got one. Just waiting for it to work.' The room erupted with laughter, giving them a break from the uphill battle they were facing.

Kath was kept busy jotting everything down. Babies cried out every now and then. They were nursed on laps, or slept in nearby prams while toddlers crawled over chairs and ended up hanging off someone else's leg. People picked up kids who weren't their own, consoled crying ones who'd hurt themselves or told others off if they were misbehaving. It was fascinating to watch how a small community worked together. People cared. They loved their community, they were outraged over the government's decision and the effect it would have on their kids, the town and its future. What a wonderful place it must be to raise a family, Natalie thought. But Gary would never leave the city. He would never fit into a place like this and she had to wonder if the locals would ever accept him.

Towards the end, the CWA ladies started shuffling about in the kitchen, putting out plates of scones and savouries, tea and coffee, while the kids seemed to swarm in like flies, waiting with greedy expressions for the go-ahead to eat.

'All right, folks, I think that's us done for tonight. Thanks for coming and please remember the next meeting. I'll try to email you all and we'll have notices at the shop and through the school.'

'Maybe in the local papers too,' said Kath loudly.

Lauren nodded. 'Thanks, everyone. Supper's up.'

The hall filled with the sound of the chairs scraping along the wooden floor. Voices grew louder as everyone began to talk and then louder again as they tried to talk over each other. Nat felt like she was being passed along like a newborn baby, with every person wanting her, whether it was to discuss their kids at school or just trying to find out some more personal information about her. What part of Perth was she from, had she set a wedding date, what did she think of Lake Biddy? By the time she made it to the kitchen, the kids and adolescents had mowed through most of the food. Nat reached for the last sausage roll.

'Once you have one of them you won't be the same again,' said Drew shooting her a smile. 'Mrs Harrison makes them and they are mouth-watering. I was actually about to tackle you to the ground for it.'

'That good, hey?' Nat bit into the flaky pastry. 'Oh my god,' she mumbled before shoving the rest of it into her mouth.

'I did warn you. She makes up two batches because they go like hot cakes. You're lucky you managed to score the last one.'

'More like unlucky. Now I want more.' Nat couldn't stop herself from sucking the tips of her fingers.

'I can suggest Margie's caramel slice,' said Drew pointing to it. 'Or Ida's chocolate marshmallow balls, and then there are Joyce's pinwheels.'

Nat raised her eyebrows. 'You know what everyone has made?'

Drew shrugged. 'Everyone does.' He stepped closer to Natalie. 'I can also tell you not to eat the chocolate cake on the end.'

Nat noticed there was only one piece missing, which was strange as it looked so good. 'Why?'

'Mrs Niles made that and her eyesight is shocking. She often gets the flours mixed up or uses cornflour instead of icing sugar. You never know what you're going to get.'

Nat laughed but she didn't get to thank Drew before he was accosted by some of the married ladies. They peppered him with questions about how he was going and offers to help if he needed it. Nat got the feeling this might be the first big outing for Drew and Billy since his mum had passed away. His eyes flicked to her, begging for a reprieve, and she wondered if she should try to save him.

'My daughter Stacy is up over the weekend. You remember Stacy, Drew? She's a dental assistant now. Do you want to come over for dinner on Saturday?' said a lady with shoulder-length dyed black hair and lipstick two shades too dark for her.

'Um, actually, I'm quite busy. Sorry,' said Drew.

This time when he glanced at Nat she caught the little nod of his head and the pleading frown. It wasn't nice, watching a man squirm as if sitting in a boiling pot while witches feasted upon him with hungry eyes. A meat market of sorts. Without thinking, Nat stepped across and grabbed Drew's arm.

'Drew, Billy's looking for you, I think he fell over,' she said, hoping her face didn't go red with the lie.

'Oh, right,' he said, diving out of the circle of women. 'I'll catch up with you all later,' said Drew before they headed for the outside doors.

'Thank you. I was starting to think you weren't going to get the hint,' he whispered as he nodded to a bloke he knew.

'Yeah, sorry.'

Outside it was dark but they could hear the kids' voices as they ran around, playing between the cars.

'Come this way,' said Drew before he yelled out Billy's name.

He led her to his ute and seconds later Billy turned up puffing with gravel dust smudged on his face. 'Yeah, Dad? Is it time to go?'

'Remember we had something for someone?'

At his father's words Billy glanced at Nat and in the outside light at the hall she could see his face in raptures.

'Oh, yes! Natty, we made you something,' Billy said brightly.

He reached for her hand and held it. 'You'll love it.'

Drew motioned to the back of his ute. Nat tried to focus on what she saw. Timber and wire in some kind of box shape.

'What is it?'

'It's a chicken coop for your yard so now you can collect your own fresh eggs,' said Billy. 'Dad and I made it for you.'

Now that she knew what she was looking at, the whole thing began to make sense. It was amazing. It actually brought a lump to her throat. These Saddler boys, who she hadn't known that long, had made her something so special, from the heart, knowing how much it would mean to her. How was that possible?

'What do you think? Is it okay?' pressed Billy. He moved the cage and she could hear the chooks' protests. 'I've given you Henny and Penny. You can just see them roosting. Two chooks should be enough, right?'

She had real chooks too? 'Oh, Billy,' said Nat, dropping down to his height. 'It's the most amazing gift anyone's ever given me. Are you sure you want to part with Henny and Penny?'

Billy pulled a face. 'We have so many chooks.'

'Well, thank you. I will take great care of them and you can visit them anytime.'

'Are you heading home now?' asked Drew. 'I'll drop this off now if you like.'

'That would be great.'

Billy rode with her, and when they parked at her house Drew immediately got out and started lifting the chicken coop.

'Billy?' he called.

'Coming!'

Billy ran to hold the other end and together they brought it up the driveway to the back of the house. Nat turned on her outside lights before coming back to open the back gate. The boys put the small hutch on the edge of the lawn.

'Sorry, girls, my lawn is still getting going,' she said, bending down to talk to the hens, who'd been stirred up by the transportation. Now she could see them in the light: two beautiful hens with soft feathers, some on their feet, which she'd never seen before. 'What breed are they? I've only really known the Isa Browns. They never had the feathers on the feet.'

Drew disappeared while Billy knelt down beside her. 'These are silky bantams. Nan said they were more bantams but the silky bits are the feathered feet and black skin. And they have pretty feathers. I thought you'd like the pretty ones.'

'I do. I love them so much. Which one is Henny?'

As Billy showed her which chook was which, Drew came back and dumped a few bags down beside them.

'One has wheat, the other some layer pellets and shells. Make sure you find a good bin to store it in or you'll have the mice in eating it,' said Drew.

Nat stood up and smiled at the kind-hearted man. 'I don't know how to thank you.'

'Least we could do for all the shed help.'

Nat realised she hadn't been very hospitable. 'Would you like a drink?'

'No, I'm right, thanks. We should be hitting the road. Take me forever to get this boy ready for bed.'

'Oh, Dad. Can't we stay a little bit, please?'

'No, you have school tomorrow and so does Natty.'

The way Drew said her nickname made her grin. 'Yes, I must get ready. Then I'll be out over the weekend to help in the shed.'

'Again? For real?'

'If that's okay with you, Billy?' Nat knew it would be.

'Sure is, Natty. I can't wait.' Billy spun around to face his dad. 'Can I show her the bike track, Dad?'

'How about we leave that for another time, okay? Say good-bye and jump in the ute.'

'Goodbye, Natty. See you tomorrow.' Billy rushed off to the ute. She was about to walk Drew out when the phone rang inside the house.

'Thanks, Drew. I'll see you on the weekend.'

'Righto.' He waved as he ducked around the side of the house.

Nat sprinted inside to get the phone. 'Hello?'

'Hey, sis, how's things in the big dust bowl?'

'Jase, hey, big bro. What are you up to?'

'Oh, you know, just sorting out a media contract with Foxtel. It's actually more exciting than it sounds.'

'Yeah, I'm sure,' she teased. But he did sound excited. He loved his job, working alongside their dad. Nat had never been offered a position in the company; her future had been sorted by her mum before she'd finished high school: marry a wealthy man, grace the social pages and run a perfect house. She'd set her mum's plans back by becoming a teacher.

'How's things with you?' asked Jason.

Delighted that someone cared enough to ask, Nat told him everything. 'Oh, it's gorgeous here, Jase. I love my kids; they all have their own little traits and try so hard to please me. You should see all the things they have given me – drawings and special bits are filling up my house. Oh, and I have new chooks. Two, to be exact.' She told him all about Henny and Penny and promised to text him a photo of them. 'I've also been doing sheep work. Learnt how to throw a fleece.'

'No way,' said Jason.

'Yes way. You wouldn't bloody recognise me in my farm clothes, being a rousie.' Then she had to tell him what a rousie did, and all about the Saddler farm. For once she knew something her big brother didn't and it felt fantastic. 'Oh, but we've just found out they want to close the school, Jase. It's awful. It's going to hurt this town so much. I'm helping them to keep it open. The whole community is rallying together. And you must try Mrs Harrison's homemade sausage rolls. To. Die. For!'

Jason laughed. 'Well, sounds like I'm going to have to come back down there. You paint a great picture, sis, and you sound so happy. I'm feeling rather jealous.' Now it was her turn to laugh. 'It's good to know you're doing okay. I miss you, though. I promise to call more often, or at least I'll try. I'll definitely be thinking about it,' he said with a chuckle.

'Thanks, Jase. I love you too, big bro.'

After the phone call Nat changed into her PJs and sat outside with her new pets. They were probably trying to sleep but she talked to them anyway. Henny and Penny were the new loves of her life.

Chapter 15

THE phone rang just as she was about to slip on her farm boots. Damn. Who would be calling her on a Saturday morning? Gary's picture flashed up on her phone.

'Gary? I thought you'd be in a conference by now.'

'I am, just on a break. Been the first chance I've had to call you.' He sounded agitated. It was very unusual for him to call while away on business. He usually preferred to catch up when he got back.

'Is everything all right?'

'You tell me.'

'Everything is fine here,' she said cautiously.

'What's this I hear about you doing sheep work out on a farm, baby?'

'I'm just helping out some friends.'

'The way Jason tells it, you're turning into a country bumpkin. Sweetheart, you don't have to try to fit in.' Gary paused but she knew he had more to say. 'This guy – Jason said he's single?'

'Yes, he's just lost his mum. His son's in my class and needs a little attention and I'm helping out.'

'I thought you went out there to teach, not become a station hand. Baby, don't overdo it.' Nat flinched at the patronising tone. Why was he acting like this? 'I fly back tonight and was hoping to see you,' he went on. 'Look, I have to go. I'll talk to you later. I love you.'

Then he hung up. Nat stared at her phone. Maybe sharing stuff with her brother hadn't been a great idea. Jason and Gary were good friends, even more so since the engagement.

With a deep breath she slipped her phone in her pocket and looked at her boots. Maybe she shouldn't go out to the farm today. She didn't want to upset Gary, but she didn't like this possessive side of him. And she had so enjoyed spending time out there. She felt so comfortable with Drew. And she didn't want to disappoint Billy.

Nat slipped on her boots and reached for her keys. Lucky she hadn't mentioned to Jason just how good-looking Drew was.

Out at the farm, shearing was in full swing. It was a hot day and would be stifling in this shed after lunch. Nat didn't know how anyone kept working through this ridiculous heat. Billy and Drew looked as if they'd been at this for hours already.

'Hey, Natty.'

Billy's grin was infectious and his enthusiastic wave always made her feel so special. 'Morning, Billy. Shall we see if I can remember how to do it?' Billy's dedication to helping his father never ceased to amaze her.

They headed over to where Drew was shearing. His fitted blue singlet clung to his damp skin and even in this heat he wore pants. His hair curled at the base of his neck where it was damp with sweat.

'Welcome back,' he said, looking up with a grin. His blue eyes were bright and alive as if he had just been skydiving, not shearing endless sheep. 'A sucker for punishment, aren't ya?'

Nat smiled. 'I think you are. Crazy shearing in this heat.'

'That's all right. We have dams for swimming.'

Nat screwed up her face. 'I did bring my bathers, just in case I was desperate.'

Drew laughed, then he went back to shearing with a smile on his face, as if he knew something she didn't.

Nat worked hard and the next few hours disappeared quickly. They stopped for lunch, eating the chicken wraps she'd made for them all.

'That's half the flavour,' she said when she caught Drew pulling out the cucumber from his.

'I can't eat spewcumber,' he said with a grimace. He held it out for Turbo, who took one sniff and walked away. 'See, if a dog won't eat it, it must be crap.' His lips turned up into an innocent smile. 'But I eat everything else.'

Nat pressed her lips together to hide her grin before focusing on Billy. 'What about you? What don't you like to eat?' she asked him.

'I don't like snotoli.'

'Mum overcooked the broccoli one night and it turned to mush,' Drew explained. 'Billy here said it resembled snot and he hasn't eaten it since then. Damn near put me off it for life too.'

'Gosh, is dinner at your place always this . . . exciting?'

'Come on, surely there's something you don't like to eat?' Drew asked.

'Like liver? Yuck,' said Billy pulling a face.

'I eat most things, but to tell you the truth I can't seem to like oysters. Gary loves them but I struggle to get them down and end up just swallowing them whole.' Nat felt her throat constrict as if trying to keep one of those slimy suckers down.

'What's an oyster?' said Billy.

Nat explained it while Drew finished his second wrap. She'd brought an extra just in case and was glad she had as Drew seemed to inhale his food. Must be all that energy he expended in the shed.

'Gary get to his conference okay?' asked Drew.

'Yeah. He rang this morning. I'd told my brother about all this,' said Nat, gesturing to the shed full of wool, sheep and smells she was getting used to. 'And then he told Gary. And now Gary's worried.'

'About what?' Drew frowned.

That fact that Drew didn't get it showed just how safe she was here with him. Why couldn't Gary understand?

'It's just different to what he knows. He didn't really want me to come out here in the first place.'

'To Lake Biddy?'

She nodded.

'But you still came?'

'Yeah. I just had to do this for myself, you know? Before life takes over.'

'You make it sound like there's some pressure involved, that you're not happy where it's going?' said Drew softly.

'In a way. I guess I'd hoped I could continue teaching but with my family business and Gary's, it's just not really going to work. I was able to wrangle this year because they all expect me to give it up afterwards.' Nat hadn't ever been this frank with anyone before. She couldn't voice her innermost thoughts with her family or her friends, besides Uncle Kent. They just wouldn't get it. They didn't understand her desire to be a teacher, for a start.

'That seems a bit sad that you feel you have to give up something you're passionate about,' Drew said.

'But marriage and family are about compromise, so I'll do my part,' she said.

'And what about you, Nat? I hope Gary is compromising things for you too.'

Those eyes sliced through her like the handpiece cutting the sheep's wool.

'I'm sure he is,' she said hopefully.

They sat there quietly for a moment. The tin walls creaked in the heat, flies buzzed around seeking out a cool spot and Turbo's tail pounded the floorboards every time Billy took a bite of his wrap. Nat really didn't want to be left with her thoughts so she got up and poured them all some cold water.

After a few more hours of shearing, Drew stopped the machine, putting the last ewe from his pen down the chute. 'Well, I think we've earnt a break. Who's for a swim?' said Drew.

Billy was lying in the wool in one of the bins having a rest but he shot up like he'd been stung by a wasp. 'I am. Can I take Natty on the bike track before we swim?'

Drew shrugged and gestured to Nat.

'Okay, you'd better show me this bike track. It's all I've heard about for ages.'

They went outside into the hot sun and Billy got on his little motorbike. 'Mine is a 50cc but you can take Dad's quad bike,' he said, pointing to a big red four-wheeled bike.

'Oh, I've never ridden a bike before,' she said and then wondered if she'd have to ride on the back with Drew.

'Here, it's pretty easy.' Drew showed her how to start it and change gears, where the brake was, and then let her head off.

She was hesitant at first but Drew just seemed to have this faith in her ability to give it a go. She took off around the shearing shed and felt her nerves disappear at the sheer elation of having the wind in her face and the thrill of something new. She pulled up next to Drew after a few laps.

'That was cool,' she said, mimicking Billy's catch phrase.

'Well, I think you're set to tackle the bike track. Don't hurt yourself,' he said with a wink and handed over a helmet.

'Follow me, Natty!' yelled Billy. His red helmet made him easy to spot.

He took her towards a patch of bush and soon she found herself riding along a little track, dodging trees, flying over mounds of dirt, weaving around dead branches and then more jumps that made her stomach roll. They did it three times, and each time she got faster and took more risks – but with the risk came exhilaration.

Pulling up back at the shed she had a smile from ear to ear. 'I feel like a kid,' she said, whipping off the helmet and feeling like her face was fried from the wind.

'You look like one,' said Drew. 'Time for a swim now.'

She grabbed her bathers out of the car and got changed in the small toilet beside the shearing shed.

'Ready?' asked Drew as he walked towards her in a low-hanging pair of blue-and-black boardies.

'I guess so.' Nat saw Drew's eyes drop to her simple one-piece black halter-neck bathers. She'd gone conservative.

'Don't mind my sock tan. Comes with the job,' he said.

It wasn't really his sock tan that was holding her attention. It was the smooth, tanned body that was firm with hard-earned muscles. And when he reached out and scooped up Billy, his arms rippled like a Muay Thai fighter's.

'This way.'

He led them towards another shed. Nat was a little confused as she thought they'd need the ute to get to the dam. It wasn't until Drew walked inside the big machinery shed that she saw what was on the ground beside a red machine with two massive wheels and two small ones at the back.

'Is that a pool?' she asked.

'Yep. Bush style.'

'It took a whole load of water from the truck,' said Billy, who had picked up a black tube.

Nat had a feeling it was a tube from a car tyre. But the pool was a massive blue tarp draped over square hay bales. Straw was littered everywhere, but the water was clear. It looked so much more inviting than a muddy dam.

'Last one in's a rotten egg!' Billy jumped in with a splash and a squeal.

Nat followed and found the water temperature perfectly refreshing. It was deep enough that it reached above her chest when sitting down. Perfect for leaning back against the covered bale. 'Drew, this is fabulous.'

'Yeah, it beats driving to Lake Grace to use the public pool.'

Billy paddled about while Nat and Drew sat there talking about saving the school, the farm versus the city and all sorts of everyday things.

'I went to an all-girls private school and it was okay. I enjoyed sport and hanging out with my friends. Uni was even better, especially when I got to do my prac in real classrooms. We had a local tavern that was our hangout and they'd get these great bands in over the weekends. Can't beat live music, Drew.'

'Yeah, I got a small taste of it while I was at Muresk. So many opportunities.'

'Dad, Seth and Mallory would love this,' Billy said, swimming up between them.

'I know. Kim's bringing them over in an hour.'

'Yippee!' Billy sank into the water with his hand over his head, pretending to be a shark and nibble on their toes with his fingers.

Nat made a mental note to leave before Kim arrived, mainly because she didn't want to be the third wheel. At times it was hard to understand what they were talking about – some of the farm stuff was quite technical and they mentioned people she still wasn't familiar with. Maybe part of her was a little uncomfortable with Kim finding her at Drew's again in case she got the wrong idea; maybe Gary's phone call had put her on edge. Either way, it was nearly time for her to head home and prep some work for school on Monday.

'Aww,' said Billy when she announced her departure. 'Do you really have to go?'

'Yep, buddy, sorry. Thanks for the swim and the bike ride. I had lots of fun.'

Billy gave her a wet hug. It made sweating her butt off in the shed all worth it. The hard work was forgotten with the fun she'd had, the new things she'd experienced. Was farm life always like this?

'Thanks, Drew, I had a great time. I'll catch up with you again soon.'

Drew walked her to her car. He didn't bother with a towel and she was thankful for the last glance of this handsome man. How had Kim not made a move all these years? He only had eyes for his son, which was sweet, but it wouldn't hurt if he found someone to make their family bigger. Billy would thrive with a mother figure, someone to help take Alice's place, someone to help share Drew's workload.

'You're welcome anytime, Nat. Seriously. We love having you out. Thanks for all your help. Let me know if anything ever needs fixing and I'll try and repay the favour.'

Nat opened her car door before turning. 'Actually, now that you mention it, are you any good at putting cupboard handles back on? This morning I went to get out the coffee and pulled a bit too hard.'

'Not a problem,' he said with a smile. 'I'll come take a look next time I'm in town if you like.'

'That would be great. See you!'

Nat left the farm feeling recharged and happy – a feeling that was becoming a regular part of life in Lake Biddy.

Chapter 16

NAT was sitting outside talking to Henny and Penny when she heard a car pull up out the front. Had Drew come to fix her cupboard already?

'Hello? Natalie, are you here?'

Nat sprung up. 'Gary?' Her heart raced in surprise. Her fiancé's head appeared by the gate. He was clean-shaved, sideburns perfectly even, and his lips spread in an alluring smile. 'Oh my god, Gary, what are you doing here?' Nat hurried over to open the gate, still feeling shocked to actually see him in Lake Biddy.

'Hey, princess,' he said pulling her into his arms.

He smelt like expensive aftershave, suits and the breath mints he lived on since he'd quit smoking.

'I can't believe it,' she said, taking in his groomed hair, touching his smooth shaved jaw and gazing into his dark-coloured eyes. Gary's soft hands caressed her neck before kissing her deeply.

'I've missed you,' he whispered. He was wearing his dark-blue pinstripe suit without the jacket.

'Did you drive straight from work?'

'I just sorted a few things before I came down. Hell, is it always this hot and dry?' He clutched at his matching blue tie and gave it a jerk.

'Did you drive all the way out here? How long can you stay? You should have called me,' she said as she pulled him towards the shade of the small back verandah.

'Yeah, it's a fair drive. Not much out here, is there? And nothing is open on a Sunday.' Gary pulled a face and wiped at the sweat beading along his brow. 'I have to head back tomorrow night or early Tuesday. See how they cope without me. You do get phone signal here?' he asked before pulling out his phone and holding it up, waiting for the bars to show.

'Yes, we're lucky – there's a phone tower nearby but if you face the wrong way or you're behind the wheat bins it drops out.'

'Wheat bins?'

'The big white sheds you would have driven past. Opposite the town.'

Gary nodded but didn't seem all that interested. 'I'll get my stuff. I grabbed some things I thought you might like for dinner.' His teeth, all perfectly white and straight, shone as he smiled.

That night they had a little picnic outside, on a rug on the lawn: champagne, strawberries, chocolate, her favourite selection of sushi, all complemented by a bunch of beautiful flowers.

'This is amazing. You thought of everything.' He really was thoughtful and sweet. It was what had made her fall for him in the first place. She pushed aside her niggling thoughts of being rushed into marriage and decided to just enjoy the moment.

Gary held her hand and moved the ring on her finger, which Nat was glad she had replaced after her trip to the farm.

'I wanted it to be magical. We have so little time together.' Nearby the chooks made little noises as they moved about their coop. 'They are rather cool, aren't they? Just going about their business,' he said as he watched Henny and Penny.

'I love them. They keep me company and we'll have fresh eggs for our breakfast.'

'Hmm, I like the sound of that.' Gary snuggled closer and kissed her lips. He'd changed into his denim shorts and a white polo shirt. 'Maybe it's not so bad here.' His hand snaked up her thigh. 'Shall we take this inside? Away from your feathered friends,' he added, kissing her neck.

'Yes, I'd hate to scare the girls.'

'Is there space for both of us in that tiny room of yours?' Jumping up, Gary grabbed the bottle and the chocolates and led the way inside.

'I'll guarantee you'll like how cosy it is.' Nat gave the last of the food to the chooks and headed inside with a smile. She pushed away all the little voices that threw up caution and fear about her future. Maybe it would turn out okay and she'd be happier than she thought.

Gary stayed all Monday, working from her house while she was teaching and then coming to visit the classroom after school hours.

'Can I come in?' he said, knocking on the classroom door.

'Gary! Hi, babe. What do you think?' Nat got up and gestured to her classroom. 'You've missed all the kids; they've gone
home. But see? This is what we've been working on.' She may
have gushed a bit over the kids' work and what they were doing
but she was just so excited to be able to share her passion with
him, and for the most part he seemed really interested.

'This kid can draw,' he said of one of Liam's artworks. 'Those
chairs seem so little.' He shook his head in disbelief. 'That was us
once, sitting in those little chairs. Next it will be our kids.'

Nat was still beaming when Kath dropped by.

'So this must be Gary,' said Kath. 'Not many fellas scrub up
like that around here.' They shook hands. 'It's nice to finally
meet Natalie's fiancé. She's such a gem to have here, we're all so
thankful.'

Nat felt her cheeks flush. She hoped he could finally see how
important this job was – to her and to her colleagues.

Kath said she'd lock up, so Nat and Gary went to the shop to
buy something for dinner.

'Holy heck, check out the price of that!' he said after a quick
lap around the small shop.

Nat felt uncomfortable with how loudly he'd spoken, but felt
even worse knowing that had been her first impression too. She
was fast learning that the cost of getting things to the country
was exorbitant. Even the bread and milk seemed ridiculously
expensive, but Frank had explained just how much the trucking
company charged to deliver it. And he couldn't haggle over the
freight price or find another transport company because no one
else wanted to deliver to their little town. Struggling locals paid

the prices and did so with a smile just to keep their community shop alive. If it closed they'd have to travel 60 kilometres to the next town.

Jess walked past in a pair of torn shorts, singlet and ugg boots. Nat loved the way no one seemed to look twice at what others wore or judge them by it. It was so different to the world she came from.

'Natty!' yelled a familiar voice.

She turned just in time to collect the hug thrown at her. Billy was still in his school uniform, with long pants and long sleeves despite the heat.

'Hey, Billy, how come you're here?'

'I'm allowed an ice-cream.' His cheeks strained with his grin, then he spotted Gary and slowly took in the man beside her. His nose scrunching up. 'Who are you?'

'Billy, this is Gary, my fiancé. Gary, this is one of my students.'

Gary bent over and held out his hand. 'Nice to meet you, young man.'

Billy beamed from being greeted so formally.

'G'day, g'day,' said Drew as he came down the aisle where they were standing. 'Wondered where you'd got to, Billy. Hi, Nat.'

Drew's shorts were torn on one corner, grease stained his khaki work shirt and he smelt like fuel. But he pulled it all off with an alluring working-man look. A look she knew Gary was taking in. Nat's heart sank.

'Hi, Drew. I'd like you to meet Gary,' she said, knowing there was no way around this moment.

'Nice to finally meet you, Gary,' said Drew as they shook hands.

Nat was fascinated by the stark contrast of hands: one pale and smooth with perfect nails, the other tanned, callused and etched with dirt.

'Come on, Billy. We'd better go. Frank's waiting out back with our stuff. Grab your ice-cream.' Drew gave them a nod goodbye and turned to let them be.

'Bye, Natty.' Billy almost followed his dad before turning back. 'Hey, maybe you should bring your boyfriend out to see some shearing. He might be as funny as you were,' he said with a cheeky grin.

'Bye, Billy.' Nat waved him goodbye and was relieved when he darted off after Drew. She turned to the shelf and picked up a small jar of apricot jam. 'Did you want this for your toast in the morning, or are you happy with eggs again?' she asked Gary.

But Gary didn't answer. While they finished their shop, he smiled and spoke with the locals, who all wanted to meet him, but didn't say another word to Nat.

Back at the house, Nat changed out of her work clothes and put on shorts and a singlet. Gary seemed to have mellowed a bit, and was texting on his phone again. Nat felt nervous. The meeting in the shop would surely come up again.

'Can't you leave some of that stuff for Sharon?' she asked.

'It's Sharon I'm texting. She's trying to find a report that Dad's chasing for a meeting.' He looked up and frowned. 'Besides, she's Dad's assistant, not mine.'

'You'll need your own soon. Do you get Sharon when your dad retires?'

'Ha, Dad will die before he retires,' Gary said, a little forcefully. 'That's why I'm putting so much work into this new venture. If I can seal this new resort deal, then I want to go to Dad and ask for a partnership, or at least my own casino resort brand.'

'That sounds great.'

He was watching her as she opened the fridge door for an apple. 'I've been thinking . . . You should come home with me. You've been here long enough, you've proved your point.'

She turned to face him. 'What point would that be?'

'That you can teach. You don't need to see out the year in this backwater to prove to any of us that you can do your job. I want you at home, with me. Maybe you could finish the year at a Perth school, one close to home.'

Nat clenched the apple as she stood before him. 'No, Gary, I can't do that. These people are depending on me. They can't find another teacher at short notice and besides, I'm all involved with trying to save the school.'

'I really don't see why you're putting so much energy into this. You seem far too invested. I think they should shut the school. That way they can pool resources. It makes sense.'

'No, it doesn't!' Nat felt a void the size of an ocean beginning to form between them. How could he think that? He knew how much this job meant to her, didn't he? Had she not fought for this time and time again? Was he ever going to understand? 'That is a crap trade-off in comparison to what closing this school will do to the town. Kids on long bus rides, people leaving the district. The town needs its school, Gary, and I can't abandon my kids.'

Gary's eyes narrowed. 'Is this about that Drew guy? He's the one you've been helping, isn't he? Not quite the single old guy I was picturing.' His brown eyes took on splashes of crimson, like a red desert storm gathering across the land.

'Of course it's not about him. Don't be ridiculous. Drew and Billy are just friends in need of a little help. I want to do what's right and see out my year,' she said, trying to stand her ground. Her voice was firm but her knees were not, and neither were the fingers trying hard to hold on to the apple.

'Don't be ridiculous?' he growled, taking a step closer. 'You are my fiancée.' He was so close she could smell his minty breath and see the grey hairs in his neat sideburns.

'I'm sorry, Gary but —'

He didn't give her a chance to reply. His hand came around her neck, pulling her even closer.

'Is this just a game to you? Are you playing around on me with this guy while I'm not here?'

He squeezed her neck, her throat, and Nat felt the air rush from her lips. What was he doing? Did he not realise he was hurting her? The apple fell from her hand, bounced once on the floor and rolled under the table.

'Gary, stop!' she rasped.

He released her and stumbled back, looking almost shocked. She somehow found the chair by the table and sat down, totally focused on breathing.

'I'm sorry. I love you, babe. I just couldn't handle you cheating on me.' Gary brushed her hair back gently, causing her to flinch and jerk away from him. Had that really happened? Gary placed the bruised apple on the table in front of her. 'I just love you so much.' With that he kissed her forehead and disappeared into the lounge room.

Nat pushed the apple away as hot tears slid down her cheeks.

Chapter 17

NAT was juggling an armful of classroom materials and trying to unlock her front door when she heard her phone ring. She groaned as she ignored the phone in her bag and shunted the door open with her hip. No sooner had she stepped inside when her phone started up again.

'Seriously?' She tipped her armload onto the table. Files, sticker sheets, her pencil case and kids' schoolwork slid across the top as she dived into her bag.

'Hi, Drew,' she said cautiously. Her mind went straight to Gary and his strong fingers around her neck. She swallowed slowly and tried to ignore the reaction of her body. Drew was not at fault.

'Oh, Nat, please tell me Billy is with you,' came his agitated voice.

'Billy? No. He went home on the school bus well over an hour ago.' Nat panicked for a moment. Was she supposed to have him?

'No, he got home all right – his bag's here, but his motor-bike's gone and I can't find him. I've looked everywhere. I half hoped he'd ridden in to you for some reason; it's all I could think of. I've got Kim and Matty checking their place.' Drew sucked in a shaky breath after his rapid-fire words. 'Shit, Nat, I'm going crazy. Where could he be? What if he's hurt?'

His words caught in his throat and Nat's heart ached for him. 'Take a deep breath, Drew, and let's think about it. Have you checked the bike track?'

'Yes, twice. I've checked the sheds, all the dams. Even Turbo is still here, which is freaking me out – he's always with Billy. That's why I thought Billy might have gone to you, Turbo wouldn't have followed him that far.'

'Would he really ride on the road to me?' she asked, feeling a sickening wave churn through her stomach.

'I honestly don't know, Nat. I was at the sheds, and he always comes to me if I'm not home. It's not like him. I'm freaking out. Can you come over?'

The pleading in his voice melted her heart. 'I'll get changed and come right now. I'll check the roads on my way.'

'Thank you, Nat. Thank you so much. Call me if you find him.'

'Of course I will. See you soon.'

Nat ran to her room to change into jeans and a T-shirt and put on socks and her boots. She glanced at the small bruise on her neck, wincing more from the memory than any pain. Gary had continued on as if nothing were wrong; he had left as planned, hugging her as if he hadn't harmed her. Nat didn't know what else to do, so she just left it, even though she felt confused by his sudden outburst. But now was not the time to dwell, she thought as she rushed from her house. She had a boy to find.

She hoped to god that Billy was just somewhere unexpected. Visions of his little body sprawled and twisted on the ground, motorbike bent beside him, accosted her mind. Tears prickled as the full weight of this possibility hit home. She forced them away. It just couldn't happen.

Nat had no idea where Billy would go, and she didn't know the ins and outs of the farm. Was he hiding on purpose? Had something happened at school? Maybe he'd done something silly, and was trying to avoid the consequences. Where would he go? It wasn't until Nat was driving past the cemetery that she was hit with a sudden thought. Billy had always had someone he used to turn to. His nana.

She hit the skids and turned her car around, veering down the short gravel track towards the cemetery's entrance. Beside the gate sat one little 50cc motorbike.

'Oh, thank god.'

She pulled out her phone and dialled Drew as she watched the little figure sitting by a lone grave.

'Have you found him?' were his first words.

'Yes. I'm at the cemetery.'

'What the hell? Oh,' said Drew when he finally realised. 'I never thought of that.'

Nat told him about the picture he'd drawn of his special place when she'd first come to the school.

'I'll be right there,' said Drew.

'Take your time. I'll stay here with him. He might open up to me.' Nat knew it would take Drew at least ten minutes to reach them.

'Righto. Thanks, Natty, I really appreciate it.'

Nat made her way into the cemetery. It was a coolish afternoon; ominous clouds filled the sky, and a gentle breeze brought with it a crispness that raised the hair on her skin. She found Billy, sitting cross-legged by Alice's grave, near the bright new headstone, pulling at the tough weeds growing nearby. His voice was soft and muffled as he talked to the grave.

Her feet crunched on the gravel stones. It was a small, rustic cemetery with only a few graves and an old gazebo in the middle that was flaking its green paint like a snake shedding its skin. A cream brick wall next to it held plaques and, no doubt, ashes from past residents.

Billy's head snapped up when he heard her approach.

'Natty, what are you doing here?' he said, scrunching up his face.

'Looking for you. Your dad was worried out of his mind,' she said gently. She didn't want him to run off, thinking he was in trouble. Instead he dropped his head and remained quiet. Nat got down on the ground beside him. 'Talk to me, Billy. Are you okay? What's going on? Did you just feel like talking to your nan?'

He shrugged.

'You know how worried we were when we couldn't find you? It's very dangerous for you to ride off like that. Even I was worried you'd had an accident on your bike. I was scared you were hurt.'

His face turned up, his eyes bright. 'Oh, that wouldn't happen.

I'm real good on my bike.'

'I know you are, but sometimes unexpected things happen, like you hit a pothole or pop a tyre, or a kangaroo jumps out. A passing truck could push you off the road. Any number of things could happen. You know how sad your dad would be if any harm came to you?'

'I guess.' He glanced to the grave. 'I wish Nan was really here,' he said softly.

Nat put her arms around him and hugged him tightly. 'I know, sweetheart. I wish she was here for you too. But I'm here now and I'd like you to be able to talk to me just like you did your nan. If you want to.' His only reply was to hug her tightly. 'Your dad will be here soon,' she added.

Billy sat up and turned back to the grave, rigid. 'I don't want to see him.'

'Your dad? Why not? Has something happened? You don't have to worry, he's not angry. He's just happy you're safe.' He shrugged again. 'Please tell me what's wrong, Billy. I'm here to help. You can trust me.'

'Can I go home with you?' he asked, his eyes pleading.

She reached out and stroked his head around his ears, just like her mum used to do when she was little. 'Sure, of course. But will you tell me what's up? Is it the kids at school or something to do with your dad?'

He nodded. Nat couldn't figure out which bit she'd got right. She was trying to think of another question when Billy glanced up at her.

'Do dads lie?'

'Lie? Not usually. Why, what would your dad lie about?'

'He said my mum was dead, like Nan.' His eyes watched her so intently, Nat was almost too scared to say something wrong.

'You don't believe him?' Nat felt way out of her depth. Billy really should be talking to Drew about this.

'She said she was my mum.'

'Who did?'

'The lady at the bus stop today. She got out of her car to talk to me. I thought she was lost, 'cos I've never seen her before. But she said she was my mum.'

Holy crap. Nat's mind swam with thoughts. Was this woman trying to abduct Billy? Or was she really his mum? 'What did you do, Billy?'

'I just said that I don't talk to strangers and got on my bike. Why would she say that?'

Nat was at a loss. Had Drew been lying all this time? Or was this lady seriously misguided? 'I don't know, Billy. Maybe she was just confused.' She stood up and held out her hand. 'How about we take you home to the farm and get something to eat? Maybe I can make you my famous mac and cheese. I'll tell your dad to come grab your motorbike.'

Billy grabbed her hand, jumping up. 'You eat mac and cheese?'

'It was my favourite meal when I was about your age. Now I try to eat healthier but I think we deserve a treat, don't you?' She was rewarded with a grin as they started walking to her car. 'I like to use lots of cheese. Do you like pasta?'

'Yeah, Dad makes a carbonara with lots of bacon. It's my favourite.'

'Goodo.' Nat tapped a quick text to Drew to let him know their plan.

Back at the farm, Nat told Billy to go change out of his school clothes and quickly rang Drew.

'What's up?'

Nat didn't have time to fill him in but just asked if it was okay if she stayed and made dinner.

'Of course, but it's me who should be making you dinner,' he said. 'I'm sorry I dragged you into this.'

Nat was actually dragged into it further than she wanted, but she didn't mention that. At some stage tonight, when Billy wasn't around, she would have to explain about the woman.

'I'll talk to you later,' she said quickly as Billy returned in jeans and monster truck T-shirt. Slipping her phone away, she clapped her hands together. 'Okay, I need a helper to show me where everything is. Up to the task?'

'Yep,' said Billy as he walked to the pantry door. Inside he pulled out a little stool, which he used to reach some aprons. 'Nan uses these when we cook. You can wear her flowery one. This one's mine.' He pulled a black one that said 'chef in training' over his head.

'You've done this before, haven't you?' she said while tying up the apron. Billy gave the apron a longing glance and she wondered if he really was okay with her using it.

But he held out his hands and turned them over, moving onto the next thing. 'We have to wash our hands first.'

'Yes, you're right. Where do we do that?'

As she followed him to the laundry she felt a pang of sadness that such an amazing kid was growing up without his nana or his mother. That they got to miss out on all his smiles, his silly jokes and that laughter. They wouldn't get to see him grow into an amazing man, just like his father, or see him get married and have his own children. Nat made a mental note to call her parents when she got home. Crazy and overbearing they may be, but they were her parents and they loved her.

Just like she felt about Billy. This funny, wonderfully different, unique, sweet boy was already bringing her so much joy, and she knew, without a doubt, he had stolen a place in her heart.

Chapter 18

DREW paused by the door, taking in the scene before him. Natalie and Billy, with aprons on, working together in the kitchen. It made his chest ache and yet brought him this surreal happiness. For the first time, Drew thought about what it would be like to have someone for Billy, and someone for himself. Someone as caring and fascinating as Natalie, who would make coming home special. Seeing them together made him realise what they'd both been missing out on over the years. Maybe having his mum around had disguised their needs and wants. For the first time in a long time he yearned to wake up beside a beautiful woman, the same one every morning – one to share his thoughts, his dreams and fears with freely.

He'd always put Billy's needs first, worrying about bringing someone new into their home, but now he saw that it could be a good thing. Billy shone when he was with Nat, and she was so gentle, accepting and loving with him. This old house certainly missed a woman's touch.

'Hey, Dad, we're making mac and cheese for tea. I hope you're hungry,' he said, quoting one of Alice's many sayings.

'Sure am.' Drew walked over to Billy and knelt down in front of him. He saw his son's face drop as he remembered he'd done something wrong. Drew held his arms gently so Billy couldn't run away but smiled to ease his son's anxiety. 'You had me so worried today. Promise me you won't do that again? I'll take you to Nan anytime you need; you just have to ask.'

Billy nodded.

'Good. I love you.' Drew pulled him into a tight hug. He smelt like cheese and soap but also like innocence and childhood. It was hard to realise his little boy was growing up right before his eyes.

Nat was watching them, her delicate fingers on her lips, her eyes shining with emotion.

'Right, I'd better not hold you up,' he said, ruffling Billy's hair.

Drew left to wash up and found himself wondering how life would be if he was married to a woman like Nat. Maybe he should keep his eyes open, be willing to let someone in. He almost laughed – he was so out of the game he wouldn't know how to go about it.

Later that night, after tea, he mentioned it to Nat while Billy was taking a shower and they did the dishes. He'd just finished teasing her about the faint hickey on her neck. Seeing Nat go all shy and flushed made him move on to his own problems.

'And so you're worried you can't remember how to date?' she asked.

'Yeah, is that silly? I've been so focused on the farm and Billy over the last eight years.'

'Drew,' Nat laughed, 'you wouldn't have to do anything, the girls would come to you. There're quite a few who would jump at the chance,' she said, shaking her head.

Drew picked up a pot and started to dry it while he tried to get his head around Nat's words. 'No, there aren't. Are there?'

'Drew, you're the town catch. There are a few girls who've been hoping you'll notice them. I won't name names but just believe me when I say you'd have no trouble finding a few dates.'

'Yeah, but it's not just dates I want. I think I'd like to find a wife, and mother for Billy, maybe have more kids. Billy was cool as a baby, the cutest dude ever. I miss that,' he said truthfully.

'You're a good dad, it would be a shame if you didn't have more kids.'

'Thanks. Some days I'm not so sure. It's hard enough running a farm, let alone raising a kid. There are no manuals and they constantly change.' Drew put his tea towel down and leant his hip against the sink as he faced Nat. 'Like today, what was that really about? I've been dying to ask but not in front of Billy.'

Nat glanced towards the bathroom and put her finger to her lips. 'When he's asleep.'

Drew was even more curious now, but he nodded. 'Okay.' He liked the idea that Nat was going to hang around for longer.

Moments later, Billy came out in his green Scooby Doo

pyjamas, his hair still damp, and sat up at the breakfast bar watching them do the dishes.

'Did you brush your teeth?' Drew asked. Billy showed him. 'Good. Say goodnight to Natty and I'll tuck you in.'

'Can Natty tuck me in too?'

Drew didn't get to answer, Nat beat him to it.

'I'd love to. Let's go,' she said, drying her hands.

Billy hopped into bed and Drew kissed him and pulled his doona up around him. 'Night, my boy.'

'Night, Dad. I'm sorry I ran away,' Billy said softly.

'I know, mate. You scared me, but I'm glad you're back home. Now get some rest.'

Stepping back, he waited by the door and watched as Nat knelt by the bed and stroked his son's head with soft fingers. Billy closed his eyes in sheer delight and for Drew it brought back strong memories of Alice doing the same. Drew felt his throat constrict, his eyes blurring, and he made a quick exit back to the safety of the kitchen.

He got out two beers and waited for Nat to return. As she walked back down the passageway he was struck by how well she seemed to fit in his house. Not something he would have thought when he'd first met her.

'Thanks for that, Natty.' He handed her a cold beer. 'Come, we'll sit outside on the verandah.'

Outside it was dark and the night was still. Drew liked sitting out at night, enjoying the quiet – except for Turbo barking at the odd fox.

'It's nice here,' said Nat, sitting beside him on the wooden bench.

Drew nodded. He could just make out Nat's features from the inside lights. Her brow was creased, not a look she wore often. 'What's bothering you?' he asked.

'How did you know something was bothering me?'

'Come on, spit it out.'

She sighed as she played with the label on her beer. 'Okay. Billy ran off because a lady came up to him saying he was her mother.'

It took a few moments for her words to sink in. His heart began to race. 'Simone was here?' he said, feeling sick to his stomach.

'Simone?'

Drew leant forward, elbows on his knees, his beer clasped in one hand while the other ran through his hair as he tried to process the news.

'Is Billy's mother alive?'

He could sense Nat's hand on his shoulder but he felt like he was in a separate galaxy. All he could think about was Simone. Was she here, had it really been her? Why had she come back? Did she want Billy? His gut clenched and his beer soured in his mouth. Never. He would not lose his son.

He became aware of Nat's voice. She was sitting closer and shaking him gently with both hands.

'Drew? Are you okay?'

'Sorry.' He didn't move and neither did Nat. She waited patiently. 'Yes, his mum is alive,' he eventually whispered.

'So you did lie to Billy? That's what had him torn up.'

Nat's words hurt him more than any knife wound could as he

thought of his son so confused and upset. 'Ah, shit. What a mess.'

After a moment, Drew sat back and looked at Nat. Her kind green eyes were like sparkly gems in the light. They cleared his mind for a moment. 'I met Simone when I was in my first year at Muresk. We partied hard, and she was always the life of the party. We did all sorts of reckless things. I found out Simone was into some heavy stuff and had some crazy issues.' The next bit was hard. 'Then out of the blue my dad, Bill, died. Car crash. I was supposed to finish uni and join him on the farm until he was too old to work, and then it would be mine. Instead I got it at eighteen. I hadn't even finished a semester at uni.'

Drew stopped to sip his beer, even though it had lost all its taste. He needed to wet his dry lips. Nat was facing him, her hand resting on his thigh in support.

'So I packed up and came straight home. Mum was a mess, I was still grieving and had a farm to figure out how to run. Of course, there was plenty of help. Matt, Kim and their dad did so much for me in those early days. I don't know how I got through it; maybe being so busy helped.

'Anyway, it was only about four or five months later that Simone rang me. She said she'd just found out she was pregnant and it was too late for an abortion. She was freaking out. Said it was mine and the dates seemed to fit. She didn't want a baby and planned to give it up. After talking with Mum we knew we didn't want that so we got her to come to the farm, and we looked after her until Billy was born and then she left. Just like that. She didn't even want to look at him. She turned her head away, wouldn't acknowledge him. He was just a harmless baby. That proved to me that he needed us, our protection and love.' Drew shook his head. 'To think she couldn't even hold him, wouldn't, even though we tried.'

Nat let out a breath.

'So you can see why it seemed easier to tell Billy his mum had died. I couldn't bear telling him his mum never wanted him. I couldn't do that to him. Now it seems I did the wrong thing. I never thought Simone would come back for him. She's never reached out before.'

'No contact at all?'

'Nothing. Now eight years later she's decided she wants to be his mum? I don't think so. She gave her rights up when she left him with me. I'll lose this farm before I lose my boy and that's not something I'd ever want to part with either.'

Drew knew his voice was raised and he sounded mad. He was flitting between throwing his beer in anger and punching the verandah post, or bursting into tears. Either one would probably have Nat running for her car. Instead, he put his beer down and fisted his eyes. His head felt like an overinflated truck tube.

'Have you got any legal documents, anything in writing that stipulates she didn't want . . . him?'

Nat stuttering over the words made him realise how much she'd come to care for Billy. She couldn't fathom how anyone could give him up either. It made Drew sit up and attempt a smile. 'We have a bit of paper somewhere, which says she didn't want any ties to Billy. I'm not sure if it will hold up in court. I'll have to try to find it now.' Alice would have put it somewhere safe, but where?

'Mum wanted proper documents drawn up but when Simone had Billy she checked herself out of the hospital before she could sign them and then we were so busy with a newborn and a farm I never got around to chasing her up. God, I felt like I was drowning every day for ages. I had lots of learning to do with Billy and the farm. I'm so lucky Mum was there. In a way Billy saved us both after Dad's death. He gave us purpose, light and so much joy. Lots of hard times too but they don't seem to be the bits you remember.'

'Sounds like Billy was meant to be here,' said Nat softly, squeezing his leg. 'What are you going to do now?'

Drew blinked as he tried to focus on her high cheekbones and full lips. She was holding him up right now, keeping him from falling into the unknown abyss. 'I don't know. I'm so glad you're here, I'd have no one to talk to otherwise. Not many know about Simone. We tried to keep her hidden, didn't want the district to talk, but they probably all knew at the time. After she had Billy and disappeared, we went on as normal. Rumours would have been rife and when they finally got up the nerve to ask we just said she'd died giving birth. It stopped heaps of questions. We didn't want Billy finding out about his mum years later from some kid at school so we tried to control the situation.'

'What about Kim and Lauren?'

'No, Kim was so young herself and Lauren was busy with Seth. Matt was the only one I confided in, and that was a while later. Matt is loyal to a fault and I don't even know if he's told Lauren the truth. Even if he has, it hasn't got around town, that I know of. They love Billy too.'

He sighed. He'd have to find that bit of paper, then see what he could do legally. Man, his head hurt, and the mac and cheese was rolling around in his stomach like lumps of polystyrene in off milk. 'I'm going to be at that bus stop every day now. Maybe she's been watching him for a while. Oh, Nat.'

'It's okay. If you're with him here, then I'll keep an eye out for him at school. I'll have a little chat with him tomorrow and see if he can remember what colour car she was in and I'll watch out for it. What does Simone look like? Do you have a photo?'

'No, I don't. She was always changing her hair so I'd hate to guess.'

'Doesn't matter,' said Nat. 'My uncle is a lawyer. Is it okay if I talk to him about what your options are? Or I could get him to give you a call?'

Drew didn't know what to say. He had to slow down, take some long, deep breaths before he lost control. 'Nat,' he managed to say, but it came out more of a squeak. 'Thank you.'

They talked for a little longer, until Drew was feeling calmer, before she said she'd better go home. He walked her to the car under the light of the moon, their feet crunching on the gravel the only sound.

'I don't know what I would have done without you today, Natty,' said Drew as they stood by the car. 'You certainly are a special person and I'm so glad Billy and I have you in our corner.'

'Anytime, Drew. I'll do whatever I can to help.'

Then she leant over and gave him a hug. It was tight and soothing, and he felt himself melt into her arms, into her sweet scent. He hadn't had a hug like this since his mum had passed, and boy, did he need one now.

'I really needed this,' he said, his voice straining with emotion again.

She rubbed his back and nodded, then eventually pulled away. 'Try to get some sleep. Call me if you need. Bye, Drew.'

'Bye, Natty.'

He watched her drive away in the dark, her lights bright in the night and that powerful motor of hers waking up the sleeping birds. He stayed for a while in the night, thinking, processing, and when he dropped his head down to his shoulder he could still smell Nat's perfume. It lingered like a life-preserver floating on the water, waiting in case Drew ever needed to grab it.

Chapter 19

THE rest of the week went off without any problems and the next week Nat knew Billy would be safe at home with Drew, on first-term school holidays. They'd talked on the phone Friday night as Drew was unsure how to tell Billy about his mum and Nat had offered her thoughts.

'You could tell him the truth, that his mum wasn't ready to raise a baby. And that you didn't want to upset him so you thought it would be better to say she'd died. Make sure he knows it's not his fault she left.' Whether it was sound advice or not she wasn't sure, but Drew promised he'd call her and fill her in. He'd invited her out to the farm again but she had to go back to Perth for the weekend as one of her friends was having a birthday party.

And Gary was home, wanting her to visit, which she was feeling confused and even a little scared about. It had only been a few days since Gary had left. He'd called and sent emails, but seeing him was a different thing altogether. He was behaving as if nothing had happened and Nat was starting to wonder if it really had. It felt like a strange horror movie she'd watched months ago. Surely he would never do it again? The look of shock on his face when he'd realised, she knew it had scared him as much as it had her.

Nat made her visit to the city shorter by leaving Lake Biddy on Saturday morning. She arrived at her parents' place just before lunch.

'Darling, it's so good to see you. Have you been using your moisturiser? Your skin looks dry. It's that bush heat and sun. Are you wearing sunscreen?' said Jennifer as she hugged her only daughter. 'You need to visit Sally while you're home,' she added, touching the ends of Nat's hair. Sally was her mum's preferred hairdresser.

Nat brushed her mum's comments aside. She was used to it. 'Hey, Mum. How are you? Is lunch ready?' Nat stepped inside, pulling her Louis Vuitton bag with her. This wasn't her childhood house, which was probably why it didn't feel like home. It was very grand, with its sweeping staircases and expensive art, but felt somehow cold to her. The first house she'd grown up in was still extravagant compared with the homes in Lake Biddy, but it was smaller than this one and the kids' art had hung from the fridge. Their toys had made it feel lived in and loved. This house looked like something out of a magazine. Nothing was ever out of place, thanks to Samuel, the gardener, and Carla, their housekeeper, who worked every day of the week. Mum liked it all to be perfect in case a friend dropped around to visit. Nat always thought they couldn't be much of a friend then if they couldn't handle a bit of 'living'.

Maybe that's why she loved the warmth of Drew's house. You could tell they lived there; they had their stamp on everything, from the pile of farm magazines on the table to the stack of dishes on the sink and Billy's schoolwork on display, his little stool tucked in the corner and the toys scattered about.

The only thing in her parents' house that showed something about them was the family portrait that hung in the lounge room, but it was a professional one. Not like the candid shots on Drew's fridge and on his walls, showing laughter and life.

Jennifer shut the door and walked off into the kitchen area, her heels on the marble echoing throughout the spacious house. 'Yes, I'm just about to serve it up, your father should be down any minute. Go wash up.'

Nat put her bag in her room and went to her ensuite to freshen up. With its Italian tiles and extravagant accents, it was a far cry from her little bathroom in Lake Biddy. For good measure she tied her hair back so it wouldn't be a focal point for her mum. She went to her balcony and looked at the ocean view that had eased her mind over the past seven years. It had been her escape. She must get down there for a walk along the beach. Maybe take a jar of sand back for Billy, or some shells if she could find any.

Nat joined her mum at the table, which had some steamed fish and salads already dished up and crystal glasses filled with her mum's favourite wine.

'Wait for your father,' said Jennifer as Nat was about to pop a cherry tomato in her mouth.

'Hello, darling!' Her father came down from his office upstairs. The tallest in the family, he almost had to duck his head under the low archway. Even on the weekend he wore work slacks and a dress shirt.

'The country air must agree with you,' he said, holding her at arm's length and giving her the once-over. 'You look so radiant.'

'It's the sun, Vincent,' said Jennifer.

'No, it's not. Look at her, she looks happy.'

'Thanks, Dad. I am happy. I love my job.'

'So tell us how it's all going.' Vincent gestured to the table and they all began to eat.

'Gary said they are going to close down your school,' Jennifer said before Nat could start. 'Does that mean you'll be back here sooner? Can we bring the wedding forward?'

'No, Mum. They won't close us down midway through a year, it would disrupt the kids. I was thinking if we can save it, I might do a second year.' Nat regretted the slip straight away. Her mum looked as if she'd just said she'd shacked up with a woman, wanted dreadies and turned vegan.

'Natalie! You can't do that to Gary, or to us. We've been waiting for this wedding for ages.'

'Mum, we've only been engaged for a month.'

'You're lucky Gary let you go at all. He's been so good about all of this.'

Nat clenched her teeth but let that one go through to the keeper. She started to share her news and her enthusiasm but conversation soon turned to the latest gossip in Jennifer's circle of friends. A divorce, someone's daughter's pregnancy scare and stress over not getting an invitation to a birthday party. Nat tried to listen but found her mind wandering back to Lake Biddy. Had her time there created a gulf between her and her parents? Or had it always been there, and she just hadn't noticed?

After the meal, Nat said goodbye to her parents and got in her car. Driving towards Gary's place gave her another feeling. Was it anxiety? Would he mention their last encounter? Would he bring up Drew again?

Gary just must have been so far out of his comfort zone in Lake Biddy. It really wasn't like him at all.

Gary pulled into his driveway just as Nat was getting out of her car.

'Hey, beautiful,' he said with his mega smile, and Nat caught herself thinking of Drew's crooked incisor that showed when he smiled. Quickly she pushed the thought from her mind.

'Hi, Gary. Just back from the office?'

'The gym actually,' he said, pulling out his gym bag. 'Must keep in shape for my lady.' He wrapped his arms around her and kissed her with everything he had.

'Hmm, I missed that,' said Nat, eventually relaxing. But did she believe her own words? She wasn't sure.

'So what's Alisha got planned for her birthday? Can I come?' he asked as they walked arm in arm up the paved pathway to his apartment. They'd discussed buying a house with a yard once they were married. Nat wanted room for kids, and Gary wanted a home gym and lap pool.

'Do you want to? I wasn't sure . . . you don't really like her, do you? I think we're going out to her favourite restaurant and then on to a few clubs. You can come; others are coming with partners.'

'I've got the night off and want to spend it with you, if that's okay.' He stopped to open his door, pausing to brush strands of hair back from her face. 'I miss you so much.'

'Well, that'd be great. I'd like you to come. I left my stuff at Mum's but I'd rather get dressed here so we can go together.'

'We'll get it later. First we have some catching up to do.' Gary shut the door and swept her up in his arms, carting her off to his room.

That night as Nat was putting on her make-up she heard Gary call out, 'Your phone's ringing!'

'Is it Alisha again?' she asked, coming out of the bathroom with her lipstick in her hand.

Gary was by the table where her phone sat. He glanced up when she got closer and his eyes suddenly darkened. Nat felt her body spasm. Warning bells were ringing loudly but it was too late. His hand snapped out, gripping her neck and forcing her forwards. His other hand dug into her shoulder, fingers like metal rods trying to pierce her skin as they worked together to push her face down to her phone.

'Why is *he* calling you?' Gary demanded. She saw Drew's name on the phone just before the call finally ended. 'I thought I sorted this out. Did you not understand me before? I don't tolerate betrayal.'

Not this again, please, not this again, Nat chanted over and over in her mind. 'Gary, please,' she begged as calmly as she could while her heart raced. She fought the pain he was inflicting, even though she wanted to cry out. This was ten times worse than last time. Her neck felt like it was in a vice and breathing was hard, which made trying to speak even harder. 'It's not what you think. His ex is trying to take his son away and I told him that Uncle Kent could help him.'

Gary squeezed harder. 'You're lying.'

She had to try to remain calm so she could talk her way out of this. She needed Gary to understand so he'd let her go. 'I'm not, I swear.' She used her hands to pull at his fingers, letting some much-needed air in so she could continue to speak. 'Call Uncle Kent and ask him. I'm going there tomorrow to pick up all the paperwork he's put together for Drew.'

'Why would he call now?'

'I don't know. Maybe his ex came back, maybe she's taken his son. I said to call if there was an emergency.' Nat had to spin it however she could. She couldn't fathom this terrifying situation she suddenly found herself in. 'Please, Gary, stop. You're hurting me.' Suddenly she felt hatred for Gary surge through her like a wave of sickness. This wasn't love, was it?

As he watched her pleading face his fingers started to relax and eventually he took his hands away, yet she could still feel where they'd been, leaving their mark, reminding her what her friendship with Drew could cost her.

'Kent's one of the best,' said Gary, walking back to the kitchen to get another beer.

While his back was turned Nat put her phone on silent and crept back to the bathroom to finish putting on her make-up. Her hands were shaking like a jackhammer. Tears threatened to ruin all her work and she didn't even bother with mascara. In that moment, Nat couldn't care less about her appearance.

'Taxi's here, my love,' said Gary five minutes later. 'You ready?'

His voice was upbeat, as if he was still looking forward to tonight. How could he change so quickly? Nat didn't want to go out with him, was too afraid to even talk to him for fear of bursting into tears. Was this really happening to her, to them? How could he be like this, so loving in one minute and so cruel the next? Was this really the man she was going to marry? Could she still even contemplate a future with him?

Maybe it was her fault – she should never have spent so much time with Drew. She thought it was innocent, but she did find herself thinking about him more than she should. Maybe Gary would feel safer once they were married. Perhaps it would all stop then. He had never been like this before. She used to be able to talk with guys, even flirt over drinks and he'd be there doing the same with the ladies, but the moment the engagement ring had gone on her finger it was like he owned her. If only she had someone she could talk to about it. Her parents would never believe her. They loved Gary.

Later, in the taxi ride on the way to the restaurant, he held her hand so tenderly, and she began to wonder if it all hadn't been quite so bad as she'd thought. He hadn't hit her, after all, just been too strong with his grip. As he helped her out of the taxi and guided her to the restaurant, she was all too aware of his hand on her back.

'Hello, Natalie!' Alisha rushed over to them. 'Gosh, you look great. Is that for me?' she said as she took the gift bag Nat handed over after their hugs.

'You know it is,' said Nat, happy to be among friends.

'Happy birthday, Alisha, you look gorgeous,' said Gary, giving her a peck on the cheek.

'Great of you both to come. I miss Nat being around.' Alisha's bright red lips turned down but it didn't mar her beauty. She owned a fashion boutique in South Perth and never left the house looking anything but fabulous. With deep tanned skin, from regular spray-tanning appointments, and luscious dark hair, thanks to Pablo, her hairdresser, Alisha was cover-girl perfect. Nat knew her from school, when they'd both been pimple-faced girls agonising over guys and trying to be noticed.

'I miss you, Lish. When are you going to come visit me and meet my kids?' Nat asked as they linked arms and walked towards the other guests at Alisha's favourite restaurant. You had to book way in advance but it was always worth it: the food was prepared by an award-winning chef and no expense had been spared on the elegant dining area. There were plush chairs, Egyptian cotton napkins and tablecloths in contrasting blues, grey marble on the floor and gorgeous chandeliers that gave the room a hint of warmth. Two big tables had been pushed together in the far corner, decorated with extra candles and fresh flowers, and Nat recognised some of their mutual friends from school. Gary sat down and picked up a conversation with one of the guys at the table.

'I'm just going to the ladies',' said Nat after ordering her drink. She checked Gary was deep in conversation and slipped around the corner to the toilets. Once inside, she sent Drew a text apologising for missing his call and asking whether it was important. Then she checked her neck for marks. There was nothing really noticeable yet, but it was sore to touch. Or maybe that was the horrific memory that came with it. She shuddered. Nat was having trouble linking those horrible moments with her current life. With a hard look at herself in the mirror she sighed, reapplied her lipstick and left. Each time she ducked off to the bathroom she checked her phone, worried Simone was back or that something had happened. When Gary went to the bar to get the next round of drinks she was relieved to see a message waiting from Drew.

> I just wanted to talk about how Billy took the news. That's all. Hope you're having a good time.

> I am. I'll call you when I get home on Sunday. :)

Then she deleted all the messages and put her phone away. Pasting on a smile, she went and drained the last bit of wine from her glass, ready for the replacement. Gary came back and held out another wine, but his fingers, splayed around the cold glass, stole her focus and for a moment she couldn't move.

'Natalie, this one's yours,' said Gary, moving the glass in front of her face.

'Oh, thanks,' she managed to say but by that time he'd placed it on the table for her so he could hand out the others he carried. She felt relieved that she didn't have to touch those fingers. She reached for her glass and nearly drank the whole lot in one gulp, stopping only because Alisha was watching her.

'I think we should hit some nightclubs later. Who's in?' Alisha demanded, her eyes still on Nat.

'I think you read my mind,' Nat replied with a smile.

Each glass seemed to numb the anxiety that was sitting in her mind, replaying events and threatening to drive her mad. Each glass made the dark side of Gary grow hazy until it disappeared, and all that mattered was laughing with her friends.

They made it to Kent's with two minutes to spare. A strong coffee was holding Nat together and she'd put on a scarf at the last minute because she could see some bruising. Probably not enough for anyone else to notice, but Natalie could and that was enough. In a way she hoped Gary understood why it was there, that it was all because of him. But he made no comment. Luckily Gary was driving, as the traffic would have been too much to handle with her mind so scattered. He had wanted to come with her this morning, and although she didn't want to spend any more time with him, as she needed some time alone to think, she didn't feel she could say no. At least this way he'd see that she was telling the truth and that she really was just helping Drew. And her parents might start asking questions if she came to lunch alone again.

'There's my girl,' said Uncle Kent as he rushed out to greet her, throwing his arms out and pulling her in tight. 'Hmm, someone had a big night,' he said.

'She was rather entertaining,' said Gary, putting his arm around her.

Nat felt uncomfortable, but relaxed a bit as he caressed her shoulder gently. 'Sorry I can't stay long, Uncle Kent, but I have to see Mum again before I leave. It's good to see you.' She loved that he wore jeans and his favourite Queen T-shirt.

'Come on inside, and I'll get you that stuff for Drew.'

'Thanks. He really appreciates it, and so do I. Billy is one of my favourites,' she said, heading into Kent's spacious brick home.

'I gathered. It's all I seem to hear about. You need to hurry up and have kids of your own.'

'As soon as I can get Nat to come back to the city, we will,' said Gary quickly.

'Kids make you realise what's important in life. How you should cherish your moments and make smiles while you can.' Kent went into his office, which was the opposite of his brother's. Kent had an old desk, covered with files and papers, a penholder that she'd made in primary school along with a paperweight from her brother. Boxes were stacked against the walls and his bookshelf was overflowing, but at least it looked used.

'It hasn't changed in here a bit, Uncle Kent. When are you going to throw this out?' she asked, picking up the glass jar, which had sequins and red hearts glued onto it.

'Never,' he said, taking it and putting it back in its spot. 'I still remember the day you gave that to me. Such a bundle of joy you were. You'd sit on the floor, colouring in for ages while I worked. I couldn't resist your smiles and we'd always end up playing tea parties.'

'With real tea,' said Nat. How could she not have idolised him, growing up?

'Here it is.' Kent handed over a folder. 'It has information on the Family Law Act, section 65E, and the forms for parenting orders. My card's in there and he can call me anytime.'

Nat hugged her uncle again. 'Thank you. Love you heaps.' Nat resisted the urge to wave the forms in Gary's face.

They had a quick cuppa with Kent and then went to her parents' house for lunch.

'When will you be back, darling?' asked Jennifer, passing the prawn salad to her husband. 'Oh, and I love that scarf. It brings out your eyes beautifully.'

Nat clammed up at the mention of the scarf but relaxed with her mum's compliment. 'I'm not sure, Mum. You can always come and visit.'

'We'd never get down there with your father's work. Even Gary finds it hard, don't you, love?'

It was a load of rubbish: if they wanted to make the effort Nat knew they could. For once she decided to call her mother out.

'You managed to find time to visit Jason when he was in Melbourne for that week, yet you can't find the time to drive out to Lake Biddy?'

Jennifer looked flustered for a moment. 'Yes, but that was Melbourne, darling.'

Nat sighed. 'Well, if you can find some time, you're always welcome to come and stay. It would give me an excuse to take you to some local tourist spots.' Ones Nat hadn't even got around to checking out yet either.

'We'll think about it,' said her mum before turning to Gary. 'So, love, how are things with you? How's the new resort deal coming along? Do you think it's viable? Does your father agree with your proposal?'

Gary flinched at the last question. Nat knew it irked him that at his age he still had to run everything by his dad.

'Yes, Tony sounds rather impressed with this new resort plan,' added her dad. 'He told me just yesterday that you've done a lot of work investigating this, Gary. I think he's seeing just how capable you are.'

'Did he mention anything about a partnership?' asked Gary, clearly happy with this news.

'He didn't, but I have a feeling he was seriously thinking about it.'

They peppered Gary with more questions than they had asked her. Nat stared at the food on her plate, not hungry, not really seeing it at all. He was already their son. How could she deprive them of officially having him in the family? She wondered if they'd ever forgive her if she broke Gary's heart. Would they even listen if she tried to explain why? Right now she didn't know what to do or what to think. It was all too hard and too scary. Maybe she just needed more time to think about it.

Yes, she decided. A little more time.

Chapter 20

NAT called Drew on Sunday night as promised. He was concerned that Billy didn't seem that fazed about his mum; in fact he hadn't reacted at all. Nat tried to reassure Drew, and to let him know that Billy might just need time to let it all sink in. It was a short conversation because his neighbour Doris dropped by and Drew had to go. But it had been nice to hear his voice, nice that he appreciated her opinion and input. And talking to him was better than talking to Gary. She needed space to think, to recover, and to figure out what she should do. How long until Gary realised she was avoiding him? How would he react? she wondered. At least she had work to distract her a little.

Nat didn't talk to Drew again until the meeting on Wednesday night at the school. It was just a small crowd of those who were determined to fight for the school, including Lauren, the school staff and the parents on the P & C committee.

'Heck, how long till school is back?' said Mel, rubbing at her forehead. Nat saw that she had food stuck to the side of her face.

Another mum pointed it out and Mel almost burst into tears. 'Jaxon is so bloody hard to feed at the moment. I wear more than he eats. I'm seriously over kids. Who bloody wanted six? I'm sure it wasn't me.'

'I know, my two are driving me nuts. How about you bring Ruby and Jack over tomorrow for the day. Give both our kids something to do,' Lauren offered.

Mel smiled. 'Lozzy, you're the best. That would be great.'

'Come around ten and we can have a cuppa too.' Lauren squeezed Mel's shoulder and Nat could have sworn Mel's eyes sparkled with more life.

Nat was busy watching Lauren, thinking about how amazing she was, when someone touched her shoulder.

'Hey, you,' said Drew.

He'd sneaked in just as the meeting had started so she hadn't had a chance to speak to him yet. Looks like he'd found her first. 'Hi, Drew. Where's Billy?'

'Kim's looking after him for me.'

Nat wondered if Kim did that at her own place or whether she went to Drew's. She wasn't sure why that thought had even entered her mind. 'Have you had a chance to look at the stuff from my uncle?'

'Yeah, it's painful to read. Just about need a translator. But it's good to have, thank you.'

'Anytime.'

Drew looked at her silk scarf and tugged the end of it. 'It's not winter yet.' His smile faltered as he noticed the bruises. Nat tried to grab the scarf but Drew pulled it completely off. 'Jesus, Nat, that's no hickey.' He leant in closer, so close she could smell soap and deodorant. 'Are those finger marks?' he hissed quietly. He took her arm and walked her out of the senior room and down to the junior room, where they were alone.

'Drew, it's nothing,' she said, worried about how he'd react. He looked like one of her students, about to explode because they couldn't get their feelings out.

His fingers gently touched her neck. 'Natty, what the hell are these from? And don't lie to me.'

Nat tried to shrug him away and snatch back her scarf. 'It's nothing, you don't have to worry about it.'

'Like hell! Tell me who did this.'

Nat stood there, unable to lie to him but also unable to share her secret. She hadn't told a soul and wasn't sure if she could even get the words out. She felt weak.

Drew crossed his arms but Nat wasn't afraid of him, even if he did look like he wanted to murder someone. Instead of pressuring her, he swore softly and walked away. Just like that, leaving Nat all alone and on the verge of tears. Why couldn't she speak about it? Was she worried Drew would look at her differently? Was she worried what Gary would do?

When she was calm enough to return to the senior room, half the people had left.

'Hey, there you are, Nat,' said Lauren. 'I just want to go over the things to prepare for our Department visit. Do you mind?'

'No,' said Nat, but she did. She wanted to escape to the safety of her home, where no one could see the shame she felt burning her cheeks and neck. She hardly took in what Lauren asked, just nodded in the appropriate spots. 'We'll talk again soon,' Nat promised. 'But I have to head off.'

Lauren reached for her arm. 'Are you okay, Nat? You seem a bit distracted. Anything I can help with? This isn't too much for you, is it?'

'No, not at all. I'm just expecting a call from Gary soon and don't want to miss it. Sorry. We'll catch up later.'

'For sure. Bye.' Lauren pulled her in for a quick hug. It surprised Nat but made her feel better. She headed home a little less tense.

She'd only been home for five minutes when there was a knock at the door. Assuming it was Lauren, she opened the door with a prepared smile. It slid from her face when she saw Drew standing there in a grey T-shirt that had a rabbit standing in front of a light bulb making a human hand in the shadow. It was quite cute – the shirt and, if she was honest, the face of the man standing before her.

'I'm sorry, Nat. I didn't mean to yell at you.' His brow creased in anguish. 'I got halfway home when I realised I couldn't leave it like that. I'm really sorry. It's not your fault. None of this is your fault.'

She wasn't sure about that. But she automatically opened the door, letting him in. He strode past her and made himself at home at the dining table. She sat down beside him, unsure of what to say or do.

Drew slid his hand to hers and held it. It felt so right, but at the same time she knew how Gary would react if he saw it. 'You've been there for me, Nat, and now I want to be here for you. I wish I could help you. It's just I can't handle abuse of any sort. You see, the reason I don't want Simone around Billy is because she's an addict and she nearly killed him.'

'What?' A world without Billy didn't seem possible.

'When I first met Simone she was a good-time girl, but eventually I learnt that was just a front. Her dad bashed her mum real bad when she was nine. He did a stint in jail and never came back. Her mum fell apart, and her occasional drug use became an addiction. She was on antidepressants as well and so Simone grew up in a crazy world, and it wasn't till after she'd come back pregnant that I realised how bad she was. She couldn't give up smoking, but we made her give up the other drugs and alcohol. She had no choice, we almost kept her prisoner, trying to dry her out. It wasn't pretty; it was hard on us all. I don't even know what damage she caused in those four months she didn't realise she was pregnant.'

Nat could only imagine.

'A few times we were unprepared and she found alcohol and drank herself silly, or called her sellers and begged them to deliver whatever they had. God knows what it did to Billy. We were lucky she didn't lose him. I grew to hate her then, hate the fact that she couldn't put the baby first instead of herself.'

Drew stopped and they sat there quietly. He still held her hand, his thumb rubbing circles. She wasn't sure who it was soothing, him or her. She knew he was sharing in the hope that she would too. The lump in her throat was still there but it had eased, maybe from Drew's touch or his closeness, which swathed her in his scent.

Nat managed to find her voice, and some courage. 'Gary's never done anything like this before,' she whispered. But as she said it, she thought about the time he came to Lake Biddy. She had told herself that he hadn't really meant to hurt her, that it hadn't been that bad. But now she wondered whether it had been a warning sign, and she'd missed it. 'I don't know if it's a one-off or whether he has a violent streak that will always come out when he's jealous.'

'Why was he jealous?'

If Drew was livid, his voice didn't betray it. Would it change after she told him? Did she dare?

'He saw you trying to call my mobile . . .'

Drew's face fell. 'Are you serious? I'm the cause of this?'

'After meeting you in the shop he felt threatened.'

'Jesus. I'm so sorry, Nat.'

'It's not your fault. You've been a perfect gentleman. Gary is just taking things too far.'

'Too damn right he's gone too far. Have you told anyone else? Your parents, your uncle, or your friends?'

Nat shook her head in turn.

'Do you stand up to him?' Her body broke out in a sweat just thinking about standing up to Gary. With wide eyes she shook her head firmly. 'Are you scared of how far he'll go?'

Yes, she was. Tight knots twisted in her stomach just thinking about it.

'I'm guessing yes,' said Drew. 'Nat, you can't put up with this.

What if he gets worse? What if this is just the tip of the iceberg?'

'I know. But he's not just my fiancé. Our families have been tied together since before I can remember. I'm not sure they'd believe me if I told them. And I still care for him. I think.'

'I can't make you stand up to him, nor can I make you share this with your family, but I want you to think about it. Please, Natty. If you're waiting around, hoping he'll change, don't. People like that never do.'

Was she just waiting for it all to go away? What if Gary always had this possessive streak? What if he never got better? What if it got even worse?

Drew let go of her hand and moved closer. Holding her face in his hands he stared her down with his brilliant blue eyes and she felt hypnotised by them. Her questions drifted away to nothing as Drew became her focus.

'You deserve better, Natty. You're an amazing person with such a big heart. Don't let him ruin that. Please.'

A tear slipped out, trailing hot down her cheek. Drew swiped it away with his thumb before he pulled her into a hug.

'Please don't tell anyone,' she begged through her tears. 'I just need some time to sort it out.' His strong arms, reassuringly tight around her, caused her to cry as if she'd bottled up ten years' worth of tears. As he rubbed her back she clung to him, and with each sob she started to feel better, as if she'd released something buried deep down in her heart.

Eventually she pulled away and went to get a tissue. 'I'm sorry,' she said, gesturing to his damp shirt before blowing her nose.

Drew smiled, that imperfect but alluring grin that made the world seem so much better.

'Don't worry about it. You can use my shoulder anytime. I guess I'd better get going. Kim will be wondering what's taking so long.'

Nat frowned. 'Yes, you'd better get back. Thank you. I'll talk to you later?' she said, walking him to the door.

'You'd better.' Drew paused, reaching out and lightly brushing her bruised neck. It sent tingles down her skin.

'Think about it, okay?' he said. 'You know it's wrong but I understand if it's hard. I'll be here for you, anytime.' Then he leant forward and kissed her on the cheek before walking back to his ute.

Chapter 21

DREW sat on a crate in his shed, hammer in hand as he looked at the seeder bar. He could hear Billy riding around on his motorbike, Turbo yapping at the back tyre and causing all the pink-and-grey galahs to squawk and fly from gum tree to gum tree. He was still sitting in that same spot ten minutes later, not having moved a muscle, when someone spoke.

'You know, to fix something you actually have to use the hammer,' said Matty with a chuckle. 'You okay? You look like you're on another planet.'

Matt sat on the edge of the seeder bar, his belly almost resting on his lap. He was in his work clothes, covered in grease, and Drew figured he'd been getting his machinery ready for seeding too.

'I probably was.' Drew put the hammer down and rested his elbows on his knees. 'You finished all your jobs?'

Matt's deep laugh echoed around the large tin shed. 'You're a funny bastard.' It was their standard gag. A farmer's work was never done and job lists seemed endless. Drew cracked a smile but Matt frowned, turning serious. 'Is it Simone? Has she come back?'

'Nah, not yet. I'm prepared, though. Nat got me some lawyer stuff to read so I can figure out my options.' It had caused him many sleepless nights, but now something else had him worried.

'Spit it out, Sadds. What's on your mind?' Matt stood up in the afternoon light. The sun was starting to set, bringing a cool chill. 'Will this need a beer? I've brought some coldies.'

Drew nodded. He needed a friend.

Matt came back from his ute with his jumper on and two cold beers in stubby holders. Those stubby holders spent their lives rolling around his ute but it meant he always had them handy. As usual, Matt had the Pingaring Gumtree Tavern one, leaving Drew his usual red Elders one.

Drew cracked open his beer can and guzzled a big mouthful while Matt made himself comfortable.

'So what's got your knickers in a twist, besides Simone? Billy isn't acting up?' asked Matt.

'No, actually. He's been pretty understanding. I keep waiting for him to erupt as I'm not sure how he's processed it. Maybe he's happy knowing he has a mum. I don't know. I guess I just have to wait and see.'

'So if it's not the little Sadds worrying you, then the only thing I can think of is a certain attractive teacher.' Drew couldn't meet Matt's eyes. 'I'm right, aren't I?'

Drew raised a shoulder in a half attempt of a shrug.

'Actually, it was Lozzy. She seemed to think something was

going on. I thought she was daft. Are you two . . .?'

'No, nothing like that, Matty. She's a great friend, really helped me out and she's having some trouble of her own. I guess that's what's chewing my mind up.'

'She in strife?' His eyebrows shot up like two hairy caterpillars. 'Can we help?'

'Nah, it's something she has to figure out on her own, I guess. I can't make her do the right thing. But hell, it's killing me that I can't do anything to help.'

'Uh-huh.' Matt studied him for a solid five seconds before commenting, 'Yeah, I see it now. I reckon Lozzy's right. You have a thing for her, don't you?'

Drew glanced out the shed at the setting sun, seeing Nat's hair in the soft golden hues. He did care for Nat – she was amazing. But it wasn't until that night, after he'd left her house, after he'd kissed her cheek, that he'd realised just how much he felt. It had driven him crazy ever since. 'It didn't start out like that, but all of a sudden it's like she's hit me over the head with a lump of wood. Whammo. Now that I've realised how I feel, I don't know how to stop it.'

'She's engaged, Drew,' Matt said seriously.

'I know that. And he's a dick.' Matt's expression changed at his description of Gary but he didn't ask why. 'It's not like I'm gonna do anything. It's just me. I have to get this under control.' He knew it was a combination of all the little things: seeing her with Billy, being able to talk to her so easily, having her supportive and caring nature in their home.

'Do you think she feels the same way?'

He sipped his beer as he thought about Matt's question. 'I don't think so.' He hung his head and felt like he was crying into his beer. 'Am I horrible for wanting what I can't have?' he whispered.

Matt cleared his throat. It was some deep conversation for them to be having while sober. 'Nah, mate. I think you're just human. And if her fiancé really is a dick, then maybe she'd be better off without him. Don't beat yourself up about it. She is a honey,' he said with a smile.

Drew had to agree, considering her face was all he could see when he closed his eyes at night. Then there was her sweet perfume, which stirred him into recklessness.

Billy's motorbike roared past. He did a circle then drove it into the shed, parking it up and switching it off. 'Hiya, Uncle Matt. Are you here alone?'

'Yeah, I am. Sorry, mate.'

Billy sat beside him on the metal bar. 'Are you going anywhere for the school holidays?' he asked eagerly.

'Lozzy might take the kids down to Bremer Bay and I know she was going to see if you wanted to go too.'

'Oh, yeah! Dad, can I?' Billy shot him a wide-eyed, hopeful look.

'I'm sure that will be okay. I'll talk to Aunty Loz about it later. *No* hounding me about it, okay?'

'Yes, Dad. I won't mention it again.'

But Drew knew that Billy would be bugging him about it the moment Matt left and then again back at the house, and over dinner. Billy didn't realise it but he was worse than a broken record. He was a persistent little bugger; he'd give his son that. It was one of the things that made him hard to handle at school – his friends grew tired of his continuously repeating the same stories. Once he'd started you couldn't interrupt him; even if you told him you'd heard it already, he still had to finish it. He'd follow you around, talking and not picking up on social cues, like when people had had enough. That's why Drew needed the school to stay open. The kids here understood he was a little different and they tolerated him. At a new school, with kids who didn't know him, hadn't grown up with him, he would be teased more. And Drew hated that thought.

'I'm going home to watch TV. Bye, Uncle Matt.'

'Bye, Billy,' said Matt, roughing up his hair.

'Okay, I'll be ten minutes,' said Drew before Billy put on his helmet and rode back to the house.

'Did you see the forecast?' said Matt. 'Looks like our opening rains are coming. You ready to get this girl out in the paddock?' Matt's thick hand gestured towards the tractor beside him.

The seeder bar was already hooked onto the Case tractor. It was oiled, watered, and had been checked for leaky hoses. 'I'm as ready as I'll ever be, I guess. It's the seeding part that worries me. It's hard enough putting a crop in all hours of the day without having to look after Billy. I'm not sure how I'm going to do it. I was thinking of employing someone to look after him and make my meals but I'm worried about how Billy would take that.'

'He'd be all right . . . eventually. And you know Loz will help out. She's got two to look after. What's one more?'

'I know, but she does so much already.'

'Why don't you ask Natalie?' said Matt teasingly.

Drew smiled at the mention of her name. 'It had crossed my

mind.' It would ensure he got to see her.

'Maybe between Loz, Nat and Doris, it can be done. Share the load?'

Doris had been Alice's best friend. She'd helped nurse Alice when she got really sick and, after she'd gone, Doris would often pop over and put dinner in the fridge for them. Drew had tried to hire her over harvest to help with the cooking but she wouldn't hear of it. Instead she made him roast dinners, which gave him plenty of meat for lunches, and helped him catch up on some housework. She was a diamond in the rough, old Doris. She lived in a ramshackle house on her departed husband's farm and drove over in her buggered ute that had no lights, except for the torch she held out the window at night, and no brakes. She often said it was God's will where she stopped. Billy thought she was the funniest lady out, with her short grey hair, missing teeth and holey trackpants.

The idea of having all three ladies helping had merit, though. Actually, it was just the thought of having a certain green-eyed beauty around more often that got his blood moving faster.

'You know, that's not a bad idea, Richo. Seems you're useful after all,' he said with a wink.

'Now that I've solved all ya problems, I'd better head home to my own. Bloody hormonal woman, grumpy and stubborn . . . and I'm just talking about my bloody sister!' Matt laughed at his own joke as he stood up and headed to his ute. He took off, arm waving out the window.

Drew finished his beer and decided that he'd talk to Nat about seeding, to see if she was keen. Hopefully, the thought of Gary's reaction wouldn't scare her off.

Chapter 22

THE first day back after school holidays was a boisterous one. The kids were excited over the classroom Hogwarts decorations, running around the room as they spotted more things from the broomsticks, house-coloured sashes, cauldrons and witches hats, spiders and pictures of the Hogwarts castle on the board. Then morning news went for over half an hour.

'We went to Albany and saw the whale place and the fort on the hill,' said Issac.

'My dad cut his finger nearly off with a bit of tin and got ten stitches,' said Ruby.

'No, he got five stitches, Ruby,' her older brother butted in.

'We went to Bali and everyone got sick except for me,' said Ava.

It was like an intersection in India in Nat's classroom, all the kids eager to tell news as loudly and as quickly as they could. It took a few days for the novelty of school holidays to wear off. During the week, Nat kept a lookout for Simone, as promised, and helped Kath plan letters to save the school. They drafted a letter to invite the minister out to Lake Biddy and rang all the other nearby rural schools up for closure to see what things they were doing.

'And you have to help me with Bogan Bingo,' Lauren had begged after school one day.

'Bogan what?'

'Bingo.' Lauren smiled innocently. 'It's an after-seeding celebration night for everyone to get together and unwind. Plus we're raising money for the P & C.'

'There never seems to be a dull moment in this small town,' Nat had replied. 'Ida was just telling me about the Holt Rock Hoedown, something about country music in a shearing shed on someone's farm?'

'Haha, yep. Just bring ya swag, tent or caravan for a night of fun. You should come. I know you don't dig country music but it's more than that. It's the atmosphere, the friendly faces and the laughs. Maybe together we can work on getting Drew there. He's due for a night out,' Lauren had said.

The Hoedown was starting to sound better, Nat had thought, then felt immediately guilty for being disloyal to Gary. She still wasn't talking to him, but he really did seem to be trying to make amends for his actions. He had started to text, at first wondering if she was okay because she wasn't replying, then eventually starting to say how sorry he was.

Princess, I just love you so much and I momentarily lost the plot. I'm so sorry. I just couldn't handle losing you to anyone, not after what I went through with my last girlfriend. You are

my life. Please talk to me. Please tell me that you're okay?
I promise never to let that happen again. Baby, please, tell me
what I can do to make it better?

Nat eventually texted back, saying that she just needed time.
Now every morning she'd get an *I love you* or a *Good morning,
princess*. She still wasn't sure whether she could trust him again,
but she appreciated how hard he was trying.

It was the last week in April, on a Tuesday, when Nat noticed
a lady standing by the school gate. A slim figure in a big knitted
black jumper with a dark-green beanie over her straight brown
hair. She had a long fringe and was sucking on a cigarette even
though it was starting to rain. Nat's gut told her that this was
Simone. By the road she saw a dark sedan, much like the one
Billy had described.

Nat approached her slowly, so as not to scare her. 'Hello.'

'Hi,' she replied, but her eyes were watching the kids.

'Are you Simone?'

Her dark eyes flicked to Nat. It was hard to tell what colour
they were, with the shadows around her eyes. There was confusion and then panic in them as she started to back away.

'Simone, wait. Please.' Nat didn't want her disappearing
again. 'For Billy's sake.'

That caught her attention. She stepped closer to the fence.
'That's his name? My boy is called Billy?'

Nat cringed at her words as a wave of smoke nearly choked
her. It was hard not to instantly dislike her, especially knowing
the whole story. Nat clenched her teeth and dug her nails into

her palms. *Calm breath*, she told herself. 'You can't be here, Simone. You need to talk to Drew. He knows you're around and that you've tried to see Billy.' Nat couldn't bring herself to say 'your son'.

'I just want to see him, see how he's grown.'

Now was not the time for Nat to give her a lecture on how she gave all those rights up. 'Please, go and see Drew now. He's at the farm and he needs to talk to you. You can't come around here again or the school will have to call the police. Do you understand?' They stood there in the light rain, the fence between them, like two fighters sizing each other up before a bout.

Simone's eyes narrowed. Her skin was patchy and lifeless. She would have been very beautiful once but the abuse was evident on her body. Her jumper sleeves were pushed up, revealing scars and marks mixed in with tattoos.

'Yeah, I guess I can't put it off, can I? At least I still remember how to get there.' Simone turned but paused, swinging back again. 'Is Drew well? Is he still a looker? Is his mum still ruling the roost?'

Nat shrugged. She wasn't going to give Simone anything. 'You'll see soon enough.' It actually turned her stomach to think of Billy's mum at home with Drew, the family back together again. Nat realised she felt a bit jealous.

Simone left and Nat waited until she'd turned down the road towards Drew's farm. Quickly she went back to her phone and called him.

'Nat? Is everything okay?' said Drew, always fearing the

worst when someone called from school.

'Simone was here. I told her she had to come to see you.'

'Shit.'

'Did I do the wrong thing?' she asked, worried.

'No, Natty, not at all. I'm just afraid. Actually, I'm terrified of facing her again.' His voice was strained.

'Is there anything I can do? Would you like me to bring Billy back to my house?'

'Actually that would be awesome, if you could. I don't really want him seeing her again until we sort this out. Thanks, Nat. Hopefully it's not for too long. I'll come get him when she leaves. I have something I want to discuss with you anyway.'

'Okay. Well, why don't you come in for dinner then? Billy will be fine with me for however long, you don't need to worry.'

'Um, yeah, I've actually got chops defrosted so maybe another time, but thanks anyway.' There was an awkward silence then Drew finally spoke again. 'Umm, I'd better go and get the paperwork out for Simone. I'll catch up with you soon. Thanks for having Billy. I owe ya, again.'

Nat could picture his smile. 'Okay, good luck, Drew.'

They hung up and Nat stared at her phone, hoping it would give her answers as to why Drew didn't want to come for dinner. Did he have Gary in the back of his mind? Maybe she was reading too much into it. He could just be stressed, or maybe the chops really did need cooking. There was just something about his voice, an uncertainty she'd never heard before. With a sigh she put her phone away, feeling a nag of disappointment.

The bell rang and, within minutes, flushed faces came pouring into the classroom. 'Walk, Noah, please. Zara, you forgot your hat. Mia, can you clean the board for me, please? Thank you.' Mia smiled as if she'd been picked first for a team. It was a chore yet the kids didn't see it as one. Even the senior room kids liked to use the blackboard, despite Grace having an interactive whiteboard. The kids made their way to their desks, animated, talking excitedly about games they'd been playing over the lunchbreak. Nat watched Billy put his hat on the hook before gesturing him aside.

'Guess what?'

'What?'

'You're not on the bus this afternoon. Can you guess who you're going to stay with?'

Billy's tiny eyebrows knitted together as he thought long and hard. He was still trying to process the fact that he wasn't on the bus.

'Henny and Penny have been waiting to see you,' she hinted.

His face lit up. 'Oh, am I coming to your house after school?'

'Yes, you are. Is that okay? You don't mind hanging out with me and the chooks?'

Billy's mouth and nose twitched together. It was his latest thing. Last week it had been clearing his throat every two seconds. As one tic went, another would take its place, and he didn't even realise he was doing it. It had taken Nat a while to notice, most could be just passed off as normal reactions, but now that she was aware she could watch them come and go. Nat did wonder if it was stress or anxiety causing them, or whether it was just some nerve issues. Drew often pointed it out gently, making him aware of it and eventually he'd stop, only to start doing something different instead.

'Yay!' he said. 'I like your place.'

He skipped to his chair and she overheard him telling his classmates that he was going to Miss Wright's house after school. It won him some envious smiles.

After school finished and she'd let the bus driver know Billy wasn't going to be on, she finished off some work while Billy coloured in a picture, and then they walked hand in hand back to her house. He had his schoolbag, and Nat was carrying the leather bag she'd bought especially to cart her stuff to and from school. It was still fresh outside and Nat was thankful for her high-heeled boots, jeans and soft pink cashmere jumper. The locals had already warned her that it got freezing in winter, especially when the frosts were around. Drew had offered to get her some wood for the tiny potbelly fire in her house. He wasn't the only one to offer, either. Wazza and Pansy had been as sweet as pie in the shop the other day, offering their services. Frank had smacked them with his straw broom and told them off for hounding his customers. They had then complained that they were his customers too. It was all in jest and Nat loved the banter that the locals seemed to have running all the time.

'How about you catch up with Henny and Penny for a bit while I put together an afternoon snack for us?'

'Okay.' Billy dropped his schoolbag and crawled down onto the lawn, calling out to the chooks. He talked to them while she ducked inside.

They had hummus, carrot sticks and rice crackers at the little table setting on her back patio while they watched the chooks.

'This is real fancy,' said Billy, scooping up a big blob of dip on the end of his carrot.

'I'm glad you approve. Now afterwards, shall we get your homework out of the way? Then maybe we can play a game or you could walk me to the shop for some groceries and the mail?'

'Okay,' he mumbled, munching the food in his mouth.

All afternoon Nat kept checking her phone in case Drew called.

'Natty?' asked Billy, drawing her attention back from the patch of dirt she'd been staring at.

Nat was finding it hard to focus on Billy's stories when her mind kept disappearing. Looking at him, she realised this probably wasn't the first time he'd called her name. 'Hmm, yep?'

'My dad's here.'

She stood up and turned around to the gate to see Drew letting himself in.

'Hey,' she said with a smile, which he returned before focusing on Billy.

'Hey, mate. Hope you've been good for Natty.'

Billy nodded and Drew told him to go get his stuff so they could head home. 'Thanks, Nat.'

'No worries, he was no problem at all. How did it go?' she asked quickly while Billy was inside.

'Okay, I guess. She just wants to see him occasionally. She doesn't want to take him away, so that's a start.'

'You going to let them meet?'

'Guess I have to, otherwise Billy might hate me later for keeping her away. But I still wouldn't mind getting the forms filled out so it's all official and it stipulates he's mine and she gets a day a month or so many hours' visitation. I want his time with her limited.'

'I understand,' said Nat quickly as Billy came out of the house with his schoolbag on his back.

'Natty helped me do my homework, Dad, and my other assignment, and we had a fancy snack and played.' Billy grinned, looking from adult to adult.

'Nice one.' Drew scratched the stubble on his jaw. Nat knew that was a sure sign something was on his mind. 'Um, I've got seeding coming up and it's the first time with Mum gone.' Drew put his hands on Billy's shoulders, keeping him close. 'And I'm not sure how I'm going to cope. Harvest was pretty hard going but between Loz and Doris we got through. But seeding's a bit different; I don't have to wait for the right temperature to seed so it's usually crazy hours getting it all in. Anyway, to cut a long story short, I'm hoping that you wouldn't mind looking after Billy on occasion, if it's not too much trouble, and only to help give Loz and Doris a break.' Drew's face was turning pink but he kept eye contact while he spoke.

Nat didn't hesitate. 'Of course.'

'Um, okay. Are you sure?' He seemed a little relieved and shocked at the same time.

'Yes, of course. He can stay with me after school. If he's up to staying the night he's welcome to stay —'

'Can I, Dad? Can I stay here?' Billy cut in.

'I guess. We might need a trial run first,' Drew said, shooting Nat a warning gaze.

'I don't mind having him for as long as you need.' Nat knew Gary wouldn't mind as it was just Billy and she'd love the company. 'He'd be no trouble here, if that's what you're worried about?'

'I'm more worried about putting you out. Seeding can go for a while.' He pulled a face.

'Well, don't. I want to help.' Nat put her hand on his arm to reinforce her point, causing him to flinch slightly. She drew her hand away, a bit puzzled. 'Call me and we'll sort out the details?'

'Yeah, I will.' Drew's chest rose with his deep breath. His long-sleeved blue-checked shirt strangely made him look very appealing, even though there was dirt on the shoulder, as if he'd been crawling under something. He smelt like grease and fuel, and for some reason she liked that.

Drew's eyes were bright as he watched her for a moment. It was as if he was trying to read her thoughts, or connect with her on another level. She felt the hair rise at the nape of her neck. 'Come on, Billy,' he said eventually. 'Let's head home. We have chores to do.' His lips curled into a smile and he thanked her again.

Drew had a way of making Nat feel amazing just by being himself, and she realised that she was attracted to him. She could try to deny it but her body had a mind of its own. How could she avoid it when he was such a handsome man with such a big heart?

Nat saw them to the gate, then watched as they walked off towards Drew's ute, Billy talking non-stop. Such a sweet sight. She was already looking forward to spending time with Billy, to having a little person around the house.

Chapter 23

'SETH, if I see you without your motorbike helmet on, you are banned for a week, got it?' yelled Lauren as Seth and Billy darted past them towards their waiting bikes.

It was just over two weeks into seeding and Nat had gone to Lauren's to drop off Billy for the weekend. To make things easier on Drew she'd taken Billy for the weeknights, and he'd settled in well at her place. She'd been able to help him with his homework, even slotting in some extra work to improve his spelling and maths. But it was good to take him to the Richards' for the weekend. He was getting comfortable with her and tested her patience sometimes.

'Kids, I tell ya,' said Lauren as they stood outside with their cups of coffee.

Lauren and Matt had a nice home and farm. Matt's parents had moved to Albany, semi-retired, leaving Matt and Kim to take over their established property. Kim had their house to herself, and Lauren and Matt had a beautiful home surrounded by massive lilac trees, lots of lawn and a pool. How Lauren managed to keep her kids alive, the gardens flourishing, the farm maintained, while fulfilling all her community roles as well, Nat had no clue.

'Thanks for this, I needed a real coffee.' Nat sipped the perfect brew from Lauren's fancy coffee machine in the 'Moms love Vampires' *Twilight* mug. Lauren's mug had 'World's Greatest Mum' on it. They stood at the side of the house on the wide verandah, watching the boys ride around the silos and machinery sheds. Mallory and her pink teddy were on a small quad bike, both wearing matching pink tutus.

'Anytime. You're always welcome,' said Lauren. They talked about how Billy was going, about how Seth and Mallory were progressing at school. 'Hey, have you got your outfit sorted for the Bogan Bingo night?'

'Not really. Jeans and a black T-shirt, I was thinking.'

'Oh, here, come and borrow one of my old checked shirts. Actually, you can keep it. I doubt I'll ever fit back into it.' Lauren took Nat into her room and pulled out some shirts. 'Here's my old favourite T-shirt. You should wear this with this red check, be perfect. Real bogan style,' she said with a chuckle.

The black T-shirt fitted snuggly. It had a Def Leppard album cover on the front, and the checked shirt went well too. 'Thanks, Lozzy, I could use these when I head out to the farm. You sure you don't want to keep them?'

'Nah, I haven't worn that T-shirt since before the kids. I'm still trying to lose the pregnancy weight, even ten years on,' she said with a chuckle. 'I kept that shirt for sentimental reasons but I'd rather see it getting used. I was a wild thing when I met Matt.

Man, did we have a good time. B & S balls, paddock parties and shed dos. Body doesn't cope with that much alcohol any more,' she said with a frown.

They ended up rolling around in fits of giggles when Lauren showed her Matt's mullet wig and black moustache, which they had to try on.

'I'm going to colour in some teeth as well. Gosh, it's going to be a good night, hopefully full of laughs. These guys will need a break after seeding. They work like crazy.'

Nat realised that the P & C did lots of events like the Bogan Bingo to bring the community together, give farmers a chance to get together and talk, as well as raising money for things that the school needed, like some new play equipment. Although if they couldn't save the school it would all be for nothing. They fell silent and Nat wondered if Lauren was thinking the same thing.

Back outside they checked on the kids again. A white ute was coming along the back lane. '*Kids!*' yelled Lauren, suddenly waving her arms like she'd just seen a big redback spider on her shoulder. Nat had to resist putting her hands over her ringing ears.

The kids saw her and stopped, taking off their helmets so they could hear her.

Lauren pointed to the car. 'Doris is coming, stay over by the sheds until her car has stopped, okay?'

'All right!' came their reply as they drove further towards the sheds.

Nat turned to watch the approaching car. 'Doris is a card. I've seen her in the shop a few times. I've never met anyone with so much character. She has her own style but such a big heart.'

'I know. I'm glad you see it. Other people see a messy-looking ragbag old lady in a clapped-out ute. But by god does she make the world a better place. Heart bigger than the wheat belt, that's for sure,' said Lauren.

Doris tooted her horn as she came towards the house. It was limp and sick-sounding, as if submerged in water. The ute was already coasting, Doris's foot no doubt trying to find some sort of brakes. It pulled up just two metres past them. Doris was good at judging its roll-to-a-stop distance.

The kids came swarming back like bees to honey when they knew the coast was clear, each one giving Doris a hug as she got out. They came away with big slices of chocolate crackle, all of them wasting no time in biting into them.

'Hi, Doris,' said Nat as they walked around the ute to greet her. Doris was wearing her Redback boots, brown trackpants with holes, some patched, some not, and a green flannel shirt with a torn pocket on it. There was a chook feather stuck in her hair, Nat noticed, as Doris reached into her ute.

'Here ya are, Lozzy. I did some baking yesterday.'

Doris produced a cardboard box full of old Tupperware containers. The original Tupperware. It must be good stuff if it could take the beating Doris had no doubt given it over the years.

'Thank you, Doris, I really appreciate it,' said Lauren.

Nat peeked inside and her mouth watered. 'What have you got in there, Doris?'

'Choc-chip cookies, caramel slice, choc crackles, sausage rolls, pinwheels, some silverside and Matty's favourite jam slice.'

'Oh, he'll love that. Matt can always tell the difference

between mine and Doris's jam slice. I swear I follow the recipe.'

'That's ya problem, girly,' said Doris. She tapped the side of her head with a crooked finger, which looked as if it had been jammed in a door once or maybe twice. 'It's all tucked up in 'ere. I don't follow no recipes any more.' Then she laughed a dry, booming laugh that would have seemed more at home on a large drunk man. 'I've made a heap for Drew as well, just dropped them off at the house on my way over. Make sure you take some for young Billy next week.'

'I will, thanks, Doris.' Nat wondered if Doris knew that Lauren and Drew both put money into her shop account for all the food she bought to feed them with. Drew had explained once that he'd tried to buy her expensive gifts as a way to say thanks at Christmas but Doris never needed anything. She didn't like new clothes or jewellery. She was a woman of the land and didn't see the point of material things unless it was more Tupperware, tea towels or ingredients to cook with. Last year Drew had a cow slaughtered and filled up Doris's big freezers with enough meat to last her ages. He said it had brought the woman to tears and it had made him chuffed to find the right present. Mind you, she'd used a lot of that meat making him stews and casseroles over the year, he'd said.

'Lozzy, I've also baked Kim's favourite curry puffs. Make sure Matt doesn't get his mitts on them,' Doris ordered. 'Now, if you'll excuse me, I'd better get back. I've got some meat defrosting and Angus was eyeing it off.' Angus was Doris's Jack Russell.

Doris swung her large body back into the ute and it started with a cough, leaving a black trail of smoke as she drove off.

One of the ute's non-working spotlights rolled around, hanging on by its wires.

Lauren put the food inside and they washed up their cups.

'Do you want to come and see what Kim is building Drew for his birthday? She's so bloody talented.'

'Yeah, sure. When is his birthday?'

'Twenty-sixth of June.'

Nat locked that away for future use and followed Lauren to the big shed nearest the house. It had huge sliding doors on the front and a workshop at one end. 'Massive shed,' said Nat. The ceilings were high and the workshop had a mezzanine floor, no doubt for extra storage.

'Okay, here it is, but you have to swear you won't tell Drew. All the kids have been sworn to secrecy too.' Lauren gave her a warning look, making her freckles turn golden in the light.

'Cross my heart,' said Nat before stepping inside to see a gigantic mash-up of junk metal. But Kim's magical eye had turned all the rusty leftover machinery parts into something great. 'Oh my god. It's amazing.' Nat walked closer to the sculpture. It was a dragon, it had to be. A long tail curled with a point at the end, and one metal wing out one side, the other yet to be constructed.

'I'm glad you like it,' came Kim's voice behind them.

'Hey, Kim, what're you doing? Something break?' asked Lauren worriedly.

Kim stood at the shed door in dirty jeans and a thick blue work jumper with the collar of her checked shirt folded out over the top. She moved inside and grabbed some tools as she spoke. 'Yeah, tyre on the seeder bar bloody came off. Have to fix it.'

'Before you get back I'll run home and get you some food to take. Doris has just been,' said Lauren.

Kim's coffee-coloured eyes swirled with delight as she groaned. 'Curry puffs?'

'You bet. I'll be back in a tick.'

Lauren left and Kim put the toolbox by the door then wheeled across a big thing, which Nat guessed was a welder.

'This is truly amazing, Kim. Drew is going to love it.'

Kim stepped up next to her and smiled. 'Thanks, Nat. Still have a bit to go. I want to have some curls of smoke and fire coming out of his mouth. Luckily I've watched *How to Train Your Dragon* with the kids enough times.'

'How ever did you do it?'

'Well, the scales are made from the points we used on the seeder – they're what dig into the ground, so these are all the old ones. Did a drive around the community, picking them up. Bits of leftover steel and wire, old tools, cogs from various machinery, fingers from old header combs – you name it, I've probably used it.'

'You have such a talent, Kim. You could make a fortune selling these in the city. Have you thought about it?' asked Nat. She felt small next to Kim, who was so accomplished and had strength and ability in spades.

'Nah. I've done a few things for the shire. They wanted some metal animals to put along the main street in Lake Grace, so that will be my next project when I have time. They won't be as big as this bugger, but this guy's going at the front of Drew's farm gate. So it needed to be grand.'

Kim's face radiated as she spoke. Drew really was blind as a

215

bat when it came to Kim's feelings. The love she was putting into this dragon was further evidence. Nat didn't want to ask about the amount of time she'd spent on it. 'Why a dragon, though?'

'Drew's farm is called Dragon Rock, so I thought it was fitting.'

Nat remembered him telling her that over dinner one night. It was because he was near the Dragon Rock reserve. 'You are so amazing, Kim. I envy you,' said Nat truthfully. How Drew could have resisted her all these years she had no clue.

Kim turned to face Nat, her brow creased and her eyes pained. 'Yeah, but it still doesn't get me the man I want, does it? Yet you've caught his eye,' she said frankly.

Nat was taken by surprise. 'Who, Drew?'

'I've seen the way he looks at you. In all these years he's never seen me that way and for that I envy you.'

Nat's mouth fell open. Kim must be mistaken, surely. 'But I'm engaged.' It was all that she could think of to say while her mind was trying to sort itself out.

'Yeah, well, Drew's not. And besides, sometimes you can't help who you fall for.'

Nat knew Kim meant herself as well. 'You really think he likes me? He's never said anything or done anything,' Nat said.

'He wouldn't, he's too much of a gentleman and he wouldn't want to get hurt in case he lost you as a friend. Believe me when I tell you that. I've had years of debating the same issue. I'd rather have Drew as a friend than lose him altogether. I know he doesn't feel that way about me. I knew it when I saw the way he looked at you.'

Kim cleared her throat and picked up some kind of Darth

Vader helmet before facing Nat, fixing her to the spot with a stare to scare all tough men. 'I like you, Nat, but if you break his heart or Billy's you'll have me to answer to. Are we clear?'

Nat could only nod. The change in Kim, so protective and fierce. She could do nothing but admire her more.

'Good. I'll see you later.' She left the shed, loading up her tools on the ute outside.

Nat could hear Lauren's voice chatting to Kim as she handed over Doris's treats and helping her load up the welder. But Nat could only sit down on the old oil drum, not even bothering with a rag, while she tried to swallow this news. Drew. Could he really feel that way about her?

Nat thought over their talks and meetings, looking for signs that he felt more. The only thing she could come up with was the night he kissed her cheek. It had been out of the blue, yet it had felt so comfortable. And his eyes, so tender and vibrant, had reached right into her soul. And it was true, things had been different between them since then. Like the time he'd flinched when she'd touched him. Maybe he'd felt that zap with the connection? She certainly hadn't been able to deny it, engaged or not.

Here she was with a smile on her face. Knowing that she meant something to Drew made her feel alive. But it could never be more than friendship, could it? She would be gone after this year, then married and having babies of her own. With Gary. She didn't know how she felt about that at this point but, regardless, she couldn't live in the country full time. It was impossible.

Lake Biddy full time? Forever? That had never entered her mind.

Until now.

Chapter 24

DREW was feeling dead on his feet. The inside of his Case tractor had been his home for the past nineteen days straight and
probably would be for the same time again, if there were no
interruptions and problems. Really, he'd been lucky to go for
this long, getting enough rain to keep going but not so much
that he couldn't get back on the paddocks. It helped knowing
that Billy was in good hands. Except for today. He'd grown sixty
ulcers just thinking about today. Simone had called last week,
obeying his rules of calling before turning up, and she'd asked if
she could come out and meet Billy properly.

What could he do? Say no? He'd thought about it and was
ready to have her cut from his life completely, but then he'd
thought about Alice. A life without knowing his mum . . . Of
course Simone was never going to be an Alice, but she was all
Billy had. If he was putting his son first, then he knew Billy had
a right to at least meet her – if only on Drew's terms. He was
also mindful that Simone could well be crazy enough to steal

Billy away one day. It was a far better option to keep her on good terms for now, at least until he could get the paperwork sorted and the law on his side. Someone like Simone could vanish with Billy in the blink of an eye. His stomach contorted with the thought, almost forcing his lunch back up. Doris's roast meat and pickle sandwiches were awesome, but he didn't want to experience them a second time.

Drew finished out the line he was on before pulling up and shutting everything down. He walked across the paddock, over the earth he'd just seeded with Bullock barley, and jumped in his ute, which was parked by the truck filled with fertiliser.

Billy would be getting off the bus any minute and Drew wanted to have another talk with him before Simone arrived. He'd told her to be at the farm after four but he wasn't counting on her being early or even on time. It wasn't something Simone had ever been good at.

Drew found himself speeding along the farm tracks too fast, his nerves making his foot go down while his mind was elsewhere. He slowed down and tried to get to the house in one piece. As Drew pulled up, he noticed dust from the little motorbike, indicating Billy wasn't far away either. Drew got out and waited. He felt like collapsing in a pile of jumbled nerves and anxiety but instead he remained upright, thanks to the ute, and forced a smile as Billy parked his bike and took off his helmet.

'Hey, Dad.'

Billy hung his helmet on the handlebar, then stepped into Drew's waist and hugged him tightly, his schoolbag still stuck to him like a turtle shell. And Billy didn't let go; his little arms clung like a vice. Could he sense Drew's fear, or was he frightened himself? Drew knelt down in the dirt so he could face his son, see the tiny freckles, the long eyelashes that Alice had always remarked on, the tiny scar on his forehead from when he had tripped and fallen as a toddler. But it was his bright blue eyes that gripped his heart. Alice had said they were wise eyes, as if Billy had been here before. They sparkled as if each one held a galaxy full of planets and stars, such wonder beyond imagination.

'It'll be okay, Dad,' said Billy as he patted Drew's shoulder. 'I love you.'

Drew bit his lip. His eyes glazed with tears but he blinked them away. He couldn't afford to break down now. He couldn't put his fears onto his son. He wondered what Billy was thinking, standing there tall and strong, ready to face what was to come, while Drew felt the opposite. Ah, the innocence of childhood.

'I know, buddy. And I'll always love you. Are you ready to meet Simone?' Drew couldn't bring himself to call Simone his mother and preferred Billy to call her by her name too. She had not earned the right to be called Mum. She had a lot to prove before that would ever happen. 'Do you have any questions for me? Or anything you want to ask her as well?' Drew stood up and guided Billy inside with a gentle hand on his shoulder.

'Will she like me, Dad?'

His question was like a shovel to the big toe. This is why he wanted Simone 'gone' – so she couldn't bring out all these feelings of insecurity for Billy. 'Of course she'll like you! What's not to like? Natty thinks you're awesome.'

His smile grew wide. 'I wish Natty could be my mum.'

Drew stumbled along the path, almost tripping up. He was shocked by Billy's statement yet had to agree. Billy was thriving, being with Nat while he was seeding. He could tell they were growing close. Nat would make an amazing mum, just like Alice. He wanted that for Billy, not Simone, whose life was a wreck, whose addiction came first over love and family. How could he ever trust her?

Once they were inside they made a Milo and waited. Neither of them was capable of starting any jobs. Even folding washing seemed impossible.

Turbo barked and Drew checked his watch. Simone was practically on time. He didn't know how he felt about that. Did he dare believe she'd improved? In a way he'd hoped she was still the unreliable person she'd always been. It would make hating her easier, make keeping Billy easier.

'She's here,' Billy said with a mixture of excitement and panic. His eyes were wide like plates.

Drew just felt dread. It sat in his stomach like black tar.

Simone was standing by her car when they walked out. She wore black skinny jeans and a big knitted grey jumper. Her straight hair hung down and the light made the red highlights brighter. She was wearing the same dark-green beanie as last time and her fringe almost covered her eyes. A cigarette was burning away between her stained fingers.

Billy was hanging on to Drew's waist, hiding behind him and peering around his body like he used to do when he was younger. Drew would be happy if he stayed like this, wary of Simone, never giving her his heart, because Drew couldn't guarantee she wouldn't rip it into shreds.

'Hi, Simone.'

'Hey, Drew.' She sucked a big drag from her smoke and butted it out on the ground with her sneaker. 'Hi, Billy,' she said, bending down.

Billy didn't speak. His hand gripped Drew's jeans, pulling on his leg hairs, but he wasn't about to complain.

They all stood awkwardly by her car. It was eerily still; even the birds remained quiet. It made Drew more nervous and fidgety. 'Shall we go and grab a seat? Did you want a coffee?'

Simone smiled and Drew saw the fun, cheeky girl he'd first met. God, it felt like a lifetime ago. They'd been so intimate back then but now she was like a stranger. Billy had changed him so much, for the better.

'A coffee would be great, thanks. Thanks for letting me come visit, too. It's the only time I get off work,' she added, following them to the back verandah.

'Where are you working?'

'I'm managing the small IGA store near my place. I've been there a while.'

Drew nodded and told her to have a seat on the chair outside. He didn't want her in his house. For all he knew she could be casing the joint, chasing some quick cash. He didn't want her to see their life, their home, or be a part of it.

'I'll just get the coffee. How do you like it?'

'White with two, thanks.'

'Righto. Turbo will keep you company,' he said before

ducking inside, Billy still clinging to him.

'She's different, Dad,' whispered Billy, glancing at the glass door while Drew turned on the kettle. 'She smokes.' Billy screwed up his face. 'She smells. Do I have to hug her?'

'No, you don't have to do anything you don't want to. You don't even have to talk to her. But if she asks you a question, it's rude not to answer,' Drew added, trying to be a good parent when really he wanted to say the opposite. If Billy decided to scream at her, tell her he never wanted to see her ever again . . . well, that would be just fine and dandy by him.

Back outside, he handed Simone her cup. She embraced it with her hands, her jumper sleeves so long they just about covered her fingers.

'Thanks.'

Billy crawled onto Drew's lap but faced Simone. Drew could tell his son was curious. He was gazing at Simone and it was making her uncomfortable. Good.

'He has your eyes,' said Simone. 'But I think he has my nose.'

'Yeah.' It was the only part of Billy he was willing to give her credit for. Other than that he didn't want to see Simone's genes. Billy was all Saddler in personality. He hoped it stayed that way.

'He looks a bit like my brother when he was little.'

They made horrible small talk, but most of the time was spent in silence while Billy openly stared at her.

Billy moved to whisper in Drew's ear, his bony bottom digging into Drew's thigh. But it was the question Billy had whispered that caused him to flinch.

Drew cleared his throat. 'Um, Billy wants to know why you

want to see him now, after all this time.' Actually it had been the first question Drew had asked her last time. Why now?

'Well, I've always thought about you. Wondered what you looked like, how tall you were getting. I couldn't really come before because I wasn't very healthy. But now,' Simone gave him a big smile, 'I'm healthy, I have a job, a house, a partner and it was time to see you.'

Drew's ears picked up at the mention of a partner. What kind of bloke was he? He didn't want some other guy near his son.

Billy whispered to Drew, 'She's still not very healthy if she smokes.'

Whether or not Simone heard it, she didn't say.

'Also my mum passed away a month ago,' she added.

'Sorry, Simone,' Drew said softly.

She shrugged. 'I know she was struggling but she was my mum and I loved her. I guess it was saying goodbye to her and remembering the good and the bad that made me think more about Billy. Made me want to reach out and right a few wrongs.'

Drew nodded. He didn't really know what to say. He'd told her about Alice on her last visit. Simone had glanced around, looking for her, the fear evident on her face. Alice could be a tough cookie when it was called for so Simone had a right to be afraid of coming back to face her. When Drew said she'd passed away he'd been annoyed at the relief he'd seen surge through her body. But Drew was older now; he could be just as tough as his mum if need be.

Drew was relieved Simone didn't spell out her issues to Billy, and the real reasons behind walking away from him. He didn't want his young son knowing anything about drugs or the harsh realities of life just yet. Simone said she was clean, had been for over a year now, but to Drew that wasn't enough. A year was nothing when most of her life had been on drugs.

'Can you tell me about yourself? What you like to do? Do you have pets?' Simone asked Billy softly. She put her cup down and focused on the child wriggling in Drew's arms.

He looked up at Drew with those big eyes. He could tell he was torn about what to do. Drew gave him a reassuring smile. Billy returned it before facing Simone again.

'I have Turbo and chooks and my yabbies,' said Billy slowly. 'And I like riding my motorbike.'

'Oh, wow, you have a motorbike. Where do you ride it? You must be very clever,' she said.

Simone had always been good at getting people to talk and she worked her magic on Billy. She pretended to be in raptures as he told her about the bike track. Slowly he opened up, but he remained on Drew's lap, which Drew liked.

'Can I see you again?' Simone's question was put to both of them. 'Maybe you could come and stay with me?'

Billy shrugged and Drew silently cursed. Over his dead body.

'Say goodbye, Billy, and then it's time for you to have a shower,' said Drew. He needed to talk to Simone. He wanted her to know his plans.

'Bye, Billy.' Simone stood up, her arms held out as if she was hopeful for a hug.

Billy held up his hand and gave her a funny little wave. 'Bye.' He slipped off Drew's knee and ran inside.

'Look, Simone,' said Drew as they reached her car. 'I've let you see him but I won't ever let him out of my sight. He will not be staying with you unless I'm there. I can't risk it.'

Simone's face paled. 'But he's mine too.'

'You gave up that right, remember? I still have the letter you wrote, giving him up.'

'But I didn't sign any legal paperwork,' she countered. 'That letter won't stand.'

Drew should have kept the possessive anger from his voice but it was much too hard.

'That's why I'm going through the courts now. I want it legal and binding. You may have given birth to him but you are not his mother. We can do visitations but I will be there for every one of them.'

'I won't hurt him, Drew.'

'You already have, just by being here,' he said crossly.

'You can't keep me from him. I'm clean now. I deserve a second chance.'

Drew scoffed; she'd already had a hundred chances. He wasn't stupid.

'I don't care. I want the courts involved. I don't care how high I have to go. You'd be better off just going back to your life than fighting me on this.' Drew hoped that was enough to scare her. He knew she wouldn't have the money to fight him, not when he had the farm. He'd sell his kidney if it meant keeping Billy.

'Why are you being a bastard about this, Drew?' Simone's voice rose to a high pitch.

'You're the one who nearly killed him. You didn't want him.

Why are you doing this to us? Go back to the city and forget about us. It's served you well for the last eight years.'

'I sank into depression after having Billy. I missed my child. It took me a while to realise it. I admit I went off the deep end but I was trying to forget it. Trying to forget him. But I couldn't. And I'm finally clean, finally thinking clear, and I want to know my boy.'

'He's not your boy,' Drew growled. If he were a dog he would have his hackles raised and he'd be ready to sink his teeth into her leg.

'And he's probably not even yours either,' spat Simone.

Her words whipped him back like a gale-force wind. '*What?*'

'You heard me. After you went back to the farm there were others. Who knew which one was really the father? But I knew you would help me out. You were always good to me back then. So I came to you, said it was yours, but I don't really know.'

'You're fucking kidding me! Are you just being a bitch, or what?' It couldn't be true. Billy had his eyes – a lighter blue, but still they were similar, and his walk was the same as Drew's. Not that that was genetics, but still.

'The courts won't let you have him if he's not even yours. If you let me see him, then I won't say he's not yours,' she said. Her dark eyes were challenging him, but was it just a bluff?

'He's mine regardless,' he said, summoning a strength he didn't feel. Don't come back here unannounced or I'll call the cops. I'll make your life hell, Simone, so don't push me on this.'

'I want to be in my son's life. I gave birth to him, I know he's mine,' she said, opening her car door and getting in. 'I won't give up either, Drew. You need to let me be in his life. It's the easy option for all of us. You really want to lose your farm over this?'

'Goodbye, Simone.' Drew shoved her door closed and turned away. If she didn't leave now, he was going to do something stupid. He clung to the side of his ute, breathing heavily and waiting as her car started and drove off. He turned to watch and make sure she left Dragon Rock for good. When there was no more dust, Drew turned around and punched the door of his old ute as hard as he could, cursing loudly enough to scare the nearby birds. Then he punched it again for good measure. The pain was sweet relief, flooding his body and momentarily voiding his brain of thought for all of two seconds. Then his knuckles began to throb and bleed where he'd split the skin.

This was not happening.

Simone had to be lying. Yet a small part in the back of Drew's mind kept yelling out that it was totally possible. This was Simone, after all. She didn't take their break-up well; she'd probably spent the month afterwards in a drug haze, sleeping with anyone who looked half interested. The idea churned in his stomach and he wanted to hit something again. The crumpled door of his ute just wouldn't do. How would he explain the big dent he'd already put there?

Drew swore and sank down onto the ground. Tears came, not from the possible broken bones in his fist but from the tearing of his heart. Billy was his son in every way. There was no way he would give him up, even if he wasn't his. How could Simone do this to him again? She'd thrown his life into chaos in seconds. He swiped at his face with rough hands but the tears came faster, blurring his sight. He wished his parents were here. How was he going to fight this on his own? How was he going to keep this from affecting Billy? Where the hell did he start?

A wet tongue ran along his arm. He pulled his hands away from his face to see a blurry Turbo, who licked him again. He nudged his head in close, curious.

Turbo glanced back to the house and Drew realised sitting here feeling sorry for himself wasn't going to help his son. *His* son. As he fought back another wave of tears, he got up, using Turbo as a crutch. 'Thanks, boy.' Drew lifted his shirt and wiped his face. Turbo was right. Billy was inside, needing a father. And he was the man for the job, regardless of what some DNA test might say.

Chapter 25

DRIVING through the farm gate to return Billy after he'd spent the week with her, Nat tried to imagine how awesome it would look with Kim's big dragon standing nearby. The sculpture was sure to attract new orders for her. Nat wondered how Kim ever found the time.

'Are you excited to see Dad?' Nat asked Billy as they drove onto the farm. He had a broad smile on his face.

'Yeah! And I miss Turbo.'

Nat drove to the shed, as Drew had suggested via text message. He was loading up the grain truck and would take Billy back out with him.

'I see him, I see him!' said Billy, pointing.

Billy was out the door the moment she stopped the car. Drew turned off a motor, ran to Billy and flung him up into the air, then hugged him tightly. Nat found herself grinning at this reunion between father and son.

'Hey,' she said as she approached them. Drew put Billy down

and Nat noticed his hand. 'Oh my god. What happened?' She reached for his arm but he jerked it away.

'It's nothing. Just me and machinery don't mix.'

Drew put his hand behind his back but she'd already seen the split knuckles, the puffy, dark bruising. How was he working with it in that state? 'Have you seen the doctor? It could be broken.'

'Nat, it's fine.' Drew's eyes went back to Billy, avoiding Nat's gaze. He'd been doing that since she'd arrived. 'Man, did I miss you.' He rubbed the top of his son's head with his good hand.

'Turbo, I missed you too, buddy,' Billy said as the dog jumped up to lick his face. He ran off, Turbo barking and chasing him.

Nat stepped towards Drew. She just wanted to stand a bit closer; whether it was so she could smell him, or make him look at her, or even just because she felt a pull towards him, she wasn't sure. But she'd missed his company. Seeding was horrible.

'I've packed Billy and you some snacks to have while you're on the tractor. His iPod is charged too so you should be set for a fair while.' Drew had offered to take her for a spin once but it hadn't eventuated. Maybe because there wasn't much room in the tractor.

'Thanks, Nat, I really appreciate it.' Finally he turned his deep blue eyes in her direction. 'I couldn't do it without you.' The stubble on his chin was getting quite long and his hair was looking scruffy. 'Didn't let Billy out of your sight?' he asked softly.

'No. I did as you asked. He's never been alone or out of my sight, even at school while he played. I've kept a lookout for her car as well.' Nat was itching to ask him again about the meeting.

By Billy's account it all went nicely. Yet Drew had made sure she was on protection duty and hadn't explained why.

'Thanks. I just don't want her near him until we have everything legalised. I don't want her in his life, Nat,' said Drew as he watched Billy try to catch Turbo's tail. Turbo was dancing around him, tauntingly waving his tail at him before bounding away. 'I can't see Simone bringing anything good into his life, not until I know she's really changed. But even then . . .' His words dropped away.

'Are you okay?' Her gut said something wasn't right.

'Yeah, all good. Should get this seeding done by next week. Just in time for the Bogan Bingo night. I think we'll all need a break by then. You included,' he said, changing the subject.

'Billy's been great, don't worry about him. We've been getting on brilliantly. He isn't a problem at all.'

'Are you off to the city now?' Drew's brow creased.

'No, we're having a meeting with the Pingaring, Karlgarin and Mount Walker schools, which are on the closure list. I'm heading to Lozzy's after here and she's driving us. It could be a long afternoon.' Nat knew she should really get going but she didn't want to leave Drew just yet.

'You going back tomorrow? To the city?' he clarified.

'Ah, yeah. Everyone wants to see me and I can't go home next weekend with the bingo on. Lozzy would kill me.' She didn't mention Gary. Since that night Drew had kissed her cheek she'd been careful to hardly mention Gary at all. Drew's eyes always flashed with a dark fury and she hated seeing him like that. Plus, it made her feel uncomfortable; she didn't like talking about

Gary or what happened. She'd only just started to reply to his emails. Nat thought it was only fair that she tell him how she felt, how he'd made her feel. Nat hoped it was a step in the right direction, getting Gary to realise she was scared.

'Did Lozzy tell you about the meeting at the school last week with the local minister?'

'Yeah, Matt mentioned it was quite hostile.'

'It was crazy. I know they were there to do a job and just tell us why it was happening but the passion from the community, it was amazing. I felt sorry for him in a way, but I hope he went back with a real understanding of our position.'

'He might,' said Drew. 'But it would mean shit to the others. I doubt that bloke could make the Ed Department see our point of view. We really need to tell them in person.'

'You're so right. Lozzy and I think we should take a few of us to meet the minister in Perth and go and meet these people making the decisions. Take signs and our petitions. We need to make a noise, otherwise they'll just roll us over.'

'Squeaky wheel always gets the grease.'

Nat smiled at Drew, who was finally talking to her like he used to, like they were a team again. 'Totally,' she agreed.

'So have you decided what you're going to do about Gary, then?'

The unexpected comment came so suddenly it almost knocked the air from her lungs. 'What?'

Drew glanced at Billy, who'd raced off to his motorbike for a quick ride, before stepping closer to Nat. He held her arm with his good hand and set his sapphire eyes on her like trained targets. 'I'm not going to sit back and watch you become a punching bag, Nat. If I have to nag you until you do something about it, then I will. Even if it means losing you as a friend.'

Her heart thudded with a slow, painful beat.

'I know you're scared, Nat. I just want to make sure you're not burying your head in the sand.'

He didn't know what her situation was. It wasn't that simple. 'Just leave it be, Drew,' she said a little harshly.

'Am I pissing you off? Are you angry?'

She wasn't sure what she was feeling, whether she wanted to scream at him or just run away and hide.

'Drew,' she growled in warning.

'Good. I want you to be pissed off, because that's how I feel. I won't see you hurt again, Nat. I'll be checking up on you next week.'

She pulled her arm from his grip and then closed her eyes so she didn't have to see him and those eyes that were reading her thoughts. Turning, she headed back to her car while trying to gather her thoughts and her breathing. Why was she so upset? She knew Drew was only looking out for her, but she felt ashamed and silly. Why did she feel like this was all her fault?

Billy's motorbike came to a skid beside her and she jumped. He tore off his helmet. 'Bye, Natty, thank you for having me.' He jumped off the bike and hugged her tightly.

'Anytime, Billy. I loved having you.'

Freckles moved on his cheeks as he squinted into the afternoon sun. 'Can I come back one day?'

She brushed some dust from his cheek and smiled. 'Of course

you can. Be good for your dad now, okay? I'll see you at school next week.'

He hugged her again and murmured something into her red coat. She was sure she heard the words 'wish' and 'mum'. But the breeze was whipping around them, taking his words. He let her go and Nat continued to her car, determined not to look back. It wasn't until she was behind the safety of her tinted window and driving away that she finally turned back to watch Drew. He was by the truck, filling the bin with grain.

She waited, and waited. At the last minute she saw him turn his head to watch her go and it filled her with relief.

It wasn't until twenty minutes later that she got a text message from Drew.

I'm sorry. I'm still your friend. Here anytime you need. I just care. Ok?

Nat grinned. She felt like hugging her phone.

I know. Thanks. I'm here for you too. I'll always be your friend. :)

Chapter 26

NAT pulled on her black skinny jeans, Lauren's tight black T-shirt and the red-checked shirt over the top. Already she felt like a bogan. It certainly made getting ready easy – there were just her work boots to go. She'd left her hair out but added a bit of wax so she was rocking a Kurt Cobain look.

She hurried to the hall to see if Lauren needed a hand with the last-minute details. They'd set up the hall earlier in the day with Aussie flags, AC/DC posters, eskies, ugg boots and blow-up guitars. Lauren had bought posters of muscle cars off eBay, along with checked flags. By the time they'd finished putting them all up, along with setting up tables with stubby holders and pistons with tea lights on top, the hall was looking awesome. Red and black streamers were twisted along the walls and hung from the ceiling – anything to try to hide the cracks. Stepping inside now, she could hear AC/DC's 'Thunderstruck' already blaring from the speakers. Nat couldn't help but smile at the transformation. It was going to be a fun night.

'Hey, there ya are, Nazza,' yelled Lauren.

Nat chuckled at Lauren's red leopard-print leggings and Guns N' Roses singlet. Everything was hanging out, but it made the look even better. She wore black thongs and a massive blond curly wig. 'Hi, I'm Shazza,' she said cheekily, putting on a real ocker voice. 'Mazza is out the back, bringing in the auction items with Drewie.'

'Kids all happy?' Nat asked.

'Yep. They'll be fine with Doris. No doubt she'll be feeding them too much and letting them be total ferals, but it's worth it for a night off.'

Matt walked in carrying a large framed Dockers football jumper. It had been signed by Nat Fyfe for the auction, as they were raising money for the P & C. They were all staying optimistic and positive about the school closure. Matt wore boardies, thongs, a VB singlet and a blue flannel shirt. He'd blacked out a few teeth and his mullet wig made Nat chuckle again.

Drew followed him in torn jeans, white singlet and blue-checked shirt. Nat couldn't pick anything wrong with what he was wearing. He still looked hot. Until he stuck a black handle-bar moustache on his face.

'That is shocking,' she said as they set up the auction items by the nearby table, laid with the coloured bingo balls and ball roller.

'You love it,' teased Drew, giving his fake facial hair a wiggle.

His right hand was looking much better than when she'd seen him last week. The swelling had gone and only a light tinge remained of the bruise. They'd texted and talked a few times since that day, their friendship back on track. Billy had spent the last week between Doris and Lauren, Drew wanting to give Natalie a break. But truth be told, she had missed the little guy's company.

As they brought in the last of the auction items, of which most had been donated by local businesses, people turned up with their big eskies full of ice and drinks, ready for a night out. They posed for photos, laughing, with the blow-up guitars. Nat took a selfie with Drew, Lauren and Matt.

It was hilarious to see the members of the community, young and old, getting into the bogan spirit. And after they'd all had a few drinks, Nat was seeing more than she ever expected. The young lads like Dicko and Wazza were a riot, giving the air guitar competition a red-hot go. Pansy had overdone it and was passed out on the ground outside and they hadn't even made it to the auction yet. Ross, the principal, Scott, the pub owner, and Frank from the shop were some of the surprises. Who knew Ross was a massive AC/DC fan? He'd come dressed like Angus. There was even some impromptu singing to great rock songs in between the bingo rounds. Matt had started a trend by dotting a yellow spot on Lauren's ample bosom with a bingo fluoro marker; towards the end of the night, several people had fluorescent spots on them. At one point, Nat was laughing so hard she was trying not to spit out her wine, which was served in a middy glass and stubby holder, and Drew squished a pink splodge on her forehead.

His eyes shot open and his mouth made an O. 'It was an accident. Your head bumped into my marker.'

'You little . . .'

'What? Shit? Arsehole? Come on, Nazza,' he slurred slightly. 'Give me your best shot. Don't play nice. It's bogan night, remember.'

'You wanker,' she said with a giggle. She snatched up her orange marker and launched at Drew. Her chair slid out from under her, sending her flailing and falling on top of him, at which point they both fell on the floor, laughing hysterically. Luckily they didn't take the plastic tablecloth with them. Even on the floor, Nat wrestled with Drew as they both waved their markers at each other. She got him on the cheek, then he got her on the nose, and she laughed harder when she got him on the mouth. And then he got her a beauty down her neck. Eventually they wore themselves out – that and they ran out of bare skin to mark.

'You look like a bloody Oompa Loompa,' cackled Lauren. She was bent over, her phone in her hand, trying to snap pictures between peals of laughter. 'Oh my lordy, you two are the funniest things. Come on, I need a photo.'

Nat pressed her face next to Drew's, still lying almost on top of him, and they smiled for the camera.

'Say "Shazza"!' said Lauren, clicking away madly.

Nat looked at Drew's face and realised she'd missed a few spots. 'Wait, hang on. Don't move.' She held his face with one hand while she coloured in the bare spots, just like her kids would do at school. She poked her tongue out the corner of her mouth, as if she was painting the *Mona Lisa*. 'There, done. Now you're a real Oompa Loompa.'

Nat realised he'd been watching her, in a way that made her

blood overheat. Then she realised she was still pressed against him. Suddenly she couldn't think, her head swimming. She scrambled up and righted her chair, leaving Drew to get up on his own. 'Phew, that was hard work.' His face was completely coloured in. 'Do I get to shout "bingo" now?' she asked, pointing to Drew.

Lauren and Matt burst out laughing, Matt spraying some beer across the table while Lauren was clutching her sides.

As it turned out, no one on their table won at bingo, but they all pooled their money together to get a box of goodies from the shop. The chocolates and marshmallows were already being sorted for a bonfire.

'At our place one weekend,' said Lauren. 'You have to come, Nazza. You haven't experienced country life until you've sat at a roaring bonfire during winter underneath the stars. Bloody magic.'

'Well, how could I say no to that?'

'Maybe we should do that for Drew's birthday. A big bonfire bash,' said Matt, whose mullet had slid sideways and now looked like a ferret trying to climb his head.

'I like that plan. You gonna bring the food and beer too?' asked Drew as he leant on the table, unfazed that his face was completely orange. Everyone in the hall was past caring. Wigs were skewiff, moustaches were found in various places like foreheads and backsides, and their table wasn't the only one playing human bingo with the markers.

'The kids would love roasting marshmallows, and we can do some damper for you, Nat. Alice taught Billy how to make the best damper. That kid will probably grow up to be a chef, not a farmer,' said Lauren teasingly. 'Set up a restaurant in the city.'

'At least you know it wouldn't be vegan food. He could do surf and turfs, real man's food. Yum,' said Matt, licking his lips.

'He wants to be a farmer, just like his dad,' said Nat. She smiled at Drew but his brow creased. 'He's a natural. He told me that all he wants to do is stay on the farm with his animals and you.' Nat thought her words would make Drew happy, yet she saw tears fill his eyes.

Abruptly he got up, grabbed his beer and headed off outside. Confused, Nat turned to Lauren and Matt for answers but they were too busy laughing at Wazza, who was trying to unbutton his checked shirt, one eye squeezed shut as if he was seeing double.

Drew had gone through the double doors out the side and Nat's gut feeling had her rising to follow him.

Outside, the cold night air was like a slap in the face, her breath misting. It was quiet – no kids running around, just cars parked outside the hall. The sky was bright with stars and Nat had a moment to appreciate the way they sparkled. There were so many she almost wondered if she was seeing double like Wazza. She searched the parking area and found Drew sitting on an upturned bathtub. She had no clue what it was doing outside the hall. Drew's shoulders were hunched and as she walked towards him they appeared to be shaking. Were her eyes playing tricks on her?

It wasn't until his beer bottle fell to the ground and his hands came up to his face that she paused, mid-step. In the light she saw a grown man falling to pieces, and it broke her heart. Should she give him space? Every part of her wanted to run to him and hold him tight. Without waiting a moment more, she stepped towards him, sat on the bath and wrapped her arms around him.

'Oh, Drew,' she said softly as she rubbed his arms. 'What's going on?'

At the sound of her voice his body turned towards her, his head resting against her shoulder, and his crying became softer. She waited, holding him tight and whispering, 'It's okay. I'm here, Drew.'

'I'm sorry,' he said eventually, wiping his face and sniffing back tears.

'Talk to me.'

He sat up but didn't move away.

'It's Billy,' he said, blinking back fresh tears. 'Simone thinks he's not mine. No.' He shook his head fiercely. 'He is mine, but she thinks he's not my biological son.'

Her mind went blank. What did she say to that? It was such an incredible blow. Straight away she started thinking about the resemblances between them – had she imagined them? 'I just can't believe it's true. Are you going to get a DNA test done?'

He shrugged. 'I don't know. I'm scared. I mean, it's not going to change how I feel about him, but to the courts . . .' He gazed at her with huge, tormented eyes that she couldn't look away from. 'What if Simone gets custody? I can't live without him.'

Nat reached up, holding his face, trying to smooth away his worry lines. Tears fell, but they were hers; she felt the wet path they made down her cheeks but she didn't want to let go of Drew to wipe them away.

'Billy is my life. I'm so scared I'm going to lose him.'

They sat watching each other cry by the dim light. 'You won't lose him, Drew,' Nat whispered as she tried to talk calmly through her emotions. 'You need to find out for sure and if it's bad news then we can fight for him. You bloody well fight, Drew, I know you won't let him go.'

Drew rested his forehead against Nat's as they both tried to calm themselves through deep breaths.

'I'm sorry, Natty,' he said as he began to wipe away her tears.

Nat closed her eyes briefly, consumed by the gut-wrenching feelings that washed over her. She felt Drew's pain and fear along with her own despair at what this could do to Billy, who she loved so dearly. And then there was the soothing flutter that Drew's caresses brought as his thumbs traced across her skin. It felt so right when his lips suddenly found hers. For a moment she forgot the ache in her heart and sought relief. Drew kissed her harder and she welcomed it. His mouth opened, so warm, tasting of beer and salty tears. She gripped his checked shirt, holding him closer as the kiss reached mind-blowing intensity. He tasted so good that she just wanted to crawl into his shirt and under his skin. Her body was alive; every cell was on fire and reacting to his touch.

Drew pulled away suddenly, leaving Nat's lips open, slightly bruised and raw but still wanting more.

'Shit, I'm sorry, Nat. I'm so sorry.' Drew stood up. Shoved his hands deep into his pockets.

She searched Drew's face, saw his anguish even though he wouldn't meet her gaze. He apologised again and walked off towards the street, away from the hall.

Nat touched her lips, still in a state of shock. Sitting there on an upturned bathtub, looking up at the stars while people yahooed inside the hall and rock music played, Nat had a very strange feeling. It was like she was alive and in tune with the world. Something was so right about this moment. Had someone spiked her drink? Maybe the wine had really gone to her head. Nat didn't care. She just looked up at the stars as if they held the answers to the universe, and felt as if time was standing still.

Nat drove out to Drew's the weekend after bingo. He hadn't texted, nor had he replied to her messages. She'd been so worried about his state of mind. He was dealing with Simone's revelation, and probably the guilt from kissing her that night. Drew was the kind of person who would punish himself for overstepping the mark. She didn't want him to. And if she was honest, it wasn't all his fault: she'd got carried away in the moment too and she'd take it all back if it would fix their friendship. The only thing left was to face him, and so she was heading out to the farm.

She found him at the shed alone. Drew didn't meet her eyes straight away, just kept working on the motor between his dirty hands as she approached.

'Drew, we need to talk,' she said. 'I need to know you're okay. Are we still friends?' She tried to keep the pleading from her voice.

His head shot up then, those eyes so blue latching on to hers. 'You still want to be my friend?' he replied, his voice full of surprise. Nat nodded and his shoulders relaxed a little. 'I'm really sorry, Nat. I shouldn't have done that. My head was a mess. I don't want to compromise our friendship, it was way out of line.'

She saw confusion and hurt glistening in the dark centres of his eyes. It *had* been out of line – she was engaged – yet the kiss had been amazing. Nat was confused herself. She'd been stewing over it all week. Maybe it was her uncertainty about Gary that was messing with her. Was Drew an escape? Is that why she liked to be with him? Had liked kissing him? He was handsome; had she just lost herself in the moment? She had been tipsy, had that just amplified things? She was also worried: what if Gary found out? What would happen then?

'I get why it happened,' she said. 'My head hasn't really been in the right place either. You've had a lot to deal with. I just wish you'd come to me about it instead of bottling it up.'

His eyes dropped again. 'I didn't want to acknowledge it, Nat. If I said it out loud, would it become real? I couldn't tell anyone. It was stuck in my throat like a lump of steel.'

'Next time just come and find me. I'm sure if we sit long enough, you'll be able to find the words.'

'I appreciate that, Nat. I really do. I didn't want to burden you with any more, then I nearly wrecked everything.'

Nat wondered if he was thinking of the kiss, like she was. It seemed so surreal. 'I said I'd always be your friend,' she said, 'and I meant it.' She could only offer friendship and it seemed that's all Drew wanted too, even though they'd kissed and even though Kim seemed to think Drew liked her. She'd thought of walking away, putting space between them to please Gary but just this week alone had been hard without Drew to chat to. He'd become a friend she could depend on and she loved being involved with his and Billy's life. She didn't want to give that up.

Their eyes met and held, as if repairing the line of friendship.

'Okay,' he said eventually. He gave her that smile she'd grown to love and it warmed her body. 'Friends,' he agreed.

'So, have you sent for a DNA test? Are you going to tell Billy? What's happening, Drew? Tell me everything.'

His eyebrows shot up with all her questions. After a second he wiped his hands down his work pants and nodded to a stack of old tyres by the shed. 'Come and sit down and you can interrogate me properly,' he said teasingly. 'Okay. No, I haven't done a DNA test, wouldn't know where to start, and no, I don't want to tell Billy, not yet.' Drew finished with a sigh. He picked at the strips of rubber and wire showing on the bald tyre he sat on.

'What do you think about Uncle Kent helping? Do you mind if I give him a call and see what he thinks?'

Drew agreed and she wasted no time whipping out her phone to call her uncle.

'Thanks, Uncle Kent,' she said, after filling him in. 'I'll talk to you soon.' Nat smiled at Drew. 'Well, he thinks it would be best if you got a legal DNA test done, so it would hold up in court, which means you need a doctor or qualified nurse to be present at the testing.'

Drew pulled a face. 'I can't visit the local doctor's surgery.

246

This would no doubt spread through town faster than 10 kilos of butter on a forty-degree day.'

Nat knew he was thinking it would end up getting to Billy at some point. 'Why don't you come to Perth and get it done? Uncle Kent can organise the kit and make an appointment for when we go up to meet the minister. What do you think?'

'Sounds like a great idea, Natty. Will he mind?'

Nat got out her phone once more. 'Hi, Uncle Kent, it's me again,' she said with a grin. Drew watched her intently as she spoke, and she couldn't help watching him too. She asked if her uncle could sort out an appointment and gave him the date.

'Sure thing, possum. Do your friends want to stay here with me? They are very welcome. Any friends of yours are friends of mine, and I'd love to meet these two that you talk about so much, especially Billy.'

Nat was hoping Drew couldn't hear both ends of the conversation. 'Thanks, I'll take you up on that. We both really appreciate it. I'll stay in touch. Love you.'

'Bye, Natty. Love you too.'

Nat hung up with a smile.

'You almost glow when you talk to your uncle. I can see how much he means to you,' said Drew.

'Yes, he's amazing. And he's also offered you a bed at his place the night before so we can all be together. I always try to stay a night here and there with Uncle Kent. It's the best way to catch up and I know how much he loves it. If you stay, you'll have more time to ask questions and pick his brains. Plus he would love to meet Billy. I may have mentioned him quite a bit.'

'He's a good kid but I may be biased,' said Drew.

'Do you want to tell Billy about all this?' she asked. Shadows like storm clouds swept across Drew's eyes, and Nat regretted making that happen.

'I don't want to. What if it gets him all upset and then the DNA results turn out fine? All that anxiety and worry for nothing. I can't do that to him. It's torturing me enough. I want to save him from all of this.'

'I agree. At this point, why worry him?' Nat wanted to reach over and wrap her hands over his, which were pulling madly at the rubber on the old tyre. She felt his frustration and fear. But she didn't reach out to him, it was all too soon after that kiss.

'Yep. Find out the results and then jump that hurdle if we have to.' Drew clasped his hands together as if he'd seen her watching them. 'Thanks, Nat. I'm glad you came out.'

They shared a smile. 'Me too.'

Chapter 27

NAT watched her students, hard at work on a maths worksheet. It felt like months since the bingo night, but only two and a half weeks had passed. In that time, school had been in full swing. And her emails with Gary had become a healing of sorts. They were back to sharing things. Nat told him about her kids at school and Gary told her about his work. It felt like they were starting to repair the cracks in their relationship. Gary had begged for another chance and Nat wanted him to have that. She'd always believed people needed second chances: everyone was human and made mistakes and bad choices even if they weren't bad people. Besides, the whole family situation was something she didn't want to face, and if Gary sorted himself out and got help then maybe she wouldn't have to.

Drew appeared in her mind, so ruggedly handsome and so different from Gary. It wasn't illegal to appreciate another man's physique, or for his smile to make you feel great. Having a friend of the opposite sex was bound to have its complications but Nat kept all those feelings locked away. Nat had made a commitment to Gary and she would honour that. Her friendship with Drew didn't mean more than it should. With a deep breath she pushed him from her thoughts.

Nat went to help Isaac, who had his hand raised. Isaac wore the Harry Potter black robe and glasses for being student of the week.

'I can't get this one,' he said with a frown.

Nat was about to explain when there was a knock on the classroom door. A man in work pants and checked shirt stood there. Nat had seen him around but wasn't sure who he was, and none of the kids got up so he couldn't have been one of their dads.

'Hello,' said Nat as she joined him by the door. 'Can I help you?'

'Hi, Natalie, I'm Grant Greenwood, Kath's son. She said I should drop by and show the kids these little guys.'

Grant picked up a box he had sitting on the bench by the door, and inside Nat saw three baby pigs. 'Oh my gosh, they are gorgeous.' She'd never touched a real pig, let alone a piglet. 'How wonderful!' Nat turned to the class. 'Children, we have a visitor today, with some special friends. Can you quickly gather on the mat, please? First, let's say good morning to Mr Greenwood.' Lots of little voices greeted Grant as they rushed to the mat, fidgeting with energy.

'Good morning, kids,' he said, pulling out one soft pink bundle.

'Oh, wow!'

'So cute.'

The kids crowded around and all had turns at holding the piglets while Grant told them about the animals and answered all their questions. Nat was fascinated by their noses, and the feel of their skin. Grant wasn't the first person to drop by with animals. Some parents had brought in little chickens or new puppies for their child's news. Ava's mum had brought in a baby kangaroo they were looking after. Liam had freaked her out by bringing in a huge, long snakeskin, but nothing had been worse than the dead rabbit Jack had caught in a trap by his mum's vegie garden. Nat had found it quite confronting, but the kids were strangely okay about seeing a dead animal. They seemed to understand the cycle of life out here, and even though the rabbit was dead they all felt its fur and checked out its feet before Nat made them all scrub their hands.

Nat walked Grant to the door when show-and-tell was over. 'Thank you so much for bringing them in. It's wonderful for the kids to learn firsthand like this; they are at such a great advantage.'

'Yes, they are. That's what's so great about our small rural schools,' he said.

Nat thought about Grant's words and realised just how right he was. 'I'm going to mention just that to the minister tomorrow when we get to Perth.'

'Good luck with that,' said Grant. 'I'll have my fingers crossed. Be sad to see this place go to ruin.'

Nat agreed. She just hoped it was enough.

The following day they closed the school so that a delegation of the P & C executives and others could board one of the school buses and head to Perth to meet with the Minister for Education. This was their last-ditch effort to keep their school open. Not many voiced it out loud but they all knew a lot was riding on this trip. When they arrived they would be meeting with their local MP, the Honourable Terry Waldron, who would help speak on their behalf. Lauren had been in discussions with Terry for the past few weeks, helping to get this visit with the minister.

Nat had worn her favourite pants suit for the occasion. She was going to follow the bus in her car because she was staying the night in Perth, and had someone filling in for her at school tomorrow. She had a good reason: Drew and Billy were staying in the city to do the DNA testing.

At the school, the team piled into the waiting bus.

'All right now, no mucking about or Kath will haul your butt to the front of the bus. Ross and Bob, I don't think you two should be down the back. It smells like trouble,' said Lauren, trying to keep up morale with light-hearted banter. 'Grace, you can be in charge of I-spy.'

'Can I come with you, Natty?' asked Billy as he reached for her hand. 'It will be boring on the bus.'

'I'll have you know, us oldies can be quite fun,' said Lauren, who'd overheard him.

Billy looked over to Nat, his question repeated in his soft eyes.

'Of course you can, if it's okay with your dad. I'd like some company.'

It was all organised, and the bus, with Nat following, left

Lake Biddy for the city. As they drove, Drew waved from the back of the bus from time to time, and Billy frantically returned the wave.

Four hours later they stopped at the car park nearest to the minister's office in West Perth and everyone poured out of the bus with creased clothes, stretching sore muscles.

'Bloody hell, how do you do it?' asked Lauren as she gave Nat the once-over.

'Do what?'

'Look like you stepped out of a magazine advert. Do you have seats that iron your clothes as you drive? Your car is pretty fancy, probably does that and more, hey?' said Lauren cheekily.

Lauren and Matt knew about the DNA test – maybe Kim too, Nat wasn't sure. Drew had told them as he wanted more pairs of eyes out, in case Simone returned. It was handy having them in on the secret, as they could help cover why Drew was staying in the city, if anyone asked. The story was that Drew and Billy were being tested for scabby mouth, after finding out that some sheep had it. Hopefully no one did ask, but Drew was doubtful: it was the country, and everyone knew everything, from the cars they drove to the moment they upgraded their tractors or planted something new. Nothing escaped the curious locals.

'Okay, everyone,' said Lauren clapping. 'Let's get this party started.'

They walked in a clump along the footpath, up the street to the minister's office, where they were meeting Terry. Nat felt the nerves of the crowd bouncing around like a hand grenade no one wanted to hold. So much depended on this; people were determined yet scared. Nat wished she could make it go away for them all. In a very short time these people had become her friends. They'd welcomed her into their town and trusted her with their children. She understood their worry about the future of their community so much more than when she'd first arrived. Oh, how she'd taken so much for granted, living in the city.

'There's Tuck, I mean Terry,' said Lauren, waving to their local MP. He wore a suit for the occasion and a nice blue tie, and returned Lauren's wave. It would be hard to miss the Lake Biddy crew – pick the crowd of scared, tired and creased country folk.

'G'day, Lauren. How was the trip?'

'We survived it,' Lauren said with a tired smile. 'Everyone, this is Terry —'

'Call me Tuck,' he cut in.

'Tuck.' Lauren continued to introduce Tuck to their party. Tuck already knew Bob, the shire president, and the CEO, Jim.

'So are we ready to meet the minister?' he asked.

There were some mumbled replies from the nervous pack.

'I think we are.' Lauren didn't sound so sure as she shuffled folders containing all their paperwork – the census of future children for the school, the benefits of keeping it open and the effects of closing it.

Nat had made sure it had all been typed up to look professional and important. Lots of copies too, in case they got filed accidentally. She was desperately hoping it would work. She looked at the faces around her. Ross, Kath, Grace, Lauren, Drew, Cynthia, the shire president and the shire CEO, as well as the older, respected members of the community who were on various boards. They held the future in their hands and you could tell each one felt that burden. What if they didn't succeed?

'Let's go,' said Nat, and led them through the doors with purpose.

At the main reception they were directed to the minister's office. It wasn't small, but there were so many of them they all had to squish inside.

A tall man stood up behind his desk and buttoned his dark grey suit. He wore a dark blue tie, and his hair was short and almost silver. His face was lean but pale, as if he never went outside.

'Minister,' said Tuck, stepping forward to shake his hand. 'These are the delegates from Lake Biddy.' He went on to introduce each person, then handed over to Lauren to speak first.

She showed the minister their proposed numbers for the school, the well-above-average marks and the high number who had made it into the Primary Extension and Challenge program. She listed all the awards the children had accumulated in the past five years – the state maths awards, the Vi Barham award for academic excellence, and so much more. For its small number of children, the school had some impressive statistics.

'The kids are getting great support and extra care from the smaller-sized school. These results just prove that,' she finished.

The shire CEO went next, stating the implications for the town if the school shut, and finally it was Kath's turn.

'Minister, I've worked as the registrar for nearly thirty years. I've seen my kids and my grandkids through this school and I'd like to see my great-grandkids go here as well. There is so much love in this school and the kids benefit hugely from the smaller classes. They have a great empathy and ability to tolerate and support their fellow class members, whether they are senior room or junior room children. They get to experience things that many other kids don't, from seeing farm animals in the classrooms to understanding just where their food comes from. I'd hate to see our children suffer the longer hours spent away from home on the buses, or worse – families moving away to another town for school.' Kath pulled out a tissue and dabbed at her eyes. Nat found herself blinking rapidly.

'It is the heart of our town and community,' Kath went on. 'It connects us all because we have all been schooled there. It is a part of us and Lake Biddy. We fight this decision with our whole hearts.'

The minister nodded his head. 'I understand and I appreciate the long drive you took to get here today. It has been very useful to hear firsthand from you all. We plan to close the school not just for economic reasons, but also for the best interests of the children. Next year your numbers will be very low and that means less social interaction for the children. It is a big part of learning.' He adjusted his tie as he looked down at the papers they'd given him. 'I will seriously look these over and have another think before anything is confirmed.'

Tuck stepped forward. 'Thank you, Minister, and thank you for your time.'

'Yes, thank you for listening to us,' said Lauren.

Nat could feel the energy leaving the room – they'd come in with so much gusto and now that they'd all had their say, it felt flat. Some looked frustrated, and others looked worried, probably wondering if they'd done enough. Nat felt exhausted. Were their voices loud enough to be heard?

'Thanks, Tuck. We appreciate your help,' said Lauren, shaking his hand.

'I just hope it works.' He glanced at his watch. 'I've got to head off for a meeting but please call me if I can help with anything.'

'Will do.'

'Thanks, Tuck,' they all said as he left, merging with the people on the footpath.

Like a bunch of tumbleweed sitting in the middle of the road, they huddled together, out of place.

'I need a drink,' said Ross.

'That minister has already made his mind up,' said James, who was on the P & C. 'I doubt anything we said would change his mind.'

'Yeah, he didn't seem to care about what we had to say,' said Kath. 'Tuck did a great job, though.'

'Yep. Nice speech, by the way, Kath,' added James as he patted her shoulder. 'But the mallee roots in my woodheap have more emotion than that pollie bastard. How are we supposed to get through to them? They just don't care. He makes all the right sounds but do you really think he's going to rethink this? It all comes down to the figures. I wish we could take something away from them, something that would affect their whole way of life,' grumbled James. 'Then they might get it.'

'I'm depressed,' said Grace, 'I need chocolate.'

'Can we drive the bus through a bottle-o for the way home?' asked Bob. 'I could go a cold one or two.'

'Will the bus fit through Hungry Jack's? I need a Whopper,' said James.

Their banter was continuous as they climbed back aboard. An eight-hour round trip, for such a short meeting.

'Do you need a lift, Drew?' asked Eric, who'd offered to drive the team to Perth, seeing as though it was his bus.

'That's okay, Eric. I'll drop them off on my way home,' said Nat quickly. 'Jump in, guys,' she said to Drew and Billy.

'Do you think we made a difference?' asked Drew as they waved goodbye to the busload of country folk.

'Fingers crossed, I guess. Hard to know. I think if they've made their decision for their budget, then nothing we do can change their mind. I hope I'm wrong.'

'So do I, Nat, so do I.'

Thirty minutes later, after driving through McDonald's for lunch at Billy's request, she pulled into Uncle Kent's driveway. She wasn't surprised to see his car, as he did most of his work from home.

'Nice place,' said Drew.

'Wow,' Billy added.

Nat hoped they never saw her parents' place. They'd probably think it was such a waste of money.

'Come on, Uncle Kent's home. You'll love him.'

Nat knocked on the large oak door. It swung open moments later. Uncle Kent stood there in his business suit, minus his jacket, and his blue tie was pulled loose. He was barefoot.

'Natty, come in, love.' Uncle Kent's eyes glistened with joy. 'Give me a hug, possum.'

Embracing her uncle was one of Nat's greatest pleasures. He was the only one in her family who gave sincere hugs that made her feel loved for who she was.

'Uncle Kent, this is Drew and Billy.'

Kent and Drew shook hands and Billy stepped forward with his hand held out too. 'Hello, Uncle Kent,' he said with gusto.

Kent laughed and shook his hand. 'Well, aren't you just the gentleman? Come in, come in. Have you had something to eat?'

'Yes, thanks,' said Drew.

'Nat, I've got some leftover honey chicken with crispy noodles in the fridge, if you're peckish?' said Kent. He glanced at Drew. 'She tries to eat well but I know her weaknesses and try to make sure she indulges as often as possible,' he said with a wink. 'Anyone for a drink?'

They walked into the kitchen dining area and Drew stopped by the fridge, admiring the faded artwork and old photos on it.

'Is that you, Natty?' He pointed to a photo of a young girl covered in a dark-brown mess. It was all over her face and hands. 'And you told me you never got dirty,' he said when she nodded.

'Hey, it doesn't count when it's chocolate cake. Uncle Kent used to let me lick the bowl every time.' She smiled at her uncle, who was watching Drew with great interest.

'You want to see more, Drew? I have a great collection of Natty,' said Kent.

'No!' Nat cried. 'Don't you dare . . .'

Kent laughed before turning to Billy. 'Can I get you anything, young Billy?' Billy shook his head. 'Well, how about you go and look in that oak chest over there and see if anything takes your fancy?' Kent waved him on and eventually Billy headed to the box and opened up the lid. Inside were a heap of Nat and Jason's old toys. Kent never let anything go, his excuse being that he had such a big house to fill.

While Billy entertained himself, they sat around the table, talking softly.

'The kit's here,' said Kent. 'Once it's done, the results will be emailed in five to seven working days. The signed hard copy will be posted out later.'

'So we'll know for sure in a week. It'll be my birthday around then. I hope I get what I wish for,' said Drew.

Nat wanted to reach out and grasp his hand but she didn't. That was something she only did when they were alone, as some people might take it the wrong way.

'Try not to worry. Once we know the outcome, then we can take the next steps needed.'

'Thanks, Kent. I really appreciate everything you're doing for us.'

'Uncle Kent's the best. You couldn't be in better hands,' said Nat.

'How much do I owe you for sorting this all out?' Drew asked.

Kent waved him off. 'No, I won't hear of it. You just worry about looking after your boy instead. You are lucky to have him.'

Her uncle then looked at Nat and she felt his longing to have had kids of his own. He had so much love to give.

'Nat, go show Drew to his room. I've got a few depositions to get through, but make yourself at home.'

'I always do, Uncle Kent.' Nat kissed his check and he sighed happily.

Nat took Drew through to the guest room. The other spare room was hers – always was and always would be.

'Wow, this is just too much, Nat,' said Drew as he dumped their bags. 'Your uncle is an amazing guy. I don't know what I was expecting. Someone like Gary, I guess, but Kent is so down to earth. Now I know where you get that from,' he said with a smile. 'It all makes sense now.'

'Yeah, he's a special guy.' Nat reached out and touched his arm. 'Whatever the outcome, in your heart Billy is your son and Uncle Kent will make sure it stays that way.'

Drew swallowed hard and his eyes softened like gems under the water. 'I hope you're right, Natty. I really do.'

Chapter 28

THEY had been at Kent's for nearly an hour when he announced he had to head out to meet a client.

'How about we go do something too?' said Nat. 'We could go to the zoo?'

Billy's head snapped up. 'The zoo? Can we, Dad, can we?' he begged. 'I've never been,' he added to Nat.

'Actually you have,' chuckled Drew. 'You were nearly three but I guess it's time we went back. Are you sure?' he asked Nat. He didn't want to put her out.

'I wouldn't have mentioned it otherwise.' She gave him a teasing smile. 'Come on, we can spend the whole afternoon there. Uncle Kent always took me. I think it's time I went back too.'

Drew shrugged. 'Fine by me. What do you think, Billy?'

Billy jumped up in the air as if auditioning for a Toyota ad.

'Great. Have fun,' said Kent. 'I'll see you for dinner. I have stuff in the fridge for your favourite seafood pasta dish, Natty. If I beat you home, I'll cook. If you beat me home, I will be forever grateful.' Kent kissed her forehead and then left.

After collecting their bits and pieces, they left too, with Nat at the wheel.

'This is going to be so cool. I hope we can see the giraffes. Do you think they'll let us feed them, Natty? Or the elephants. Do you think they have baby ones? What are your favourites?' Billy's hands waved around as he fired questions to Nat from the back seat. His eyes sparkled brightly and the smile only left his face when he rattled off more excited questions, sometimes not even waiting for her answers.

At the zoo Billy grabbed onto both of their hands and they walked as fast as his little legs would go. The tiny penguins and the big crocodile had him in awe and made Drew wish he'd done this sooner. When he went to the city it was for a purpose – shopping, picking up parts, appointments. They got in and they got out. Staying longer meant more money for accommodation and food, so doing things like this seemed to go on the backburner. Yet it was making some awesome memories. Memories he may need to cling on to, depending on the outcome of this test tomorrow and how it all ended up in the courts. God, he didn't want to think about the worst-case scenario but it kept creeping into his mind.

'Drew?' said Natalie softly, nudging his shoulder. 'Drew.'

Straight away he picked up her worried tone. He met her eyes while Billy was busy watching the orangutans. 'Is it that obvious?'

Nat smiled, but he could tell she was concerned. 'A little. You're getting that worry line.' She pressed her thumb against his forehead and gave it a gentle rub.

Drew instantly felt his body relax. Just being beside Natalie made him happy: to see her smile, hear her voice, and watch the way she moved. He was happy with just that, or so he told himself, but then she would touch him. Oh, it did things to his body that he couldn't control. Made him feel alive, soaring high in the sky like a bird on the breeze and made parts of him wake from their deep slumber. How had he lived this long without feeling this excitement, desire and longing?

She'd probably stop if she knew, but he didn't want her to stop. Each bit of contact, be it a brush as she walked past or a touch of her hand when she passed a plate, every single time he felt it and cherished it. He craved to reach out now and brush her hair back, to run his fingers through its silkiness and then caress her skin. He knew how damn soft it was too. And he knew just how perfect her lips were. And how amazing she tasted. He felt his desire build like a steam engine, except there was no release.

Drew gritted his teeth and almost shook his head to clear his mind. He resisted the urge to curse from his frustration. It was okay to manage being around Natalie, until he began torturing himself like this. Wanting her so much. Some days it grew and grew until he was crazy with want. His body burnt with the ache. Then some days his heart felt so heavy and lonely.

She can only be a friend. Words he muttered often to keep himself in check.

He'd come to the conclusion, after many, many nights of thinking, that he'd rather have Nat in his life as a friend than not at all. He would suffer the pain of not being able to hold her or kiss her again, just to be able to stand near her and be there for every smile and every glance from those teal eyes that cut straight to his soul. Some pain was worth enduring.

'I'm sorry,' he whispered. He knew he had to push all that, as well as tomorrow's test, from his mind.

'I know it's hard but now's a time to forget and enjoy.' Nat glanced at Billy and smiled in such a tender way it made his throat constrict. Her unspoken words echoed inside his head.

God almighty, she was an angel, he thought. How did such a beautiful creature end up in his life? And how did she understand him so well?

He realised that Natalie and Billy were his ticket to forgetting his worries. And as they walked around the zoo, his mood improved tenfold.

'Dad, look at that one, the one scratching his butt,' said Billy, laughing.

The rest of their time at the zoo passed in a blur of animals. Drew took many photos with his phone, but every one of them had either Billy or Nat in it. No fancy animals could compare with the amazing humans by his side. He walked around the zoo feeling ten feet tall, and every time Nat smiled at him adrenaline shot around his body.

'Dad, can we come back again one day?' Billy begged at closing time.

'I'm sure your dad will bring you back,' said Nat, giving Billy a wink.

If Drew got to keep his son, then he'd bring him back every

bloody year. Hell, he'd do it every month if it would help the universe make Billy his forever.

Back at Kent's, Drew got Billy started in the shower.

'You can swing ten cats in here, Dad!' Billy exclaimed.

Then Drew joined Nat in the kitchen. 'Can I help you with the pasta?'

'Sure, can you stir this?'

Drew reached for the wooden spoon, his hand brushing her fingers. Then her hands caressed his hips as she moved him to the side so she could get into the pot cupboard. Yep, helping her cook was much more fun than watching from the table.

'Thanks.'

'You look like a chook scratching around down there,' he said teasingly.

Nat grunted as she dived to the back of the cupboard again, metal pots clanging loudly. 'You would too. Uncle Kent has no order,' she said with a laugh before standing up with the pot she was after. 'Bingo.' Nat filled it with water, added a touch of oil and salt. 'Jason and I used to love coming here. We were allowed to pull out the pots and turn them into drum sets. Uncle Kent would get down on the floor with us for hours and play. Sometimes we'd turn up and he'd have a treasure hunt set up for us, and one time he turned the backyard into a camping oasis. He would take us to the beach, teach us to boogie board and how to make the best sandcastles.'

'It sounds like a great childhood,' said Drew as Nat added salt and pepper to the bacon that he was stirring.

'Oh, it was. I'd hate to think of what I'd be like without him. Uncle Kent showed us real life. He took us to zoos and parks, and also to the seedy parts of town. He pointed out that life was hard for some. We learnt a lot of lessons from him and he did it in a way that stayed with us.'

'Like what?'

'Well, this one time he stopped and sat with this homeless guy who was always on this street corner not far from his favourite coffee shop. Uncle Kent would buy him a coffee and muffin each time he went there, and sit with Bert – that was his name. Jason used to call him a bum and a hobo, but not after we met Bert and learnt about his amazing life and the family he'd lost. Made us less judgemental. Bert passed away a year ago and Uncle Kent paid for his funeral.'

Drew had stopped stirring, so moved by Nat's story.

'Well, something smells amazing,' said Kent, coming through the door. He put his briefcase down, threw his jacket aside and pulled off his tie.

'It's nearly ready. You have time to wash up,' said Nat.

'Great.' Kent headed off to his room.

Drew handed over the spoon so Nat could add the cream and mix the pasta through. 'I'll set the table.' Drew found the utensils and Nat helped him with the rest.

They were just setting the bowls down on the table when Kent reappeared with trackpants and a Kiss T-shirt on.

'Billy, come and eat, please,' said Drew, pulling out his chair for him. Billy left the Lego truck he was making and joined them.

'I love pasta,' said Billy, reaching for his fork and stabbing a big noodle.

'Me too, Billy,' said Kent. He winked at Nat. 'I told her, Drew, that she needs to ditch that man she's engaged to and live her life, or live with me so I can come home to cooked meals.' He gave Nat a wink. 'Thanks, possum. It looks amazing.' He picked up his fork and shovelled in a mouthful like he hadn't eaten all day.

Nat started up a conversation about the zoo but Drew was still clinging to Kent's words about Gary. Kent just got better and better, in his book. If worst came to worst and Nat didn't get out of the relationship, then Drew would have an ally in Kent, someone to go to. Already his chest felt lighter, knowing he had another course of action. The banter around the table as they ate made Drew feel a part of a family he'd been missing. The smile on Billy's face and the ease he felt with both Nat and Kent just made this more enticing. How would he cope when she left at the end of the year? Would they still stay in touch? Would Gary allow him and Billy to visit? Would Nat still be with Gary then? Could Gary change? Drew gritted his teeth; he disliked where his train of thought was going. He shook it off and tried to stay in this moment, this perfect family moment.

The next morning Billy and Drew sat in the doctor's office, the DNA kit open on the bench. It was less scary than a hospital but the room still had a sterile smell that made him uneasy.

'Dad, do we really have to do this scabby test?' said Billy after the doctor had swabbed his mouth.

Ignoring the doctor's sideways glance, Drew explained. 'Sure do, bud. When sheep have scabby mouth it's actually contagious and we can catch it. So we need to be tested. It's all routine, mate, nothing to worry about.'

The doctor shot Drew an understanding smile.

Billy watched in awe as the doctor swabbed Drew's mouth, and then everything was signed off and packed away.

'Now, the results will be emailed to the address on the form in around a week. I hope it's what you want,' said the doctor in his South African accent.

'Cheers, doc,' said Drew.

Nat was sitting in the waiting room by a pile of old magazines and a screaming child. She stood up the moment she saw them.

'See? Easy, hey?' she said to Billy.

'I don't think I've got scabby mouth,' he said loudly while his tongue flicked around his mouth.

Drew wasn't about to tell him the lesions would more likely be on his hands. After Billy's outburst he watched the expressions change on the two people waiting to see the doctor and tried hard not to laugh. 'Come on, let's go home.'

They climbed into Nat's car and left the city behind them, but those swabs were at the forefront of Drew's mind again. It was a shame he couldn't leave all that in Perth as well. Billy slept most of the way, due to a late night playing Monopoly as Kent had insisted. No one had won; they'd given up when Billy started to fall asleep at the table. Drew could tell Kent didn't want Nat to leave and that he cherished every moment with her.

He wondered if Kent saw the same feelings in Drew. Could he tell how much Drew cared for Nat? Was Drew that easy to read?

All these thoughts churned through his mind, making the trip home a quiet one. Even with Billy asleep they didn't want to risk talking about the DNA test, or Simone.

Drew had a quick nap himself, feeling tired from all the stress and worry, and the late-night Monopoly. He ended up dreaming about Natalie. About when he'd walked past her room earlier that morning and peeped through the gap in her door. Her sage green covers were covering her body but her golden hair splashed across a matching sage pillow. That had been enough to turn him on. And that vision was the last image in his mind when he woke up in the car. It made it hard to look at Nat without feeling the burning desire from his dream that stirred him awake.

'It's good to be home,' said Drew, clearing his throat and trying to gather his senses as Nat drove towards his house.

'It even makes me happy, getting back to Lake Biddy.'

'Really? This feels like home to you?' he asked, rubbing his eyes and sitting up.

'Yeah, it does. Or at least it feels like it's mine.'

'Do you want to stay for tea?' asked Drew. He didn't want her to leave just yet. He'd enjoyed being with her for nearly two days. He was feeling addicted and wasn't ready to rip off that bandaid just yet.

'Thanks, but I really should get home and get my lesson plan sorted for tomorrow.'

'How about long enough for a cold beer?'

'Okay, then. How can I pass up a coldie?'

Drew laughed. 'You're starting to sound like a local now. You've been hanging around Lozzy too long,' he said teasingly.

'Dad, are we home?' came a groggy voice from the back.

'Sure are, buddy. Ready to see Turbo?'

When they pulled up, Drew unpacked the car and sent Billy off to let Turbo out of his kennel and then to check the chooks.

This would give him a quiet moment with Nat, and he wasted no time in ditching their bags inside and returning with two beers so they could sit outside in the afternoon sun. Even though it was cold, the clouds were gone, letting the weak sun warm them up a little.

'I suppose you're going a bit crazy?' asked Nat, sitting beside him.

He could smell her sweet fragrance, and he sucked it in like a smoker chasing a nicotine hit. Yeah, he was going crazy all right. If he didn't keep his thoughts down, he'd find himself sitting beside her with throbbing body parts.

'Just a bit,' he said, shifting in the seat. 'But thanks for being there and for all your help. Kent is great.'

'I know.' Her grin showed how much she agreed. 'Are you really worried?'

'You mean have I thought about the chances of her being right? Every day. Every second. But I don't need some paper to tell me he's my son. I know it here,' he said, banging his chest. 'I won't give up the fight.'

'He's one lucky boy to have you.'

They drank their beers in silence for a moment. Drew closed his eyes, drawing strength and peace from the woman beside him.

Billy came back and headed inside to watch some TV, breaking the tranquillity.

'So, next week, hey?' said Nat.

'Next week?' said Drew, playing dumb.

'A year older, Drew. Getting closer to thirty,' she teased.

'Hmm, don't remind me. Do you know what Matty and Lozzy have planned, besides this bonfire? Knowing them, they have something horrible in mind as well. Invite the whole district or something crazy.'

'Ha, I doubt it. But it's bound to be memorable with Loz on the job. Don't worry. Loz tells me you can't go wrong with a bonfire.' Nat flicked her hair back and Drew caught the lavender scent of her shampoo. 'I'm quite excited. Apparently roasting marshmallows is a given.'

'It is, and you'll have all three kids trying to show you the best way to cook 'em. Don't listen to any of them. They charcoal them. What you need is coals. Come to me, I'll show you the right way.'

'I'll keep that in mind,' said Nat as she stood up and drained the last of her beer. 'Well, I'd better go. Thanks for this.' She put it on the little glass table.

Drew did the same and stood before her. 'I seem to thank you a lot, Natty. Don't know where I'd be without you around. This year would have been bloody tough.'

'You have plenty of people who love you, willing to help. But I'm glad I could be one of them too.' She smiled and threw her arms around him, hugging him tightly.

Drew melted into her arms. He hadn't expected this – he'd

hoped, maybe. And she didn't pull away straight away, instead rubbing his back.

'I know it's hard but try to relax and not think about it, Drew. Okay?'

He kept waiting for her to pull away; he would hug her all night long if he could. His hands were splayed across her back and they itched to run lower down her red coat. But if he pulled her too close, she'd feel more than she'd bargained for. As if reading his thoughts, Nat released him and he dropped his arms. It was a good, long hug. Enough to get him through until the next one, if he was lucky.

He walked her to her car as usual.

'Cheers, Natty.' He held her door open for her.

'Bye, Drew.'

He stood and watched her go until the last fleck of dust settled back on the ground.

Chapter 29

NAT texted Drew every afternoon to ask if he had the DNA results – that is, if he didn't send her one first. She had set up Drew's email on his phone so he would know as soon as it came in. It had been a very long, drawn-out week and Drew must have been showing signs of strain. Ida at the shop had commented to Natalie on Drew's scruffier-than-usual appearance and slightly withdrawn behaviour. 'He was just staring at the frozen peas with the door wide open. Ended up waving my hand in front of his face. Do you think it has anything to do with the scabby mouth?'

'Oh, I'm not sure,' Nat had said, trying to keep a straight face.

More than ever, Nat was dying to go out to the farm and comfort him, but Drew had said Kim had been dropping around each night to keep him company. She was relieved that he wasn't alone, and yet irritated at the same time. Nat wanted to be the one by his side – she'd been there at the DNA testing, she'd been the one he'd come to first. It killed her having to take a back seat. But she didn't dig too deep into her feelings, for fear of what she'd find. Besides, she was focusing on rebuilding her relationship with Gary, so maybe the week apart from Drew was a good thing.

But by the time Friday night came around, bonfire time for Drew's birthday, she was champing at the bit to see him.

She arrived early, as per Kim's plans. Nat was to keep Drew distracted so Kim and Matt could transport the dragon and set it up by the front gates. Lauren was setting up the bonfire next to it.

Driving up to the sheds, Nat felt her stomach clench with nerves. She wondered why . . . Was it finally seeing Drew after such a long week apart? Or maybe she was scared of the test results. Maybe Drew knew already and didn't want to share. She hoped he wouldn't hide things from her.

Drew was standing by his ute, wearing jeans, boots and a blue-checked shirt that made his eyes brighter. Nat was fast becoming a fan of the flannel shirt. Her friends would be horrified. But the whole ensemble fit Drew just perfectly. A real man who was good with his hands, worked the soil and fed the country. She couldn't deny there was something very sexy about that.

His blond tips sat up as if he'd just scrunched them with hair wax. It was a look other guys would pay big bucks for, yet on Drew it was all natural. His crooked-toothed smile appeared and she felt her lips tug up automatically. It was so good to see him.

Nat grabbed her gift from the car as she got out. The air was crisp, the sky was clear and it would get even colder as the sun disappeared. But for now it clung on to the earth, shooting yellow rays across the land like giant fingers.

'Happy birthday, Drew,' she said, hugging him tightly and risking a quick kiss on the cheek. It was hard to do that and not recall the bingo kiss. Pulling back from his arms and trying to hide the blush she could feel burning its way up her face, she shoved the gift into his chest. 'This is for you.'

'Natty, you shouldn't have. But thanks.' He shook the little box. 'Should I open it now?'

'Yes, of course. Where is Billy?'

'He's been with Lozzy all arvo. I'm sure they're cooking up something rotten. I told Billy he had to warn me if it was something I wouldn't like. Big parties aren't my thing.' Drew pulled on the blue bow.

'Don't worry, it's nothing big. Just your close friends,' said Nat.

Carefully she watched Drew open the box. His eyes glassed over with sentiment when he saw his gift.

'Oh my god. Zoo passes for the next couple of years! Nat, you shouldn't have.'

'Yes, I should have, because I know you'll be keeping your promise to Billy and going back there soon. I'm that sure of it.' She waited a moment, while Drew blinked rapidly. He didn't speak and she could tell he was trying to gain control.

'I . . . this is . . . Natty.' Drew gave up and threw his arms around her again.

She felt his lips brush her cheek and it made her shiver. 'Have you got good news to celebrate?' she asked cautiously. She felt

Drew stiffen. He let her go and stepped back, leaning against the door of his ute.

'I got the email,' he said softly.

Nerves fluttered along her skin. 'Well? What did it say?' She searched his face for the answer and felt a wave of sickness. He didn't look happy. 'Oh, Drew.' Her heart was going to break.

Drew grabbed her hand and gave it a squeeze. 'Nat, I haven't read it yet. I still don't know.'

'You haven't read it? Why not?'

'I'm scared.' His eyes latched on to her as if he was drowning. 'It's my birthday, Nat. Everyone is here. How can I celebrate if I open this and find out it's not what I want to hear? I just don't think I could deal with it.'

'You told me the outcome didn't matter.'

'I know. Doesn't mean it won't gut me. Just the thought of having to tell him . . . I'm not sure I could do it.'

'Do you want me to read it?'

'I was going to wait till tomorrow, or maybe Monday . . .'

Nat held out her hand and wiggled her fingers. Drew handed over his phone without complaint.

She found the email and opened it, reading quickly as she felt Drew's gaze burn holes in her. Nat lifted her eyes. 'Billy is all yours.'

'Oh my god, for real?' Tears filled his eyes. He put his hand over his mouth as he grinned with happiness.

Nat read the email out loud, which was hard through watery eyes. 'You can rest easy now, Drew. You got your birthday wish.' She leant against him and his arms immediately wrapped her up.

'This is the best feeling ever,' he said as his hands rubbed her back.

Nat realised their hugs were becoming longer but they felt so comforting and right. She loved the smell of him, so earthy, manly and strong.

'You know, this jacket is nice and all,' said Drew, holding her at arm's length and giving her red coat the once-over. 'But it's not bonfire-approved.'

'What do you mean? Will it burn?'

Drew chuckled. 'If you stand too close, it will. But I mean it's far too good to have fire smoke all over it. You'd have to get this dry-cleaned, hey?'

'I see your point.' Dry-cleaning had to be taken to Lake Grace. A long way to go just to get a jacket done.

Drew opened his ute and reached over to the passenger side. 'Here, you can wear this work one. It doesn't matter how it smells.'

He held up a black jacket with *Summit Fertiliser* written on it. Nat unbuttoned her red coat, handed it to Drew and put on the one he supplied. It was big but so comfy, and it smelt like Drew as well as grease or fuel or something farm-related.

'Thanks.' She put her red coat back in her car and pulled out the beers she'd brought.

'Here. Time for a birthday drink,' she said, handing a cold stubby over.

The beers hissed as they cracked them open. Leaning against the bonnet of the ute, they watched the sun creep its way down. It was going to be dark soon. Nat checked her phone for Kim's okay. She'd want Drew to see his dragon in the daylight. Maybe they were having trouble shifting it.

As if by magic, her phone lit up.

Bring birthday boy. We are ready.

'Looks like it's time for us to go.'

Nat took her car and Drew drove his ute down to his front gate. Nat could already see large red flames. Lauren hadn't wasted any time; it looked like it was roaring. How were they supposed to stand next to that without singeing something?

Doris, Kim, Matt, Lozzy and the kids were all sitting around the fire in deckchairs. A table was set up on the side with bread and sauce plus the damper Billy would make for them all, and some spuds wrapped in foil. But the thing that demanded their attention was the dragon.

They had it set up just inside the gates and it was awesome, almost gothic, in the dying light. Nat instantly turned to Drew, wanting to see his expression when he saw it. Everyone else had got up out of their chairs and walked towards him.

'Happy birthday, Sadds,' said Matty and Kim.

Drew's mouth dropped open as he walked towards the massive metal structure. 'What?' He glanced at Kim, shaking his head in disbelief. 'Wow.'

They all gathered around the clawed feet of the dragon, looking up at its wings and sharp teeth. The teeth, Nat realised, were the ends of old flat screwdrivers and spanners.

'Kim, it's . . .' Drew was speechless and everyone laughed.

'It's bloody amazing is what it is,' said Doris, who rapped her knuckles against it like it was the hard shell of an army tank.

'You like her?' asked Kim, standing beside Drew in boots, jeans, green flannel shirt and a similar jacket to the one Nat wore. Those two looked like they belonged together. Drew pulled Kim into a hug and Nat found she had to glance away.

'I like the claws best,' said Billy.

At his son's voice, Drew let Kim go and picked Billy up. 'Hey, mate.'

Billy squirmed in the embrace, clearly embarrassed at the sudden affection. But Nat knew why Drew needed to hug his son. *His* son.

'Dad,' Billy complained, so Drew let him go.

'How about we get the birthday boy a drink?' said Matty, slapping Drew's shoulder.

'I'll get the sausages cooking,' said Lauren.

'Billy, is it time to put the damper on?' asked Doris.

Billy shrugged. 'Seth, wanna play spotlight?'

'Can I play too?' asked Mallory.

The kids disappeared looking for torches and Doris mumbled to herself as she went back to the fire.

Nat felt awkward being left with Drew and Kim, so she went to help Lauren.

'Nah, I'm fine, Nat. Grab a seat, enjoy the fire and the stars,' said Lauren, pointing up.

Nat leant back in the chair. She had to admit the stars looked pretty spectacular now the sun was gone. As each minute passed she could see more, twinkling in the black night like diamonds.

The flames sent up little sparks and the warmth they gave out made her feel cosy and content. The smoke from the fire wafted about, mixing with the crisp night air, and together they made an unforgettable scent. While Lauren fossicked about over at the table, Nat sat and watched Drew through the flames.

'The dragon looks amazing with the firelight flicking over it, hey?' said Matt, handing her another beer.

'It sure does. Kinda brings it to life. Kim is incredible.'

'Yeah, the ol' sis is a chip off the old block, all right.'

Kim was still with Drew. They were talking, smiling and standing really close to each other. Nat tightened her grip on her cold beer. Kim squealed and threw her arms around Drew and they hugged for ages. Nat guessed he'd told her the news about Billy. Which he was entitled to . . . she was one of his best friends and all. But still, did they need to hug for that long? Kim's lips were moving. Were they whispering sweet nothings to each other?

Matt said something but she barely registered it; her focus was on Drew and the acid feeling in her stomach. The beer was not agreeing with her. And she felt restless all of a sudden.

Something crossed her line of vision. 'Hey, lovey. Wanna help me drink this bottle of wine?' asked Lauren.

Moisture was running down the outside of the bottle. Wine felt like the perfect solution to how she was feeling right now. Nat glanced up at her new friend.

'Hell, yeah.'

Chapter 30

'BY the look on someone's face I'd say we're making them uncomfortably jealous,' said Kim against Drew's ear.

'What?' he said. Drew went to move but Kim gripped him like a vice. She was one strong woman.

'Don't move, you idiot, and you can't look either.'

'What are you going on about, Kimmy?'

'Natalie. Who do you think?'

'Natalie is jealous? Of us?'

'Yes, you dummy. Glad you could catch up.' Kim dug her chin into his shoulder. 'You like her and she likes you. Isn't it time you did something about it?'

Drew pulled back so he could see Kim's face. She really was a pretty girl. Her skin was flawless and tanned, her eyes lively, and she had a smile that always brightened his day. He couldn't imagine life without her. 'What do you mean, I like her? Have you been talking to your brother?'

'No, why? I already knew. So does Loz.'

'Jesus, is it that obvious?' Drew clamped his hand over his forehead as if it would hide the bold letters of Nat's name stamped there.

'Yeah, it's that obvious. I've never seen you look at anyone the way you look at her, Sadds. I know you so well. You've fallen for her, haven't you?'

Drew thought back to when Nat mentioned her theory on Kim. He studied her now and, sure enough, the way her eyes caressed his face said it all. How could he have not seen that?

This revelation only made answering her question that much harder. He simply nodded his head. Sadness flickered across her coffee-coloured eyes and Drew felt awful.

Kim stroked his face before moving her hand to his shoulder. 'Then why aren't you telling her this?'

'I can't go chasing another man's bride. What would that make me?'

'It makes you a man in love. And from what I see here, she cares for you too. Maybe if you put your cards on the table, she might break off her engagement. Did you ever think of that?'

'Or she doesn't and it ruins our friendship.'

Kim looked at the dirt and kicked at a stone. 'Yeah, I get that. But maybe some things are worth the risk.'

'She'll be going back to the city at the end of the year anyway. We knew at the start she wasn't the sort to stay out here long, even though she's making a good go of it. And anyway,' he added half-heartedly. 'Life's been great so far, why complicate it?'

'Andrew, you know what your mother would say to that.'

He smiled. Kim was right. Things would have been so much

easier if he'd fallen in love with Kim instead. Didn't they say you should marry your best friend? Maybe they could work on it, see how it went. But even as he thought that, Nat's face swam before him and his heart ached. His heart wanted only her.

Drew tugged on her ponytail, like he used to when they were younger. 'I'm sorry, Kim. I'm sorry I didn't realise.' He didn't know what else to say. This wasn't stuff they normally talked about.

'It's not your fault, Sadds. That's life. You're still my friend. At least, I hope so?'

'God, yeah. I can't survive without you. You know that, right?' He loved her, just differently, but he couldn't bring himself to say it. He hoped this would suffice. The light of the fire danced across Kim's smiling face. She was still happy to be his friend. Thank god. He put his arm around her and directed her back to the fire, where their chairs waited.

'Yeah, I guess you'd be a bloody wreck without me around to pick up the pieces. Who'd weld up all your broken crap?'

'That crap you speak of is offended and so am I,' he said in jest. Everything was right again in the world. Kim was by his side and Billy was his son. And across from him sat Natalie. Gorgeous Natalie with those eyes that made his blood simmer.

'Where are the kids?' he asked as they sat down.

'Hopefully getting lost,' said Matty with a chuckle.

'Guess I can tell you the good news, then. Billy's mine.'

Lauren, with her super hearing, gave out a whoop.

'Bloody good news, Drew,' Matt said. 'I knew he had to be. No one else could have spawned such a mini you.'

Lauren turned the sausages over quickly, then hugged Drew. 'I knew it. She was just blowing smoke to make you back off. Take her through the courts, Drew. We'll all be behind you.'

'Yeah, I guess I need to call Kent and see what my next move is,' he said, glancing at Nat.

Nat took a big swig from her wine glass and set those eyes on him. 'I sent him a text with the good news. He's delighted and waiting for your call.' Nat didn't give him her usual smile as she turned back to the fire.

Soon the girls were serving up snags in bread and then they were singing happy birthday to him by the fire as Lauren produced his favourite lemon cheesecake. 'Thanks, Lozzy,' he said, feeling as if his mum were there too.

'Alice made it every year. I don't see why the tradition can't continue.'

'Mum would have loved this. The dragon, the fire, all of us together – all of it,' he said.

Doris dabbed at her eye with the ratty sleeve of her jacket. 'Aye, that she would have. And she would be making sure we didn't burn the bloody damper,' she added with a deep chuckle. 'Miss you, Alice,' she murmured, glancing up at the stars.

It was a perfect night. The kids sat by the fire with their sticks, poking at the coals, waiting for the marshmallows. The stars were bright in the clear sky. Drew had a massive dragon at his front gate, and if that didn't scare away the thieves, nothing would. And he had his most treasured friends and family around the huge bonfire. Sometimes the simple things in life were just what the doctor ordered.

It was great to see Nat having a ball trying to roast marshmallows with the kids. The flames flickered across her face, making him love her more by the second. He tried to catch her eye but she was so focused on the children, so he ended up chatting with Kim and Matty for most of the night.

Doris started to tell some yarns of the old days, the things they did to survive on the land back when her Fred was alive. Drew had heard many of them before but every now and then Doris mentioned something new, like the time Fred had ridden his bike all through the night just to see Doris, only to find she'd fallen asleep waiting for him. Looking at Doris now, it was hard to picture a teenage version.

'Did I tell you what happened yesterday?' she said now.

Everyone gave her a blank stare.

'I had my chooks out for a scratch, and my dogs, they're well behaved. They leave the girls alone. Only, I had a visit from old Tom up the road. Didn't think nothin' of his dog Crackers, who'd jumped off to play with me dogs. Anyway, not long later I heard me girls cacklin' up a storm. Then Crackers goes past with one in his mouth, proud as punch, the little bugger.'

'Was it dead?' asked Seth.

'Well, I chased Crackers. Around the house I go and when I get around the corner I find Crackers digging a hole to bury the chook in his mouth. But right next to this hole is a pair of chicken feet sticking out of the dirt. He'd already buried one and was going back for a second! I started growling at him, thinking my girls were gone, when the feet sticking out of the ground wiggled. Bloody hell, I thought. Quick smart I plucked that chook from the dirt and there was my Betsy alive and well. A little dirty but alive and well.'

'Crackers had buried her alive?' said Matt in awe.

Drew was starting to laugh and the kids were already rolling around on the ground, nearly skewering each other with their marshmallow sticks.

'Yep. Didn't kill none, just liked burying 'em for later, I reckon. Warned old Tom to keep him on a chain next time.'

That was Doris. A story for every occasion.

A few wines later, Natalie stood up. 'Well, I best head home while I'm still sober enough to drive.'

Everyone tried to convince her to stay but she shook her head. 'It's been a fantastic night. Thank you all so much. But I'd better get home.' She hugged Lauren goodbye. 'Hope you had a great birthday, Drew.'

Sadly she waved and walked off to her car. He was hoping for a hug but maybe the crowd was too large for that. He wanted to walk her to her car, to get that hug and maybe brush his lips against her neck, but it was too late now.

Kim leant over his shoulder, slipping another beer into his hands. 'Don't let her get away,' she whispered.

Her words stayed with him all night.

Chapter 31

IT was ten minutes to lunchtime and the kids were struggling to stay focused on their maths. The younger ones had coloured counters in front of them, which Mia was using to make a pretty flower. Some of the older ones were counting on fingers and Billy and Isaac were staring at the walls as if they held the answers.

It was the last day of school before term two finished. Nat couldn't blame them for being unfocused. She was already thinking about her time in the city. Two weeks with Gary. He'd been the perfect fiancé lately – phone calls, romantic emails, gifts in the mail – which was all fine but the apprehension was building in her stomach at the thought of going home and seeing him in person.

Her phone vibrated and she glanced at it. Another message from Drew.

Are you avoiding me, Natty?

Nat closed her eyes and breathed deeply. Yes, she was avoiding him. Ever since the bonfire last week Nat had realised she needed to step back. To give him and Kim a chance to connect, which, based on their form that night, was finally happening. She couldn't have Drew all to herself, not when she was committed to someone else. And Drew was much better suited to Kim than he was to a city girl like Nat. So she was trying to let him go. At least that's what she was telling herself. It wasn't that she was jealous of them and punishing Drew by being distant.

All good, just busy with kids. See you after holidays.

She hoped that would stop any more texts. She just didn't want to deal with them any more. Which was funny, considering every time her phone buzzed she almost pounced on it, hoping it was from Drew. Like she did now.

Righto. Have a safe trip. Stay in touch.

Yeah, right, she thought after reading his reply. Gosh, she was just all over the place. Nat couldn't even make sense of her own mind. She had fifty frogs in there just jumping from one thought to another, none sitting long enough for her to get a grip on her feelings. Even the kids had picked up on her tense mood.

'All right. Let's pack up.'

'But I haven't finished,' Ruby said in a whiney voice. Her deep red lips pushed together as if ready to cry from the stress.

'It's okay, Ruby. You don't have to finish it. If you want, you

289

can take it home to complete.' Nat stood up and flattened out her knitted tunic, which went over her black leggings and boots. 'When you're all packed up let's have a game of heads down, thumbs up.'

'Yay!' said a chorus of voices and the packing became almost frantic.

Within moments their desks were clean and they were all sitting up like perfect soldiers. 'Okay. Liam, Lucy and Noah, you can go first, because I saw you all working hard today and using lovely manners.'

The three kids sprang from their seats and headed to the front. While they played, Nat packed up her desk and got the afternoon artwork organised. Her phone sat silently at the end of her desk like a big hairy spider. She hated any spider bigger than her thumbnail.

The lunch bell went and the kids rushed back to their desks. Nat let them go and then followed the urgency of little bodies that went straight for their bags, pulling out sandwiches or leftover pasta from their lunchboxes. Jack seemed to inhale his egg sandwich in one go. 'Jack, sit down to eat or you'll get indigestion.' He glanced outside. 'Everyone else has to eat too. The footballs aren't going anywhere.'

Jack eyeballed her for a second, then sat his bum down on the bench next to Billy. Billy sat there quietly, eating his wholemeal sandwich slowly. He never played football with the boys, instead wandering around on his own or tagging between Mallory and Seth. Some days he was happy to be in the sandpit by himself, building roads and dams around pretend paddocks. Looking at him was a reminder of Drew. One she couldn't handle at the moment.

When they'd all eaten Nat headed for the staffroom, only to find Kath in there, holding some paper with tears rolling down her cheeks. Grace had her hand on Kath's shoulder, and her eyes were glassy but she was blinking fast.

Nat's heart sank. 'Is everything okay?'

Kath started to talk, but decided after a fresh round of tears that she couldn't and waved her hand at Grace.

'It's official. The Lake Biddy school will close at the end of the year.' Grace took some deep, steadying breaths but the tremble in her lips remained. 'It is with great regret, yada yada yada,' Grace read from the letter over Kath's shoulder. 'No point reading the rest of the spiel, not going to change things or make us feel any better.'

'You're kidding me. I was so sure it would stay open. Hell, we did everything we could.' Nat felt like she'd let them all down. She stood at the open door and watched the kids in the long corridor, eating their lunches, talking excitedly. Their work hanging up on windows and walls. The colours and sounds. How sad to lose it, how bloody sad for the whole community. 'I don't get it. How could they?'

Kath dabbed at her tears and passed over the letter. 'They just couldn't see the worth in keeping it open while our numbers drop, even though they'll be picking up in five years. What am I going to do for work now? I love this job.' Kath reached for another tissue.

'Does Lauren know?' Nat couldn't move from her position

watching the kids. There was so much life in this little building. What would become of it? How soon until it was falling down and overrun by spiders? Just that thought made her want to cry. She'd become so attached to this place, which felt so much like home. She felt for the kids, for the parents, for the staff and for the community. It was losing part of its history, the place they'd been schooled and dreamt their kids would be too. Lauren had shown her where Drew and Matty had carved their names into one of the old gum trees in the playground when they were little boys. And above their names were their dads' names, almost unrecognisable. A legacy of sorts.

'No, I haven't been able to get myself together to notify anyone. I figured, what's the rush? Nothing we can do about it now,' said Kath, reaching for a chocolate biscuit. Her lunch sat untouched in its container beside her.

Nat felt the urge to join her on a chocolate binge. They fell quiet, thinking their own sad thoughts. Lake Biddy just wouldn't be the same place without its school. Parents wouldn't come to town to do their shopping. They'd go into Lake Grace instead and shop when they picked their kids up. Poor Ida and Frank were really going to feel it. They scarcely scraped through as it was. Sometimes Nat just wished she could give them all some money to get them in a more comfortable spot. Her parents wouldn't miss it. Yet knowing Frank and Ida, she realised they wouldn't take handouts and were happy with their life, even the day-to-day struggles. It seemed to be what the town was built on: hard work, grit and determination. And a lot of volunteer sweat, passion and dedication to the community. How could you come to

Lake Biddy and not fall in love with the place? This small community had touched her heart in so many ways.

Soon all the kids cleared out to play and Nat, Kath and Grace moved to the big windows to watch them and eat their own lunches. Ross was out on duty but Nat always tried to keep an eye out for Simone, even now.

'You know, we should do something special. Something to celebrate the school.' Nat turned to face Kath. 'How about a time capsule? Each student puts something in, and the staff too. And then we can bury it, as if we're burying a part of us all with the school.'

Grace clasped her hands together and Kath looked like she was about to cry again.

'That's a wonderful idea,' said Grace. 'A way to say goodbye.'

'While I'm in Perth over the holidays I can find out what's available, maybe look at prices for a plaque.' Nat needed a mission to keep her focused on something positive, to keep her mind off Drew and the sad news about the school. 'I'll go ring Lozzy and have a chat about it. She's going to be so upset.' Nat also wanted to hear her friend's voice. She couldn't turn to Drew, even though that's what she wanted most.

She was in the classroom on the phone to Lauren when the bell went and kids started coming in. 'I have to go, Lozzy, the kids are back in. Yep, I'll call you from Perth. We'll get it sorted. I know, it sucks. Talk soon. Bye.'

Nat got up and took a moment to think about what she had to do. 'Art. We're doing art, kids. Time to get out your paint shirts.' The kids flitted about the classroom getting organised, excited for the easy lesson. Nat used this time to gather her senses.

'Right. Now, today you are simply going to paint whatever you would like. Maybe it's something you want to do on the holidays or something special. It's all up to you,' said Nat as she handed out A3 paper. 'Then you'll be writing about your picture.' Emily had spent some of the lunch break putting out the paints while Nat had been chatting with Lauren.

'Also . . .' Nat trailed off as she got to Billy's spot and found it empty. His chair was still tucked in. She glanced around the room. 'Has anyone seen Billy?'

The kids looked around.

'Toilet?' said Seth.

'Can you please go and check? Thanks, Seth.' Nat wasn't worried. It was quite common for kids to have to go at the most inappropriate times. Billy was one of the worst.

She was helping Ruby decide what to paint when Seth came back. 'I can't find him, Miss Wright. I checked the toilets and the playground.' Seth's eyebrows met and he looked so much like Matt.

'Oh. Okay. Um, Emily?' she asked the aide who was down the back washing up some spilled paint. 'Can you keep an eye on the class, please?'

'No worries,' said Emily, who dried her hands and joined the kids.

Nat walked out and checked with Grace that Billy wasn't in her class. Then she checked with Kath in the office. 'What about you, Ross? Did you see him while on duty?'

She didn't want to panic, but her heart was starting to race.

Normally a kid would have popped up by now. Grace had told her about one boy a few years ago who'd got upset over an incident in the playground and had simply walked home – 5 kilometres away. Sure enough, they found him alone in the kitchen, eating cereal. They could laugh about it now but Nat was sure Billy wouldn't do that; his home was over 20 kilometres away. Unless he'd gone to her house? Maybe something scared him enough to seek another shelter?

'I recall seeing him playing in the sandpit,' said Ross.

'I'm going to run home and see if he's there. Can you take over my class, please, Ross? Emily is watching them at the moment.'

He stood up straight away, his face full of concern. 'Yes, you go. Then we might have to let Drew know.'

'I'll call Kath if I find him.' Nat rushed back into her class to get her phone and keys. Before she left she asked the class if anyone had noticed if Billy had been upset.

'Or did anyone notice a lady by the fence, someone you've never seen before?' Nat asked, feeling like she was going to be sick. Surely not. She didn't want to believe Simone could have taken him away. And Nat was supposed to be watching out for Billy. Drew would kill her. Nat was about to drop the F-bomb when she remembered the room was full of kids.

'I didn't,' said Seth, who was one of the oldest in the class.

All the little faces watched her, and she could tell they were picking up on her concern so she tried to smile. 'That's okay. We'll find him. Finish your work,' she said as calmly as she could before rushing out past Ross. 'I don't care what they do,' she mumbled before jogging up the corridor and out the door.

She checked her house, looked around for Simone's car, and even stopped at the shop to see if Ida had noticed anything or seen Billy. Nat came up totally empty. She needed to call Drew. She hurried back to the school, hoping to find he'd just been asleep in the cement tube or busy building a teepee near the bush reserve behind the school. It had to be something like that. God, she hoped so.

She caught up with Ross and Kath: still nothing.

'Grace, can I quickly ask the senior kids something?' Nat said, popping her head in the door.

'Yeah, sure. Kids, listen up, please. Miss Wright has a question.'

The older kids lifted their heads. 'I just need to know if anyone saw a woman standing by the fence at lunchtime, maybe wearing a green beanie. She may have been talking to Billy. Can anyone recall someone hanging around?'

Summer, an eleven-year-old with bird earrings, shot her hand up. 'I did, miss. She was smoking and it was wafting towards us where we were doing handstands on the lawn.'

Oh, god. Nat clutched the cupboard under the blackboard for support, her knees becoming two-minute noodles of the soggy kind.

'She was wearing a beanie, I think,' added Summer.

Grace came over and put her hand on Nat's arm. 'Are you okay? You look like you're about to be sick.'

'Oh, no.' Nat's stomach was rolling, her head pounding so hard she was struggling to think.

Grace's voice seemed so distant. 'Thanks, Summer. Guys, continue with your work. I'll just be a minute.' Grace helped her outside, away from all the prying eyes. 'What's going on, Nat?' she demanded softly.

'I think Billy's been taken.' Nat felt clammy and faint. The world was starting to spin. What did she do now?

The next thing she knew she was sitting on the senior's bench and Grace was shoving a glass of water under her nose. 'Nat, please, what is going on? You've got us all worried. What do you mean Billy's been taken?'

'Us' turned out to be Kath and Ross, hovering in her peripheral vision.

Nat looked at them and felt the weight of the world come crashing down on her. Tears blurred her vision. 'I have to tell Drew.' Nat broke down and sobbed into her hands.

Chapter 32

DREW was driving like a madman, racing towards the school. God protect anyone on the road ahead, human or animal.

Kath had called him. 'Drew, can you get to the school as soon as possible?' Her tone alone had made the hairs on the back of his neck stand up. And then she'd said, 'We can't find Billy.'

He'd dropped the fencing gear, left it all sitting in the paddock and raced off in his ute. Turbo would just head back to the house and wait. Kath had not wanted to go over the specifics on the phone, but he had to assume Simone had taken his son. His foot kept pressing harder against the accelerator. What he wouldn't give for Nat's car right now, instead of this old ute that hadn't gone so fast in its whole life.

He slowed through town and finally pulled up at the school. Ripping off his jacket, as he was nearly sweating from the stress, he ran through the school gates.

'Drew,' called Grace, who was sitting in the undercover area with Nat. 'We're over here.'

Drew pulled up short when he saw the state Nat was in. Red eyes, tear-stained face, and white as a freshly shorn sheep. He bent down in front of her but Nat wouldn't look at him.

'It's all my fault,' said Nat in a trance-like state. 'I was meant to be watching him and I got distracted. I'm so sorry. It's all my fault.' Her voice was so raw it broke his heart, but Drew wasn't really processing anyone's words yet.

Nat flicked her eyes up and they latched on to his. 'I'm so sorry, Drew,' she sobbed. 'I think Simone took him.'

Drew fell back onto his heels, as if blown from an exploding grenade. His worst fear had been confirmed.

'Who's Simone?' said Grace.

Nat drew in a breath. 'Billy's mum,' she said. 'I was supposed to be keeping watch. Can we call the police, get them to look for the car? She'd be on her way back to Perth. We can probably track her route.' Her voice grew stronger, more determined. 'I'll call. I know the car and what she looks like.'

Drew was struck cold, frozen, but on the inside there was a volcano of lava lashing up. He wanted to burst, scream and shout, swear and kill something, someone, preferably Simone.

Kath and Ross came and went, water was offered to him, Lauren turned up, then Matt and Kim, but he couldn't move. The world moved around him as if on high speed while he sat there, the cramp in his legs nothing to the pain that was pulling him apart on the inside.

'Drew,' said Kim. She slapped his face to rouse him. 'Drew.'

He didn't even feel the slap but he blinked until he could focus on Kim. 'Billy?'

'The police are looking for them. Come on, it's time to go home. Kids are about to finish school.'

'I need to find Billy. I need to go to Perth,' Drew said as Kim and Matt practically dragged him up onto his feet.

'We will, mate. We will,' said Matt.

'I'm so sorry, Drew.'

He turned at Nat's gutted voice. She was still so beautiful but he didn't know what to say to her, couldn't think of the words, so he just turned and left with Kim and Matt. He couldn't even give her a reassuring smile. He was just a shell.

Before he knew it they were at his place and packing up some gear.

'We're both coming with you. We'll bloody knock on every door we can. I know the police are probably already doing it but . . . shit,' said Matt as he grabbed Drew's packed bag. 'Can you wait ten while Kim whizzes home to grab our stuff?'

Kim didn't even wait for his reply. One minute she was there beside him, the next she was gone. Everything seemed to flash past in chunks, like he was watching a badly scratched movie. Nothing was fluid or in sync. Take Billy from Drew's life and he just couldn't function properly. If they didn't find him, would he feel like this forever?

'We'll get him back, Drew. Don't you worry. We'll find him even if we have to search every bloody house with a fine-tooth comb. She can't hide from us forever.'

When Kim returned they hit the road. He was in no state to drive; he just stared out the window the whole way, not game to think about his son being missing because if he did, if he let those floodgates open, he wasn't sure he'd be able to shut them. And who knew how long it would take before it would run dry?

Chapter 33

'SO have you been to Wave Rock?' Simone asked Billy as they sped through the outskirts of town.

'Yeah, but not for ages. We have a few rocks on the farm that I play on with Seth.'

'Who is Seth?' she asked and was pleased when Billy replied excitedly, telling her about his best friends who lived next door and all the things they got up to, from building bush cubbies to racing their bikes.

'Are we going to my house?' Billy asked at one point as he glanced around, trying to work out where they were.

'We're going to Wave Rock first. I'll get your ice-cream there and we can have a look around together. Make some memories,' she said with a smile.

Billy looked at her strangely. 'But I don't want to go to Wave Rock. I want to go home,' he said softly. 'You said we were going to Dad.'

'We are, Billy. After our ice-cream, remember?'

Simone could hardly believe that this little boy was made from her DNA, grown inside her belly, that she'd given birth to him after nine hours of labour. It had all been so sudden, in the end. One minute she was walking around Drew's house cursing the heat and her swollen ankles, and the next she'd been struck down with pain so intense she'd craved a hit of any sort. For five months Alice had hovered over her like a prison guard – *don't do this, don't do that, you must eat this, it's good for the baby.* Simone had grown to dislike the child, as life in the Saddler household had become unbearable. It was all about the baby. When he was born she'd been so relieved it was all over, relieved she could be herself again.

Yet the memory of that white room, the doctor and nurses, the blood and the newborn baby cries had always stayed with her, no matter how hard she'd tried to burn them from her mind with whatever concoction she could find.

She could still remember the moment the doctor had lifted him up to her, saying, 'It's a boy!' Simone hadn't wanted to know, hadn't wanted to see him either, but it had been too late. His little body was there, all red and mucky. She'd turned her head away then, hot tears running from her eyes. Not because of any love that was swamping her, but from relief that it was all finally over. At last she could have her life back – and they could have the baby.

But later Simone had been curious about the boy. It was surreal to think he'd been the baby growing inside her all that time. But because she refused to hold him or be near him, she'd severed whatever bond may have grown. As soon as she'd felt up to walking, she took the meagre possessions she had left and escaped back to the city.

Suffering through the after-effects of her pregnancy and labour constantly reminded her of what she'd been through – breasts full and aching, a body trying to recover, and then the baby blues, which made her depression worse. Getting back to normal, the parties, the good times, had seemed to ease her mind. She at least felt free. The way Alice had lorded over her and gone on and on about the child and its health – well, she'd been glad to be rid of him. In a way she'd been jealous of the love and devotion they'd given an unborn child when Simone struggled to get anything from her own mum.

It wasn't until her mum passed away from a drug overdose that she recalled any happy childhood memories of her own. Going for ice-cream, visits to the beach. Some of those times were to escape her dad when he was in a foul mood but it had brought them closer together. Simone often wondered, if her mum had really loved her, why hadn't she left her abusive husband and started a new life?

Here she was now, facing her own son and trying to make amends. Her mum had never left her, after all, no matter how bad things had got.

Simone pulled out a cigarette and lit it.

Billy gaped at her. 'You can't smoke in a car,' he said. 'We'll choke. Smoking kills you. Gives you cancer. I don't want cancer.'

The kid was going on and on. Simone saw the horror on his face; it looked as if he might jump out the car, so she wound down her window and threw her cigarette out.

'That's littering. You're lucky it's not summer or you could have started a fire.'

'Jesus, kid, who are you? The goody-two-shoes police?' The sooner they could get to Wave Rock, the better. She was dying for a ciggie. 'Can I stop and have a smoke?' she asked him.

He shook his head and crossed his arms. 'I want my dad. Can we go home now?'

'But we haven't had our ice-cream yet, and I promised you two, remember?' Maybe she should just stop and have a quick smoke before her nerves went crazy.

'I don't want one. I just want to go home.' His bottom lip dropped.

'Well, I want to see Wave Rock and have an ice-cream, so we'll keep going.'

Simone's mother had brought her up on tough love and she knew that with a firm hand Billy would understand and get over it. Once he got his ice-cream it would be fine.

She glanced across and saw big fat tears falling down his face.

'Let's put on some music, hey? What do you like to listen to?' Simone turned up the radio. She ignored his crying and sang along. Soon he'd give up trying to get her attention.

'I want my dad,' he sobbed, but she ignored his hiccups and snotty nose. He just wanted his own way but she guessed he'd be fine after a treat.

'We're nearly there. I wonder if they still have the animals there. We could see the white kangaroo.' She might as well have been talking to herself. Billy just cried even more. This kid was persistent.

And it only got worse. By the time they arrived in Hyden, he was in near hysterics. He wouldn't get out of the car so she left him there while she had a quick smoke then went to get the ice-cream.

'Here, buddy, just what you wanted,' she said, opening the car door. But he didn't move, wouldn't even look at her. 'Okay, then. Suit yourself.' She left the ice-cream on the ground for him. 'Well, I'm going to have a look around the rock. Come with me if you like. It will be fun.'

He stayed put, so she turned and headed to the rock. As she walked through the bush and climbed over the rock, looking for tadpoles in the little pools, she wondered if he was hoeing into the ice-cream.

But on her return she found it where she'd left it, melted into a mess on the ground. Billy was asleep in the front seat, snot and tears smeared over his face. The kid had been crying non-stop for over an hour – no wonder he'd crashed.

He would be better when he woke up, she thought. He just needed time to realise he was fine with her, that they could be a family.

Simone went to buy some chocolate before waking him up.

'Hey, Billy, wanna come and look at the animals with me?'

He sat up with a start, looking around and trying to get his bearings. 'Where's my dad? I want my dad,' he said, starting to cry again.

'No, Billy, enough crying. You'll have no tears left soon.' She reached out for his arm to pull him out of the car. 'Come on, you'll feel better if we go see something.'

'I don't want to,' he said. 'No!' he screamed when she pulled him from the car.

She let him go and he fell to the ground, sobbing, and that's when she saw the dark patch spreading across his school pants. She was hit with the strong smell of urine.

Billy didn't seem to care that he'd wet himself; he just lay there on the ground with more tears and snot. What was it with this kid? Surely he was too old to be wetting his pants. Didn't kids stop that before they got to school?

'Damn it, Billy. You don't have any other pants to wear. Now what are we going to do?'

Simone didn't know what to do with him. She hadn't even changed nappies, so there was no way she wanted to be changing a grown boy's pants. She couldn't call her mum. Instead she lit up another cigarette and watched him. 'You're just making this harder on yourself, kid. It doesn't have to be like this.'

Simone's earlier thoughts of having her son with her, doing the family thing, lots of laughs and fun, all suddenly slipped away, replaced by the cold reality. But she didn't want to give up just yet. He had to come around. She just had to be patient. TV, she suddenly thought. Kids love TV.

Somehow she managed to get him back into the car, and they drove to the Hyden motel, where she booked a room for them. She couldn't coax him from the car so she ended up carrying him, crying and screaming, to the room. Luckily the place was quiet, so no one would pay them any attention. Simone had seen plenty of unruly kids before, anyway. People would just think he was misbehaving.

She put him down on the floor and turned on the TV. Billy curled up into a ball and kept crying for his dad. Her friend had a ten-year-old boy and she'd looked after him a few times. He'd never been this difficult. Even when his mum hadn't returned as promised, even two days later, he'd never become this hysterical.

Simone left him and went downtown to buy some bourbon UDLs to get her through, and a heap more snacks and chips from the roadhouse. When she returned he was asleep on the floor.

'Hey, little dude. You hungry?' she said, shaking him gently.

He opened his eyes but they were blank.

'Come on, you need to eat or at least drink something.' She piled it up beside him and went to sit on the bed, hoping he might eat if she wasn't watching.

Man, what had she done wrong? Was this kid just different? He did seem a little strange but she'd just put that down to him being shy.

As she went back outside for a smoke, she noticed he hadn't touched anything. The way they were going, Billy was going to win this round. Simone wasn't sure how much longer she could keep this up. Is this what being a parent was all about? If it was, she wasn't sure her nerves could take it. Just as well she'd bought another two packets of cigarettes. With a sigh, she opened her next can and took a big drink. It was going to be a long night.

Chapter 34

THE following morning Nat woke up feeling like she had a massive hangover. Her eyes were so puffy she could hardly see out of them, her head pounded from dehydration and her mouth was like a desert. And the kicker was that she was supposed to go to Perth today. Gary was expecting her but she couldn't leave, not with Billy gone. She had to call Gary and say she couldn't make it, but how would he react when he heard it was because of Drew and Billy? Would he jump to conclusions or would he be understanding? It was the last thing she felt like doing so she put the call off, and rang Drew instead.

'Natty?'

'Hey, Drew, any news?'

She heard him sigh heavily. 'No, I was going to ask you the same thing.' He groaned. 'I fucking hate this. I feel so useless. I can't eat, I can't sleep, I can't even think straight. If it wasn't for Kim and Matt I doubt I could even operate. I just see Billy's face, his smile, and wonder if I'll ever see it again. I even hear his laugh and think he's right behind me. It leaves me devastated each time I turn and it's not him.'

'I'm sorry, Drew. I wish I could tell you good news. I feel so awful. I can't tell you how sorry I am.' Tears sprang up and Nat felt herself going to pieces again. 'I feel like I've failed you,' she croaked. If she didn't get the words out now, she never would.

'Oh, Natty. Don't . . . I . . .' he started. 'Hang on.'

Kim's voice replaced Drew's. 'Nat? It's Kim. Drew just has to answer more questions for the police. Don't worry, we're taking good care of him.' Kim sounded tired too.

'Thanks, Kim. Please keep me posted if you can.' They hung up and Nat stared at her phone while silent tears fell. What had he been about to say? Would he ever forgive her?

After a shower she forced herself to go to the shop to collect her mail, and buy lots of chocolate for comfort. As if chocolate could make her feel better. She wanted to go driving around looking for Billy, or at least camp out at the police station for news. She was useless and it was infuriating.

At the shop she got out and walked inside, oblivious to the creases in her shirt, to her messy hair and puffy face. She was worse than what the cat dragged in but it didn't matter, nothing mattered without Billy.

'Hi, Natalie, how are . . . Oh, are you okay?' Jess stopped chewing her gum long enough to drop her mouth open in shock.

Nat nodded. 'Can I get my mail, please, Jess?'

'Um, sure.'

Nat took the two bills and then walked around the shop, but the one thing she wanted she couldn't buy. *How to Find a*

Missing Kid: Complete Kit or *Finding a Child for Dummies*.

'Oh, there ya are, lovie,' said Ida, who came from the private section of the shop. She waddled when she walked but she exuded warmth and love. 'Oh, pet, come here. I just heard all about it.'

Why was Nat not surprised? How much Ida knew she wasn't sure, and she wasn't about to ask either.

Ida wrapped her soft arms around her and Nat could do nothing but fight the tears that threatened to fall. She wanted her mum, but her mum wouldn't understand. What she needed was Uncle Kent's arms around her. He'd brush her hair and rub her back, just like he always did when she was devastated over anything, from boyfriend break-ups to Jason pulling the heads off her Barbie dolls.

'Is this why you were asking about the car yesterday?' asked Ida, now holding her at arm's length.

Nat nodded. 'Can you keep asking the locals if they saw it? Maybe we can find which way out of town it went.'

'I can do better than that, lovie. I just saw it go past when I put the wheelie bin by the road.'

What? Was it possible? Nat double-checked that Ida had seen the exact make, model and colour.

'Yep, that was it. Headed north out of town.'

Nat's mind was sparking like cut electricity lines. Was it really Simone? Could she be headed back to Drew's place? Would Billy be with her? 'Thanks, Ida, you're amazing. I have to go.'

Without waiting for a goodbye, Nat ran from the shop to her car, throwing her mail across the seat. She drove to Drew's with her stomach riding up in her throat, hardly able to breathe. Her phone taunted her; she wanted to call Drew, but she didn't want to get his hopes up. This wasn't a sure thing yet. She'd hate to make him feel worse.

The dragon at Drew's gate seemed to guard it like a knight in armour and she wished it was real so it could chomp Simone into a million pieces, or at least flame-grill her. At the house she was instantly upset to see no sign of a car. Damn.

Movement caught her eye and her heart skipped a beat, but it was only Turbo bounding towards her from the car shed near the house. She got out to pat him, not worrying about dog hair or the dust prints he left on her clothes when he tried to jump up. 'Hey, Turbo. Did they forget about you in the rush?' She wondered if he was hungry. 'Come on, then.'

She walked up to the sheds where his kennel was, Turbo trotting beside her with a hopeful expression, tongue flopping out of his mouth. He seemed so excited. Would he still be happy if he knew his playmate was gone?

They drew closer to Turbo's kennel, and Nat pulled up short when something crossed her path. *Billy!*

'I can't find my dad,' sobbed Billy. His face and eyes were redder than Nat's, and tears and snot mixed together with dirt from his hands. And he smelt like urine.

'Oh my god, Billy.' Nat dropped to her knees and pulled him to her. He sagged against her and they both sobbed silently. 'Oh, my boy. Where have you been?' she said softly while running her fingers through his hair soothingly. Slowly Billy began to calm to just the odd hiccup and sniff. 'You're safe now. I'm here.' She rocked him against her, ignoring the mess he was leaving on her shirt and the wetness of his pants.

'Would you like to go inside and have a warm shower and I'll make us a Milo?'

'I want my dad,' he said, threatening to cry again.

His words squeezed her heart. Whatever had he been through? 'Dad's not far away. He went to Perth to look for you but he'll come right back when he knows you're here. Is that okay? Can you wait here with me until then?'

He nodded eventually but she could tell he wouldn't be right again until he had Drew. Poor kid looked so weak and exhausted.

Nat didn't want to push him for details about what had happened for fear it would upset him. He would open up when he was ready, and probably not until Drew was back and he felt safe again.

'Let's call him now, shall we? He'd love to hear your voice.'

Billy nodded emphatically, and Nat dialled Drew's phone number. She was a little shocked to hear Kim's voice.

'Hi, Nat. What's up?'

Did Drew not want to speak to her again? Was he angry with her for losing Billy? Hopefully this news would at least help him forgive her over time.

'Hi, Kim. Is Drew close by?'

'Yeah, we're just about to visit Simone's mum, if she still lives there.' Kim sounded tired yet determined.

'I have Billy here, he's back home,' Nat said quickly, not wanting to keep them waiting on good news.

'You have Billy?' squeaked Kim.

The phone made a funny sound and then she heard Drew's voice. 'You have Billy?' he practically yelled down the phone. She could hear all the emotion contained in that one question.

'Yes, Drew, he's here. We're at your place. I'll put him on.'

Nat wriggled her nose at the urine smell as she handed her phone to Billy. Her knees were sore but she didn't stand up. She wanted to be as close to Billy as possible.

'Dad?' said Billy. His face lit up as he heard his father's voice and she could only imagine just how happy Drew would be at this moment. If only she could see his face.

Billy nodded lots, shrugged his shoulders and said very little. Nat had a feeling he was a bit traumatised and didn't want to speak about what had happened. She hopped it didn't leave any lasting scars.

'Dad wants to speak to you,' he said, handing the phone back after a while.

'Drew?'

'Hi, Nat. Has he said anything to you about what happened?'

'No, nothing. It will come. Maybe when you get home.'

'We're going to notify the police and head straight back. They may want to talk to Billy too. Matt is calling Lozzy, so she'll be there shortly. Are you right to watch him till then?'

Nat felt a little offended at the question, like she was being quickly replaced. She couldn't help feeling she was being punished. 'Of course. I'll get him in the shower.'

'Shower, why?'

'I'll tell you later,' she said, wary of Billy eavesdropping.

'Nat, how did you find him? What happened?'

Nat told him the story: Ida at the shop, finding Turbo and then Billy. 'I'm guessing she brought him back,' she said, and she saw Billy's eyes drop to the ground.

'We'll find out more soon enough. I'm just glad he's home.' He sighed like someone had just lifted a truck from his shoulders. 'Right now I'm hoping the police can get Simone and bring her in for questioning.'

'It's only going to help your case.' Uncle Kent would have a field day with this.

'That's what I'm hoping. All right, we're going to get moving so I can get home to my boy. We might pass you on the road,' he said. 'Thanks, Natty, for being there.'

The use of her nickname and the gentle tone in his words made her cup the phone closer to her ear. 'It's the least I could do. I still feel really bad,' she admitted.

'We'll talk about it later, hey? Matt said Lozzy's left now. Give Billy a hug from me. See ya.'

'I will. Bye, Drew.' She lingered over his words for a minute before the smell of Billy brought her back to reality.

'Okay, Dad's on his way home. Aunty Loz is coming over, so let's get you in the shower.'

She let Billy undress and didn't touch his dirty clothes in case they were needed for evidence. She scooped them into a plastic garbage bag and left them on the table for Drew.

'Natty, don't leave,' Billy begged from behind the shower curtain.

'I'm still right here. You make sure you wash properly,' she said, trying to be normal. He needed routine and stability.

He was towelling off when she heard Lauren pull up.

'Can you get dressed while I go see Lozzy?'

The water dropped from his hair as he nodded.

'Good, then we'll make a nice hot chocolate and see if Dad has any of those wafer biscuits you like.'

Lauren ran into the house like a woman on a mission. She saw Nat's happy face and pulled her into a hug. 'Oh, thank god. He's really here?'

'Yep, just getting dressed. He hasn't said anything yet and I haven't wanted to push him. I'll leave that for Drew, I think. And he'll have to talk to the police, no doubt,' she said in rushed whispers.

'Yeah, good plan. I'll see if he wants to come home and play with Seth and Mallory. Might take his mind off things.' Lauren pressed her hand against her forehead.

Nat told her about the clothes on the table so she could pass it on to Drew.

'Jesus, I wonder what happened. Billy sometimes does that when he gets really distressed,' said Lauren. 'I can only imagine how awful it was for him.' They talked as they made the Milo in a travel mug and got biscuits ready.

'Aunty Loz,' cried Billy as he ran to her.

Lauren picked him up and squeezed the life out of him, her eyes glistening with tears. 'Oh, my Billy boy, it's so good to see you.' She glanced at Nat, and they shared an understanding smile.

Eventually she put him down. 'Wanna come home and play with the kids until Dad gets back?'

'Yeah,' he said noncommittally. He really just wanted his dad.

'Can I have my Milo first?'

'Yeah, of course,' Nat said.

After his Milo and about eight biscuits, Lauren put her hand on Billy's shoulder. 'Say goodbye to Natty. She's off to Perth now.'

It was Nat's turn for the tight hug. He smelt shower-fresh, and tucked into her arms perfectly. Someone was looking out for them all.

Lauren and Billy drove off and Nat went home to pack for Perth, feeling much better than when she'd woken up. She might smell slightly and have snot down the front of her shirt, but she'd wear it gladly, because it reminded her that Billy was really home.

Chapter 35

NAT sat on Gary's balcony, a hot coffee cupped in her hands, gazing out over the city of Perth. Cars moved along the freeway like busy ants, their lights on as the afternoon grew dark from the cloud cover. She had to admit, she loved this view. And it was even better when Gary was at work and she could appreciate it without that tiny niggle in the back of her mind. It had been a week and a half of nothing but normality with Gary, as if the whole thing had never happened. She'd stuck to her promise to give him a second chance, and he had been a perfect gentleman. But the tiny niggle persisted. It was fear, she knew. Fear that the violent man may reappear.

He was at work during the days but Nat kept busy making plans for the next school term. And Alisha kept dragging her off for coffee. Just this morning she'd rocked up and begged for Nat's help in picking some seats for her boutique. They'd had a great time trying to find that perfect piece that would complement her shop and give it extra class. Nat was happy that she'd spotted the white leather chair for her friend. Plus it was nice to get out of Gary's home; his masculine stamp was on everything from the dark towels and bedspreads to the minimal, modern furniture and the lack of personal items. It wasn't her home. They had talked about buying a home with more rooms and space for children but Gary wanted to wait until after they were married.

For a moment she wished she was back with Henny and Penny, who she'd left at home alone. She'd let them have the run of her backyard, and Lauren had promised to check on them before she left on holidays. Henny had become quite tame, and would even rest on Nat's lap, letting her stroke her soft feathers. If only Henny was here now . . . she could use some therapeutic chook time.

Her dad was busy with work and her mum was busy with salon appointments, clubs and charity events. Not that she could talk to them about what had happened in Lake Biddy with Billy. They'd only use it as another black mark against the town, a reason she should come back to Perth. No one understood and she was finding it hard to cope with her feelings about Drew and Billy. The only person she could talk to was Uncle Kent, and they hadn't had a chance to catch up properly. They had seen each other at her parents' place for dinner but it had been too hard to talk privately with him, especially with Jason monopolising his time.

Her first few days back in the city had been the worst. She felt like she'd been torn away from Billy and everything that had happened. Like she'd run away from them right when they needed support. After moping around Gary's apartment, gorging on food and coffee for two days, she eventually rang Lauren to chat and see how Billy was doing.

'You should just call Drew,' she'd said.

'I can't.' He had to call her first, or at least text. And he'd done neither. Even though they'd seemed to part amicably, Nat felt a huge ocean churning between them.

'He doesn't hold you responsible, Nat,' said Lauren for the second time.

Yet Nat held herself responsible. Maybe she needed to forgive herself before Drew could? But she didn't want to let herself off that easily. The guilt ate her up whenever she had a quiet moment.

'Has Billy said much?'

'Not a lot. Hey, I gotta go, Nat. We're off soon and Matt is stomping around like a bear with a sore head because the car still isn't packed. We'll have a good natter when we all get back.'

Damn it. Nat had a feeling Lauren was trying to make her call Drew herself. Maybe Kim would tell her.

To call Drew or not to call Drew? Nat had gone with the latter but even now she fought with the notion of calling him. Her fingers itched to leave the warm coffee cup and reach for her phone. But she was scared. What if he didn't want to talk to her? What if Gary found out she'd called him?

Her phone rang again and she jumped at it.

'Oh, hi, Uncle Kent,' she said with a sigh.

'Sorry, pet. Did I get you at a bad time?'

'No, I'm fine. Just a lot on my mind at the moment.'

'Well, how about you come around to dinner tonight? I'm

making a roast. It's time we caught up properly,' he said. 'I don't like the thought of you wasting away at Gary's.'

'I'd love to. Need a hand with dinner?'

'No, pet, it's all under control. Just come at six. Can't wait to see you.'

He made a kiss sound into the phone before he hung up. Nat smiled in anticipation.

When it was time to go to her uncle's place, she rang Gary.

'Hi, honey, how are you going?'

'Not that good. I'll be home late. Have tea without me, babe.'

'Actually Uncle Kent has invited me over for dinner. I'm sure you're welcome too, if you finish up early.'

'Thanks, I might swing by if it's not too late, otherwise I'll just head home and grab some of Chong's number twelve.'

'All right. I'll talk to you later then.'

Nat tidied up the kitchen and put her hair in a plait. She didn't bother putting on make-up or changing out of her jeans, singlet and the blue-and-white checked shirt of Alice's that Drew had given her. It was fast becoming a favourite – it was soft and warm, and it didn't matter if it got dirty. She put on a pair of dress boots, as she'd left the work boots at home in Lake Biddy, and drove to her uncle's.

She knocked once before opening the door and stepping inside.

'I'm here, Uncle Kent,' she called out just as the mouth-watering smell of roast hit her. 'Oh, yum, it smells divine.' She headed towards the kitchen when something came screaming towards her and hit her at waist height.

'Natty!'

'Billy? What are you doing here?' She hugged him back and couldn't help smiling at his angelic face. 'You look happy!'

'We went to the zoo today. I got to see the giraffes again.' His eyes sparkled.

'Hey, Natty.'

Drew appeared, leaning against the wall in worn jeans that hugged his lean thighs and a grey polo shirt that made his eyes a little darker. His strong arms were crossed against his chest and she could only think one thing: *Whoa.* He was gorgeous. Nat stepped towards him, Billy still hanging off her side, and the closer she got, the more intense his earthy, just-rained scent was. 'Drew, what are you guys doing here?'

Uncle Kent appeared with that cheeky, knowing smile of his. 'They're my guests for a few days. I thought you'd like to join us for dinner,' he said, giving her a hug and squishing Billy in the process as he refused to leave her side.

'We're matching,' said Billy. His flannel pyjamas had a blue-and-white check too.

'So we are,' she said, ruffling his hair, which was long overdue for a trim.

'Come and sit. I'm just about to serve up, and no, I don't need any help. Sit,' Kent ordered.

'You were the last people I expected to see here,' she said to Drew as they took their places. The table was set with cutlery, a full gravy boat and everything they'd need for dinner and more.

Uncle Kent always went all out when it came to eating. There was a reason his belly was expanding.

'We had some court business to sort so Kent suggested we come up and stay with him. It's school holidays and I wanted to do some fun stuff with Billy.' He gave her a look that said, *Anything to help him forget.* 'So we've been to the zoo, Scitech, the movies —'

Billy cut in to tell her all about watching this new movie and the massive popcorn he'd had, and how they'd gone to Adventure World afterwards. 'Dad went on the water slides with me but not the scary roller-coaster. People were screaming and they went up and down and inside out!'

They chatted through dinner, discussing bits and pieces but not the topics that Nat was dying to talk about. It wasn't until they were finished that Kent asked Billy to help him set up Monopoly while Nat and Drew cleaned up.

'I've been meaning to call,' she said, meeting his eyes after piling dishes into her arms.

Drew picked up the empty gravy boat and sauces. 'Why haven't you?' he asked frankly. Those tantalising sapphires bored holes in her but she didn't mind – she'd missed them, and was glad to see them full of life again.

She walked to the kitchen and dumped everything on the bench to sort for the dishwasher. 'I think I was scared.' She couldn't meet his eyes but she did feel she owed him the truth. 'I didn't know if I was forgiven, or maybe I hadn't really forgiven myself and didn't think I was entitled to know how Billy was going.' Good, now she'd said what was on her mind.

'Oh, Natty.' Drew reached for her, pulling her closer but keeping his hand on her arm. 'I don't blame you one bit.'

'But I saw the way you looked at me —'

Drew almost growled as he interrupted her. 'That wasn't about you. I just couldn't deal with what was going on. Didn't mean I blamed you. Your job wasn't to watch Billy twenty-four seven. Simone was determined to take him.'

Relief flooded through her and she felt like heavy shackles had been unlocked from her wrists. 'So what happened with Simone?' she whispered.

Drew glanced through to the far room, where Billy was busy laughing at something Kent had said or done.

'Billy said she'd told him she would take him back to the farm, because we were all going to have dinner together. So he eventually went with her, and she took him to Hyden. She was going to spend the day with him at the rock. I think she hoped he'd grow to like her, you know – be intrigued by his mum. But when he realised she wasn't taking him back to me, he got upset. She booked a hotel room but had a hell of a time trying to keep him quiet. He probably had one of his attacks. He would have panicked and shut down. So she dropped him back at the farm and went home. I don't think she planned to run off with him . . . just wanted to get to know him. The police took her at the station and she told them that it had just been some bonding time and then she'd returned him. That there was no law that said she couldn't see her son.'

'What?'

'Yeah, she tried to spin it to her advantage but the state Billy

324

was in when she left him at the farm speaks for itself. I'm so glad you went out there and found him, Nat. Imagine how long he'd have been there, alone, before I came home or Doris went to feed Turbo? I think his meltdown freaked Simone out and she couldn't cope. She never could handle anything too hard. Which is lucky for us. I think when he soiled himself she realised she couldn't manage him. He's not your average kid,' Drew said with that crooked-toothed smile.

'Yeah, he's above average, hitting the pretty-darn-special bracket,' said Nat, and Drew broke into a grin.

'There's the Natty I miss.'

Nat frowned. 'What do you mean?'

'You've been different since the bonfire. I'm not silly. What's going on?'

Having him stare at her was like being strapped to a lie detector. She couldn't make something up, nor could she look away. There was only one option left. 'I guess I was just trying to give you some time with Kim. You guys were looking very close.' Damn, were her cheeks getting hot?

'We are close, but it will never be more than that. That's what we were talking about.'

'You were?'

'Yep. Kim understands. I did actually think about giving it a go, now that I know how she feels.'

Nat's breath caught in her throat as the seconds ticked by like minutes. 'And?' she managed to ask.

'And I realised it's not fair on her. I don't feel that way about Kim and she deserves someone who does. Kim will always be in my life, she's one of my best friends. Just like I need to have you in my life.'

Nat's stomach flipped and a current zapped through her body. His words made her feel alive.

'Natty, can we go back to how we were before? I treasure our friendship and I miss you.'

Friends. Yes, she knew that's all it could be. Yet she felt a trace of disappointment. Drew was watching her hopefully, his blond tips sitting at funny angles that her fingers itched to touch. 'I'd like that very much.' She kept her hands busy by wrapping them around him and hugging him tightly. Drew did the same and she melted into the safety of his arms. His strength, his scent, his warmth, all felt like home.

'Hello, Nat? Kent? It's just . . .' Gary's words fell away as Nat sprang back from Drew's arms.

'*Gary?*'

'Natalie?' He stood frozen for a moment, glancing between Nat and Drew. 'Nat, I think we should leave,' he said, his face impassive.

'Gary, I . . .' She was about to say she could explain but he was already heading for the front door. 'Oh, shit. I'd better go sort that out,' Nat said to Drew and turned to leave.

Drew latched on to her hand. 'Natty, don't go,' he whispered. 'I'm worried.'

'I'll be fine,' she said. 'I just need to explain it to him. It'll be okay. He knows what's at risk. This is his chance to prove to me that he really has changed. I'll call you tomorrow. It's okay, Drew.'

She hoped it would be. This would be the turning point for Gary. She had given him a second chance and she hoped he would think about his behaviour. With all the talking and emails and apologies, Nat was feeling optimistic that they could work this out. She had to see it through, and that meant going with Gary now.

'Please say goodbye to Billy and Uncle Kent for me.' Shaking Drew's hand free, she followed Gary, but felt as if she'd just left her life vest behind. She didn't dare turn back to see Drew's face.

Already she was wondering how to convince Gary that it was just a hug between friends. Even though, now, she wondered if she was fooling herself. Nat cared deeply for Drew. How was she going to keep everything calm when she knew Gary's suspicions were justified? He had the right to be pissed off. But he didn't have the right to hurt her. She just hoped he wouldn't get so angry that they couldn't discuss it rationally. She had to hope that he'd changed.

Lifting her chin, she walked past Gary and into the night.

Chapter 36

NAT felt terror slowly working its way through her veins. Gary's face was set like marble, except his eyes, which darkened further and further as they drove home. Instead of calming down as she'd hoped, he seemed to be getting angrier. She could feel tension radiating from his body as he sat ramrod straight, muscles bunched in his white office shirt. Nat resisted the urge to press herself against the passenger-side door but in her mind she was turning to liquid and pouring into the gap between the seat and door.

The streetlights flashed past. 'Gary, we need to talk this through,' she said as calmly as she could, but it came out a little strained and jumpy due to the fact that her heart was in her throat. Should she reach over and hold his hand, reassure him? She was so uncertain about how he would react. Second chances were scary.

He didn't say anything at all until he pulled into his parking spot and shut off the car.

'Come inside and we'll talk,' he said gruffly.

Nat opened her door with a shaking hand and moved slower than a turtle. Her mind was going faster than a rabbit, trying to guess what was to come and figure out how to explain what Gary had seen. She was torn between hope that he had changed and fear that he hadn't. Her belly was a jumble of twisted barbed wire as she walked behind him on the lit pebbled pathway. Inside, Gary strode to the large glass wall and looked out over the city lights. He stood there with his hands clenched by his sides.

'Gary, you need to calm down. There was no need to insist I come home without saying goodbye to Uncle Kent. He was right there with Billy. Nothing sordid was going on.' She stood behind a chair, using it for balance, using it to hide her shaking body, using it as a shield and wondering if it would be enough.

Gary turned and the force of his gaze hit her like a slap. 'Nothing going on? His hands were all over you. You were draped over him,' he said angrily. 'What else have you been doing?' he said, stepping towards her and locking his hands onto her arms. He dragged her from behind the chair, putting her firmly in front of him.

'Gary, this is your second chance. You promised me you'd never lose control again. Please. I need you to be the Gary I said I would marry.'

A hand snapped up and clenched her jaw hard, dragging her face close to his. Her teeth ached from the pressure.

'Second chance? What about your second chance? For all I know, you're sleeping in his bed.'

Nat tried to pull back. 'No, I'm not. Gary, let me go. You're hurting me,' she begged. 'You promised me you'd never hurt me again.'

'You wouldn't know what real pain is,' he said, letting her jaw go but gripping her neck instead. He pushed her back towards the bedroom while she struggled for breath. She tripped over a rug and fell to the ground, getting a brief reprieve as she slipped from his grasp. She crawled along the floor, trying to get away, when she felt a blinding pain in her ribs. Curling into a ball, she cried out as he kicked her again, his shoe hard and unforgiving. Tears sprang forth, her world going blurry.

'Gary, no, please,' she whimpered. 'You promised me. You promised.'

'When are you going to learn that I don't share? I will not be humiliated. I promised to behave but you were all over him. It was . . . disgusting. I will not have you doing it behind my back and making me a laughing stock.' Gary reached down and dragged her up by her neck, both hands tight.

Natalie feared her windpipe was being crushed as he pulled her to the bed. Could her lungs collapse? Each breath was a struggle.

As her world grew dark, she wondered how she could have let this happen to her. Again. Gary had blown his second chance. He was not the man she wanted to marry. Not by a long shot. The shame was so intense she wanted to die from it. She didn't even know who Gary was, and as she finally passed out into darkness she felt a moment of relief that it was over.

Chapter 37

DREW paced around Kent's house like a caged lion. On his tenth lap Kent stepped into his path.

'Drew, what's going on? Where's Nat?'

'It's a mess. Nat and I had cleared the air, we were friends again and having a hug when Gary walked in,' he said, struggling to keep the fire from his voice.

Kent stood there as if waiting for the punchline. 'And? What's wrong with that?'

'I'm worried I've made it worse for Nat.'

'Why? With Gary? Was he upset? Didn't you just explain?'

'You don't get it. Gary's a hothead. He can't think clearly when he's jealous. He all but dragged her home.' Drew so badly wanted to tell him that Gary had been hurting Nat, but that would mean breaking a promise. 'Can you call her, please?'

Kent frowned. 'What do you mean? What aren't you telling me, Drew?'

Drew didn't reply but Kent pulled out his mobile and rang

Nat. He glanced at Drew. 'No answer, but that's not surprising, is it, if they're talking things over?'

Drew ground his teeth together.

'Is there something going on between you and Nat?'

Drew shot his hands up as if under arrest. 'No, of course not. We're just good friends.'

'I can see that,' said Kent. He glanced back to check Billy was still occupied. 'And I can also see how much she means to you.'

His words seemed to hang in the air like a thick morning fog. Drew didn't know how to reply, but couldn't bring himself to deny it. It felt like a shootout in a Western as they eyeballed each other.

'Do you love her?' Kent asked softly.

Again Drew didn't know what to say. Could he admit to Kent that he loved his niece, the one who was engaged to be married to another man? After everything Kent had done for him and Billy, Drew owed him the truth. 'Yes. Yes, I do.'

A smile grew on Kent's face, completely confusing Drew. 'I knew it. They say men don't notice stuff, but I noticed.'

Drew bit the inside of his cheek. 'I haven't done anything about it,' he eventually said, but then he remembered the kiss.

'You don't want to tell her?' Kent asked. 'You should.'

Why did everyone keep saying that? Would telling her really change anything? Gary was abusive and she still hadn't left him. Why would she leave him for Drew and live a plain life in the middle of nowhere, away from everything she knew?

'I'm not sure it would work between us,' Drew said truthfully. He didn't want to try it and then be devastated when she went back to the city. It had happened to a few of the guys in the district. But then again, others were still happily married to their city gals. 'She shouldn't marry Gary regardless. He's bad news.'

'Well, that we can agree on. I think he's too selfish, doesn't put Nat first. And I have a feeling she's doing it more out of family duty than anything. She's always wanted to please everyone. But I want her to please herself. I've tried to tell her that I think she's trapping herself by getting married but she won't listen. Just thinks it's an old man's mumblings.'

Drew agreed with Kent but was too afraid to say so.

'Can we play Monomoney now?' Billy asked, appearing in the doorway. He still couldn't pronounce Monopoly correctly.

'Um, not just yet, can you watch some TV instead, or play with the Lego? Thanks, buddy.' Drew was relieved for the distraction from his conversation with Kent as he was scared he was close to spilling Nat's secret. What a world of trouble he'd be in then. And they'd just fixed their relationship; he didn't want to bust it up again. He was so torn. He wanted to drive to Gary's and see for himself if she was all right. But what if she was fine and he just made it worse? He could call the police but he knew Nat would hate that.

Try as he might, Monopoly couldn't hold his interest. He kept looking at his phone, wondering if Nat would call him, if Gary might be hurting her, wondering whether he should text her and see if she was all right. But if Gary was hovering over her phone . . . Damn it. Images of Nat with bad bruises swam through his mind like thick globs of poisonous algae.

'*Daaaad*, it's your go again,' Billy whined, holding the dice out for him.

Kent squinted at Drew, no doubt trying to read his mind. 'I'm sorry, mate. I'm going to have to call it a night. I'm tired,' Drew said.

They packed up and all went to bed, but Drew couldn't sleep. He tossed and turned, looked at his phone, then tossed and turned some more. Maybe he could get Kent to ring her in the morning, just to see she was okay. At some ungodly hour Drew fell asleep, only to wake early and start fretting all over again.

Kent found him sitting at the kitchen bench at seven o'clock, staring at his strong black coffee. It was his third cup.

'Morning. You look hung-over,' said Kent, scratching his belly through his royal-blue robe. He wore matching slippers.

'I didn't sleep that well. Um, Kent,' he started while Kent fixed himself a coffee. 'Is there any chance you could call Nat this morning and see how she is?'

Kent's eyes narrowed. 'Why are you so worried about her? What are you not telling me?'

'I can't call because the last time I did, Gary saw and went ballistic. Please, Kent. Just give her a quick call and see if she sounds all right.'

After studying him for a few seconds, Kent picked up his mobile and dialled Nat. 'Voicemail again. She's probably still asleep.'

Drew made him try again at eight, and when there was still no answer, Drew begged him to try Gary's home phone.

Kent went looking for the number, as he'd never needed to call it before. Drew waited anxiously as Kent dialled the numbers.

'Hi, Gary, it's Kent. Just chasing Natalie. Can I speak to her, please?'

Drew had to resist pressing his ear up to Kent's phone and was relieved when he could hear that she had answered.

'Hi, possum. Is your phone off? I've been trying to call. Are you okay? You sound raspy, are you getting a cold?'

Drew froze. Raspy? He saw red as he instantly imagined Gary's hands pressed around Nat's throat. Breathing heavily, Drew got up and paced the kitchen. He wanted to hit something, mainly Gary's face.

Kent touched his shoulder and he just about hit the roof.

'Sorry, Drew. Didn't mean to scare you. It's okay, she seems fine.'

'No, you don't get it,' he said, going back to pacing. 'She's not going to say anything different while he's there. And her throat, I bet that bastard's hurt her again. I'll bloody kill him,' he growled.

Kent gripped his shoulders and shook him a little. 'What do you mean, hurt her again? Drew?'

He couldn't hold it in any more. He felt like a boiling kettle, whistle going mad with the steam. If he wasn't taken off the heat he was going to blow. 'Nat doesn't want anyone to know, but Gary is abusive.' There, he'd said it. He felt his body start to deflate. 'I'm going against her wishes but I will not sit back while he keeps hurting her, Kent, and she won't get help. It's time to make her.'

'Are you sure? She would have said something, she would have come to me,' he said, looking hurt.

'She doesn't want anyone to know; she made me promise not to tell. But I can't hide it, not if it means she'll keep getting hurt. I threatened to tell if she didn't do something about it. She wanted time, but I don't think he's going to get any better, Kent, I really don't.'

'How can you be so sure? Gary's been a family friend for years. His dad and my brother have been best friends since childhood.'

'Trust me, the bruises on her neck were real. He wants to own her, not marry her. We have to do something,' he pleaded.

Kent looked as if he wanted to trust him but it was hard to believe something you hadn't seen with your own eyes. Drew understood why Natalie hadn't told her parents. If Kent was struggling to believe it, how would her parents react? Maybe knowing that Drew loved Natalie didn't help either. Maybe Kent thought he was just trying to break them up.

'It's okay. I believe you, Drew. I can see your worry and even though I find it hard to wrap my head around, I believe you. What shall we do?'

'We go get her.'

Within minutes they had Billy packed up in the car. The drive to Gary's apartment felt like a three-hour trip and Drew's nails were not going to last. Every red light made him feel like getting out and running, except he didn't know which way to go.

'Is this Natty's house?' said Billy as they pulled up in a park bay.

'It's Gary's place,' said Drew.

'Look, you stay here, I'll go in first, in case seeing you makes things worse,' said Kent.

Drew didn't like it but he nodded. He wanted to run in there and tear strips off Gary. His heart was pounding in his mouth as he waited, and all too soon Kent was back.

'Well?'

'They're not here.'

Drew thought the worst and felt panic start to strangle his airway. Where could they be? His mind went straight to the worst-case scenarios.

'Don't stress. I rang Nat and she said they're on their way to her parents'. She had something important to tell them. And that is where we're going now too.'

So then Drew had to contain himself for the drive to Nat's parents' place. More nails chewed.

Kent parked behind a shiny Mercedes while Drew and Billy gawked out the car window like open-mouthed clowns in a side-show alley.

'It's massive,' said Drew. The house was a grand two-storey mix of stone and rendering. It had tall pillars at the entry, making it look like some fancy American plantation house. The lawn out the front was immaculately maintained with shaped bushes and hedges. Perfectly pruned shrubs sat like lollipops down the side of the circular driveway, which was paved in colours that matched the house. Recently planted flowers gave a burst of colour to the green of the larger established trees and maples. 'I've never seen anything like it.'

'It's just a house,' said Kent. 'And a cold one at that. Let's go.'

Billy got out of the car and clung to Drew's leg, no doubt feeling like he'd landed on a movie set.

One of the massive double jarrah doors was still open and they all marched straight in.

'Kent, what are you doing here?' said a tall man wearing a suit.

It took Drew a moment to adjust to his white marble surroundings and to focus on the man by the door. He could see the resemblance to Nat, and where she got her height. He suddenly felt very underdressed in jeans and his best Target T-shirt. His mum had always bought his clothes from the Target Country store in Narrogin or Big W when she went to the city. Now Drew would have to do his own clothes shopping. It was something that filled him with dread.

'Vince, I'd like you to meet Drew and Billy, friends of mine.'

Vincent didn't bat an eyelid as he shook their hands. Maybe Kent often brought strays over.

'Nice to meet you, come in. I'm Vincent. How are you, young man?' Vincent said to Billy.

'Your house is . . .' Billy walked in and saw the grand staircase. 'Wow.'

Drew could tell by the look on his face that he was itching to go up the stairs. For a country boy, stairs were a thing of wonder, as were escalators and elevators.

'You can go and have a look around, if you like. Climb the stairs?' said Vincent.

Billy glanced at Drew for his approval. 'Sure, buddy, it's okay. I'll be right here.'

As Billy headed up the stairs, a woman came towards them, her heels clicking on the floor, her figure wrapped in a dark-green pants suit with a soft-pink silk scarf. 'Who is it, darling? Oh, hi, Kent.' She stood beside Vincent.

Uncomfortable, out of place and awkward were words that came to mind as Drew stood there in the mansion alongside Nat's parents.

'Darling, this is Drew, and that's Billy heading up the stairs. The people Kent's been helping.'

'Right,' said Jennifer vaguely. She didn't seem to know who they were and probably didn't care, but Drew was surprised that Vincent knew of them. He seemed like a very smart, clued-in man. Not surprising, really, when you saw what he'd made of his life.

'We came to see Natalie,' said Kent.

Vincent frowned. 'Oh, she's just arrived. We were about to sit down.'

Jennifer and Vincent guided them into the massive sitting room off to the side. Gary and Nat were seated inside, Nat looking at a picture on the wall while Gary was using his phone. She was all dressed up in heels, grey linen slacks and her button-up red coat with a thick grey scarf. She was mesmerisingly beautiful and then she turned and Drew saw the pain on her face. It left him breathless.

'What are you doing here?' said Gary, the lines on his face doubling as he caught sight of them. He shot a glance at Natalie, obviously thinking she had something to do with this arrangement.

All Drew saw was an angry man who was looking cornered. It spelled danger.

'We came to see Natalie,' said Kent, standing beside Drew.

'I think we should go home, Nat. I'm not feeling well,' said Gary, reaching for his jacket.

'No, I need to tell my parents something,' said Nat softly.

'Yes, stay,' said Kent, playing the game. He stepped towards Nat and held out his hands. 'Here, let me take your coat, Natty.'

Nat was like a fox in the spotlight. She undid her coat while Kent waited with his hand outstretched.

'And the scarf,' said Kent. 'It's much too warm for that in here.'

Nat's eyes flicked to Drew and he knew what she was thinking.

'Nat, it's time we went,' said Gary again, reaching for her arm. She flinched.

'How about you just back off, mate?' said Drew, louder than he intended.

'I beg your pardon? This is none of your business.' Gary puffed up his chest and snatched her coat from Kent's hands.

Drew stepped forward and reached for the scarf around Nat's neck. He had to know for sure. But her hand quickly clutched at his, stopping him from removing it.

'I told Kent. I'm sorry, but I'm worried about you,' he whispered to her.

Nat's gaze went straight through to his core. He could see her pain and yet there was a flicker of something stronger too.

'It's okay, Drew. I'll do it. It's why I made Gary bring me here,' she said, squaring her shoulders. 'It's time to tell my parents.'

'Tell us what?' said Jennifer.

He saw her determination to stand up for herself and it melted his heart. After taking a beating, here she stood, facing her parents, facing all her fears. Truly, she had guts.

With a careful hand she unravelled the scarf. 'I'm here to tell you that I'm not marrying Gary,' she said, turning to her parents. 'He hurts me,' she added in a shaky whisper.

Drew didn't even have to move closer to see the bruising that had started to colour already, and he noticed the split lip under the thick layer of makeup.

'You bastard,' he said, turning to Gary. Everything seemed to glow red, like an alarm was going off in a nuclear plant.

'What on earth?' said Jennifer.

'See, Kent? Your proof,' said Drew, 'although Nat's word should be enough for all of us.'

'I'm sorry I didn't tell you, Uncle Kent. I felt so ashamed,' said Nat. 'But I refuse to let it continue.' She slipped the ring off her finger.

'Oh my lord,' whispered Kent, stepping closer.

'Gary, I don't want to marry you any more,' Nat said firmly as a tear slipped down her face. 'I trusted you and you hurt me, more than once. I can't marry someone I don't trust or even like any more. It's over.'

Her words were like a thousand cuts to Drew's heart, each one more painful than the last. Gary had hurt her. He wished he could have prevented it. Wished he could inflict the same pain on Gary, plus more for good measure.

Gary gripped Nat's arm and pulled her towards him, her

heels clattering along the floor in protest. 'No, we'll talk about this at home, princess.'

'Get your hands off her,' said Drew, pulling Gary's arm away. He would never let him lay a finger on her ever again.

'Piss off, she's my fiancée.'

'Not any more, she's not.' Drew snapped. Pulling his fist back, he punched Gary hard in the face, sending him crumpling to the floor. 'You prick.'

'Oh my god,' said Jennifer, horrified.

'What is going on?' roared Vincent. 'Natalie?'

'I'm not going to apologise,' said Drew, shaking his fist out. He shot a hate-filled look at Gary, whose mouth was bleeding. He stayed on the floor like the weak man he was. He faced Vincent. 'I won't see Natalie harmed, I won't let this prick lay another hand on her. I love her too much for that.'

He heard Nat's gasp before Gary said, 'I knew it.'

Drew stepped towards Gary and pointed to him. 'You touch her again and I swear to god, I'll come back. I don't care who you are.'

He stepped around the congregation and Gary's blood, which looked so vibrant against the white floor. Drew's hand hurt but it was so worth it. He didn't want to look at Nat, to see the disappointment in her eyes, the hurt caused by his broken promise, so he kept his eyes down. 'I'm sorry, Natty. I really am,' he whispered on his way past her. 'I had to tell Kent.'

He got to the door and called out, 'Billy, it's time to go.' His son came jumping down the stairs, oblivious to all that had happened.

'Dad, they have so many stairs,' he said, taking Drew's hand. He stopped and looked up. 'But we didn't get to see Natty?'

'She's busy. We'll catch her later. Come on.' He gave him a gentle tug.

Billy struggled to keep up with Drew's pace once they were outside in the crisp air as they headed out into the street. He pulled out his phone to call for a taxi.

'How about we go to Macca's for dinner and then drive home?' said Drew, finally able to breathe.

Billy smiled and nodded.

It was going to take all his effort not to stomp around to the end of the street while he waited for a taxi. He may have just lost one of his best friends, the woman he loved. But he'd be damned if he was going to let her suffer any more at the hands of that monster. God knew what else he'd done to her. Drew felt ill at the thought. He just needed to get home. Back to the farm, back to normal, simple life, back to just him and Billy, taking on the world.

Chapter 38

NAT felt like she was watching a movie, but it seemed she had the starring role.

'What in god's name is going on?' said Vincent. 'Natalie? Is this true? Gary? Would someone please explain?'

He helped Gary up while Jennifer ran off, no doubt to get a towel to clean the floor.

Nat stood there in a fog, trying to put the whole puzzle together. 'That was Drew. He's a friend from Lake Biddy.' A friend who'd said he loved her. Drew's words kept running through her mind, over and over.

'Have you been sleeping with him?' said Gary, wiping his mouth with the hand towel Jennifer offered to him. 'Tell me,' he growled.

'How about you just back off or I'll slap some legal jargon on your arse,' said Kent, coming to stand beside Nat protectively. Then he turned around and inspected her neck. 'Has he hurt you anywhere else?' he demanded, his brow creasing as he looked at her bruising flesh.

Nat couldn't bring herself to mention the pain in her ribs, or the fear of reaching the point of passing out. Maybe she'd be able to speak up eventually but it was still too soon, too raw. So she just nodded and dropped her eyes to the floor.

Uncle Kent lifted her chin with his finger so she'd look at him. 'Don't you do that! You are not at fault here – that bastard is.' His voice softened as he pushed back a strand of her hair. 'Oh, Natty, why didn't you come to us? No one should ever have to put up with this. No one.'

Her dad sucked in a breath as he inspected her bruises. Her mum joined him, her mouth open, as if she couldn't believe this was happening in her house.

Nat looked at Gary. She felt repulsed by him, couldn't see the man she'd once thought she loved. Had she ever loved him? She looked down at the ridiculous ring in her hand. There was no sadness at no longer wearing it, just a sense of finally being free.

'Gary, we're over. I gave you a second chance and you blew it. Never again will I put myself in danger. I never want to see you again. You need help.'

'Are you just going to let her?' Gary posed the question to her parents.

'Dad, I will not marry him, no matter what you guys want.' Nat lifted up her blouse to show the bruising to her ribs.

'Oh my,' said Jennifer. Nat had never seen her mum so shaken or shocked. 'He did this to you? Oh, my baby girl.' She touched her daughter's face, her eyes brimming with tears.

'Gary? How could you?' said Vincent, turning to Gary. 'Get out of our house.'

'She deserved it,' said Gary as he swiped the ring from Nat's hand. 'She was all over that guy, making a fool of herself.' He took his jacket and left, slamming the door as loudly as Drew had.

'Who is he?' Jennifer said staring at the closed door. She looked confused and torn. It was how Nat had been feeling since the first time Gary had hurt her.

Nat turned to her parents. 'I do care for Drew, maybe a little too much, but I was trying to give Gary a proper chance. I really was trying —'

'It doesn't matter what you did, darling,' Jennifer cut in. 'You didn't deserve this. No one does.'

Nat nodded slowly. 'I need to live my own life, and that means doing what's right for me. I know Gary's like family to you but I will not marry someone like him. I want to continue teaching and I want you to be happy that I'm happy.'

'Honey, we do want you to be happy,' said Vincent. He gently touched her neck, then pulled her into his arms. 'I can't believe it. My poor darling, you should have said something sooner. I'm so sorry.'

Jennifer brushed her hair back. 'Oh, Natalie. No man who does that is worth it, no matter who he is.' She stroked her daughter's hair like she used to when Nat was little.

After a moment, Nat pulled back. 'I'm sorry. I just need some time. I'll be at Uncle Kent's. I'm sorry, Dad. I know this will be hard on you with Tony.' She wondered what Gary's dad would think when he heard the news. The business would be in for some serious fallout.

'Stay and talk, sweetheart,' Vincent begged.

'No, I need some time to think. I will come back, but right now I'm not quite sure I can talk about anything.'

Vincent nodded, tears glistening. He hugged his wife tightly. 'We'll be here, waiting.'

'Thanks.'

'Come on, possum. Let's get a strong coffee,' said Kent, wrapping his arm around her.

She knew Kent would have a million questions for her, and he'd want her to take legal action against Gary for what he'd done to her. Nat wasn't sure how she felt about that yet. Did she really want the news all over the city?

'I'm sorry,' she whispered again as she walked away from her parents, who stood, dazed, with a bloody, red mess by their feet. It was such a far cry from the perfect family picture they liked to display.

Chapter 39

'DAD, Natty wasn't at school today,' said Billy as he came into the house and threw his schoolbag on the floor.

'Billy, don't do that. Get out your lunchbox and homework if you have any, please.' Billy grunted but did as he was told while Drew finished making some Saos with Vegemite, tomato and cheese. 'So who was teaching then?'

It was the first day back at school after term break and Drew had been waiting for this day to find out how Nat was. He hadn't counted on her not coming back. His chest ached as if his heart was tearing away, threatening to fall into the black cavity below and shrivel up.

It had all been made worse by the lack of contact. No simple text to say she was okay. Not that he'd sent any either. He knew she would still be angry with him for spilling the beans, but he couldn't take it back now and, quite frankly, he didn't want to. No one should endure abuse of any sort.

'Mr Penith did. It wasn't too bad, I guess,' Billy said, dropping his empty lunchbox in the sink and reaching for a Sao. 'Is Natty coming back, Dad?' Billy asked, putting his biscuit down. He didn't look that hungry any more.

'I don't know, mate. Maybe.'

Billy put his little hand on top of Drew's. Drew stared at one big, callused hand and one small one. They actually had the same hands; he could see it plain as day. The same shape, the same knuckles and nails. It was the most perfect thing to see. He put his other hand on top of Billy's and then Billy put his other hand on Drew's and soon they were playing a game and laughing. It felt good to laugh. He hadn't done it much since arriving home. It was hard to get back into the swing of life without Nat. He saw her in his mind so clearly. Would that eventually fade? Would he stop seeing her by the shed, or sitting on the back verandah, or playing with Billy?

Turbo began barking. 'Someone's here,' said Billy, cocking his head to the side.

'Might be Kimmy.' Drew went outside, eager to see Kim's smile and to have her company.

It was cool outside, raising the hairs on his arms, but the smell was so crisp and fresh from recent rains. He would leave footprints in the gravel until the next shower came through – which wouldn't be far away, judging by the deep blue of the sky.

'Hi, Drew.'

That voice. He dropped his eyes from the sky to see Natalie walking towards him. Her hair was out, blowing in the gentle breeze, and she wore jeans that hugged her so perfectly. He stopped and stared. The dark blue of the sky made her hair bright like a halo, and the green of the freshly washed trees made a vibrant border together with the rusty red of the gravel where she stood. *Just breathe*, he told himself. *Just breathe.*

'You weren't at school today.' It was the first thing that came to mind.

'I had some things to sort in Perth that couldn't be put off.'

'So you haven't quit?'

She shook her head. 'I have the year to finish out.'

He took one step closer. He needed to explain, to say his bit. 'I've thought about it a lot, Nat, and I'm not sorry about what I said and what I did. I'd do it all again, even though I broke my promise.'

Nat stepped closer and put her hand on his chest. His eyes dropped to her hand, pressing against his heart. He could hear it beating, over their breathing, over the birds squawking in the trees, and over the rustling of the breeze around them, which swept her hair to one side.

'Did you mean it?'

'What?' He was having trouble keeping up. Her touch alone was driving him insane, not to mention her scent. She was intoxicating and he was feeling drunk.

'Did you mean it when you said you loved me?' Her green eyes were intense, but he saw no evidence that she hated him.

'Aren't you angry with me? For telling —'

'Drew, answer me. Yes or no.'

Her words were so forceful he replied automatically, like a child in trouble. 'Yes, yes, I did mean it. I love you. Crazy in love with you.'

The strangest thing happened. Natalie smiled and reached for his face, caressing him with both hands. 'I was hoping that's what you meant.'

And then she kissed him. Soft lips melted against his and then there was an explosion of flavour as she deepened the kiss. Drew felt like he was in the deep end, struggling to stay afloat.

'I don't get it,' he said when they stopped for air.

Nat gave him a little smile that made his knees threaten to give way.

'I love you too, Drew. I think I have for a while but I was fighting it. I don't know why. I can't imagine life without you or Billy.'

'You want me?' he whispered.

'Like there's no tomorrow. I've made a few changes in my life. It's time to make myself happy and that means being with you and Billy.' She ran a finger across his lips then down his jaw before plunging her hand into his hair at the base of his neck.

'You've just made me the happiest farmer in the world,' he said. He knew he was probably grinning like a fool. She made him feel things worth feeling. Pulling her against him, her curves nestling in tightly, he shifted her hair so he could kiss her neck. The bruises had gone but he was gentle. No one would ever hurt her again. He kissed up towards her ear, then along her jaw until he reached her lips. By now she was pressing against him harder and breathing heavily. He kissed her like he'd been dying to since that night at the hall, but this time it was better; this time she was his to kiss.

'Dad? What are you doing?'

Drew stopped and smiled. 'Hold that thought,' he whispered before turning around to Billy. 'Guess who's back?' He stepped sideways so his son could see his favourite teacher.

'Natty!'

Billy ran towards her, wrapping his arms around her waist. It may have just been the best day of Drew's life.

Chapter 40

THE hot day carried a hint of eucalyptus and a mix of ladies' perfumes as hundreds of people gathered on the lawn by the primary school. Bright summer dresses added pizazz to the school that usually saw only blue uniforms. The whole community had turned up and then some. People had come from far and wide, back to the tiny school they'd all attended. All eyes were turned to the shire president, who stood by a lectern.

'This school opened in 1917 and today we celebrate its last day, only a few years short of its one hundredth year. It is with sadness that we say goodbye but we will all look back with fond memories, and it will always be a part of Lake Biddy's history.'

Nat felt a lump rising in her throat. Looking around at others – some mopping at tears with wet tissues and others fighting the waterworks – made it even harder to keep a lid on her own emotions. She pressed into Drew's side, seeking his support even though it was almost too hot to make body contact. He kissed her forehead and tightened his grip around her shoulders. It was the end of an era for this tiny town. Who could know the lasting effects the school closure would have?

The president finished his speech and Lauren, as president of the P & C, got up with Ross to put the large time capsule into the ground. The plaque Nat had had made was on display, ready to be attached to the small brick wall that would mark the capsule's resting place. Everyone at the school had put bits in there: work, stories, photos and much more, to be opened up in twenty years' time.

After the official part was over, the crowd mingled around the building where old work was on display. They talked excitedly like kids on the first day of school. Drew was constantly introducing her to past members of the community who'd come back especially for this day.

'Hey, look, this is one of the old stories I wrote in Miss Page's class,' he said, pointing to some old lined paper.

'The Day I Ate a Pig,' read Billy. 'Dad that looks so old,' he added with a giggle.

People laughed at the old work and the book of punishment. Deciding who had got the cane the most was a huge source of entertainment.

'I don't want to change schools,' said Billy, sitting on the senior room bench.

'Neither do I,' said Nat. She knew change was hard for Billy. 'But we will do it together, hey? I'll still be your teacher,' she said, trying to tickle him.

'Mallory is glad you're coming too,' said Lauren, joining them. 'She's stressing about the hour-long bus ride to school already,' she whispered to Nat so Billy didn't hear. They didn't want him having anxiety about it too.

Luckily Nat had got a job at the Lake Grace school where most of the kids would be going. She'd take them in with her if they didn't settle on the bus, but Drew reassured her they'd get used to it eventually. Lake Grace had received extra government funding for the students transferring from Lake Biddy, a plus for them but not so much for Lake Biddy's problems. At least the school grounds were being taken under the shire's wing and would become the local community centre and playgroup.

'Your folks still coming up on the weekend?' asked Lauren.

'Yep. Mum *has* to help organise the engagement party. I told her I want a low-key country one.' Nat pulled a face. 'I'm not really sure she understands what that means,' she added with a laugh.

'Don't worry, we'll have her in flannel before you can shout Prada. Kent seems to have taken to the lifestyle. Matt said he's coming to drive the header at harvest?'

'Well, he wants to try. He's besotted with all the big machinery. I think he's found a new love. I'm just glad he loves coming to visit. He dotes on Billy.' Nat smiled. 'You know, it's so great to have my city world mixing with my country one, and I'm so relieved that Mum and Dad are being supportive. I feel like they finally see me.'

'I'm happy for you, Nat,' said Lauren. 'How are things with Gary's family?'

'It's still strained between Dad and Tony, even though Tony is so angry with Gary. He's insisting that Gary seeks help. Plus he's given me his word that Gary won't get away with what he's done and won't be allowed to hurt anyone else. At this stage I won't press charges, I'm going to see how this pans out. And Dad has also promised that I never have to be near Gary again unless I want to. I don't think he'll be invited to any more family get-togethers.'

'Are you sure, Nat? I would have reported him straight off.'

'I'm giving Gary and his family the chance to work it out. For him to get better.' Nat was moving on with her life. She had a new home, a new family, a new son and a wonderful community to share it all with.

'And Simone?' asked Lauren quietly while Billy was distracted with Mallory.

'Well, Drew has sole custody but she still has visitation rights. She hasn't asked to see him yet, and Drew doesn't think we'll see much of her. Billy was more than she bargained for. But if she does want to make contact at least it's on our terms.' Nat liked saying 'our terms'; Billy was as much hers as Drew was. They were both her Saddler boys.

Nat was delighted to be his new mum. Billy wanted to start calling her 'mum'. Glancing at his cherubic face, she felt her emotions swell, remembering when he'd asked her. He was trying it out at home but in public 'Natty' still came out first. It would take time but they had plenty of it.

'Hi, Natalie. I just heard the news – congratulations,' said Ida, bustling up to them and giving out a warm hug.

Billy grabbed Nat's hand and held it out to Ida. 'Here's the ring,' he said proudly. 'I helped Dad pick it.'

Nat watched the small solitaire diamond sparkle in the sunlight that flooded into the school's corridor. It was the most exquisite thing she'd ever seen and it was never going to come off her finger.

A week ago she'd gone out to the farm for dinner, and Billy had rushed up to her and made her put on a blindfold. He'd helped her to the house, but she'd nearly tripped up the steps as Billy had been so keen to get her inside. 'You can take off the blindfold now,' he'd said while still holding her hand. The house was clean, the lights were off and candles were glowing from the table and benches. A heady aroma filled her nose from the flowers arranged around the room.

Then Drew had appeared, dressed in black slacks and a black dress shirt. He was delicious. He produced a bunch of red roses before kissing her.

'Dad, can we do it now?' Billy had asked.

'I thought we were going to wait until after dinner?'

'But I can't wait,' Billy had said, fidgeting.

'You know what? I can't either.'

Nat had smiled, watching the two of them and wondering what they were up to, when Billy had held up a little red box. He knelt down on one knee, then Drew followed suit.

'Natalie Wright, you are the love of our lives. Will you marry us?'

'Please,' Billy had added. 'Dad, you need to use your manners,' he'd whispered.

Through her tears and laughter Nat had managed to get out her 'yes'.

She pulled herself back to the school and found herself smiling at the memory. It was still so fresh in her mind. Her Saddler boys, proposing together. She couldn't imagine one without the other.

Nat glanced around the corridor. People from the district milled around them, some hovering near the food table with plates, talking and catching up with locals they hadn't seen in ages. The sausage rolls were long gone and one lone chocolate cake remained.

But it was the figure of her future husband, leaning against the wall and watching her with vibrant sapphire eyes, that held her focus. His crooked-toothed smile that she loved so much was suggesting what he wanted to do with her later and it sent tingles of anticipation through her body. Her farmer, who looked so delectable in a flannel shirt and nothing else. So bad was her addiction that anytime Drew wore a flannel checked shirt she found him ten times more irresistible. She was madly in love with this farmer. She didn't think it was possible to get enough of Drew and the amazing thing was that she had her whole life to put the theory to the test.

And then there was Billy, the coolest kid, who had stolen her heart first. Maybe the community had won her over next. Uncle Kent had said it was worth its weight in gold. It was like an extended family, where everyone cared about their town and the people in it. You couldn't buy love like that.

'Come on, Natty, it's time to let the balloons go,' said Drew, holding out his hand.

She took it and gripped tightly just as Billy reached for her other hand. Together they headed outside into the afternoon sun, so bright and pure. As they walked across the lawn towards

Frank, who was passing out the helium balloons in the school's colours, Billy tugged her arm so she'd look at him.

'Yes, Billy?'

'I told Dad I wanted you to be my mum,' he said, showing all his teeth. 'And now you are.'

'Really?' she said, caressing his sweet, angelic face.

'And I wanted you to be my wife,' said Drew. 'And soon you will be.' He winked and shot her that smile she'd instantly adored.

Her chest felt like it was bursting with all the love. Pulling them close, she wrapped her arms around them. 'I love you both, very much.'

People ambled past them, some commenting on how sweet a picture they made, others smiling or making happy sounds. Yet to Nat it felt like the three of them were in a world of their own.

Acknowledgements

This story was close to my heart, because my community lost our small primary school in 1998. Soon after that, the nearby school of Karlgarin where I was working as a teacher's aid closed. Thanks to Jim Stewart and Rosie Argent for sharing the nitty gritty part of what they went through then. Also, thanks to the Honourable Terry 'Tuck' Waldron MLA for the chat. All those little details you supplied help. Writing this brought back memories of Aunty Kate (Kath White) and her work at our little school over many years. And thanks, Aunty Lorna, for the poem, it is one of my favourites.

To Ali Watts and Jo Rosenberg, where would I be without you both? Thanks for polishing this so it could shine. Thank you, Maria Matina, for being a wonderful publicist who always seems to make the time. Also thanks to Louise, Fay, Clem, Julia, Kym and the many other Penguins who have helped me out. You are all invaluable.

Thanks to my friends and family for the support, help, guidance, coffee, stories, laughs ... all of it is needed and greatly appreciated. Tooey, I just had to put your ute in there! It was gold, as were all the other little stories that make it into the book

ACKNOWLEDGEMENTS

from real life. (Karl and Nic, your dog with the chooks – classic.) And if you're wondering, yes: people probably are too afraid to talk to me. Who knows what could end up in my next book?

A big thank you to the readers who make this possible. You guys are fantastic. Please feel free to follow my author page on Facebook, my many sunset photos on Instagram or my random Tweets.

@fiona_palmer
fionapalmer.com